TRIPWIRE

a J.T. Ryan Thriller

A Novel
By

Lee Gimenez

RRP

River Ridge Press

TRIPWIRE
by
Lee Gimenez

This is a work of fiction. The names, characters, places, incidents, and dialogues are products of the author's imagination and are not to be construed as real. Any resemblance to actual persons, living or dead, is entirely coincidental.

Printed in the United States of America.

Published by
River Ridge Press
P.O. Box 501173
Atlanta, Georgia 31150

Cover photos: Grindstone Media Group
used under license from Shutterstock, Inc.

Cover design: Judith Gimenez

ISBN-13: 978-0-578-91312-4

Novels by Lee Gimenez

Tripwire

Blacksnow Zero

The Sigma Conspiracy

Crossfire

Fireball

FBI Code Red

The Media Murders

Skyflash

Killing West

The Washington Ultimatum

The Nanotech Murders

Death on Zanath

Virtual Thoughtstream

Azul 7

Terralus 4

The Tomorrow Solution

Lee Gimenez

TRIPWIRE

a J.T. Ryan Thriller

Lee Gimenez

Chapter 1

Atlanta, Georgia

"You look gorgeous," J.T. Ryan said, as he walked into the bride's preparation room of the church.

Erin Welch turned away from the mirror and faced him. "I bet you say that to all the girls, J.T."

Ryan strode closer to her, taking in her whole appearance. She was radiant in her flowing, white wedding dress, her long brunette hair framing her sculpted good looks.

"No, I'm serious," he said. "You look great."

"Really? I'm nervous as hell."

"Just pre-wedding jitters."

Erin nodded. "You're right."

Ryan grinned. "I'm always right."

"You're such a smartass, John Taylor Ryan. That's going to get you killed one day." Erin faced the mirror again and smoothed down the folds of her long, flowing dress.

"Thank you, Erin. For asking me to walk you down the aisle. That means a lot to me."

She stared at him for a long moment. "Another one of your sarcastic comments?"

"No, I'm being totally serious now."

Erin nodded. "My father passed away years ago. You're the only man I admire enough to give me away at my wedding."

"If I didn't mention it before, your fiancée is a great catch. Atlanta's District Attorney with aspirations to be governor one day."

"Thanks, J.T. I love him very much and he loves me. That's what matters."

Ryan smiled, taking in her beauty. "Your fiancée is a very lucky man. You're quite a catch yourself."

She returned the smile, approached him and adjusted his tuxedo tie and picked off a piece of lint from his jacket lapel. Then she looked up into his eyes. "Did you ever wonder if you and I would get together?"

"We work together all the time, Erin."

"Not that way – in a personal way ...."

Ryan grinned. "It would have never worked out. You're Assistant Director of the FBI and hire me as a security consultant. In effect, I report to you."

"That's bullshit and you know it. I may hire you, but you're always your own boss." She laughed. "Hell, most of the time it feels like I'm working for you."

There was a knock at the open doorway and Erin's maid of honor came into the room. "The service starts in 15 minutes," she said.

"Okay," Erin replied. She turned to Ryan. "Now, shoo, J.T. I've got to finish getting ready."

Ryan gave her a half-salute. "Yes, ma'am."

***

It was a postcard perfect day for the wedding, Ryan thought, watching from the first pew of the church as the priest began the ceremony. Bright sunlight streamed into the large chapel through the room's stained-glass windows, giving the event a warm glow. The multitude of lit candles at the altar also added a festive feel to the occasion. Incense was burning in the church, creating its own pleasant aroma, which combined with the sweet scent from the arrays of flowers that adorned the chapel.

As Ryan looked around the church, he realized the wedding was well-attended. All of the pews were full and everyone was dressed up for the occasion.

The priest recited the opening prayers and began a sermon, as the bride and groom stood in front of him at the altar. Ryan was so close that he could hear every word and noticed the smiles of joy on the faces of Erin and her fiancée.

What a perfect day, Ryan thought. *I'm happy for you, Erin. You deserve this.*

Suddenly Ryan heard two muffled thuds.

Erin's fiancée clutched his chest, his knees buckled and he collapsed to the floor. Blood began to pool on the altar's marble floor.

Erin screamed, her white dress now spattered with bright red blood.

Then all hell broke loose in the chapel, people shouting, as everyone in the crowded church panicked and ran for the exits.

Ryan opened his tuxedo jacket and pulled his pistol from a hip holster. He frantically gazed around the room, desperately looking for the gunman. But all he saw were the church attendees yelling and fleeing in the confused pandemonium.

Ryan sprinted to the altar and crouched protectively in front of Erin, who was on her knees, hugging her fiancée's lifeless body.

Blood was everywhere.

Chapter 2

Los Alamos National Laboratory
Los Alamos, New Mexico

The military convoy cleared the last checkpoint and exited through the high-security gate of the facility. Twenty minutes later the convoy was headed west on the highway. It was well past midnight and traffic was light on the desolate road.

This part of New Mexico was sparsely populated. It was also heavily wooded, the forest seemingly endless in every direction.

The truck convoy abruptly slowed down and Captain Keating, who was in the third truck of the eight vehicle column, radioed to the lead Humvee. "What's the holdup, Sergeant?"

"Sir, looks like there's some road construction going on, up ahead," the reply came.

Keating, who was in the front passenger seat, glanced at his truck's NAV screen, then scanned the notes on his clipboard. "There's nothing scheduled, Sergeant. We should have clear sailing to Albuquerque."

"I'm aware of that, sir. But there's a road block and construction signs. I can see a bulldozer and a concrete mixing truck up ahead. And two guys in Department of Transportation uniforms are on the road holding up Stop signs."

Captain Keating radioed up to the helicopter flying overhead and confirmed the road construction on the highway.

"Damn," Keating said, glancing at his watch. The route had been scheduled with a tight timeframe. He knew the colonel at Kirtland Air Force base would be pissed.

Keating contacted the lead Humvee again. "Okay, Sergeant. Get out of your vehicle and go check this out. And tell those D.O.T. clowns we're in a hurry."

"Yes, sir. I'll take care of it," came back the reply.

A minute later Captain Keating heard a deafening explosion from up ahead and saw a blinding fireball lighting up the night sky.

Seconds later his own truck exploded, killing the captain and the driver instantly.

The echo of the nighttime blasts could be heard for miles.

Chapter 3

The Oval Office
The White House
Washington, D.C.

J.T. Ryan had been to the White House several times before. The last time was two years ago, when he, Erin Welch, and several CIA officers had been assigned by President Steve Harris to a top-secret task force.

As Ryan waited for the President to arrive, he studied the other two people in the room. Sitting to his left was Alex Miller, a senior CIA officer, and to his right was General Foster, the administration's Chief of Staff. All three men where sitting on wingback leather chairs that fronted Resolute, the Oval Office's famed wooden desk.

It was a storm-filled day in Washington, the turbulent, dark sky casting a gloom into the room from the three tall windows behind the desk.

Just then the office door opened and President Harris strode in, flanked by two Secret Service agents. The visitors all stood as the President made his way around his desk and sat down.

"Please sit," Harris said to his guests. Then he dismissed the Secret Service agents, who left and closed the door behind them.

"Thank you for flying into D.C. on such short notice," the President began. "But it couldn't be avoided. We have a major national security crisis on our hands."

Ryan had figured as much when he'd received the call from the White House yesterday. But hearing it directly from the President himself added a gravity to the meeting he hadn't felt before.

President Harris gave Ryan a hard look. "Where's Erin? She's supposed to be here as well. I specifically asked for her."

"Yes, sir," Ryan said. "Unfortunately, she couldn't be here today."

The President's eyes flashed in anger. "Why the hell not?"

"Sir," Ryan replied, "Erin Welch's fiancée was murdered two days ago. During the wedding ceremony, right before they took their vows, a gunman opened fire and assassinated him."

"My God. I didn't know. Was the assassin captured?"

"I'm afraid not, sir. After the shooting the church was bedlam. Everyone in attendance panicked and fled. In the confusion the killer got away. I assisted Atlanta PD trying to find him or her, but we came up empty. Since Erin's fiancée was the District Attorney for the area, we suspect it could be a revenge killing for putting some criminal behind bars."

The President nodded. "All right. Now I understand why she's not here. She was a key part of the task force last time. Hopefully she'll be able to join the team eventually." He turned toward Alex Miller. "Alex, since you're Deputy Director of the CIA's Special Operations division, I want you to head up the task force. You'll have free reign to staff it as you see fit."

"Yes, Mr. President," Miller replied. "I want to use the same operative from before. Rachel West, one of my best. She's in-route back to the U.S. from Australia."

Harris pointed to General Foster. "The General, as my Chief of Staff, will be your main contact. He'll make sure I'm kept up to date on everything."

The President turned his gaze back to Ryan. "In light of Erin's absence, and since I don't trust many of the top people at the FBI, I have no choice but to deputize you as an official FBI agent."

Ryan grinned. "Do I get a badge and everything?"

The President's face reddened and he glared at Ryan. "This is the reason I needed Erin here. To keep you in line, Ryan. I know you're the best at what you do. And I also know you think you're a hotshot because you were a Delta Force Tier 1 operative. But you're also a smartass. And I don't like smartasses."

Ryan winced, realizing he'd crossed the line. "I'm sorry, Mr. President."

Harris glanced at Miller. "Since you're in charge of the task force, Ryan will report to you. I expect you to keep him in line. I know we couldn't have solved the last crisis without Ryan's help, but he's also a loose cannon."

Miller nodded. "Of course, Mr. President."

Ryan could tell by Miller's pleased expression that the man was relishing his new authority.

The President placed his hands flat on the desk in front of him. "Now that we've got the logistics out of the way, I want to fill you in what we're facing. Foster, give these gentlemen what we have so far."

Foster reached into his briefcase, pulled out two manila folders and handed one each to Ryan and Miller.

"What I'm going to tell you," the President said, "is all top-secret information, not to be shared with anyone not on this team. Is that understood?"

Ryan and the CIA man both nodded.

"Good." Harris paused a moment as if to organize his thoughts. Ryan studied the President closely. Steve Harris was an imposing man, well over six feet, almost as tall as Ryan's own 6'4". Like himself, Harris was powerfully built, but unlike Ryan who was all hard-packed muscle, the President had a paunch. Harris had a full head of black hair, a square jaw and blue eyes. He reminded Ryan of photos he'd seen of J.F.K.

"Yesterday," the President began, "an Air Force truck convoy carrying sophisticated military weapons was attacked. During the attack, six of the vehicles were destroyed, killing all the personnel inside. A helicopter that was escorting the convoy was also shot down. But even more alarming, two of the trucks were stolen. These were the vehicles carrying the weapons. And they've vanished without a trace."

"What kind of weapons were in the stolen trucks?" Ryan asked.

Harris massaged his temple with a hand as if trying to rub away a growing headache. "That's the part that's most alarming," Harris said. "The part that turns this event into a national security crisis. Those trucks were carrying ten suitcase-size nuclear bombs. They had just been manufactured at Los Alamos National Laboratory. They were being transported to Kirtland Air Force Base in Albuquerque. From there they were being sent to our armed forces in Germany and South Korea."

Ryan and Miller exchanged glances, then Ryan said, "I didn't know the U.S. was still making those types of weapons." He recalled what he knew about the original program, named 'Green Light'.

"You're right," Harris replied. "The W-54 program, also known as Green Light, was shut down in 1985. But it was reactivated since you left Army service. It's been kept top-secret. Only a few people know it exists. Just a limited number of employees at Los Alamos, a few military officers, and senior people at the Pentagon."

"I wasn't aware it had been reactivated," CIA Deputy Director Miller said.

"As I mentioned before," the President responded, "the existence of the program is only shared on a need-to-know basis. The W-54 program was created in the 1950's in response to the rise of the Soviet Union. At the time, the U.S was worried that Germany would be overrun by the Russians after World War II. Our scientists were able to miniaturize a nuclear device to a very small size. Although they're called 'suitcase-bombs', they're actually carried on backpacks by soldiers. They're low-yield because of their small size, but they can still do quite a bit of damage."

Harris paused a moment, then said, "The W-54 program was also called 'Green Light' because teams of Army Green Berets and Navy SEALs were the ones that positioned them in the battlefield."

Harris stared at Ryan and then Miller. "So you can see why this is a national security crisis. So far, we've been able to keep this theft quiet. We don't want the country to panic. We've told the media that the explosions were from a gasoline tanker truck that accidently caught fire and detonated."

"Sir," Ryan said, "since this is a major crisis, I'm sure you've deployed all of our national security resources to investigate?"

"Of course. General Foster is coordinating with the directors of the FBI, CIA, DHS, and DIA to search for these criminals."

"Then why do you need us?" Ryan asked.

The President steepled his hands on the desk. "The W-54 program at Los Alamos is top-secret. Someone leaked the information. It could be someone that works at the intelligence agencies. I suspect deep-state government agents."

"We took all of them down two years ago," Miller interjected.

"That's what we thought at the time," Harris said. "Now I think there's more." He shook his head slowly. "It seems like every time I clean up the bureaucratic deadwood and deep-state traitors in D.C., there's more beneath the surface. D.C. is a deep swamp, a very deep swamp. Anyway, enough about that. I want you, Ryan and Alex, to run a parallel investigation and report back to me."

The President pointed a finger at Miller. "I don't want the CIA Director to know you're working on this."

"Yes, sir," Miller said.

Harris then gazed at Ryan. "And this applies to you also. You report your progress to Alex Miller, and General Foster, and to me. No one else. Is that understood?"

"Of course, Mr. President. What about Erin? Can I read her into this operation?"

"Yes. I'm hoping that once she processes her grief she'll be able to join the team."

Ryan heard thunder and glanced out the windows, as lighting bolts lit up the ominous, almost-black sky over Washington.

The President turned and also stared out the windows, then addressed the group again. "General Foster and I both believe the weapons were stolen by terrorists. Who they are is unknown. That's our job now. To find and capture these terrorists before the bombs are detonated." Harris massaged his temple again. "There's something else I need to tell you, something that makes the situation even more dire. The attack on the Air Force convoy was conducted with great precision. Our lead trucks and the ones at the rear, and our helicopter were targeted and destroyed quickly and efficiently, before any of our defensive measures could be deployed. We're dealing with highly sophisticated terrorists. Diabolical killers who are capable of anything."

Ryan swallowed hard as the President's words sank in. He recalled the events years ago, when on September 11, 2001, terrorists highjacked planes and crashed them into Manhattan's World Trade Center buildings and the Pentagon. For a moment Ryan visualized something similar happening, except this time the planes would be carrying nuclear weapons.

He shuddered at the thought.

Chapter 4

Atlanta, Georgia

J.T. Ryan rang the buzzer at the front door of the townhouse and waited. The home was located in Buckhead, an exclusive area of Atlanta.

Moments later he heard a deadbolt unlocking and the door opened. Erin Welch stood there, looking haggard, exhausted and defeated. Her eyes were red-rimmed as if she'd been crying for hours, her long hair was disheveled, and she was wearing wrinkled gym pants and a baggy old sweater. Erin was usually an immaculate dresser, always sporting Dior dresses or Ralph Lauren suits.

Without saying a word, she stepped aside and motioned him in.

Ryan strode into the foyer and tried to come up with something to say to comfort her. All he could manage was, "I'm very sorry, Erin."

She nodded and pointed toward the kitchen. "I'm having coffee. Want some?"

"Sure."

He followed her into the high-end kitchen. After grabbing a cup from the coffee pot that was brewing, he sat across from her at the marble-topped dinette table.

"Is there anything you need?" asked Ryan. "Anything I can do for you?"

Erin shook her head and wiped away a tear. "No. There's nothing anyone can do." She stared down at the table. "It's ironic. One of the happiest days of my life turned into the worst."

He searched for words to ease her pain. "I'm sorry for your loss."

Erin nodded. "The funeral is this Saturday."

"I wish I could be there, Erin. But now that I'm on the President's task force...my time isn't my own. I just came back to Atlanta to pack some clothes and to see you. I'm booked on a flight tonight to Langley. Alex Miller is heading up the team and we'll be working out of his location."

"How did the meeting go?"

"It's a bad situation, Erin. Really bad."

"Can you read me into the operation?"

"Of course," Ryan said. "The President hopes you'll eventually join the task force."

She shook her head. "That's not going to happen. Not now, anyway." Her facial expression changed from anguish to fierce and determined. "I've got a killer to catch. If it's the last thing I do. I'm going to find and kill the bastard who did it."

Ryan had already figured this was what Erin would do. She was too good an FBI agent to do anything else.

Erin stood, poured herself another cup of coffee and sat back down. "Tell me about it, J.T. Tell me about the crisis."

Ryan spent the next half hour detailing everything he had learned at the White House meeting. When he was done, he leaned back in his seat and took a sip of his now cold coffee.

"Damn," she said. "It is bad."

"Yeah, it is." He reached out and covered her hand with one of his. "I don't want you to worry about it. You've got enough on your plate, Erin." Trying to lighten the mood from the crisis and her fiancée's murder, he smiled. "Anyway, now that I'm on the investigation, it's going to be easy to solve."

She gave him a puzzled look. "It is? How do you figure that?"

His grin widened. "I'm Superman, remember? I can leap over tall buildings and bullets bounce off my chest."

Erin shook her head as a small smile settled on her face. "You're too much, John Taylor Ryan."

"I guess I am. By the way, you were right about me being a smartass would get me in trouble. During the meeting at the Oval Office, I made a joke. President Harris was not amused. Not one bit."

She folded her arms in front of her. "Serves you right, buster."

"I can promise you, it won't happen again. Harris told Miller to keep me in line."

She nodded. "You better watch yourself, J.T. He's a lot tougher boss than I am."

"I know."

They spent another hour talking, then Ryan glanced at his watch. "Damn. I've got to go. My flight's leaving soon."

They stood, and he looked into her red-rimmed eyes and saw the pain there. He knew the grief would be with her for a long time.

"If you need anything," he said, "anything at all, call me on my cell. Day or night, okay?"

"Okay. Thank you for being my friend."

He nodded. "Of course."

Erin wiped a tear, then in a low voice said, "Can you please hold me. Just for a minute?"

They embraced for a long moment and he stroked her long hair. He tried to think of something he could say to ease her pain, but knew there was nothing.

Eventually she broke off the embrace and murmured, "I need to be alone now, J.T."

"I understand. I'll see my way out. Take care of yourself, Erin."

She nodded and then stared down at the highly-polished hardwood floors.

He turned and by the time he opened the front door to leave, he heard her sobbing. He almost turned back to try to comfort her, but realized there was nothing he could do for her. Sometimes in life you have to deal with grief all on your own.

Chapter 5

Vancouver, Canada

The woman was gazing out the floor-to-ceiling windows of her penthouse office on the 80th floor. From her vantage point, Vancouver's modern skyline was visible, as well as the tranquil waters of the stunning harbor. It was a crystal-clear day and the azure sky contrasted with the lighter blue of the bay. To her left was the Canada Place buildings, a waterside architectural marvel of glass and white sails that housed a hotel, a convention center, a trade center, and a cruise ship terminal. Also visible was Stanley Park, one of her favorite spots to walk. In the far distance she could also make out the Lions Gate Bridge, the suspension overpass that connected the harbor area to the mountains north of the city. She loved the view, and had the office tower built at this location to give her the sight.

There was a knock from behind her and she turned to look. Her assistant was at the open doorway of her office. "Your encrypted teleconference connection is online," he said.

"Thank you, Shawn," the woman replied. She pressed several buttons on the panel by the wall which opaqued the windows to black, then automatically slid down a custom-made titanium curtain over the glass. This made the whole office a Sensitive Compartmented Information Facility, or SCIF. SCIF's prevented all types of electronic eavesdropping.

After closing the door to her office, the woman went to the computer on her desk and turned on the monitor. The screen came to life and she clicked on the encrypted teleconferencing icon.

The colonel's face filled the screen. Multiple large scars covered his facial features, the result of a car accident years ago. As usual, the man was wearing a poorly-fitting business suit. The scarring on his face made him a hideous-looking man, she had always thought. But she had hired him for his efficiency, not his appearance. And he was highly efficient.

"Good afternoon, Lexi," he said in heavily-accented English.

"Actually it's morning here, Colonel."

"Of course. I have a progress report for you."

"Positive news, I hope."

The colonel nodded. "Very good news. The operation was flawless. All of our objectives were met."

Lexi smiled. "You have done well. Where are the packages now?"

"All ten devices are in a safe location."

"Excellent, Colonel. I'll wire your payment today. By the way, I've heard no news about the attack and theft."

"I believe the American authorities want to keep it quiet – to prevent panic. They issued a statement that a gasoline tanker truck caught fire and exploded."

Lexi nodded. "Makes sense."

"Your information sources were highly accurate," the colonel added. "The convoy's location and schedule was exactly as you described."

Lexi made a note on a pad on her desk, a reminder to wire her source his payment today.

"Is there anything else you need from me today, Lexi?"

The woman shook her head. "That's it for now. Wait for my further instructions."

"Of course."

She turned off the call and shut down her computer monitor. Then she went back to the wall with the floor-to-ceiling windows and reversed the SCIF process. The titanium curtain raised and disappeared into the ceiling as the glass went from black to clear.

Brilliant sunshine bathed the large room and the city's familiar skyline and harbor appeared. Lexi stood there and gazed out as she planned her next steps. She was excited and eager, savoring the moment. Operation Tripwire had finally begun. But the best was yet to come.

Chapter 6

Special Operations Division
CIA Annex Building
Langley, Virginia

Alex Miller was at his desk reading a report when he heard a rap at his door. Looking up he saw Rachel West there.

"Hey, Chief," she said with a grin.

"Have a seat, Rachel."

She pulled up a chair and sat down. "Feels good to be back at the Factory," she said. The 'Factory' was the nickname used by CIA personnel for the Special Operations Division. It was called this because it did all of the Agency's dirty laundry, including lethal 'wet work'.

Miller studied the agents' appearance. The good-looking, blue-eyed blonde was wearing jeans, running shoes, and a black polo shirt. Holstered on her hip was her Glock 43 pistol.

"We have a dress code at the Agency, young lady," he said sternly. "You are not exempt."

"Guess I forgot, boss," she replied, the grin still on her pretty face.

Miller glared.

Rachel sat straighter in the chair and her smile faded. "Sorry, boss."

"I'm sure you're wondering why I brought you back from Australia."

"Yeah. I wasn't done with that investigation."

"That's over now, Rachel. I'm putting you on something new. A national security crisis." He paused, unlocked a desk drawer, removed a folder and handed it to her. "The details are in there. President Harris has reactivated the task force. The one we were on two years ago."

"Must be something big," she said, the levity all gone from her voice.

"It is. Our task force will be running a parallel investigation to the U.S. intelligence services. The President suspects there's a leak somewhere in government and we'll report directly to him and only him."

"What about the Director of Central Intelligence? Are you telling your boss about the task force?"

Miller shook his head. "Absolutely not."

"So who's on the team besides us?"

"We'll be the nucleus. I'll add agents from the Factory as needed. Since the FBI's Erin Welch is not available, the President has put me in charge of the team. As Deputy Director of the CIA, I'll have the resources and logistics to make things happen."

"Yes, sir."

"There's someone else on the task force, Rachel. Someone you know well. Probably too well. John Ryan."

"J.T. is on the team?" she said, her grin returning.

"You can wipe that smile off your face, young lady." He pointed an index finger in her direction. "You will not have a 'personal relationship' with him until this assignment is complete. I need your total focus on eliminating this crisis. I don't want your judgment clouded by your personal feelings. Is that understood?"

"Yes, sir."

"You've disobeyed me on this issue before. And I let it slide. But only because you're one of my best agents."

"The best," she murmured.

He ignored that and in a harsh tone said, "But I will not let it slide again. If you let your emotions run loose, you will pay a price. The highest price."

"What do you mean, Alex?"

"Your employment at the CIA will be terminated."

"You can't do that!"

He glared. "Watch me."

Rachel's shoulders slumped and she nodded. "All right. I'll follow the rules."

"Good. I'm glad I'm finally getting through. Now let me brief you on this crisis."

Alex Miller spent the next hour filling her in on the Oval Office meeting and giving her additional information he had learned since then.

When he was done, he said, "Any questions?"

"How do we proceed from here?"

"This morning I was on the phone with General Foster, the President's Chief of Staff. He's coordinating with us. He's cleared your visit to Kirtland Air Force base in Albuquerque. Since the truck convoy was headed to this base, it's possible someone there is the source of the leak. You're to leave for Albuquerque immediately. I'm hoping you'll be able to determine if someone on the base is working with the terrorists."

"Yes, Alex."

"By the way, I met with J.T. Ryan this morning. I've sent him to the National Lab in Los Alamos. He's on his way there now."

Chapter 7

Los Alamos National Laboratory
Los Alamos, New Mexico

The Los Alamos National Lab was established in 1943 as the site of the Manhattan Project. The lab's single purpose was to design and build the world's first atomic bomb. Twenty-seven months later, a test atomic device was detonated 200 miles south of Los Alamos at the Trinity site. This first test bomb led to the production of the two nuclear weapons used in the bombing of Hiroshima and Nagasaki, Japan. This happened in August 1945 and resulted in the surrender of the Japanese to the Allied forces. It was also a large factor in ending World War II.

Since that time, the original lab has expanded to the current facility, which has over 12,000 employees and extensive security measures. The sprawling complex is comprised of hundreds of building and resembles a small city. Currently, it is one the world's leading centers of science and technology. It is still the site for the development of nuclear weapons for the U.S. stockpile.

J.T. Ryan was there now. After going through the extensive layers of security checks, he had been shown into the office of the lab's director, Dr. Timothy Keller.

The two men shook hands and after Ryan showed the director his newly-minted FBI credentials, Keller sat behind his desk and Ryan took the chair fronting it.

"General Foster from the White House called me," Dr. Keller said, "and told me to expect you. Said you've been given top-security clearance, so I'm free to share all classified information with you."

Ryan studied the man as he spoke. The scientist was in his late fifties, with graying hair, a slight build, and had a pallid complexion, as if he spent little time in the sun. Keller wore round, wire-frame eyeglasses which gave him an owlish appearance. Ryan knew the guy had earned multiple PhD diplomas in physics and engineering.

"Yes, the general told me he was calling you," Ryan said.

"I'm a bit confused, Agent Ryan. I've already been questioned by several agents from the FBI and the DIA."

"That's right. The task force I'm on is conducting a separate investigation. That's why I'm here."

"I see." Keller adjusted his eyeglasses with a hand. "First of all, let me say that everyone here is deeply concerned about what happened. The theft of the ten devices is shocking, as is the deaths of the forty airmen. Specially since it happened so soon after the convoy left our facility." He paused a moment. "We here at Los Alamos take great pride in our security measures. As you saw when you entered our complex, there's multiple checkpoints that visitors must pass. And each visitor has to be fully vetted before they're allowed into our facility. On top of that, all of our 12,000 employees go through rigorous background checks before being hired. So, I feel confident there was no leak of information about the convoy from anyone here at Los Alamos."

Ryan had expected the director to say something like this. That's why he had done research on his own before coming to the laboratory.

"Isn't it true, Director, that you've had several issues regarding security here at Los Alamos?"

Keller took off his glasses and began cleaning them with a handkerchief. "I'm not sure what you're referring to...."

Ryan pressed on. "Isn't it true that in 1999, one of your scientists, Wen Ho Lee, downloaded nuclear weapons codes to data tapes and removed them from the lab? That scientist was arrested, convicted, and served time in prison for his crime."

"Well, that is true."

"And isn't it also true," Ryan said, "that in 2004, hard drives containing classified weapons data went missing and was never found? I have several more instances like this that I can tell you about...."

Keller held his palms in front of him. "All right, all right. You are correct, Agent. All of these incidents you mentioned did happen."

"And a few more, sir."

"Yes, and a few more. But I still believe our security is top-notch."

"It's been my experience," Ryan said, "that any security system can be penetrated. And that some people, given the right incentive, can be bought or intimidated into releasing top-secret government information."

Keller nodded. "I would never admit this publically, but I have to agree with you. Now, how can I assist you with your investigation? I want to cooperate with you and the White House in any way I can."

Ryan leaned forward in his chair. "First, I need names, job descriptions and addresses of everyone of your employees and contractors at Los Alamos. We'll do a deep dive into their background and financials to see if we can find any incriminating evidence."

Director Keller jotted on a notepad. "Yes, we can do that. We'll put that on a flash drive for you."

"Second, I'd like to see a prototype of the actual weapons that were stolen. It'll help me visualize their size and weight. Knowing what they look like will help us locate them."

"Of course," the director replied. "I can show you one of the labs where the W-54's are stored."

For the next hour, Ryan questioned the scientist about the security procedures, hiring processes, and other details he thought might help him in the investigation.

After that, Dr. Keller ushered Ryan to one of the labs in the complex where the weapons were stored. Before going inside, they went through several security checkpoints. They also had to don protective garments that resembled Hazmat suits. Keller assured him that wearing the suits was not really necessary to prevent radiation poisoning, since each bomb was entirely cased. The suits were 'just in case' an 'unforeseeable' event happened.

Several technicians were in the lab, and after being instructed by Dr. Keller, one of them unlocked one of the large steel lockers. The technician then removed a normal-looking backpack from the locker and set it down on a table in the room.

"Go ahead and open it," Keller told the tech.

The lab guy unzipped the backpack and lifted out a black metal container, which had a control panel on the top of it.

"This is an actual W-54 nuclear device," said Keller. "It's a sixth-generation unit, much more advanced that the original W-54 bombs developed years ago. This unit was just developed this year."

"It's carried into potential battlefield areas," Keller continued, "by military units such as Army Delta Force and Navy SEAL teams. It's carried in the backpacks you see here and is often referred to as a 'backpack nuke'. This particular model has an explosive TNT equivalent of ten tons." Keller paused a moment. "As you may have guessed, this device is not armed right now. The igniter has not been activated and the timing device has not been set, so it won't explode."

"So if I pick it up," Ryan said, "and accidentally drop it on the floor, it won't go BOOM?"

Keller was not amused. "This is not a laughing matter. We don't joke about nuclear bombs."

Damn, thought Ryan. *This guy has no sense of humor.* "Sorry, Director."

Ryan stared at the W-54, amazed how compact it was. The rectangular shaped container appeared to be about 15" long, 8" wide and 8" deep. "May I pick it up?"

"Yes."

Ryan placed both hands on the sides of the metal device, grasped it tightly, and lifted it off the table. He estimated it weighed about 50 lbs, a weight that could be easily carried by well-trained soldiers for long distances.

He lowered the device back on the table , and after studying the unit's control panel, he picked up the backpack and examined it closely. It was made of a heavy-duty plastic material and had several combination locks on the opening flap. But it looked and felt like a non-descript, black pack with black straps, similar to dozens like it that are available from Wal-Mart, Target, or Amazon.

"This is amazing," he said, turning toward Dr. Keller. "That something so small could have so much destructive power."

"I agree. By the way, I should tell you something else about the W-54. Besides the explosive damage, setting off this type of device would cause a massive electronic magnetic pulse. Are you familiar with what that is?"

"An EMP?" Ryan said. "Yes, somewhat. What kind of damage are you referring to?"

"An EMP that could knock out all data transmission for hundreds of miles. TV, internet, landline, cell phone, and electronic banking would cease."

Ryan tensed and his heartbeat raced as he mulled over all the implications.

Chapter 8

Los Alamos National Laboratory
Los Alamos, New Mexico

J.T. Ryan had spent the rest of the day talking with Director Keller and then with his key people at the laboratory, probing for any weaknesses in their security measures. Now he was in the guest quarters that Keller had assigned to him during his stay. The one-bedroom efficiency was located in one of the buildings at the Los Alamos complex. The apartment's green paint and Spartan furnishings reminded Ryan of the many BOQs he had used during his years in the military.

Sitting on the bed, he powered up the new encrypted satellite cell phone that Alex Miller had given him at Langley. He punched in Miller's number and the man answered on the second ring.

"It's J.T., sir."

"What do you have for me, Ryan?"

"I've got a list of names and particulars of all the employees and contractors at Los Alamos."

"That's good."

"Sir, the list contains over 12,000 people. I'd like to have your techs analyze this group and see if they can spot discrepancies or red flags that may highlight financial problems or criminal association. I assume you can do this?"

"Of course," Miller replied, sarcasm dripping from his voice. "We are the CIA."

Ryan shook his head slowly. *This guy is a tough pill to swallow,* he mused. He went on and filled Miller in on what he'd learned from Director Keller and his top people.

Miller then said, "I just got off the phone with General Foster at the White House. He told me that it's the consensus of all of the intelligence services, including the FBI, CIA, DIA, Homeland Security, and the NSA, that the perpetrators of the attack are Islamic terrorists. They believe it is a splinter group from Al-Qaeda or ISIS. Because of that, they've dispatched hundreds of agents to the Middle East. They're blanketing Syria, Iraq, Egypt, Afghanistan and Libya, that whole area."

"Do you agree with their assessment, sir?"

"I don't know. I don't believe we have enough information yet. What do you think, Ryan?"

"I think we have to follow the evidence."

"Good. I agree with that."

"Sir, I want to send you the list of employees. I can upload the flash drive to this cell phone and text you after this call."

"Excellent."

They spoke for several more minutes, then Ryan texted Miller the data. He hung up the phone and set it on the bed. He stood and was about to go to the kitchenette and see if he could find something to eat, when his cell buzzed.

Picking up the phone he answered the call.

"It's Rachel."

"Rachel West," he said, grinning. "My favorite CIA agent."

She laughed. "How many agents do you know at the Agency?"

"Besides you, none."

"Not much of a compliment then, J.T."

Ryan chuckled, as he visualized the stunning-looking blonde. With her sculpted face, piercing blue eyes and curvaceous figure, she resembled a model not an undercover operative. She also had a razor-sharp mind and a great sense of humor.

"How long has it been, Rachel? Since we saw each other?"

"Too long. Way too long, that's for damn sure."

"Sorry I missed you when I was at Langley. After I met with Miller, he put me on a jet to Los Alamos and here I am. Where are you?"

"I got to Kirtland Air Force Base today, J.T. I spent the day talking with the top brass here."

"Find anything?"

"Nothing yet. You?"

"Too early to tell. The National Lab has had security breaches in the past, so there may be something here."

"From what I can tell, J.T., the military people at Kirtland are squared away. A lot of crew-cuts, yes ma'am, no ma'am, polished shoes and freshly pressed uniforms. I'll be here awhile but I'm not hopeful I'll find the smoking gun here."

"You're probably right about that," he said. "By the way, I just got a great idea. Los Alamos is not far from Albuquerque. Maybe we can get together. You know, have coffee or something...."

Rachel laughed in that throaty, sexy laugh of hers. "Something, something?"

"Yeah. That sounds delicious."

"I'd love to jump your bones," she said. "You know me. Question is, can you handle it?" She chuckled again. "Remember last time? I wore you out."

He visualized her again and got aroused. "God, you drive me crazy. You know that?"

"I'd love to get together," she replied, her tone somber now. "That's part of the reason I'm calling."

"Can we meet?" He glanced at his watch. "It's only a two hour drive. I could drive over, spend time with you and drive back before I start here in the a.m."

"Like I said, I wish we could. There's nothing I'd like better. But my boss read me the riot act. Told me we have to keep it professional until the task force is done."

"Miller said that?"

"Yeah, J.T."

Ryan squeezed the phone so hard it almost cracked the plastic. "Damn that bastard."

"I agree. But he told me if I disobey him this time, I'm out at the Agency."

"He'd fire you?"

"Yeah."

"I'd love to strangle that man."

"Calm down, J.T. Please...."

Ryan inhaled deeply and let it out slowly. "All right...all right."

"He's not a horrible boss. He let me skate last time when he found out we were fraternizing."

"I know he did, Rachel. All right, we'll just have to wait until the crisis is over. But it's going to be hard."

She chuckled. "How hard?"

He glanced down at the front of his pants. "Damn hard."

Rachel laughed. "Poor baby. I wish I was there now. To help you ease the tension."

He chuckled, enjoying her zesty sense of humor. "So tell me, what's the other reason you called me? I know the first reason was to give me the shitty news from Miller."

"I wanted to hear your voice," Rachel said, sounding serious now, the levity gone. "You know how I feel about you."

"I feel the same way, Rachel." They had danced around the 'L' word for a long time, both of them thinking it, but never actually saying it out loud. It was a bridge they didn't want to cross. At least not yet.

They spent the next half hour talking, reminiscing about old times, enjoying the banter, neither one wanting the call to end.

Finally they said their goodbyes and hung up.

Ryan lay on the bed and stared at the ceiling for a long time afterward.

Chapter 9

Vancouver, Canada

Lexi rode in the back seat of the Cadillac Escalade limousine as it made it's way through the city streets on the way to the cemetery. Her thoughts alternated between the operation and her upcoming visit to her husband's grave. Although he had died two years ago, she dutifully visited the site once a week.

The woman's birth name was Alexandra Ivanova. Her parents always claimed they were descendants of Russian Tsarina Anna Ivanova, who had ruled the country as Empress from 1730 until 1740. Alexandra had never been able to prove the veracity of the claim, but she had never really tried. She enjoyed the feeling of being a member of royalty. Born in St. Petersburg, Russia, Alexandra and her husband had immigrated to Canada years ago and had become Canadian citizens. She had shed her Russian name and now was known as Alexandra Atwood, or simply Lexi Atwood. She was a tall and lean woman in her forties, with classic good-looks. Lexi carried herself with a regal air and always wore extravagantly expensive clothes. Today she was wearing a custom-made Dolce & Gabbana outfit. She had a lustrous mane of long, reddish hair combed fashionably to one side. She adored the color red, and coordinated her clothing to complement her crimson tresses.

On her ring finger she still wore her wedding band and the five-carat ruby ring her husband had given her at their engagement.

The Escalade went through the cemetery's entrance gate and made its way through the manicured grounds. It slowed and moments later parked at the curb. Lexi stayed in the SUV as her bodyguards exited the vehicle and scouted the area. One of her guards opened her door and she stepped out. Glancing around, she noticed only a few people visiting the cemetery.

It was a chilly morning and she buttoned her long, leather coat. The massive headstone was just ahead and she strode toward it, the heels of her red Louboutins sinking into the soft, verdant grass. Her bodyguards stayed a discreet distance back, but they were always alert, always on watch.

When she reached the grave site she caressed the marble headstone with her hand and then slowly traced her husband's name with her fingers. Kneeling, she placed the single red rose she had brought with her at the foot of the grave. She closed her eyes and said a silent prayer.

Chapter 10

Los Alamos, New Mexico

"This is where it all happened," Bob Jackson said, as soon as they stepped out of the Chevy Impala.

J.T. Ryan gazed at the stretch of blacktop up ahead, which had yellow crime-scene tape and orange cones roping off the now-closed stretch of highway. Even from one hundred feet away the melted rubber, metal, and plastic debris was visible on the charred road. The highway was bordered by forest area on both sides, and the trees adjacent to the road were charred as well. Uniformed police were stationed by the roped-in area, guarding the crime scene. Ryan also spotted several CSI techs bagging left over debris.

"What's left of the destroyed trucks and the human remains is back at Los Alamos," Jackson said. "Our CSI lab is still processing that, looking for any trace evidence."

"Find anything?" Ryan asked.

"Nope. Not yet." Bob Jackson was the National Labs' head of security. He was a tall, rangy black man in his early fifties.

Ryan strode forward into the roped-off area and stopped in the middle of the road. He turned around 360 degrees, very slowly, as he methodically surveyed the crime scene. He pointed toward the charred treeline . "How far into the forest have you searched?"

"About a hundred feet," Jackson replied.

"I think you need to comb the area deeper into the woods. At least two hundred feet, maybe more."

"Why?"

Ryan pointed toward the treeline. "Because that's where the attackers laid in wait."

"What makes you say that?"

"That's the way I would have set it up. Block the convoy's route with the fake construction work. Then attack from both sides of the road with mortars, RPGs, and small-arms fire. The forest gave them perfect cover."

Jackson nodded. "Makes sense. You sound like a military guy. You served?"

"I did. Iraq and Afghanistan. I commanded a Delta Force unit."

"Thank you for your service," Jackson said and extended his hand.

Ryan shook it and grinned. "I appreciate that. But no thanks necessary. I loved doing it."

"I'll have the CSI team broaden the search," Jackson said. "By the way, we did find shell casings on the road. They were from our guys' rifles. As you know, we had forty Air Force airmen spread out in the convoy. There must have been a firefight."

Ryan nodded. "Yeah. I agree. The two trucks carrying the bombs were stolen, not destroyed. So the men guarding those vehicles shot it out with the terrorists. By the way, were all of the convoy's personnel accounted for?"

"They were. We found the bodies, or what was left of them, of all of our guys. So none were taken hostage."

Chapter 11

Kirtland Air Force Base
Albuquerque, New Mexico

Rachel West was tired and in a sour mood. She'd spent two days questioning dozens of key personnel and had nothing to show for it. Everyone at the base seemed squeaky clean. All except the guy sitting across from her in the conference room. There was something he was holding back, and by God, she was going to find out.

"All right, Captain Burke," Rachel said. "Let's go through it again. You were one of the officers in charge of setting up security for the convoy. Who did you tell about this operation that wasn't cleared?"

"Like I told you yesterday. No one."

She studied the captain closely, who was in his Air Force uniform. She was looking for 'tells', subtle facial clues that he was lying. Her piercing blue eyes bore into his and his gaze shifted away from her.

Rachel leaned forward in her seat. "You're lying, you son-of-a-bitch."

Burke grimaced and stood abruptly. "I am not! I resent that. This interview is over."

She glared back. "Sit down, Captain. This interview is far from over. I'm on a task force that reports to the White House. If I tell them that you're lying, your Air Force career is over."

The man appeared uncertain and sat back down.

"Now tell me the truth, Burke."

"Like I said, I spoke with no one about the convoy."

Rachel gritted her teeth and stabbed her index finger on his chest. "Lie to me again and I'll cut your balls off."

He blanched and his eyes bulged.

Then she stood. "Okay. You've left me no choice, Burke. I need to see your commanding officer at the base. I'm sure he'll be very interested in what I'll tell him."

The captain raised his hands in front of him. "No, please. There's no need for that."

"You're going to come clean now?"

He nodded.

"Start talking."

He rubbed his forehead. "I'm a married man."

"I know. I saw the ring on your finger and read your file. So you told your wife about the convoy?"

Burke shifted uneasily in his seat. "No. Not her. Someone else."

"Who, damn it?"

"A woman, here on base. We're...close."

"Now we're finally getting somewhere. So you're screwing someone. I want her name."

"Do you have to involve her?"

"This is a national security matter. Hell, yes, I have to question her."

Burke stated the woman's name and Rachel wrote it down.

"Why did you tell her?" she said.

He shrugged. "I guess...I guess I wanted to impress her. This is the first time I've been involved in something this important. I know it was wrong, but...."

"Next time, Captain, I suggest you think with your brain and not your other body part."

He nodded and stared down at the table.

Then Rachel said, "Now go find your honeypot and tell her I'm waiting for her in this conference room."

Chapter 12

Special Operations Division
CIA Annex Building
Langley, Virginia

Alex Miller was in his office when his desk phone rang. The info screen said *The White House* and he picked up the receiver.

"This is General Foster. And President Harris is with me. Is this a secure line, Miller?"

"It is, sir." Miller replied. All communications in and out of the CIA building was encrypted and scrambled.

"Good. The President and I wanted to get a status report on your investigation."

"Of course, sir. I've got J.T. Ryan at Los Alamos and Rachel West at Kirtland."

"Find anything suspicious?" the President asked.

"Not yet, Mr. President. But those two are good. If there's anything there, they'll find it."

"All right. Keep at it," the general said. "I've been in close contact with the FBI Director in D.C. His people haven't come up with anything either. As I told you last time we talked, everyone in the U.S. intelligence agencies believe the people who stole the weapons are Islamic terrorists. That's why they've deployed hundreds of agents to the Middle East."

The general paused, then said, "All of the Homeland Security and FBI offices across the U.S. are on high alert. They've done everything possible to lockdown the major cities. We all feel that when the terrorists strike, their target will be areas that are most populated."

"I agree, sir," Miller replied. "As we learned on 9/11, New York was the first target. Are you planning on letting the country know what's happening? I haven't seen anything on the news."

"I want to keep it quiet, for now," the President said. "News about stolen nukes would cause widespread panic. Until we have a better fix on who we're dealing with and what they want."

"Yes, sir," Miller said. "Have there been any ransom demands?"

"No, not yet. Which in itself is bad news. If the terrorists just wanted money in exchange for the bombs, we would know we're dealing with criminals. But since no ransom demands have come in, we believe this is much worse. Their motive may be pure hatred for America and everything we stand for. If they detonate one of these devices in Times Square during rush hour, the casualties in Manhattan would be in the hundreds of thousands, maybe more."

Chapter 13

Los Alamos National Laboratory
Los Alamos, New Mexico

J.T. Ryan was about to climb into his rented Ford Explorer when Bob Jackson flagged him down, crossed the parking lot, and strode over.

"We broadened our search at the crime scene like you suggested," the chief of security said, "and we found something."

Ryan nodded. "That's the best news I've heard today. What did you find?"

"Blood stains. Plus shell casings. Lots of them. Deep in the woods, about two hundred feet from the highway. It's clear the terrorists attacked our trucks from there."

"Any way we can trace the shell casings?"

"They were brass casings. The type used in AK-47s. But AKs are a pretty commonplace type of rifle."

"How about the blood?"

"We're working on trying to find a match," Jackson said. "But nothing yet."

"Call me when you get something."

"Will do, Ryan. Where are you headed?"

"Based on what you just told me, I've got an idea I need to check out."

"Care to share?"

Ryan smiled. "Not yet. But you'll be the first to know if it pans out."

Chapter 14

Los Alamos, New Mexico

J.T. Ryan had spent the day visiting all of the local area hospitals in the town of Los Alamos. At each place he used the same procedure. After flashing his FBI badge, he questioned each of the Emergency Room administrators, asking about anyone who had been treated for gunshot wounds in the last few days. Although GSWs were supposed to be always reported to the police, he knew sometimes things fell through the cracks, especially in the hectic environment of an ER.

By three p.m. he realized the day so far had been a bust. No GSWs had been treated at the local hospitals.

Next he turned his attention to the day clinics that are so popular these days. Using his cell phone, he looked up the locations of the 'doc-in-the-box' clinics in the area. He ignored the upscale parts of Los Alamos, and focused on the ones located in the poorer neighborhoods, figuring those treated patients on a cash basis. Any criminal with half a brain wouldn't want to leave a credit card trail.

After visiting three clinics without success, he drove deeper into a poor Hispanic neighborhood. The 'doc-in-the-box' was situated in a strip mall in the southern part of town. Finding it ten minutes later, he parked his SUV in front of the seedy-looking strip mall. The clinic was nestled between a massage parlor on one side and a tattoo shop on the other.

Ryan went into the clinic, approached the counter and held up his badge. "My name's Ryan and I'm with the FBI. I need some information."

The young Hispanic guy sitting behind the counter stared at the badge and his eyes grew wary. "How can I help you?"

"I'm looking for anyone who's been treated here for a gunshot wound in the last five days."

The Hispanic guy shook his head forcefully. "No. We've had nothing like that."

Ryan glanced at the guy's name badge which read *Roberto*.

"Listen, Roberto, I'm not with ICE. I'm not here to deport you. I'm with the FBI and I'm investigating the murder of forty people. So if you don't start telling me the truth, I'm going to arrest you right now."

The guy's eyes grew big. "Okay, okay," he said.

Ryan tapped on the computer that was in front of the guy. "Why don't you look it up."

"Oh, yeah. Sure." The guy worked at the keyboard for a couple of minutes and then he turned the computer screen around so Ryan could read it.

"See," Roberto said, "no gunshot wounds."

The agent read through the long list of patients and realized the guy was telling the truth. "Okay. Now I need to speak to the doctor in charge of this place. I want to question him as well. Go get him, will you?"

Roberto found the physician and Ryan met with him in his office. The doctor, a heavyset Hispanic man in his seventies, also confirmed what the computer records had shown. He questioned several other employees at the facility with the same result.

Ryan left the place and went back to his Ford Explorer. Although the clinic and the doctor had seemed legit, there was something about Roberto's demeanor that made him suspicious.

There was a convenience store in the strip mall. He walked over and purchased two prepared sandwiches, a bag of chips, a candy bar, and a large coffee, and ate them in his vehicle. It was the first food he'd had since breakfast and he was famished. When he was done he glanced at his watch. It was seven p.m. and the clinic closed at eight.

He settled in to wait.

Exactly one hour later he noticed the clinic's employees begin to file out of the building. Roberto came out a moment later and got into a worn-looking, ten-year-old Honda.

Ryan quickly climbed out of the Explorer, sprinted to the Honda and got in the vehicle's passenger seat.

"What...the hell?" Roberto sputtered.

"It's me again," Ryan, said with a grin.

"What...what do you want...I told you before...."

Ryan's grin faded. "And you lied to me before."

The guy shook his head. "We've treated no GSWs. You saw for yourself...."

"That may be true. But you know something."

Roberto shook his head, but his eyes blinked rapidly and his hands were shaking a bit.

"Okay, I have no choice. I'm placing you under arrest."

"No! Please! I'll be deported. The *migra* will send me back to Guatemala."

"Then start talking."

"You won't arrest me?"

"No. You have my word."

"Okay. Someone came to the clinic. Three days ago. He said he'd been cleaning his gun and it went off. I told the guy our doc at the clinic is a straight arrow – he'll report any gunshot wound."

"What happened next, Roberto?"

"The guy left."

"And that's it?"

Roberto said yes, but his eyes said no.

"Bullshit," Ryan said. "You're lying to me again. You're under arrest."

"No, please!"

"Talk then."

Roberto let out a long breath. "They guy with the wound? He's my cousin, Jorge."

"That's why you lied? To cover for him?"

"*Sí.* Yes. Before he left the clinic, I told him I could patch him up. And after work, I did. I've worked here two years and I've seen how the doc does things."

"Where do I find this Jorge?"

Roberto looked hesitant again and Ryan pulled out his badge and shoved it into the guy's face.

"Okay, okay. I tell you." And he did.

The agent put away his badge. "If you call Jorge and warn him I'm coming, I'll find you and it won't be pretty. You'll get the worst beating of your life."

Roberto nodded furiously and Ryan climbed out of the Honda and slammed the door.

***

Jorge lived in a run-down apartment complex on the south side of town. The structure's roof sagged and the exterior paint was peeling. The landscaping was non-existent.

Ryan went into the building, climbed the stairs to the second floor and located the right apartment. Bare light bulbs hung from the ceiling of the corridor, illuminating the litter strewn on the hallway.

He took out his badge and also his pistol, which was holstered at his hip under his jacket. Holding the gun at his side, he used his badge to rap on the door. "FBI. Open up."

He heard shuffling shoes from the other side and a click from the spyhole. He knew the guy inside was staring at his credentials.

The door opened a crack. "What yo' want?" The guy spoke in a heavy Hispanic accent.

"Open up, Jorge. We need to talk."

"Abou' what?"

Ryan kicked the door hard and it flung open, knocking the man inside to the floor. The agent pocketed his badge, pulled out flex-cuffs and cuffed the guy's hands behind his back. Then he dragged him into the living room and pushed him down on the dilapidated sofa. After closing and locking the front door, Ryan searched the rest of the apartment and found no one else.

He went back to the living room and stared at the wiry, tough-looking guy with the black mustache and scraggly beard. Jorge's left arm was bandaged. The man fit the description Roberto had given him.

Ryan pulled a straight back chair in front of the guy and said, "Okay, Jorge. We need to talk."

"I got nottin' to say."

"We'll see about that."

"*No hablo Ingles.*"

"Bullshit. You speak English fine."

"No talkin'."

"I'll arrest you."

He shrugged his shoulders. "Been 'rested plenty. Don' give a shit."

Ryan realized Jorge had been through the system and knew how it worked. He'd lawyer-up immediately. "You're a hard case, huh?"

Jorge gave him a crooked grin. "My brother. He the hardcase. He be here soon. You see."

"Another bullshit line. I bet you don't even have a brother. Now tell me how you got that gunshot wound on your arm."

Then, as if on cue, Ryan heard the front door unlocking and Jorge yelled, "Watch out, Manuel! Cop here!"

The agent whirled around and saw a big guy barrel into the room. He was 6' tall and built like a brick. He sported MS-13 gangbanger tattoos on his heavily-muscled arms.

Before Ryan could pull his gun, the big man was lunging toward him. Ryan hit him with a punch to his gut and Manuel staggered back. Then with his eyes full of hate, Manuel charged again, this time with both of his huge arms extended, obviously trying to bear hug him to the floor.

Ryan hit him again, this time with a powerful left-right-left combination to the guy's solar plexus and this time the man went down and stayed down.

The agent pulled out a flex-cuff and bound Manuel's hands behind his back and stuffed his handkerchief into his mouth.

After closing the front door again, Ryan took a moment to massage his knuckles. *Throwing a hard punch isn't like in the movies*, he mused. *In real life it hurts like hell.*

He went back and sat across from Jorge again. The man's eyes narrowed and his look of defiance was all gone.

"Got any other brothers, Jorge?"

The man shook his head.

"Okay. Now we talk, or do you want what Manuel got?"

The guy stared at his brother's prone body on the floor, still unconscious.

"Arrest me," the Hispanic man said. "I no resist...."

"Too late for that, my friend."

"I don' know nutin."

"You know plenty, Jorge." He reached out with a hand and squeezed hard on the man's bandaged arm.

Jorge screamed.

"How'd you get the wound?"

The guy was still wincing from the pain and Ryan squeezed harder.

"Stop! Stop!"

Ryan let go of his arm. "Talk."

"I cleanin' my gun."

The agent reached over and squeezed again, even harder. "We can do this all day."

Jorge screamed again and tears rolled down his face. A moment later he said, "You FBI. You no can do this."

Ryan grinned. "I'm a special kind of FBI agent. The kind that doesn't give a shit. Now talk." He let go of the guy's arm.

"All right," Jorge said, still gasping for breath. "A guy...a guy pay me...."

"To do what?"

"As...hired gun. Me and Manuel. And bunch of other Guatemalans. To shoot at trucks...."

"Who hired you?"

"Scary-looking dude. With funny accent."

"Hell, you've got a funny accent, Jorge."

"No. The guy not Spanish – he and others with him – foreign. They spoke...to each other...different language. Not English."

"Were they from the Middle East? They spoke Arabic?"

Jorge shrugged his shoulders. "Who know? They pay good. Ten large. Five before and five after."

"They paid you $10,000? In cash?"

Jorge nodded.

"Where do I find these guys?"

The man shrugged and Ryan squeezed his arm again and didn't stop.

Jorge screamed and a moment later passed out from the pain.

Ryan had interrogated a lot of people during his years in Special Forces and he had a feeling this guy really didn't know.

Which meant the agent was at a dead end.

Chapter 15

Vancouver, Canada

Lexi sipped coffee as she gazed out the floor-to-ceiling windows of her penthouse office on the 80th floor. It was an overcast day, the iron-gray clouds obscuring the spectacular view of the city's waterfront.

The beautiful red-haired woman turned away from the windows, crossed her massive office and went into a locked, separate room. This space contained a large workstation with three computers.

Mounted on the wall fronting the workstation were six large flat-screen televisions. All of the TVs were turned on, with the sound muted. Three of them were tuned to cable news channels, covering various events happening around the world. The other three TVs were set to business news, covering the moment-by-moment fluctuations in the U.S., European, and Asian stock markets.

Sitting at the workstation, Lexi powered up her three computers, input her passwords, and opened stock trading programs on the screens. She examined her current equity holdings, which were extensive, and mulled over her next purchase. Background music played from her sound system, and as usual it was her favorite song, the classic rock ballad *Stairway to Heaven* by Led Zeppelin.

Although she had never been educated beyond high school, Lexi had always been fascinated with financial transactions. She had left her parents home at seventeen, got an apartment in St. Petersburg, Russia and worked two jobs as a waitress. She lived frugally and saved every penny of her earnings. She also spent countless hours reading everything she could find about the stock market and finance. After having earned enough money, she plowed her savings into a brokerage account and began buying and selling stocks. To say that she was extremely successful would be an understatement.

After two years, she was a millionaire. And by the time she was twenty-five she was a billionaire, Russia's first woman to achieve this status.

Then, while attending a party with some friends, Lexi met someone, a dashing, impeccably-dressed man named Sergei Petrov. She was attracted to him immediately. They started dating, and although he was evasive about what he did for a living, he always had plenty of cash and wasn't shy about spending it. He took her to all of St. Petersburg's finest restaurants, bought her expensive jewelry, and in every respect, treated her like royalty.

Within a few months she realized she was deeply in love with Sergei and he with her. One evening while dining at Cafe Peterhof, St. Petersburg's most elegant restaurant, he presented her with a five-carat ruby ring and asked her to marry him.

She immediately said yes.

It was one of the two happiest days in her life – the other being the day she learned she had become a billionaire.

They married soon after, honeymooned in Antigua in the Caribbean and settled into his lavish estate in the suburbs of the city. Almost immediately, she realized something was wrong. Very wrong.

Suitcases full of cash started being delivered to their home. At first Sergei said they were cash payments for his 'consulting' business. But she pressed him and he finally told her the truth. Her husband was a money-launderer. But not just any run-of-the-mill money-launderer. He was the main one for Russia's Mafia, the Bratva. The Bratva is the largest crime organization in that country.

She loved him deeply and did a lot of soul-searching, and knew she could never leave him, regardless of his criminal association. They remained married.

Eventually the Russian authorities learned of his occupation and he was indicted. Before he was arrested, Sergei and Lexi fled the country, changed their identities, and settled in Vancouver. They became Canadian citizens under the names of Alexandra Atwood and Sergei Atwood.

They still had the billions they had made (she had made hers legally, him not so much) and purchased a lavish estate on Vancouver Island. Lexi went back to stock trading and her husband went back to his profession, money-laundering.

It was an idyllic life, she had thought at the time. Until three years ago when Sergei's money-laundering was uncovered. Before the couple could flee again, he was arrested, charged, convicted, and sent to prison, where he died.

Lexi was heartbroken.

She was inconsolable for months, spending her days crying non-stop. Even two years later a day didn't go by without her thinking about him and how much she missed him.

As Lexi studied her massive stock portfolio, which was displayed on the computer screens, she sipped coffee. She strategized what she would buy and sell next. Especially now, in light of her current operation. She thought about the ten packages, safely stored until she gave the colonel his orders. The packages would give her immense wealth, she knew. Or her strategy could backfire and make her penniless. She savored the thought, never one to be afraid of taking risks.

Lexi studied the screens again, her fingers caressing the keyboard, feeling the imminent excitement of another day of stock trades.

She drained her coffee cup and set it aside.

Then she clicked on her mouse to activate her very first trade, her exhilaration beginning to build. Some days the excitement became so intense it bordered on sexual. Just then the erotic thoughts of making money and sex comingled, and she felt herself getting wet.

Yes, it's going to be a good day, she thought. *A very good day.*

And Lexi was rarely wrong.

Chapter 16

FBI Field Office
Albuquerque, New Mexico

J.T. Ryan stared through the one-way glass into the interrogation room.

Two men were inside. One of them was unshaven and was wearing a baggy, orange jumpsuit and was shacked to the floor and the metal loop on the table. The other guy was dressed in a gray business suit, a blue tie, and a starched white shirt. He was clean-cut, had closed-cropped hair, and wore highly-buffed black shoes. He looked every inch an FBI agent.

After a few minutes the guy in the suit stood and walked out of the room.

"Anything?" Ryan asked.

"Nope. Nothing. Nada," the agent said. "He's all yours, J.T."

Ryan nodded. "Thanks. You don't need to hang around. I'll take it from here."

"You got it," the other man said and walked away.

Ryan entered the room and closed the door behind him. "Remember me, Jorge?" he said with a grin.

The Hispanic man in the orange jumpsuit shrugged. "*Si*. I wish I could forget."

"Just for the record," Ryan said loudly, "I'm FBI Special Agent John Taylor Ryan. And you're Jorge Rodriguez. You've been charged and are being held on numerous felony charges, including murder. You're also being charged for committing terrorist acts against the United States." Ryan glanced at the security camera on the wall by the ceiling. "You're being charged for terrorism under the Patriot Act, which means some of your civil liberties are suspended."

"*Ques eso?* What last part mean?" Jorge replied.

Ryan grinned. "It means, my friend, that you're shit out of luck."

The prisoner grimaced but said nothing.

Ryan unbuttoned his navy blazer, took it off, and draped it over the back of his chair. Then he strode to the wall, went up on his tiptoes and pushed a switch on the CCTV camera. The green light on the device turned black. Next he went to the room's window and closed the blinds.

"What 'yo doin?" Jorge said.

Ryan laughed. "Like the song says, don't worry, be happy." He rolled up the sleeves of his blue denim, button-down shirt and sat across from the other man.

"You told the agent that just left nothing new. And I'm sure he asked you politely and respectfully, as all good Bureau agents are trained to do. But I'm not as polite."

"This good cop, bad cop? I seen movie before."

"You got part of that right, Jorge. He was the good cop. But I'm mean cop."

The Hispanic man grimaced. "I told 'yo before. Everything I know."

"Maybe. Maybe not. You're a smart guy. I'm figuring you held something back, so you'd be able to cut a deal later. Except this time the only deal you're getting goes like this. We're sending you on an all-expenses paid trip to a beautiful tropical island in the Caribbean."

Jorge's eyebrows shot up. "Well, that don't soun' so bad."

Ryan grinned. "You may rethink that when I tell you where it's located."

"Where?"

Ryan's grin widened. "Guantanamo, Cuba. The prison the U.S. has there."

"Gitmo?"

"Yeah."

"*Mierda*. Shit."

Ryan laughed. "Yeah. You'll be smelling it and eating it, along with all the roaches and rats that are all over that damn place."

Jorge glared. "This no funny."

"From my side of the table it's hilarious." Ryan then turned serious. "And if the threat of Gitmo isn't enough to scare you, I'm sure I'll think of a few other things that may jar your memory."

"*Que?* Like what?" the man asked, hesitation in his voice.

Ryan removed the .357 Magnum pistol holstered at his waist and placed it on the table. Then he reached into a pocket and pulled out a 3" knife, flicked open the blade and also rested that on the table. The sharp blade of the knife gleamed from the overhead light. From Ryan's experience interrogating suspected terrorists in the Middle East, he knew the fear of pain was a more powerful motivator than the pain itself.

Ryan tapped the knife with a finger. "This has many uses, as you will soon find out. The gunshot wound on your arm. I'm sure the medics in this jail stitched it up?"

The man nodded.

"Well, stitches can pop out," Ryan continued. "Specially if they're cut. And if I squeeze your arm, you'll start bleeding out. It's a very slow and painful death."

Jorge's eyes were as big as saucers and he began screaming at the top of his lungs. "*Ayudame! Ayudame!* Help! Get me out!" over and over.

Ryan sat quietly and waited for the man to wear himself out from the yelling. When that happened a few minutes later, he said, "We're in a soundproofed room. No one can hear you."

The agent stood, picked up the knife, and began walking around the table.

"Wait!" Jorge screamed. "I talk! I talk!"

"You're sure, my friend? I don't want to waste any more time with you."

"*Si! Si!* Yes!"

Ryan sat back down and placed the knife on the table. "Okay. Let's hear it."

"The guy that hire me. He say his name Mike."

"Mike what?"

Jorge shook his head. "Don' know."

Ryan picked up the knife again.

"*Es verdad!* It true! It true!"

"Okay. What else?"

"They drive big Suburban. Black."

"Plate number?"

Jorge scrunched up his face, deep in thought. Then he said a partial license plate number.

Ryan pulled out a notebook and wrote all this down. "What else can you tell me about him?"

"Like I tol' 'yo before. He scary-looking."

"You're kind of scary-looking yourself, Jorge. Exactly what do mean? Describe him."

"His head covered with hood and scarf. But I see face – his face all scars."

"What part of it?"

"All over."

The agent wrote this down. "That's good. Now we're making progress. How did you contact him?"

"He give me cell number." Jorge then said the phone number.

Ryan jotted this down, but figured it was a burner phone, which would be a dead end. "What else?"

Jorge scrunched up his face again, obviously concentrating. "*Eso es todo.* That's all."

"You're sure?"

"*Si.*"

The agent tapped on the knife again.

"*Es verdad!* It true!" Jorge's eyes bulged with fear.

"All right. I believe you. Now relax. I just need one more thing from you."

"*Que? Que quieres?* What 'yo want?"

"I need you to listen to something I brought with me." Ryan reached into his pocket and removed a tiny tape recorder. "I'm going to play a bunch of different languages. You told me last time the man who hired you and the others with him spoke in a strange language. One you didn't understand. Right?"

Jorge nodded his head. "*Si.*"

"Okay. I'll start the tape. This conversation is in French. Tell me if it sounds similar to how they spoke."

Jorge listened and shook his head. "*No.*"

"Okay. How about this?" This conversation was in Chinese.

He shook his head again. "*No es.*"

"How about this one, Jorge?"

"No."

Ryan wrote all of this down. He continued playing a long list of conversations in different languages from around the world for the next ten minutes and the man kept shaking his head no. When he played a conversation in Arabic a minute later, Jorge held up his hand.

"This is what you heard? This language?"

Jorge shrugged. "*Es posible.* Maybe."

"But you're not 100% sure?"

He shrugged again.

Ryan jotted this down.

"We done?"

"Yes, for now, Jorge."

"Yo' still send me to Gitmo?"

"Hell, yes. But maybe I can get you a better cell. One with running water and a toilet that flushes."

Chapter 17

Vancouver, Canada

Lexi had just finished an extremely successful day buying and selling stock, her equities trading gearing up for the start of her operation. She turned off her computers and left her trading room.

Just then she heard a rap at her penthouse office door. Her assistant opened it and peered around the jam.

"You have an incoming encrypted call, Lexi."

"Thank you, Shawn. Is it the colonel?"

"No, ma'am. The other man."

Shawn closed the door behind him and Lexi spent several minutes lowering the titanium curtain over the floor-to-ceiling windows. Knowing the office was SCIF secure, she went to her computer on her desk and turned it on.

The screen came to life and she clicked on the call. Unlike her teleconferences with the colonel, this call was audio only. It was an extra step in security her informant insisted on. Based on the man's senior position in U.S. government, she understood why it was necessary. She never spoke his name during these calls, another security precaution.

"Good afternoon, Lexi," the man said in his deep baritone voice.

Lexi glanced at her voice analyzer graph, which was a small window on her computer screen. The analyzer confirmed it was him.

"Good afternoon. It's good to hear from you."

"I'm calling for several reasons," he said. "First, to thank you for the payment you wired me recently – and specially for the bonus you added."

"You earned it. The info you provided was highly accurate. The details of the truck convoy was exactly as you described. Our operation was a complete success."

"That's excellent, Lexi. I'm also calling for a different reason. Something that's somewhat concerning."

Lexi sat straighter in her chair. "What is it?" she said sharply.

"I can't confirm it, but there's a rumor going around senior intelligence levels that the President is conducting a separate investigation outside of normal channels."

Lexi gritted her teeth. "How is that even possible, damn it?"

"I can't control what the President does. No one can. He is the President, after all."

"I know that!"

"Calm down, please, Lexi. It's just a rumor."

"The fact you're telling me about it," she said, her voice harsh, "means there's something to it."

"Yes, that's true. I've heard it from several people at the White House. People I trust."

"Tell me what all this means, damn it. You're the fucking expert."

"As you know," the man said, "after September 11, 2001, President Bush created the Department of Homeland Security. That means that security investigations from all of the U.S.'s intelligence agencies are pooled. So senior people like myself have access to all of the details of terrorism related investigations."

"Okay, I understand."

"But," he continued, "if someone is working outside of normal channels, I wouldn't have access to that information."

"All right. Who's conducting this separate investigation?"

"I don't know yet, Lexi. I'm working on that right now."

"You better fucking find out! I pay you big money to be my eyes and ears in Washington. If you don't want the gravy train to stop, you damn well better find out." She paused a moment and took a deep breath to control her anger, knowing she needed the man as much as he needed her.

"Yes, Lexi. Don't worry, I will."

"I know you will," she said in a sweet tone. "I'm sorry I was rude earlier."

"That's okay. I know this is a tense time for both of us."

"It is."

"I'll keep working on this, Lexi. I'm making this my top priority."

"Thank you."

They hung up the call and the woman and leaned back in her chair. She hand brushed her long auburn hair to one side, a nervous habit from long ago. She brooded over what her informant had told her.

A moment later she made a snap decision and clicked on her mouse, initiating an encrypted call to the colonel. She located him five minutes later and his scarred face filled her computer screen.

"Colonel, I'm glad I caught you. I'm making a slight change in plans."

"What is it?"

"Where are the packages now?"

"At the safe place, Lexi. The place I stored them when I was in the U.S. last time."

"Okay. I need you to bring me one of the packages."

"To Vancouver?"

"That's right. I'll send my jet to pick you up today. Go get one of the packages and bring it to me."

The colonel scratched one of the numerous scars on his face. "But why?"

"You don't need to know, damn it. I pay you to do my dirty work. That's all. Just follow my instructions."

The colonel nodded. "Of course."

Lexi disconnected the call and turned off her computer. She sat at her desk for several minutes, mulling over her next steps. She hoped she would never have to use the package, but knew it would be good insurance if the operation failed.

It's always good to have insurance, she mused. *You never know when you'll need it.*

Chapter 18

FBI Field Office
Albuquerque, New Mexico

After he finished interrogating Jorge Rodriguez, J.T. Ryan located an empty conference room, went inside and closed the door behind him.

Pulling out his encrypted cell phone, he punched in a number.

When Alex Miller picked up, he said, "Sir, this is Ryan. I wanted to update you on my meeting with Rodriguez."

"Hopefully you were more successful than the Bureau agent who called me earlier. He found nothing new."

"Yes, sir. I did learn quite a bit. I guess I was more persuasive."

"I don't care how you did it, Ryan. In fact, it's better if I don't know. I just want results."

"Me too. One important thing I found out was that Rodriguez is pretty sure the language the terrorists were speaking was Arabic."

"I see. Then it's a good thing the FBI and CIA are blanketing the Middle East with agents."

"Yes, sir."

"Tell me something, Ryan. You said Jorge Rodriguez was 'pretty sure' it was Arabic. He's not completely sure?"

"Sir, that guy is no mental giant. And he's no linguistics specialist either. But he's the only source we have right now."

"All right. What else did you learn?"

"The terrorists were driving a black Chevrolet Suburban and I got a partial license plate number." Ryan read off what he had.

"Okay. I'll run that down on my end and let you know."

"I also got a cell phone number that Jorge called to coordinate with the terrorist. But I figure that phone is a burner." Ryan gave him that number as well. "And one other thing, the leader of the terrorist cell, the one that paid Rodriguez, said his name was 'Mike' and his face was badly scarred."

"That's good work, Ryan. That might help us locate him in the Middle East."

"Yes, sir."

"Anything else?"

"No, sir. That's it."

"Okay, Ryan. As soon as I run down the license plate and the phone number I'll call you back."

Ryan hung up and put his phone away.

Then he glanced at his watch and considered something for several moments. Coming to a decision, he left the FBI offices and drove to the outskirts of Albuquerque. He located Kirtland Air Force Base and found the Marriott Hotel, which was close to the base.

A few minutes later he knocked on a hotel room's door on the third floor.

He heard locks unfastening and the door opened. Rachel West stood there, an astonished look on her face.

"J.T.! What the hell are you doing here? I thought you were in Los Alamos."

"I was." He grinned. "But now I'm here."

She smiled back. "I can see that. Come in. Come in."

Ryan stepped inside and she closed the door behind him.

"You can put the gun away, Rachel."

She was holding a Glock at her side, pointed to the floor. "Oh, yeah." She rested the pistol on a nearby table. "Force of habit. Years of CIA training."

He nodded and studied the good-looking woman. Her long blonde hair was pulled back in a ponytail and she had on no makeup. She was wearing casual clothes – jeans, a short-sleeve polo shirt and Adidas running shoes. The blue color of her shirt matched the cerulean hue of her eyes. And as always when he saw her, she took his breath away.

"You look great, Rachel."

She grinned. "You don't look so bad yourself." Then her smile faded. "Wait a minute. How did you find me? I never told you."

"I'm an ace detective, remember?" He pulled out his FBI credentials and held it up for her to see. "And now I've got a real badge to prove it."

Rachel rolled her eyes. "It may be real. But don't let it go to your head. It's only temporary. The Feds will take it back when the crisis is over."

"We'll see."

She stepped closer to him and hugged him. "I've missed you, J.T."

He hugged her back, enjoying the warmth and sensuousness of her curves, then caressed her face gently with a hand and stared into her piercing azure eyes. "God, I've missed you too."

He kissed her softly on the lips and she returned the kiss, harder. When they broke the kiss, she whispered, "This feels good."

Ryan embraced her tightly with both of his powerful arms. "Yeah, it does. Damn good."

"Now that you've got that fancy FBI badge," she said, "does that mean you're going to arrest me and strip search me?"

He grinned. "Have you committed a felony?"

She smiled back, giving him one of her patented devilish grins. "I'm sure I have, officer. Once or twice in my deep, dark past."

"You're a bad girl, Rachel West. A dangerous girl. My mother warned me about women like you."

Rachel let out a throaty laugh. "Did she?"

"She did."

Rachel traced a finger over his lips, then slid her hand over his broad chest. Very slowly she moved her hand lower down, past his taut stomach and rested it on the front of his pants at his groin.

Ryan was instantly aroused.

She cupped the bulge in his pants. "What would your mother say about this, J.T.?"

He groaned from the pleasure.

Just then his cell phone buzzed in his jacket. "Fuck," he said, anger in his voice. "Who the hell could that be."

"Let it go to voice mail," Rachel whispered, still massaging his bulge. "You've got more important things to work on." To make her point, she squeezed him harder.

"Damn, woman, cut that out. Only a few people know the number to this cell phone." He reluctantly pulled away from her and removed the phone from his pocket.

"Ryan here," he said.

"It's Alex Miller."

Shit, he thought. *Talk about bad timing.* He grimaced and gritted his teeth.

Rachel stared at him and silently mouthed *Who?*

Ryan simply shook his head. "Yes, Director Miller."

The blonde woman's face blanched.

"I've got information for you," Miller said, "on the license plate you gave me." Miller proceeded to him the details, then asked Ryan to put his cell phone on speaker.

Ryan did and Miller's voice filled the room. "Where are you now, Ryan?"

"Right now?"

"Yes."

"Sir, I left the FBI office in Albuquerque and I'm driving back to Los Alamos."

Miller laughed, but it wasn't a pleasant laugh. In a menacing tone, Miller said, "That encrypted phone I gave you has numerous capabilities. One of these is a GPS locator, which means I know you're not on the road driving back to Los Alamos. In fact, you're in Room 325 of the Marriott Hotel near Kirtland Air Force base in Albuquerque. And I just pinged Rachel West's phone and know she is, in fact, standing no more that a few feet away from you."

Ryan shook his head slowly and ground his teeth. He watched as Rachel's face turned a deep shade of crimson.

"So the jig is up," Miller screeched. "I know Erin Welch cut you a lot of slack in the past, Ryan. But I'm a whole different animal. I will not tolerate fraternization until this whole thing is over. Am I making myself clear, Ryan?"

"Yes, sir."

"I know you can hear me, Rachel," Miller said, his voice icy. "Am I making myself clear to you also?"

"Yes, sir," she replied.

"I'd better be getting through to you, young lady," Miller added, "or they'll be hell to pay."

Rachel nodded, then lowered her eyes and faced the floor. "Yes, Director, I understand."

"All right. Now Ryan, I want you to immediately leave that hotel room and get to work on the information I gave you."

"Yes, sir."

Chapter 19

FBI Field Office
Atlanta, Georgia

Erin Welch unlocked her office door and went inside.

Her desk was covered with stacks of case reports and a pile of unread mail. It was her first day back to work from her bereavement leave and she wasn't looking forward to plowing through the mountain of paperwork. Since she was in charge of the Bureau's Atlanta office, she had close to forty agents reporting to her. And each one submitted regular progress reports.

Erin gazed out the windows of her corner office and watched as a passenger jet flew over the city's skyline, on final approach to nearby Hartsfield International.

She took off her gray linen jacket and draped it over the back of her executive chair and sat down. Turning on her laptop, she began opening the most critical emails first. Luckily she'd been able to access her work emails from home and had been able to deal with the most urgent ones from there.

There was a rap at her door and she glanced up. Her assistant, Agent Brian Donovan was standing in the open doorway.

"Welcome back," Donovan said.

"Thanks, Brian."

"I know I said this at the funeral," he added, "but I wanted to express my condolences again. I'm sorry for your loss."

Erin nodded, but said nothing, still numb from the murder of her fiancée. She knew she still looked a mess. The black circles under her puffy, red-rimmed eyes, were a testament to her lack of sleep.

"I organized your staff's progress reports as best I could," Donovan said.

Erin nodded again. "I appreciate that." Then she pointed to the bullpen area which was right outside her office. There were only a few agents in the large space. Usually the forty cubicles were mostly occupied and the bullpen was a beehive of activity.

"Where is everybody?" she asked.

"Most of the guys," Donovan said, "have been assigned to the truck convoy crisis. They're already in different parts of the Middle East. The Director of the Bureau emailed me himself, since you put me in charge during your absence."

"Of course. I remember now. I was copied on that email. I'm glad you were able to handle it."

"No problem, Erin. Can I get you anything?"

She shook her head. "No, thanks." Then she stared at the mountain of paperwork on her desk. "I just need to get back to work."

Donovan left, closed the door behind him, and walked back to his cubicle.

Chapter 20

Vancouver Island, Canada

Lexi watched from her third-story bedroom window as the helicopter flew toward her walled estate. The Eurocopter Hermes slowed, hovered over the circular landing pad in her extensive back yard, and touched down.

The high-pitched whine of the chopper's jet engines powered down, the propeller blades slowed to a lazy swirl and stopped. The Eurocopter's cabin door opened and a man wearing all black clothing and a black hood climbed out. He pulled a suitcase out of the helicopter and closed the door. Then he strode across the manicured lawn toward the estate.

A few minutes later Lexi heard a soft knock on her bedroom door and it opened partway.

"Your visitor is here, Mrs. Atwood," Sun-Yi said. The young Asian woman with the doll-like face had been Lexi's maid for years.

"Tell him I'll be right down," Lexi replied.

Sun-Yi left and Lexi finished dressing. She was wearing a crimson Armani blouse and matching skirt, set off with a wide black belt and black Louboutins. Standing in front of the full-length mirror, she brushed her long reddish tresses to one side so that the mane cascaded over one shoulder and covered the left part of her blouse.

Satisfied with her appearance, she exited her bedroom, took the elevator to the first floor and entered her spacious study.

The colonel was there, standing in front of the dormant fireplace, still holding the suitcase at his side. The black hood he was wearing was still on, covering his head and most of his face.

"Colonel," Lexi said, "I trust your flight here was uneventful."

The man nodded. "Yes, Lexi. Thank you for sending your jet to bring me to Vancouver." He paused a moment and scratched one of the scars on his face. "And the helicopter was a pleasant surprise. You didn't have one of those last time I was here."

Lexi smiled. "I got tired of taking the ferry to my office every day. The Eurocopter is much quicker." She pointed to the suitcase he was holding. "Is the package in there?"

"Yes."

Just then the door to the study opened and Sun-Yi entered. "May I get you or your guest anything?" the young Asian woman asked.

"No," Lexi said. "And we don't want to be disturbed," she added sharply.

Sun-Yi, always a shy girl, lowered her gaze to the floor. "Of course, Mrs. Atwood." She left and closed the door behind her.

Lexi faced the colonel. "Let's get down to business. And you can dispense with the hood for now – Sun-Yi won't be back until we're done."

The man nodded and pulled down the hood of his black sweatshirt. The angry scars that covered most of his face, neck, and bald head were now visible. She swallowed hard. They hadn't met in person in some time and the sight of his disfigured face was disturbing.

The colonel rested the suitcase on the coffee table fronting the fireplace. He unlocked the case and lifted the lid.

Inside was a rectangular black device with a control panel at the top.

"This is it?" she asked, a bit incredulous. "It's much smaller than I expected."

"Yes, Lexi, this is one of the W-54s. From what I understand, it's the latest model of these types of nukes." He reached into the case and pulled out a backpack. "The bomb can be carried in this pack."

"I see. How heavy is it?"

"About 50 pounds."

Lexi nodded. "Is it safe for me store it here in my home?"

"Perfectly safe. As long as you don't arm it and initiate the timer, it will never explode." He reached into his pocket, pulled out a sheet of paper and handed it to her. "These are the instructions for preparing the device. I'll leave this with you."

He then pointed out the buttons on the control pad to arm and set the timer on the weapon.

When he was done, she said, "Not difficult, is it?"

"No."

She gave him a cold grin. "Let's hope I never have to use it."

"Why did you want it here?"

"Let's just say it's insurance."

"You're the boss, Lexi."

She flashed him a harsh look. "And never forget that."

The colonel nodded.

"You can close the suitcase, Colonel. We have a few other things to discuss."

The man shut the case and looked at her expectantly. "You've decided on the location of the first explosion?"

"Not yet," Lexi said. "But I'm close. I have a few more financial transactions to make. I'll let you know soon."

"All right."

"There's something else you should be aware of, Colonel. My source in the U.S. government tells me there's a new investigation being conducted to find the stolen bombs. An inquiry being done outside of normal channels. And unfortunately for us, my source doesn't have access to the findings of this separate investigation."

"I see."

"So we have to be extra careful," she continued. "Take every precaution to keep the American authorities from learning our identities."

"I will do that. Per your instructions, the false leads have all been put in place. These leads are all dead ends."

She pointed an index finger at his face. "No fuckups, understood?"

"Yes. I understand perfectly."

Satisfied she'd made her point, she said, "My helicopter will take you back to Vancouver airport. I assume you'll be wanting to go back home?"

"Yes."

"In that case, tell the pilot of my plane," Lexi said. "And have a safe flight. You're an important part of my operation."

She paused a moment and in a sweet voice added, "I appreciate you, Colonel. I appreciate all that you do for me. I don't tell you that enough. You're not just an employee – you're much more than that to me. I consider you my friend," she added, lying. "And I'm sorry I'm such a bitch most of the time."

He nodded and she could tell he valued her softer, appreciative tone.

"By the way," Lexi added, "when you leave this room, tell Sun-Yi not to disturb me for any reason."

"Of course. I'll talk with you soon." He pulled his hood back up, left the study and closed the door behind him.

Lexi went back to the suitcase, which was still resting on the coffee table. She unlocked it and opened the lid. She studied the black metal device closely, carefully inspecting the control panel, recalling the steps the colonel had described to detonate the weapon. She marveled at the simplicity of it and was amazed how much destructive power she now had in her possession.

Before it had all been theoretical. Plans on a piece of paper and spreadsheets on a computer screen. Theoretical and far away. Her plans had been just that. But now, seeing one of the bombs close up, it was all very real.

Lexi reached out with a hand and touched the weapon.

Suddenly she felt a sexual thrill, which intensified as she slowly caressed the metal surface. It was an erotic sensation similar to what she felt when she was trading stocks and making money.

Lexi closed her eyes, the image of her dead husband's face filling her thoughts. *God, I wish you were here Sergei*, she thought. *I need you.*

She pushed the thoughts of Sergei away, knowing that could never be. She opened her eyes and kept gazing at the bomb as she continued caressing it's pebbly metal finish. Another jolt of sexual thrill coursed through her again, this time stronger, and she felt herself getting wet. The familiar, urgent itch was back. An itch for which she knew there was only one cure.

"I'm sorry, Sergei," she whispered. "For what I have to do."

Then she removed her ruby engagement ring and wedding band from her finger and placed them on the table.

Next she sat on the leather sofa and got comfortable. Pulling up her skirt, she slid her fingers under her red silk panties. She felt her wetness, the electric jolt becoming more intense by the second.

Her fingers rubbed feverishly until she groaned loudly, the ecstasy of pleasure and pain coming in several long waves.

Afterward she stretched out on the sofa and rested for ten minutes.

Now feeling energized and ready for the rest of her day, she got up from the sofa, smoothed down her dress, and put her rings back on.

Then she closed the suitcase, locked it, and dragged the case to one of the bookcases that lined the wall. This particular bookcase had a hidden, swing out feature. She opened the panel, which revealed her wall safe. After unlocking the safe, she stored the suitcase inside.

Chapter 21

Los Alamos, New Mexico

J.T. Ryan had just finished breakfast and was about to start working on the new leads he'd obtained, when his cell phone buzzed.

He slipped the phone out and took the call. "Ryan, here."

"It's me," he heard Rachel West say in a dejected tone.

"Hey, Rachel. Are you okay? You sound...."

"Like shit?"

"Yeah."

"That's because I feel like shit."

"I'm really sorry, Rachel. About the mess with Miller yesterday. It's all my fault. I should have never come to see you."

"I'm glad you did. I wanted to see you. I needed to see you."

"I know," he replied. "And I wanted it just as bad. Still, I blame myself. Don't worry, hon. After this crisis is over, I promise we'll go away together. How does St. Croix sound? I know how much you love it there. We'll soak up the sun, and swim, and sip colorful drinks all day."

"I know you too well, John Taylor Ryan. You just want to go to the beach to see me in my bikini."

"That thought never crossed my mind," he said with a chuckle.

She laughed. "Yeah. I bet."

"So. What are you working on today?"

"I'm wrapping things up here at the Air Force base. I've questioned everyone connected to the truck convoy. Several times."

"Anything?" he said.

"Zero. Less than zero. These Air force guys and gals are squeaky clean. I thought I had something a few days ago. A captain who was involved in the convoy's security was being evasive in his answers. Turns out the reason he was lying is because he's married and he bragged about his involvement with the convoy to his girlfriend. The girlfriend also works here at Kirtland. I questioned the honeypot and found out she's no terrorist and has no ties to terrorism."

"All right," he said. "I never thought there'd be anything at the Air Force base."

"Well you were right, J.T. What are you doing next?"

"I'm running down the lead of the partial license plate number. The terrorists were driving a black Suburban. Alex Miller found information on it."

"Okay. I guess we should hang up now and get to work."

"We should," he said, without enthusiasm.

"Yeah, we should get back to work," Rachel said, sounding just as dejected as at the beginning of their conversation.

Trying to lift her mood, he said, "Hey, did you hear the joke about the married couple?"

"Is this another one of your corny jokes, J.T.?"

"Yes."

"Okay. Tell me."

Ryan said, "One evening a woman and her husband were sitting on their front porch enjoying a bottle of wine together, when the woman suddenly said, 'I love you'. Surprised, the husband said, 'Is that you or the wine talking?' 'It's me,' the wife replied, 'talking to the wine'."

Rachel chuckled.

"How about this one," Ryan said. "What do marriage and tattoos have in common? Both seemed like a good idea at the time."

Rachel chuckled again.

"I got another one for you, Rachel. Why did the man get a job at a bakery? Because he kneaded dough!"

Rachel laughed. "You're too much, J.T."

"Feeling better?"

"Yeah. Thanks for that."

"I got a million more jokes," he said, laughing, "if you want to hear them."

"You're sweet. But I've reached my limit of your corny jokes."

Ryan smiled, knowing from her tone that he had cheered her up. "All right. Guess I'll have to work on my material."

"You do that, J.T. And don't give up your day job. You'd never make it as a stand-up comedian."

"Ouch! That cuts to the core."

Ryan and Rachel both laughed. Then they said their good-byes and hung up.

Chapter 22

Vancouver, Canada

Lexi was in the penthouse office on the 80th floor of her building when she heard a knock at her door. "Come in."

Her assistant Shawn opened the door and said, "An encrypted call just came in. It's not the colonel. It's the man with no name."

Lexi nodded and Shawn left and closed the door behind him.

After putting her office into SCIF mode, she took the call and stared at the screen of her computer monitor.

"I have something for you," the man said in his deep baritone. Lexi verified his identity via the voice analyzer and said, "Go ahead."

"The separate investigation that was rumored to be taking place? I've confirmed that it's true, Lexi. And I have the names of some of the participants."

"How good are your sources?"

"I trust my informants at the White House implicitly."

"Deep-state people?"

"The deepest," the man chortled. "Washington is a fucking swamp. I very deep swamp, full of snakes. Greedy snakes. Thank God for that."

"Tell me the names of the investigators," Lexi said.

"The search is being run out of the CIA's Special Operations Division. They're the outfit that does the Agency's dirty work – covert stuff – assassinations, if needed. Anyway, this division is run by the CIA's Deputy Director, a man named Alex Miller. He's been put in charge of the investigation."

"Who else?" she asked.

"An ex-Special Forces guy named John Ryan. He's a private investigator out of Atlanta who does security work for U.S. law-enforcement agencies. Apparently he's been deputized as an FBI agent."

"I see," she said. "Anyone else?"

"Yes, Lexi. The person in charge of the FBI's Atlanta office. A woman. Her name is Welch."

"Erin Welch?"

"Yes, that's right. You know her, Lexi?"

Lexi's face burned with anger. "Yeah. I know who she is. She doesn't know me, though. And more importantly, I know the bastard this Welch woman was going to marry."

"What do you want me to do now, Lexi?"

"Keep your ear to the ground. Find out all you can about this separate investigation. I need to stay one step ahead of these MFrs."

"Will do," he said. "By the way, when can I expect my next payment?"

"You're a greedy bastard, aren't you?"

The man chortled. "That's a fact."

"I'll wire you the money today."

"I appreciate that, Lexi."

She hung up the call and turned off her computer monitor. Then she picked up the handset of her desk phone and tapped in a number.

Five minutes later, Lexi's head of security was in her office, standing ramrod straight in front of her desk. The brawny Canadian man had buzz-cut blond hair and was built like a football player. In fact, he'd been a linebacker for a college team before going into security work.

"Shawn told me you needed to see me?" he said.

"Yes. Something's come up, regarding that project I assigned you a while back."

"Which one?"

"The District Attorney in Atlanta."

"Yes, Lexi, I remember. I took care of that."

Lexi tapped her red Mont Blanc pen on the desk. "And you did a good job. Who did you hire...to do the actual work?"

"A professional."

"I don't want to know his name. Can this 'professional' keep his mouth shut? Even if he's arrested and given some type of deal for cooperating?"

"It doesn't matter, Lexi. He doesn't know who I am or who you are. I hired this 'professional' thru a cut-out. A third party, using fake corporations."

Lexi nodded. "That's excellent. You do good work."

"I was trained by a master, Lexi. Your late husband, Sergei."

The red-haired woman tapped her pen on the desk again. "Sergei was a great man. And a very loving and kind husband. I miss him every minute of every single day."

"Will there be anything else, Lexi?"

"No. That'll be all. For now."

Chapter 23

Albuquerque, New Mexico

J.T. Ryan drove into the airport's parking lot, found an empty slot and parked. He went into the terminal building and located the Hertz counter, which was situated along a row of other car rental agencies.

Ryan approached the counter and flagged down the pert, young blonde girl who staffed it. She looked to be in her late teens, probably a recent high-school graduate.

"My name's Ryan," he said, holding up his badge. "I'm with the FBI and I need some information."

"Wow!" the blonde girl said, her eyebrows shooting up. "I never met an FBI agent before. That's awesome!"

He smiled and glanced at her name tag, which read *Ashley*.

"It's not as exciting as it sounds, Ashley."

"I bet you're on a big case," she said excitedly. "Are you trying to catch a serial killer?"

"Not exactly. But I do need some information."

"That's awesome! What can I do to help?"

"There was a Chevrolet Suburban that was rented out from this location. Black in color. I only have a partial plate number. I'm trying to find the person who rented it."

"Okay," Ashley replied eagerly. "I'll be glad to look it up! Do you have the date of when it was rented?"

Ryan shook his head. "I'm afraid not. But it would have been during...let's say in the last month." Ryan didn't mention anything about the man's scarred face, since it could have been one of the terrorist's associates who rented the vehicle.

"No problem, Agent Ryan!" she said in a bubbly voice. "This is so exciting. Don't worry, I'll find it for you!"

She tapped on her computer keyboard for the next five minutes, periodically jotting things down on a notepad. When she was done, Ashley looked up from her computer screen.

With a wide grin, she said, "I got it, Agent Ryan!"

"That's great. Who rented it?"

Her smile dimmed a bit. "Actually I found more than one person. We have four black Suburbans at this Hertz location and they were rented out by multiple people over the last month."

"I see."

"Here's the list," she said, handing him a sheet of paper.

"You've been extremely helpful, Ashley."

The pert young woman beamed. "That's awesome!"

"You know," he said, "you could help me even more if you would print out the rental contracts of each of the people on this list. That way I could get their full names, addresses, driver license numbers, and credit card information."

"Wow! I'd love to do that, Agent Ryan. But isn't that, like, confidential information? I know on the TV shows, the police have to get a court order, or something?"

"That's true, Ashley. But that takes time and that's one thing I don't have." He dropped his voice to a whisper. "You don't want the serial killer to get away, do you?"

Her eyes got big. "I knew it! It *is* a serial killer!"

He nodded. "Let's just keep this between us, okay? It'll be our little secret."

"Yes! This is so cool!"

"So you'll help me, Ashley?"

"Of course! I'll get right on it!" She went back to her computer and worked at her keyboard for several minutes. Moments later she handed him a stack of printouts.

"You've been extremely helpful, Ashley. Let me give you my business card. My cell phone is on there. If you can think of anything else that might assist me in the investigation, don't hesitate to call."

She nodded and took his card, a bright smile lighting up her face. "You bet, Agent Ryan! This is so awesome!"

Chapter 24

Albuquerque, New Mexico

J.T. Ryan had spent the last two days running down the names of the people on Ashley's list. Several were from right there in Albuquerque and a few others from nearby towns. He'd found no one suspicious, mostly businessmen or trades people needing a larger capacity vehicle for a few days.

Ryan was now headed to the address of the last person on the list. According to the rental car agreement, the man lived in the town of North Valley, a small city about ten miles from Albuquerque.

As soon as Ryan reached North Valley, he drove his Ford Explorer to the first gas station he found and filled up his gas tank. Then he input the man's address into the Explorer's NAV system and drove out of the Shell station.

Ryan hated relying on automated artificial intelligence devices like the NAV, but grudgingly had to admit they were more reliable and faster to use than his beloved paper maps.

Ten minutes later he was driving through an industrial area, with warehouses lining both sides of the road. There were no homes or apartment buildings from what he could see. A minute later he heard the NAVs cheerful woman's voice say, "You have arrived at your destination."

He pulled to the curb, stopped his SUV, and stared at the empty, weed-filled lot, which was nestled on two sides by old warehouse buildings. Thinking his vehicle's NAV system was incorrect, he took out his cell phone and input the man's address. But this also indicated the empty lot was where he lived.

Realizing the home address the man had put on his car rental agreement was phony, Ryan punched in Alex Miller's number and waited for him to pick up.

Miller answered on the second ring.

"Sir, this is Ryan. I've found something and I need your help with it. I've run down the list of people who rented Suburbans from the airport Hertz location. They've all checkout out, except one. A man named Timothy Smith." Ryan read off the man's address, place of employment, driver's license number, and credit card information. "Can you trace this guy from your end? I could probably find out, but I figured with your resources it would be faster."

"Good thinking," the CIA man said. "I'll check it out and call you back."

Ryan disconnected the call, rolled down his window, and settled in to wait. Fifteen minutes later his cell phone buzzed.

"It's Miller," the CIA man said. "I ran down the information you gave me. It turns out 'Timothy Smith' is as phony as a three-dollar bill. He doesn't exist. His home address is fake, as well as his place of employment. This guy must have forged his driver's license because the number is also phony. He did, however, have one thing that was real."

"What's that?" Ryan asked.

"The credit card Smith used was real. So the rental company got paid. As you know, most car rental companies put through a charge right away to make sure their vehicles aren't stolen off the lot. Hertz placed a hold on part of the rental cost the day it was rented, so no red flags went up."

"Who issued the credit card?" Ryan said.

"That's where it gets interesting. It was a Visa card issued by a Syrian bank."

"Syria? That's in the Middle East. What was the name on the credit card?"

"Tarik Logistic Exports," Miller said, "a company based in Syria. I looked them up and they list a subsidiary located in Albuquerque, New Mexico, a company we now know is a front."

"So the intelligence agencies may have been right all along in their original assessment. The terrorists are based in the Middle East."

"It sure looks that way, Ryan."

"I'm assuming you want me to head to Syria right away?"

"Negative," Miller replied. "We already have hundreds of agents blanketing that area. I'll contact the FBI Director and give him this information. They'll start investigating this Tarik Exports immediately."

"Yes, sir."

"Ryan, I want you to stay in New Mexico and keep working the case from there. You found out the Middle East connection. I have confidence you can find out more."

"Is that a compliment, sir?"

Miller didn't reply. Ryan smiled as he visualized Miller's face, which was probably scowling by now. He could almost hear the CIA man grinding his teeth.

"Don't test my patience," Miller said testily. "Just do your damn job!"

Ryan heard a click and knew the man had hung up on him. *Some people have no sense of humor,* Ryan mused.

He sat in the Explorer for the next five minutes as he sorted through his options of what to do next. Coming to a decision, he fired up the SUV and began driving out of North Valley and back toward Albuquerque.

An hour later he pulled into the city's airport parking lot, found an empty slot and parked. Going into the terminal building, he found the main office of the airport's TSA. After explaining what he was looking for to the supervisor of the Transportation Security Agency, he strode to the TSA surveillance control room, an office on the third floor.

Ryan went inside and flashed his badge to the TSA officer that was staffing the CCTV office. The guy sitting at the workstation was big and brawny and must have been a weightlifter because his biceps bulged. He was wearing a crisply starched TSA navy blue uniform and highly-polished black shoes. His name tag read *Parker*.

"I'm J.T. Ryan," he said, "I'm with the FBI and I need some information."

Parker nodded. "Yeah. My supervisor called me and said you were coming up." The man was barely suppressing a scowl. It was clear he wasn't happy that Ryan was in his control room.

"I'm working on a terrorism case." Ryan pointed to the bank of TV screens which covered a whole wall of the room. There must have been 50 CCTV monitors, the black & white images showing different parts of the airport. "I'm looking for security camera footage for the corridor where the rental car companies are located. I need the footage for two different days. The day the vehicle was picked up and the day it was dropped off at the Hertz rental place."

Parker nodded again. "That doesn't sound too hard. I just need to see your search warrant."

"Search warrant?"

"Yeah," Parker said in a hard voice. "That's a court order saying you have the authority to have the information."

"I know what it is." Ryan smiled, trying to disarm the guy's antagonistic attitude. "As I mentioned, I'm working on a terrorism case. A case that's time sensitive. Since we're both in law-enforcement, I thought we could speed things up a bit." He grinned again. "It could take me a couple of days to get that search warrant."

"Wish I could help you," Parker said. "But the rules are the rules. I still need to see that court order first." As if to prove his point, the TSA man folded his muscular arms across his brawny chest and flexed his biceps, which were clearly visible on his short sleeve shirt.

"You're not going to help me, are you Parker?"

The TSA guy gave him a tight grin. "You catch on fast." He pointed toward the office door. "There's the door. I suggest you use it."

Ryan shook his head slowly, realizing playing nice wasn't working. He turned around, walked to the door and locked it. Then he strode back to the workstation, pulled up a chair and sat across where the TSA man was sitting.

"What part of 'No' are you not understanding, Ryan?"

"I've tried being reasonable. Obviously that's not going to work. You leave me no choice, friend."

"What are you going to do?" Parker said with a sneer. "Shoot me? Remember, I got a gun too."

"Nothing so drastic," Ryan replied with a hard grin of his own. Suddenly he reached out with both hands and grabbed the TSA man by the throat and squeezed fiercely with a vice-like grip.

Parker's eyes bulged and he tried to pull away but Ryan held on, tightening his grip even more. Parker's face flushed, turning pink, then bright red as he tried to break free.

But Ryan held on, his clenching hands squeezing harder as the TSA man bucked in his chair, his eyes bulging, which were now as big as saucers.

Finally Ryan loosened his grip and Parker coughed and gasped for air, his face crimson. After several minutes, Parker was able to catch his breath, although his face was still red. He massaged his bruised neck for along moment and gave Ryan a wild-eyed stare.

"Are you crazy?" the TSA man said. "You can't do that. You can't pull that kind of shit."

"I just did," Ryan said. Then he reached into this pocket, took out a flash drive and held it up in the air. "Now. Are you going to help me or not?"

Parker nodded. "Yeah."

"That's better. Now look up the CCTV surveillance tapes for the days I told you and copy the footage on this flash drive."

Parker nodded again. Without saying another word, he started tapping on his keyboard.

Chapter 25

Los Alamos, New Mexico

After leaving the Albuquerque airport, J.T. Ryan had driven the two hours back to his guest quarters at the Los Alamos Labs complex.

He was there now, sitting at a small desk, booting up his notebook computer. Taking out the flash drive Parker had prepared for him, Ryan began scrolling through the footage of the CCTV camera. The camera angle wasn't perfect, since it covered not just the Hertz counter but also several other rental companies.

Because of that it was a long, tedious process as Ryan slowed and speed up the footage as new customers came to the Hertz counter. Luckily his notebook computer enabled him to zoom in on the visuals being shown, so he could get a fairly close look at the customer's faces.

After three hours of monotonous scrolling, which required a whole pot of coffee to stay alert, Ryan thought he spotted something. He backed up a few frames and then ran the video in slow motion as a man wearing black sweatpants and a hooded, black sweatshirt approached the Hertz counter.

Ryan zoomed in to get a better look.

Because the man's hood was pulled on, it covered most of his face. Ryan zoomed in even tighter, the image scrolling in super-slow motion as the hooded man spoke with the Hertz agent on duty. The camera angle showed both men in profile, so it was difficult to get a clear look at hooded man's facial features.

Just then the hooded man turned his head to reach for his wallet and Ryan saw what he looked like.

Which was exactly the same as Jorge Rodriguez had described him: A scary-looking guy with angry red scars covering most of his face.

Ryan froze the picture, knowing he'd found scarman.

Chapter 26

Vancouver, Canada

Lexi knew she was getting close.

She was in her stock trading room, having spent the last four hours analyzing companies to buy and sell, in preparation for the beginning of Operation Tripwire.

Once her trades were fully complete, she would give the go ahead to the colonel, the package would be moved to its location and Tripwire would begin.

Lexi sipped coffee as she studied graph charts on the three computer screens on her workstation. Then she made notes on her legal pad, reminders to herself of different strategies to utilize over the next several days. Periodically, she glanced up at the six flatscreen TVs mounted on the wall. Each TV, muted for sound, showed a different cable news channel, the screens covering various events happening around the world.

Lexi then turned to the computer resting on the left side of her workstation. She opened up one of her stock trading programs, and using the notes she had had made on the legal pad, began testing her strategy on how a company's stock price would behave when a certain event took place.

Lexi was a master at buying short, a technique used by stock traders. In effect, it meant that when you shorted a stock, you were betting the company's stock price would drop and you would profit as a result.

After spending an hour testing her theories, she knew the accuracy of her strategy was rock solid. *Nothing is guaranteed*, she mused. *But my strategy is damn good.*

Feeling energized by her success, she closed the trading programs and turned off her computers and TVs. Then she left her stock trading room, locked it, and entered the massive office, which was adjacent to her trading room.

She approached the office's floor-to-ceiling windows and gazed at the city's ultra-modern skyline and spectacular waterfront. It was past 6 p.m. and the sun was setting, a reddish glow settling over the city and the nearby mountains.

Lexi turned away from the windows and went to a nearby teak cabinet and opened it. She poured herself large glass of Merlot and took a sip. She never drank liquor when she was trading stock, realizing that was dangerous. But she loved the taste of the rich, red wine right after one of her sessions. She took another sip, larger this time, savoring the Merlot as she considered how close she was to success. She went back to the windows and stared out toward the sparkling lights of the city. She sipped the wine, relishing her accomplishments.

Tonight is special, she thought. *I'm close. Damn close.* She knew she was almost at the point of having everything in place.

Lexi felt energized. But not just energized. More than that, she felt sexually excited. Her cheeks flushed as the familiar itch came back.

She closed her eyes, memories of her late husband Sergei flooding her thoughts. The itch was stronger now, the erotic thoughts intensifying.

Her eyes snapped open, knowing only one thing would cure the itch.

Then she recalled where she was, not at her home where there was only one way to cure the itch. She was at work, in her office. A smile spread on her lips, knowing her assistant Shawn was still here. The young man, an extremely industrious employee, always worked late.

Reaching for the handset on her desk phone, she punched in his extension.

"Yes, Lexi?" he said when he picked up.

"I need you."

"Of course. Shall I bring my laptop with me? To go over the budget figures?"

"You won't need that, Shawn. Meet me in the back room in five minutes."

"I see," he replied, hesitation in his voice. "It's late, Mrs. Atwood. I really...should be heading home."

"I need you. Don't disappoint me, Shawn."

"Yes, ma'am."

Lexi hung up and walked through the sitting area in her office and into a separate room. Once a storage area, she had the space converted into a bedroom for times when she was trading stocks late into the night. The windowless room was outfitted with a king size bed, a dresser, a night table, and a liquor cabinet. Approaching the night table, she glanced at the framed photo that rested on it. The picture was of her beloved Sergei. After caressing the photo for a moment and asking for his forgiveness, she took off her five-carat ruby engagement ring and wedding band and placed them in a drawer. Then she turned on the sound system in the room and began playing her favorite song, *Stairway to Heaven*. The song was set on an endless loop, playing over and over. She set the volume low and hummed along to the words, which she had memorized long ago.

Then she inspected her appearance in the dresser mirror. Lexi was wearing a black silk Ralph Lauren blouse and a red skirt with a red belt and red Louboutins. She kicked off her heels and began combing her long, lustrous auburn hair. As usual she combed it to one side, the tresses cascading over one shoulder and covering the left part of her blouse.

There was a soft knock on the bedroom door and she turned toward it.

"Come in, Shawn."

The young man came in and closed the door behind him. A worried expression was on his face.

Lexi pointed to the liquor cabinet. "Would you like a drink?"

"No, Mrs. Atwood."

She smiled. "You don't have to be so formal, you know. We've called each other by our first names for years...."

"Yes, ma'am," he said, his voice hesitant.

She approached him and placed a palm on his arm. "Don't be nervous. It's not like this is our first time."

"Yes, I know, Mrs. Atwood... it's just... you know I don't like...to be unfaithful...to my wife...."

Lexi smiled again. "I know, honey. I think that's admirable. Sweet even. But like I've told you before. Don't think of this like you're cheating on her. Think of it like...it's part of your job. Like working on budgets." She paused and smiled. "Just more fun." She caressed his arm with a palm and admired his clean-cut looks. He was slight in build and had beautiful gray eyes.

"If it makes you feel better, Shawn, I feel guilty too, every time. But I always ask for Sergei's forgiveness first. That helps."

"Yes, Mrs. Atwood."

"Are you sure you don't want a drink first, honey?" she asked. "It'll help relax you."

Shawn nodded, went to the liquor cabinet and poured himself a large amount of wine from the decanter. He downed it quickly and faced her again.

"You know what I like, Shawn. Let's get started, okay?"

He nodded and without saying a word, began undressing. When he was done, he went to the bed, pulled off the covers, and lay flat on his back.

Grinning, Lexi sat on the bed next to him, admiring the young man's slender, almost boyish physique. Shawn was nothing like her strapping, muscular Sergei, with his horse-like cock. But still, she enjoyed Shawn's body. It had given her much pleasure over the years. *You'll never replace Sergei*, she mused. *But you certainly can cure my itch.*

Still fully dressed, Lexi lay next to him and snuggled close, placing her palm on his chest. "Hold me," she said in a low voice.

He put his arm around her tentatively. She could tell he was still nervous, his naked body shivering a bit. He was staring up at the ceiling not making eye contact with her.

"It's going to be fine, honey," she said in a soothing voice, her palm tracing his chest gently. "Don't you find me attractive?"

He closed his eyes. "Oh, God, yes. You're a gorgeous woman, Mrs. Atwood."

"Lexi. Call me Lexi. Please."

"Yes, Lexi."

"That's better. If you find me attractive, then what's the problem?"

He finally turned and faced her. "I think...I know...what we're doing is wrong."

"Well, I suppose you're right. But in life we have to make sacrifices. For the ones we love. You love your wife and your children. And you want to provide for them. You send your children to expensive private schools. Isn't that right?"

"Yes."

"You can afford to do that because I pay you extremely well. More than you can make at any other company in Canada. Isn't that right?"

"Yes."

"So, you see, Shawn. What we have is a beautifully efficient relationship. You give me what I need and I give you what you need."

"Yes, Lexi."

She caressed his chest again. "I wish we could make love like normal people do. With both of us nude. But I can't do that, Shawn. I can't dishonor Sergei that way." She glanced at her husband's photo on the nightstand, then looked at Shawn again. "And I apologize to you for that, but we have to do it this way."

"I understand, Lexi."

"I'm glad." She placed her palm on his cheek and caressed his smooth skin. "Do you know why I hired you two years ago?"

He turned his head and faced her. "Because of my business skills. My knowledge of budgets and economics."

She smiled. "Yes, of course for that. But deep down, I saw more than that for you. I did hire you because you're a genius at budgeting. Running a big company like mine, I need people I can trust. Hard working employees that I can confide in. And I've confided in you. You know a lot about my business dealings. You know about the colonel, and some other things. Not everything, of course. But I also hired you, Shawn, because to tell you the truth, I was lonely."

"You're a billionaire," he said. "You're a beautiful woman. You can have any man you want. Why me?"

She traced her fingers over his face. "You have beautiful gray eyes."

He nodded, but said nothing. He seemed more relaxed now and his body had stopped shivering.

She glanced toward his groin, saw he would need some coaxing.

"I want you to close your eyes now, Shawn. Close your eyes and relax. Okay, honey? I'll do the rest."

"Yes," he whispered, as he lay flat on his back, staring at the ceiling, his eyes closed.

Her palm slid to his chest and then lower to his abdomen and finally rested on his flaccid groin. She began massaging him gently, her excitement building as he stiffened.

He was fully ready moments later and she got off the bed, pulled up her skirt and shrugged off her red silk panties. Her cheeks reddened, her anticipation building.

Lexi got back on the bed and sat on his lap, straddling him. Reaching down with a hand she held him firmly, then inserted him inside of her. She gasped a bit, the sensation feeling delicious.

She began riding him, rocking back and forth, slowly at first, then picking up the pace. She watched his face, saw he was enjoying it now, just as much as she was. His eyes were still shut tightly, but he was breathing heavy, a low moan coming from his open mouth.

Lexi rode him harder, knowing her itch would be satisfied soon. Very, very soon. She grinned and picked up the pace.

Chapter 27

FBI Field Office
Atlanta, Georgia

"I have a theory," Erin Welch said into the phone.

"What is it?" Alex Miller replied, his voice sounding a bit tinny, a result of the encrypted phone connection.

Erin was sitting at her desk, looking toward her white board which was mounted on one wall of her office. She had spent an hour jotting notes on the board, everything she knew about the terrorism case. Miller had been sending her regular progress reports on what had transpired during her bereavement leave.

"I think," Erin continued, "that the two events are connected. The theft of the nuclear weapons and my fiancée's murder."

"What do you base that on, Erin? I just don't see it."

"It's hard to put into words. Let's just say I don't like coincidences."

"People get murdered every day," he said, sounding unconvinced.

"I've been an FBI agent for ten years. I'm not a rookie, right out of Quantico FBI school."

"I meant no disrespect."

"None taken."

"The President thinks very highly of you," the CIA man said, "and so do I. So, let's say your theory is right. What do you need from me?"

Erin looked at the tall stack of case reports on her desk. "Half my agents from this office are in the Middle East. In the mean time, crime isn't taking a vacation in this city. I've got shit piling up left and right. I've been working eighty hour weeks since I got back. I need someone to run leads down here in Atlanta and try to find a connection."

"Okay," Miller said. "I can send you someone. One of my best agents, Rachel West. She's done as much as possible at Kirtland Air force Base."

"Yeah, I know Rachel. And I agree, she's good. Although I'd rather you send me J.T."

"Sorry, Erin. That's a negative. Ryan's still working the case out of Los Alamos."

"All right. Send me Rachel. How soon can she be here?"

"I'll call her right now. She'll take the next plane to Atlanta."

"Thank you, Alex. By the way, have you heard anything from the terrorists? Any ransom demands?"

"Nothing yet. Which is worse. If they just wanted money in exchange for the weapons, we think they would have contacted us by now. The President, General Foster, and I all think the worst is going to happen. Specially since Ryan just found a strong link between the stolen bombs and the Middle East. We now think the terrorists are based in Syria – some splinter group from ISIS or Al Qaeda." Miller paused a moment, then said, "I hate to say it, but we all think they're going to set off the bombs in downtown Los Angeles, New York, and Washington D.C. Maybe even your city, Atlanta. The casualties from something like that would be hundreds of thousands, maybe millions of people."

Erin swallowed hard, realizing what the CIA man was saying was likely the truth.

"I agree with you, Alex. I'm thinking the same thing."

Chapter 28

Los Alamos, New Mexico

J.T. Ryan had just finished breakfast and left his guest quarters at the National Lab complex when his cell phone buzzed. Ryan pulled the phone from a pocket and took the call.

"It's Alex Miller," the CIA man said.

"Yes, sir."

"Ryan, I need to fill you in on a new development. Erin Welch has a theory that the theft of the weapons and her fiancée's murder are connected somehow. I'm not convinced there's anything to this. I'm thinking Welch is still grief stricken and her judgment is clouded. But still, I can't rule it out. What do think?"

Ryan mulled this over a moment. "Erin Welch is the smartest FBI agent I've ever worked with. If she thinks there's a connection, I wouldn't bet against her."

"Yeah. You're probably right. Anyway, I've sent Rachel West to Atlanta to help Welch chase down leads. Rachel's job is done at the Air Force base."

"Yes, sir. Director, have you been able to find out more about the Syrian bank? The one that issued the credit card to the terrorist?"

"Nothing yet. We've got agents on the ground in Syria, trying to find out. The problem is, Syria is a failed state. It's pretty much a lawless country. Tracking down information is damn hard."

"I understand," Ryan said. "What about the video clip I sent you? The one with scarman at the Hertz location."

"We're running that down also. Every FBI and CIA agent in the Middle East has a photograph of scarman. We'll find him. By the way, excellent work on getting that, Ryan."

"Does that mean I get a bonus?" Ryan said in an amused tone.

"Another one of your lame jokes?" Miller replied testily.

"Sorry, sir. I can't help myself sometimes."

"That's going to get you killed one day, Ryan."

"Erin tells me that all the time."

"And she's right," Miller said in a harsh voice. "Every damn time."

"Yes, sir."

"Now, enough of your bullshit. What's your next move, Ryan?"

"This morning I'm heading back to Albuquerque. There's something I need to do at the FBI office there."

"All right, Ryan. Call me immediately if you learn anything new."

"Yes, sir."

Ryan hung up and strode to his SUV in the guest quarters parking lot. Getting in the Explorer, he fired it up and drove to the exit gate of the complex.

Two hours later he was in the interrogation room at the FBI office in Albuquerque.

Across from him was a wary-looking Jorge Rodriguez, wearing a prisoner's orange jumpsuit, his hands manacled to the metal loop on the table.

Ryan grinned. "I bet you're glad to see me again."

The man shook his head. "No."

Ryan laughed. "Yeah, Jorge. I guess I'm like a bad penny. It's hard to get rid of me."

"Chingate!" Jorge spit out.

"Now, now, my Guatemalan friend. Don't be mean. And remember, I speak Spanish too. You're in a Federal building. I don't think they'd approve of you using the 'F' word here."

Jorge let out a long breath. "What 'yo want?"

"A simple thing. I just need you to make a phone call."

The prisoner's face scrunched into concentration. Then he said, "What in it for me?"

"Thought you'd ask that, Jorge. Make this phone call and I'll get you good food while you're in this place. Not the gruel you've been getting up to now."

Jorge's eyes lit up. "Yeah?"

Ryan nodded. "Big, fat juicy steaks, black beans and rice and plantains. I'm sure you'd like that."

Jorge nodded forcefully. "*Si! Si!*"

"Okay, then." Ryan pulled a cell phone from his pocket and rested it on the table. "Remember this?"

The prisoner looked at it for a moment, then said, "*Si.*"

"This is your phone, Jorge. I want you to make a call with it. A call to the guy who hired you. Scarman. The guy who said his name was Mike. I want you to call the phone number he gave you to contact him. We've tried finding whose number it is, but we suspect it was a burner phone. But I'm hoping scarman still has it. Maybe if we're lucky, he didn't dump it."

Ryan reached into his pocket and took out a piece of paper and placed it on the table.

"On this sheet," Ryan continued, "is the number to call and what I want you to say. If it goes to voice mail, then just read this and hang up. Okay?"

"*Si.*"

Using a key he'd obtained from the FBI Agent in Charge, Ryan unlocked the man's manacled hands. Then he turned on the phone and gave it to Jorge, along with the note.

"Go ahead, Jorge. And put it on speaker, so I can hear what you hear."

The man did as he was instructed and a moment later Ryan heard the phone ringing. It rang ten times without answering, then an automated female voice said in English, "Leave a message."

Ryan nodded to Jorge and the Hispanic man began reading from the sheet of paper. The statement said that his name was Jorge Rodriguez, the man Mike had hired for the attack on the truck convoy. It then said that he had been wounded in the attack and left for dead. But he had survived and was thinking of going to the FBI for a reward. If Mike didn't pay him $100,000, Jorge would give the FBI the details of the attack.

Once Jorge concluded the call and hung up, Ryan said, "You did a good job."

"*Gracias.*"

Ryan took the phone and the note back and manacled the prisoner's hands to the table again.

"*El bistec? Para mi almuerzo?*" Jorge said.

"Don't worry," Ryan said. "I'll tell the guards. You'll get steak and rice and beans for lunch today, and from now on, as much as you want."

Jorge smiled a toothy grin. "*Gracias.*"

"*De nada,*" Ryan replied, standing up.

Then he turned and left the room.

Chapter 29

Vancouver, Canada

After putting her office in SCIF mode, Lexi sat behind her desk and turned on her computer monitor. When the screen came to life, she clicked on a folder which initiated the encrypted call.

Moments later the colonel's heavily-scarred face filled the screen.

"Your email said you had something urgent to discuss," Lexi said.

"That's right," he responded as he rubbed one of the angry, red scars on his cheek.

She leaned forward in her chair. "Tell me."

"I received a phone call today. A disturbing one. When I attacked the truck convoy, I had to hire some extra men locally. The crew I took with me from here wasn't big enough."

"I remember you telling me that, Colonel. So what's the problem?"

"I received a call today, a voice-mail message, from one of the local men I hired. I thought he was dead, Lexi. During the firefight some of the locals were shot up – I did a check and figured they were dead. Apparently he survived."

Lexi's eyes flashed in anger. "You told me everything went flawlessly! You fucking lied to me!"

"I...I'm sorry...." he said, stammering a bit, as he once again nervously scratched one of his facial scars. "I thought he was dead."

Lexi ground her teeth, then gulped in several deep breaths and let them out slowly, trying to dampen her rage. After a long moment, she said, "This hired gun. Who is he?"

"An MS-13 gangbanger from Guatemala. His name is Jorge Rodriguez. His message said he was going to the FBI to finger me as the ringleader unless I pay him $100,000."

"I see." The red-haired woman mulled this over a minute. "Sounds suspicious to me, Colonel. If he talks to the authorities, he implicates himself. This smells like a setup to me."

"I agree, Lexi. But still. We have a problem. How do you want me to deal with it?"

She pondered this again. "The money part is no problem. I could wire you the money right now. But this looks like a trap. I want you to do nothing. Understood? I may be able to deal with this on my own."

The colonel nodded. "Yes, Lexi."

"By the way, did you take the precautions I told you to take when you hired the locals?"

"Yes. I memorized those phrases in Arabic and used them when I talked to my own men. I made sure I talked loud enough so that the locals I hired heard the Arabic."

"That's good, Colonel. Between that and using the credit card from the Syrian bank will disguise our locations."

Lexi paused a moment, then said, "We need to talk about something else. Something more important."

"What?"

"I'm ready," she said, a tight grin on her face. "I'm ready to put Operation Tripwire into phase one. My financial transactions are in place. I can now give you the location of the first package."

He grinned back, but he was so grotesquely disfigured that Lexi had trouble looking at his face. She glanced left of the screen to divert her eyes.

"Tell me, Lexi."

"Not over the phone. This information is too sensitive. Even with all of the encryption. We need to meet in person."

"I'll come to Vancouver then."

"No, Colonel. I'll come to you this time."

His eyebrows shot up. In an incredulous tone he said, "Are you sure about this? Is it safe for you to come here?"

"Probably not. But there's a second reason I need to go to your city. Something I haven't done in way too long."

"All right. You're the boss."

Her eyes blazed. "That's right. I am. And never forget that."

She disconnected the call and sat back in her chair, her mind focused on the conversation with the colonel. The development with the hired gun bothered her. *It's a loose end*, she thought. *And I hate loose ends. I'm too close now to let anything fuck it up.*

Clicking on a folder on her computer screen, she initiated another encrypted call, this one to her deep-state source. As always, the call was audio only, to protect the man's identity.

"Good afternoon, Lexi," the man's voice boomed in his deep baritone. "How can I be of service?"

After verifying his identity with the voice analyzer, she said, "I need you to do something for me."

"Of course."

Lexi leaned forward in her chair. "I want you to locate a man. One of the local gunmen the colonel hired. This hired gun has become a liability. He's gone rogue. I'm sure he has a criminal record in the U.S. With your resources I think you'll be able to locate him." She then went on to give him all of the details the colonel had told her about the man.

"I'll find him, Lexi. And when I do?"

"Eliminate the problem. Am I clear on this?"

"Perfectly clear, Lexi. I'll take care of it."

Chapter 30

FBI Field Office
Atlanta, Georgia

Erin Welch was in her office, speed reading reports her agents had prepared for her on pending cases. She jotted notes on a legal pad, detailing action items she wanted the agents to follow up on. Although she'd plowed through one tall stack of reports, she still had another two stacks to go through. And more came in every day, the criminal element in the city not going away any time soon.

Her desk phone rang and she picked up the handset. "Yes?"

"Your visitor is here," her assistant, Brian Donovan said. "She's in the lobby."

"Please bring her up. Thank you."

Hanging up, Erin stood and began to clear her desk as best she could, stacking the paperwork in multiple piles. A few minutes later there was a rap at her door and Erin walked to it and opened it.

After shaking hands with Rachel West, Erin sat down behind her desk as the CIA woman perched on one of the visitor's chairs.

"It's been awhile," Erin said, "since we last met."

Rachel nodded. "Over two years."

Erin gave the CIA woman an appraising look, taking in her long blonde hair, vivid blue eyes and sculpted, model-like face. She was dressed in a gray business jacket and matching slacks.

"You haven't aged a bit, Rachel. In fact you're even more gorgeous now. No wonder J.T.'s crazy about you."

Rachel smiled. "Thanks for the compliment. But you're a good-looking woman yourself."

"I'm not in your league," Erin replied, returning the smile. "Never have been, never will." Then she turned serious. "Did Miller fill you in on what I needed help with?"

"He did. You think there's a connection between the theft of the weapons and the murder of your fiancée?"

"That's right. The timing between the two events is very close to each other. I hate coincidences. They've always made me suspicious."

"I'm the same way, Erin."

The FBI agent opened a drawer and pulled out a large manila envelope and handed it to the other woman. "In there," Erin said, "is everything I have on the murder of my fiancée, Ed Roth. As you know, he was District Attorney for the Atlanta area. So obviously he made a lot of enemies along the way. I've looked up and summarized the criminal cases he prosecuted. I'm hoping we can find something from checking that out."

Erin pointed to the tall stacks of reports on her desk. "I've been buried with that shit, trying to get a handle on all of the hundreds of recent crimes in the Atlanta area, so I can't focus on one case, no matter how important it is to me."

Rachel nodded. "Understood."

"Before you get started," Erin continued, "there's something else I'd like to talk to you about. Something of a personal nature."

"Of course, Erin. Go ahead."

"It has to do with Ryan. I've known J.T. a long time. We've worked on a lot of FBI cases over the years. He's a professional. The best damn investigator I've ever dealt with. And a good and decent man." Erin paused a moment, then said, "I know the two of you are close. I just hope you don't hurt him."

A puzzled expression crossed Rachel's face. "Hurt him how?"

"Years ago, J.T. loved a woman," Erin said. "And she loved him, or so he thought. She ended the relationship and it broke his heart. He went into a deep spiral. Started drinking heavily. Eventually, with my help, he came out of it. I'd hate to see that happen to J.T. again. He doesn't deserve it."

Rachel shook her head. "I have no intention of hurting J.T. – I care a lot about him."

"Okay. I just wanted to clear the air."

"Of course. By the way, Erin, you should know that my boss has laid down the law. J.T. and I are not to 'fraternize' until this terrorism case is solved. So you see, you have nothing to worry about."

Erin gave the CIA agent a long, up-and-down look and smiled. "A woman like you can get into a man's head. Make him a little crazy. Make him do things he shouldn't."

Chapter 31

St. Petersburg, Russia

After a brief stop in Paris for refueling, the Gulfstream G700 had flown directly toward St. Petersburg.

Lexi gazed out the private jet's window at the scene below. Although they were still a mile away from the city's historic center, she could clearly make out the Winter Palace and the Hermitage Museum, their colorful facades illuminated by the morning light as it reflected from the Neva River. In the background she even spotted the beautiful onion domes of the Church of Spilled Blood.

Lexi had grown up in the area and never tired of the view. Unfortunately, since she and her husband had fled Russia, she rarely got to see it.

The Gulfstream G700 continued south, and instead of landing at Pulkovo International Airport, it landed at a private airfield to avoid Russia's strict customs and passport controls.

The jet rolled down the tarmac, approached one of the unmarked hanger buildings and went inside. Lexi unbuckled her seatbelt, stood, and went to the bathroom in the rear of the cabin, carrying a small travel bag.

As she walked down the aisle, she passed the only other people on the large jet, the four muscular, stony-faced men who constituted her security detail.

Going into the bathroom, she closed the door behind her. She looked at her reflection in the small mirror above the sink and took several items out of her travel bag. Then she began pinning up her long auburn hair. When she was done, she pulled on a wig and looked at her reflection again. The wig's short black hair transformed her appearance.

That done, Lexi took off her scarlet Versace dress and red Louboutin heels and replaced them with a non-descript gray dress and black flats. Lastly, she donned large frame black sunglasses, which further hid her identity. Satisfied with her looks, Lexi left the bathroom, nodded to her security chief, and she and all of the bodyguards deplaned. They then walked to the waiting Mercedes-Benz limousine, which was parked in a corner of the hanger building. After getting in the limo, the vehicle drove out of the building and headed for the airfield gate. Soon they were speeding toward their destination.

An hour later the Mercedes was navigating surface streets through an industrial-looking area comprised of shuttered factories and warehouses. This part of St. Petersburg was far from the prosperous shopping, exclusive townhomes, and baroque architecture of the Nevskiy Prospekt Avenue, the city's main artery.

The limo stopped at one of the old warehouses, and after Lexi's bodyguards had checked it out, she went into the building and walked up to the second floor.

Unlike the structure's decrepit exterior, the warehouse's second floor had been converted into a high-tech area divided into offices and open work areas.

She entered one of the offices, where she found the colonel standing at attention by his desk, obviously waiting for her arrival.

"It is good to see you," he said.

Lexi nodded, but said nothing in return, trying to avoid looking directly at his badly-scarred facial features, the bright burn marks much more pronounced in person than on video. She swallowed hard, and avoiding the armchair fronting his desk, she sat instead on a couch in a corner of the room. Keeping him at a distance helped her deal with his horrifyingly disfigured face.

The colonel sat behind his desk and patiently waited for her to begin the conversation. He was dressed in an ill-fitting business suit, clothing he was clearly uncomfortable wearing. She had always figured it was because the man had spent his entire adult life in a military uniform, rising in rank from a private in the infantry to a full colonel in Russia's Military Intelligence Service, the GRU (the organization was officially known as the Glavnoje Razvedyvatelnoje Upravlenije, giving it the initials GRU). The colonel's full name was Mikhail Sharpov and he was a rising star in the GRU because of his superior intelligence and cunning. But the colonel's promising career was cut short by a tragic car accident. He suffered third-degree burns on most of his upper body and head from the accident's intense fire. And although his mind was as sharp as ever, his superiors and the men he led had a difficult time accepting his grotesque facial features.

Realizing his career at the GRU was effectively over, the colonel left the military and went into private security work. Two years ago, Lexi heard about the colonel's excellent reputation and after meeting him during one of her secret trips to St. Petersburg, she hired him on the spot to work for her full time. She paid top dollar, and he in return he gave her his complete obedience. Beyond that, he felt an immense gratitude to her for giving him a new purpose in life.

When Lexi began planning Operation Tripwire, she knew he was the only man who could help her pull it off. His exemplary military background had been on full display during the truck convoy attack, ensuring its success.

"As I mentioned on our call recently," Lexi said, "I've concluded my preparations for the operation."

The colonel nodded. "You've selected the location for the first package?"

"I have." Lexi reached into a pocket, took out a sheet of paper, and walked to his desk and rested the sheet on it. "On this is the exact location and the date when I want you to do it. Read the note, memorize it, and then burn it. Understood?"

"Yes, Lexi."

"And one other thing," she said. "Maybe the most important thing. You must do this job all on your own. I want no one else involved."

A surprised expression settled on his scarred face. "I have an experienced team of men here. Men I trust. Ex-military men that have worked for me for years."

"No, Colonel. I don't want anyone to fuck this up. I trust no one but you. And only you. Are we clear on this?"

"Yes, Lexi."

"I'll send my jet to pick you up here. It'll take you to where the packages are stored. Get one and personally drive it to the location I gave you."

He nodded. "I understand."

"Excellent. Any questions?"

"No."

"In that case," she said, "I think we're done here."

"Are you going back to Vancouver now?"

She shook her head. "No. I have one more stop to make."

"In St. Petersburg?"

"Yes."

"Is that safe for you, Lexi? Police forces are everywhere. Especially here in the city. You're still a wanted criminal in Russia."

She nodded. "I know. It's a risk I have to take. It's been too long since I saw her last."

The colonel knew the woman Lexi was referring to. "Of course."

Lexi rose, and without another word, left the office. With her security team in tow, she exited the warehouse and got back in the limousine.

An hour later Lexi was striding the wide, gilded corridors of the majestic Hermitage Museum, her chief of security at her side. Unfortunately her other bodyguards had to stay in the limo, since a woman being accompanied by four men was bound to attract attention.

The Hermitage, one of the world's greatest museums, is a complex of historic buildings that included the Russian Tsars' Winter Palace. It was originally built in 1771 by Catherine the Great to house her priceless collection of paintings. Tsarina Catherine was so impressed by Raphael's frescoes in the Vatican that she had them copied onto canvass and displayed at the Hermitage.

The famed museum now included a vast collection of famous paintings by Leonardo da Vinci, Matisse, Gauguin, and Rembrandt. It also included priceless statues, carved gems, silver, gold, and porcelain pieces. The Hermitage's collection was so impressive that it rivaled Paris's Louvre and the Vatican as the world's greatest museum.

Passing a room that held several Leonardo da Vinci masterpieces, Lexi continued on to a more remote part of the museum on the second floor. Finding the right room moments later, she entered it while her security chief waited outside, knowing she preferred her privacy during this part of her visit.

Lexi approached the painting slowly, almost reverently, her flat shoes almost gliding over the beautiful marble floor.

Her heart pounded in her chest, her excitement palpable at seeing her again. It had been over a year since she had seen the painting in person and her sense of awe grew with every step she took. Finally she was standing right in front of it.

The priceless painting was of her royal ancestor from centuries ago, Empress Anna Ivanova. The Tsarina had ruled over Russia from 1730 until 1740. Anna was the daughter of Peter the Great's co-tsar Ivan. When the throne passed to her at the age of 37, she brought French and Italian culture to St. Petersburg, and was one of the most influential Russian rulers who imbued the city with its sophisticated European customs, architecture and culture.

Unlike Lexi, Anna was a plain, dowdy-looking woman. But her plain looks, captured faithfully in the painting, did little to dampen Lexi's love for her royal ancestor.

She desperately wanted to reach out and touch the priceless artwork. But she was keenly aware of the museum guard that stood in the room and the security camera mounted on the wall. Not wanting to create any kind of disturbance, Lexi resisted the temptation to touch the painting.

Instead she gazed at it for a full ten minutes, studying every brushstroke carefully, trying to memorize every detail, knowing it could be another year before she risked coming here again.

After another five minutes staring at the historic artwork, she turned around and reluctantly left the room.

Chapter 32

Los Alamos, New Mexico

J.T. Ryan was driving toward Albuquerque when his cell phone buzzed. He took out the phone and answered the call.

"Ryan here."

"It's Alex Miller," the CIA man said.

"Yes, sir."

"I've got bad news. Really bad news."

Ryan's grip on the wheel tightened. "What?"

"As you know, Jorge Rodriguez was being transferred from the FBI holding facility in Albuquerque to the prison in Guantanamo, Cuba."

"Yes, I remember."

"Well, he never got there, Ryan."

"What happened?"

"An FBI agent picked up Rodriguez this morning and was driving him to the transport jet. They never got to the airport. They're both missing along with their car."

"How the hell could that happen?" Ryan said.

"I don't know."

"That transfer was done in secret," Ryan said. "Only a few people knew it was taking place."

"That's right. It can only mean one thing."

Ryan's shoulder muscles tightened and his stomach churned. "There's a leak. Someone that works in our intelligence agencies. A deep-state mole."

"President Harris warned us this was happening," Miller said. "The secret details of the truck convoy carrying the bombs was leaked. And now this."

"What do you want me to do, sir?"

"The FBI has issued an All Points Bulletin on the missing car, the agent, and Rodriguez," Miller replied. "I want you to help with the search."

"Will do."

"I'm meeting with the Director of the FBI later today. I want to coordinate with him, figure out a way to track down this damn leak."

Chapter 33

Rural Pennsylvania

The colonel glanced at his handheld GPS tracking device and slowed down the Ford Econoline van he was driving. He estimated he was about a mile from the destination Lexi had given him.

The area he was driving through was rolling pasture land, sparsely populated. The only homes he saw were farmhouses on large properties. He continued going west, seeing almost no other vehicles along the way.

The landscape up ahead became wooded and he glanced at this GPS device again. Only a half mile to go. He continued on the county road, now driving through a forest. Moments later he spotted a dirt road to his right. He slowed the van and turned onto the road. A light blinked on the GPS and he pulled off the dirt road into a deserted area under a stand of trees.

The colonel put the van in park and turned off the engine. Climbing out of the van, he looked around the wooded area, perplexed that this was the correct location.

He scratched one of the scars on his face as he mulled it over. *Could this really be the spot?* Thinking he had made a mistake, he consulted the GPS again, and realized it was the exact location Lexi had provided.

Reaching into a pocket of his hooded sweatshirt, he pulled out an encrypted satellite phone and punched in a number.

Lexi picked up on the first ring. "Are you there, Colonel?"

"Yes. The location you gave me." He read off the GPS coordinates and also described the area, and how far he was from the nearest town. "Are you sure this is the place you wanted me to bring the first package?"

"Yes," she replied. "Are you questioning my judgment?" she added testily.

"Of course not."

"Good. Now, I want you to take the package and hide it deep in the woods where no one can find it. All right?"

"Yes, Lexi."

"When you set the timer, make sure to give yourself plenty of time to get the hell away from that place. Call me immediately and give me a status report when you've set the timer. Are you clear on this?"

"Yes."

"Excellent," she said and hung up.

The colonel put the phone away, then walked around the back of the van, unlocked the cargo door and opened it. Grabbing the backpack from the floor, he strapped it on. He closed the door and began trekking into the forest. The canopy of trees was so heavy that the ambient light was dim. Taking out a Maglite, he turned it on to light the way.

Ten minutes later he stopped.

He knelt down and brushed aside the deep pile of dead leaves covering the ground. Then he took off his backpack, laid it on the dirt and unzipped the bag.

His stomach churned at the sight of the weapon. For the last few days he had been rehearsing this exact moment, but seeing it now and knowing he was about to activate it made his heart pound.

Don't let Lexi down, he thought, pushing aside the fear. *She needs me. I can never let her down. I owe her too much.*

The colonel flicked a switch and a solid green light came on the control panel. Then he began adjusting the timer, adding minutes to the readout. When he reached the right amount, he flicked on another switch.

The control panel's solid green light began flashing.

He quickly zipped the backpack closed and shoved a large mound of dead leaves and dirt on top of it. That done, he pulled out his phone and punched in a number.

When Lexi answered, he said, "I've set the timer. The package is now activated."

"How long?" she asked.

"Two hours."

"Good. Now get the hell out of there. And thank you, Colonel. For everything. You're not just an employee. You're my friend."

"That means a lot to me," he replied and hung up.

Standing up, he quickly retraced his path, anxious to get back to his van.

Chapter 34

Vancouver, Canada

Lexi glanced at the clock on the wall, counting down the minutes. It had been almost two hours since the colonel had called.

She was at the workstation in her stock trading room, cuing up the final transactions on the stock trading software. She clicked on the mouse, getting her computer ready to activate the command.

Lexi glanced up from the computer to the six flatscreen TVs mounted on the wall. Each television showed a different cable news channel, the various stations covering different events happening currently around the world. Using a remote control, she changed three of the cable news channels to local TV stations for the Philadelphia, PA area.

Each of the local stations was broadcasting everyday events. One was showing the Philadelphia area weather and traffic, a second one had on a soap opera, while the third was broadcasting commercials.

That done, Lexi glanced at the clock again.

Two minutes to go.

She clicked on her mouse and typed in the final activation command on her stock trading program.

But she didn't press the Enter key.

She stared at the clock. One minute to go.

Her heart thundered in her chest as the seconds ticked down.

50 seconds...40 seconds...30 seconds....

Her shoulders tensed and her stomach churned, her finger hovering over the Enter key as the time ticked down the last 10 seconds.

Then 0 seconds.

She stabbed the Enter key.

The software trading program instantly activated, short selling a massive amount of company stocks. Over 200 different companies were traded. The corporations were in banking, transportation, utilities, communication, energy, and others.

Lexi looked at the TV screens to see what was happening. To her amazement, nothing had changed. The Philadelphia stations were still broadcasting traffic, daytime talk shows, and commercials.

Her faced burned. *What the hell is happening? Did the colonel fuck up? Damn him!* She gulped in a deep breath and let it out slowly to control her rage.

Lexi stared at the clock again and realized it had been less than a minute since the bomb's detonator had been activated. Since the weapon was not in the immediate Philadelphia area, it would take a few minutes for the effect to be felt there.

As if on cue, one of the local TV stations interrupted the talk show being broadcast with a news anchor.

"We've just received news," the newsman said, "that power blackouts are taking place in the area northwest of Philadelphia. We've also been informed that a bomb-like blast has been reported in that rural area. Police and fire personnel have been dispatched. Our reporters are also in route there, as well as our news helicopter. We'll bring you more details as we learn them."

The newsman paused and pressed a hand to his ear, obviously listening to what someone was telling him. "We've just been told," the news anchor said, "that the power blackout is now affecting the city of Philadelphia itself. We're also getting reports of cell phone and landline communication going down."

Lexi listened intently, savoring every word.

Fuck yes! she thought. *It's working! Exactly as I planned!*

"We're also hearing," the newsman continued, "that Internet communication is down and that computer banking has been interrupted."

Lexi glanced at the two other Philadelphia TV stations and they had also interrupted their regular programming. They were now showing news people covering the area-wide blackout. Then she gazed at the cable news channels and they too were picking up the event.

"From what we've been told," the news anchor said, "the power and communication blackout is now blanketing all of the city of Philadelphia and its suburbs. Authorities are urging citizens to stay calm." He paused a moment and touched his ear. "It's possible that even our own TV transmission may be effected by this blackout. If that were to happen –"

The newscaster was cut off in midsentence and the TV screen went dark.

Lexi stared at the other two local TV stations and within seconds they went black also. Energized and elated by what she was seeing, she glanced at the trading screens on her computer. The stock market, obviously alarmed by what was happening, was plummeting. She grinned fiercely, knowing her short selling strategy was paying off.

Lexi stared at the Dow Jones ticker as it shed a thousand points in five seconds. Then it plummeted another thousand points in three seconds.

Panic selling was taking place. The stock market was crashing.

She typed on her keyboard and pulled up a spreadsheet to see the exact figures of what her net worth was doing.

Her mouth hung open, seeing the numbers.

Today's stock-trading had pushed her net worth well past one billion. She was now closer to two billion.

It worked! It worked even better than I planned.

Chapter 35

The Oval Office
The White House
Washington, D.C.

"How many people are dead?" President Harris asked.

"We're still tallying that up," General Foster replied. "The local authorities are estimating approximately 10,000 were killed yesterday."

Harris rubbed his jaw. "Damn! That's a lot of innocent victims."

"It could have been a lot worse," Alex Miller said. "If the bomb had been detonated in downtown Philadelphia instead of a rural area, the casualties would have been hundreds of thousands."

The President nodded. "True." He faced the general. "Are we sure it was one of the nuclear weapons that were stolen?"

"Absolutely, Mr. President. It was definitely one of the W-54s. The explosive yield of the blast is exactly what we expect from a backpack bomb."

The three men were huddled in the sitting area of the Oval Office.

President Harris rubbed his jaw again. "Why did the terrorists pick a desolate area to blow up the weapon?"

"That's unknown, sir," Foster replied.

"What's the situation in Philadelphia now?" the President said. "Is there still an area wide blackout?"

Alex Miller nodded. "Yes, sir. But unlike a typical blackout where only electricity is effected, this is much worse. All electronic communication and data transmission is down. Cell phone, Internet, landlines, TV broadcast, and electronic banking are also down. And that may continue for several weeks."

The President's face flushed. "How the hell is that even possible?"

"Sir," the general said, "it's a side effect of a nuclear explosion. We've known for some time that detonation of this type of weapon can cause a massive Electronic Magnetic Pulse. In the military, we've prepared for something like this. We've outfitted naval ships with EMP blocking devices, but it's never been considered for civilian use. We would need many hundreds of thousands of these EMP blockers to protect one American city, let alone our whole country. And each EMP blocker is incredibly expensive."

President Harris nodded. "I see." He stood up from the wingback chair he was sitting in and began pacing the office.

"Sir," the general continued, "besides the casualties in Philadelphia, we have another big problem."

Harris stopped pacing. "What?"

"The shutdown in banking transactions hasn't just effected the local Philadelphia economy. It's causing a panic in the stock market. The Dow Jones Average dropped four thousand points yesterday. The New York Stock Exchange stopped trading several times during the day, but every time it resumed the massive selling continued. And we're seeing another huge drop today."

The President planted his hands on his hips. "God damn it! This situation just keeps getting worse and worse." He stabbed a finger in the air in Alex Miller's direction. "Where the hell are we with the investigation? Are we any closer to finding the terrorists?"

"Yes, sir, we are," Miller said. "J.T. Ryan found out the terrorists that pulled off the truck convoy attack appear to be based in Syria. The leader of the group is a heavily-scarred man. We've got hundreds of agents on the ground now in Syria looking for this man."

"I see. Where's Ryan now? In the Middle East?"

"No, sir. He's in New Mexico, trying to locate the whereabouts of Jorge Rodriguez, one of the perpetrators of the attack and the FBI agent who was transporting Rodriguez to Guantanamo. Both men are missing."

"Yes," the President said, "I know about that. I met with the FBI Director yesterday. He filled me in. He said both men had vanished without a trace."

The President began pacing again. "We've got to find the terrorists, damn it, before they strike again. The question is, what city will they hit next."

"Sir," Foster interjected, "since they didn't set off the first bomb in a crowded downtown area, it's going to make our job harder. Police departments across the country had been alerted to possible bombings and were on the lookout for terrorists. Most cities now have security cameras everywhere. But since a rural area was the detonation site, that makes catching the killers much more difficult."

Harris rubbed his jaw. "Either of you gentlemen have anything positive to tell me? Any theories?"

General Foster shook his head. "No, sir."

"Mr. President," Miller said, "Erin Welch thinks there's a connection between the stolen bombs and the murder of her fiancée. The two events happened about the same time. She has a theory that the perpetrators of the assassination and the convoy attack were both committed by the terrorists."

Harris sat back down. "I see." He said nothing for a long moment as he mulled this over, then said, "I trust Erin's judgment. We could have never solved the Fireball conspiracy without her. If she thinks there's a connection between both events, then we should help her find it."

Miller nodded. "Yes, sir."

"You said Ryan was in New Mexico?" the President said.

"Yes. He's assisting the FBI in trying to locate Rodriguez and the Bureau agent."

"And?"

"We're at a dead end," Miller said. "Those two men have vanished and we have no clues on their whereabouts."

"All right," Harris replied. "We'll keep the Albuquerque FBI people looking for them. In the meantime, send Ryan to Atlanta. From what I can see, he seems to be the only one that's getting results on this damn case."

"Yes, Mr. President," Miller said. "I'll take care of it."

The President went quiet for a minute, then said, "There's something about this whole business that has a bad smell to it. The transfer of the prisoner, Rodriguez, to Guantanamo was Top Secret. Only a few people knew about it. Now he and the FBI agent are missing. It can only mean one thing. There's a leak. A deep-state mole is involved. I told the FBI Director yesterday to make this one of his top priorities. We need to find the traitor. And find him fast."

Harris faced Alex Miller. "You need to do the same thing, Alex. It's possible the leak is someone at the CIA. Turn over every rock. We need to find the bastard before any more innocent Americans are killed."

"Yes, Mr. President."

Chapter 36

Atlanta, Georgia

J.T. Ryan's Delta flight touched down at 10:30 a.m., he deplaned, and strode through the Hartsfield Airport terminal on his way to the baggage area. Along the way in the concourse he spotted several TVs showing scenes from the Philadelphia area. The terrorist attack two days ago was still front page news. He shook his head slowly, angry at himself for not having already caught the criminals behind the plot.

After collecting his luggage, Ryan took the airport tram and located his Ford Explorer in the long-term parking lot.

Forty minutes later, he unlocked the door to his midtown apartment and went inside. He had been in New Mexico for weeks and the air inside smelled musty and stale. He opened all of the windows in his apartment, letting in the crisp cool air. It was October and Atlanta's great Fall weather had arrived.

After taking a shower, he changed into fresh clothes, which as usual consisted of slacks, a long-sleeve button-down shirt, and a navy blazer, with his Smith & Wesson .357 holstered at his hip. He went to his kitchen to prepare some lunch. Opening the refrigerator, he inspected the meager contents inside. There was a carton of eggs, a half-gallon of milk, two wilted tomatoes, a six-pack of Coors, and two cans of Pepsi. Checking the milk and eggs, he realized they were spoiled. Trashing them, he pulled out a bottle of JIF from his pantry and made himself two large peanut butter sandwiches. The bread was stale but edible, and he wolfed them down, along with a Pepsi.

Then he made a call to Erin Welch, left his apartment and drove to the FBI office in downtown. He went through the security checkpoint in the lobby and made his way to Erin's office on the top floor.

Ryan knocked on her open door and she waved him in.

"Welcome back to Atlanta," she said, standing up from behind her desk. "I'm glad you're here, J.T."

"Thanks," he said. "It's good to be home." He studied the good-looking woman, who still appeared as tired and worn-out as he'd seen her last. Dark circles were under her eyes, likely from a lack of sleep.

"Let's go over there," Erin said, pointing to a sitting area in the office. "As you can see my desk is a mess."

He noticed the tall stack of file folders which covered almost every inch of her desktop. There was barely any room for her laptop computer and phone.

After they sat down, Erin said, "Alex Miller called me and told me you'd be coming back to help me work the case here."

"How's that going?"

She shrugged. "Rachel's been at it for days."

"And?"

"She's all right," Erin said with a grin. "But she's no J.T. Ryan."

Ryan smiled back. "Thanks for the vote of confidence."

"Don't get me wrong," Erin continued, "Rachel's an excellent CIA agent, but I think finding my fiancée's killer is going to take someone familiar with Atlanta's criminal element. You know the seedier side of this city like the back of your hand."

He nodded. "Yeah. I see your point."

"Did you watch President Harris's address to the nation this morning?"

"No," he said, "it happened when I was on my flight. I caught a replay of it on the radio when I was driving home."

"Okay. The President did a good job in his talk trying to calm the nation after the terrorist attack. The stock market has been in a tailspin since the event happened."

"How long do your think the EMP effect will last, Erin?"

She shook her head. "I don't think anyone really knows. The Electronic Magnetic Pulse created by the bomb explosion was massive. Alex Miller thought it could take several weeks for the Philadelphia area to recover and get their communication and electronic transmission systems back online."

"In the meantime," he said, "the terrorists could strike again. We both know more than one nuclear device was stolen."

"That's a fact." She stood and pointed to the large white board mounted on the wall by the sitting area. The right side of the board was covered with handwritten notes. The left side of it was mostly blank.

"This is where we're at with the investigation," Erin said, picking up a marker and drawing a line down the middle of the white board. "My fiancée, Ed Roth, was murdered and we're now beginning to look for a connection to the terrorists." She pointed to the blank side of the board. "As you can see, we're nowhere near finding that. Which is why you're here, J.T."

Erin pointed to the side of the board that was covered with handwritten notes. "Now let's look at that part of the investigation. Ten backpack nuclear bombs were stolen while in transit from Los Alamos to Kirtland Air Force Base. The attack on the truck convoy was executed with military-style precision, indicating the terrorists are not amateurs, but in fact a sophisticated group."

"I agree."

"You found out," she continued, "that the attack was led by a man with a scarred face, a man that has Middle East connections. Syria to be exact." Erin paused, then said, "According to what Alex Miller has told me, the FBI, CIA, and Homeland Security have hundreds of agents on the ground in Syria right now. With the photo you obtained of the scarred man, they should be able to locate him and his accomplices."

"Hopefully soon, before the criminals detonate another bomb. Did Miller say anything about which city might be the next target?"

Erin shook her head. "It's anybody's guess. Any major U.S. city. It could even be Atlanta."

"Yeah, I thought the same thing. It could be Atlanta."

They spent the next hour going over the details of the case, then Erin said, "I gave Rachel the files I obtained from the District Attorney's office here in Atlanta. In them are all the cases my fiancée prosecuted. He was good at his job so he put a lot of criminals behind bars."

"I'll get with Rachel," Ryan said, "and see what progress she's made. What hotel is she staying at?"

"The Sheraton off of the 400, north of downtown."

"Yeah. I know where that is, Erin. Anything else we need to discuss?"

"No. We've covered everything. By the way, I've got a conference room on this floor that's rarely used. You and Rachel can work out of there if you like."

Ryan stood. "Thanks. I'll take you up on that."

Chapter 37

Atlanta, Georgia

J.T. Ryan left the FBI building and drove out of the downtown area and headed north on Route 400. Before going to the Sheraton he stopped at Scooters, a coffee shop in Roswell. In his opinion, they made the best coffee in the world. After getting two large to-go-cups, he drove to the hotel.

He knocked on her room door and waited. Rachel opened it a moment later, a wide smile on her pretty face. "John Taylor Ryan, you're a sight for sore eyes. Damn it, it's good to see you."

Ryan grinned back. "It's great to see you too. And I brought coffee."

She scrutinized the large cups on the plastic tray. "Hopefully, it's not the crap you make at your office."

He laughed. "Ouch! That cuts to the core. No, I brought the best brew in Atlanta. It's from a coffee shop named Scooters."

Rachel took the tray, he went inside, and she closed the door behind him.

"Erin called me a little while ago," Rachel said, "told me you were coming over."

"Yeah. I just flew in this morning and met with her. We went over the case."

She placed the tray on the table, right next to the holstered Glock that was resting there.

He pointed to the handgun. "Have you had to use it yet while you've been in Atlanta?"

She grinned. "Not yet. But the day is young."

"You sound like me," he replied with a laugh. Turning serious, he said, "I'd love to give you a hug and kiss right now — but I'm worried Alex Miller's got cameras in this room."

"I checked. No cameras, no hidden microphones. I'm willing to chance it if you are."

Ryan stepped closer to her and embraced her with both of his powerful arms. She snuggled close, her warm, curvy body pressing into his, while her head rested on his chest.

"This feels great, babe," she whispered. "I've missed you."

"And I've missed you."

She looked up into his eyes and their lips met. It was a gentle, soft kiss that lingered for a long moment.

When they separated minutes later, they both took out their cell phones and stared at the screens, fully expecting Miller to call and read them the riot act again. When no calls came, they put their phones away.

"That's strange," Rachel said.

"I agree. Maybe Miller expects us to live up to our word and decided to trust us."

Rachel gave him a devilish grin. "If he expects that, he's a silly man."

Ryan held up a hand. "I don't want you to lose your job, okay? I think we need to keep our promise."

Her mischievous grin widened. "That's going to be hard to do. Specially hard for you."

Ryan shook his head slowly, laughing at her double entendre. "You've got a bit of the devil in you, Miss West."

"Part of the reason we get along so well."

"You're right about that." He studied the good-looking woman's appearance. As usual her long blonde hair was pulled into a ponytail. She had no makeup on her sculpted, beautiful face and she was wearing simple clothes. Jeans, Adidas running shoes, and a short-sleeve polo shirt, it's blue color matching the vivid hue of her eyes. And as always when he saw her, she took his breath away.

There were two chairs by the table and they went and sat across from each other. They sipped the strong, savory coffee and held hands for several minutes, relishing being together again.

Eventually he said, "We should talk about the case."

Rachel gave him a fake pout and stuck her tongue out at him. "You're ruining the mood."

"I know. I'm sorry."

She smiled. "Just kidding. I know the job comes first." Then she pointed to the bed in the hotel room, which was covered with file folders. In a business-like tone she said, "I've spent several days going through those. Erin's fiancée, Ed Roth, was a busy man as District Attorney. He locked up hundreds of criminals. My guess is, all of them would have a vendetta against him. From everything I've read, Roth was a great DA. He made a lot of enemies along the way."

"I'm sure you're right," Ryan said.

They spent the next two hours going over the details of the criminal cases Rachel had researched. After listening to her and asking probing questions, he realized they were no closer to finding an answer.

He glanced at his watch, saw it was 8 p.m. "Obviously we're not going to find the identity of the killer tonight. We've got way too many suspects. We need to look at this from a different perspective. Tomorrow I'll go see one of my CIs here in Atlanta. She's been my confidential informant for years. She knows a lot about the criminal element. We may get a lead from that."

"Sounds good, J.T."

"You hungry? Because I'm starved. All I've had today was peanut butter sandwiches and crap airline food."

"I'm hungry too," Rachel said. "There's a restaurant at this hotel."

"No way. I want to take you out to dinner. To a great place I know. But you'll have to change. It's a nice restaurant."

She grinned. "I'd like that very much."

He returned the smile and reached out and squeezed her hand. "Me too."

Rachel stood and pointed to the door. "Now shoo. I need to freshen up and get dressed. I'll meet you in your car in fifteen minutes. What are you driving these days?"

"Ford Explorer, silver in color. It's parked in front of the hotel."

"Got it. You haven't bought that Corvette yet, huh?"

"Not yet. But I'm still thinking about it."

"Don't think about it too long, J.T. Life is short."

***

The Brookwood Grill was Ryan's favorite restaurant. He hadn't been there in years and missed it. The modern, oak-wood and natural-stone decor created an excellent, intimate setting for dining. They were seated at a table by the fireplace, the pleasant aroma of the crackling wood mixing with the mouth-watering scent of steaks in the kitchen.

"You look amazing," he said.

Rachel smiled, almost shyly. "Thank you, kind sir." She was wearing a form-fitting black cocktail dress with spaghetti straps, her lustrous blonde hair cascading over her shoulders. Her azure eyes sparkled. And she had applied a light pink lipstick and a luscious smelling perfume.

"The only question I have, Rachel, is where do you keep your gun? You certainly aren't hiding it under your dress."

She held up her cocktail purse. "I carry a .380 auto in here, for when I'm dressed like this. It's a small gun, but still plenty lethal."

"That's my girl."

Rachel frowned. "That's a sexist thing to say. And I resent it."

He realized he'd insulted her in some way. "What did I say wrong?"

"You called me a girl! I'm a woman. A thirty-five year old female. And a damn good CIA agent." She pointed an index finger at him. "I'm not a girl. Get it?"

He put his palms in front of him. "I'm really sorry. I didn't mean to insult you. Really, I didn't."

Her frown melted and she grinned. "Got you! I was just kidding about that." She reached across the table and took his hand with one of hers. "I really don't mind if you call me a girl. I think it's sweet, actually."

Ryan's tension evaporated, glad he hadn't offended her. He squeezed her hand. "I'm glad. Sometimes women are hard to decipher."

She gave him one of her mischievous grins. "Yeah, we are. Keeps you guys on your toes."

"Would you like some wine? I can order some."

"I'd prefer a vodka, J.T."

"I remember now. Absolut vodka and tonic." Ryan flagged the waiter, ordered the vodka and tonic for her and a Sam Adams for himself, and the waiter headed toward the bar area.

"I love this place," Rachel said, glancing around the intimate, beautiful decor of the restaurant. "Do you come here often?"

"A few years ago, I used to. But not now." He took a sip of water. "I need to tell you something. There's only one other woman besides you I've brought here. A very special woman. Or so I thought at the time."

"Was that Lauren?" Rachel asked. "Lauren Chase? Erin told me about what happened. She said Lauren broke up with you."

He stared down at the table. "Yes, it was Lauren. It took me a long time to get over her."

"I'm sorry you had to go through that, J.T."

He raised his eyes and looked at Rachel. "Let's not talk about that anymore. That chapters done. I've turned that page a long while ago. I'd rather talk about you." He took one of her hands and raised it to his lips and kissed it softly.

"Rachel West," he said, "CIA operative extraordinaire, the smartest woman I know, and a woman who has the prettiest blue eyes I've ever seen."

"And also a world-class marksman with a handgun," she said jokingly. "Don't forget about that. We'll go to the gun-range and compare hits. Bet I can beat you."

He shook his head. "I won't take that bet. I know better."

The waiter returned and served their drinks. When he left, Ryan picked up his glass of beer and held it up. "A toast."

She clinked her tumbler of vodka with his glass. "What are we toasting?"

"To us."

"I like the sound of that," she replied with a radiant smile. After a moment, in a somber tone she added, "And to staying alive."

He nodded, knowing exactly what she meant.

They pored over the extensive menus and she said, "What's good here?"

"Everything."

You're not helping me, J.T."

"If you want fish, the trout is excellent. And for steak, the filet mignon is the best I've ever had."

"I'll go with the trout, then. And I bet you're having the steak."

"How'd you know?"

"Because you're so predicable. You always have steak. Just like you always have beer. I'm surprised you had Sam Adams tonight. I know you prefer Coors beer."

He shook his head. "This restaurant doesn't serve Coors."

She patted his hand and grinned. "Poor baby."

He smiled back, enjoying the banter. Then he flagged the waiter, gave him their dinner order and the man moved away.

Ryan took a sip of beer. "I think we should talk about the 800 pound gorilla in the room."

"That's funny, I don't see any of those here."

"You know what I mean, Rachel."

"Do I?"

"Yes, you do."

She sighed. "Do we have to talk about it? Really? Can't we just enjoy a delicious dinner and then a beautiful evening after dinner?" She flashed a devilish grin. "You know what's going to happen tonight, don't you? It's been a long time since we've been together, in the Biblical sense, and I plan to wear you out."

"Please Rachel. We need to talk about this."

She picked up her drink and downed it quickly. "All right. But in my opinion, we ought to just do it and worry about the consequences later."

He shook his head. "You know I want to as much as you do. But I don't want you to lose your job over it."

She wrapped her arms around herself, her expression defiant. "Fuck my job."

"It's who you are. The CIA is your life."

She grimaced. "I know that, damn it."

"So it's settled then," he said. "We'll keep our promise to Miller."

"The hell we will!"

"Are you willing to get fired over this?"

"Miller will never find out, J.T."

Ryan shook his head slowly. "I don't want you to take that chance. I could never forgive myself if you were kicked out of the CIA because of me."

"I think that's really sweet. And chivalrous. And I love you for it. But my mind's made up." She reached over, picked up his glass of beer and drank it down. "Anyway, this conversation is a moot point."

"How so?"

Her sparkling azure eyes bore into his. "Do you really think you can resist me?" She grinned fiercely. "I seriously doubt it."

"What do you mean?"

"Don't be such a Boy Scout. You know exactly what I mean." She slipped her hand under the table and cupped his groin.

He closed his eyes, instantly aroused by her touch on his pants. After a moment he opened his eyes. "Please, Rachel. Don't do that here. Someone could see you."

"I don't give a fuck if they see me," she whispered, and began stroking him slowly.

Ryan groaned, his heart pounding, the bulge in his pants growing.

"Still think you can resist me, J.T.?"

"No...God no...."

A self-satisfied smile settled on her face. "I know you too well, baby. I knew you wouldn't be able to hold out." She slipped her hand from under the table and caressed his face.

"Tell me something, Rachel. Did you plan on this happening all along?"

"Of course. Why do you think I wore this sexy dress. And the high heels and perfume. And just so you know, I'm not wearing panties under my dress. I don't do that for any other man. Only you."

"You're an amazing woman, you know that?"

She gave him a mischievous grin. "You're really going to find out how amazing as soon as we leave this restaurant."

Just then the waiter came with their dinners. But as soon as he placed the dishes on the table, Ryan said, "What do think, Rachel? Should we take this to go?"

Her blue eyes blazed with intensity. "Absolutely."

The waiter took their dinners and went to package them up.

"The only question left is," Ryan said, "my apartment or your hotel?"

"Which is closest?"

"My place."

"Your place then, J.T."

Chapter 38

Vancouver, Canada

Lexi was in her penthouse office on the 80th floor when she heard her assistant's voice through the intercom.

"Excuse me, Lexi. An encrypted call just came in. It's the man with no name."

"Thank you, Shawn."

Lexi put her office into SCIF mode and took the call.

"Good morning," the man's deep baritone voice boomed. "I have new information for you."

After verifying his identity with the voice analyzer, she said, "Good news I hope."

"Mostly good, yes."

"Go ahead."

"The Federal authorities have sent hundreds of agents into Syria," he said. "They're scouring the country for Middle Eastern terrorists. They're convinced the leader of the group is based in Syria."

"That's excellent. Exactly what I wanted."

"I have one other thing," he said. "The CIA, DHS, and the FBI now have a photo of a scarred man, the man they think is the ringleader."

"Have you seen this photo?"

"Yes, Lexi. In fact I have a copy of it on my desk. But it could be anyone. It's hard to tell from the picture who it is."

"I see. Do they have the scarred man's name?"

"No. Only a photo."

She breathed a sigh of relief. "Good. Transmit me a copy of the picture."

"I'll do that."

"You said you also had some bad news?"

"Possibly bad. It's unclear to me, Lexi. It appears one of the lead agents working the case, a man named John Ryan, has been reassigned from New Mexico to Atlanta. He's working on the murder of a District Attorney there."

Lexi gritted her teeth. "I see."

"As I said, I'm not sure how all this fits into the terrorist angle and the bombs, but I wanted to alert you."

"All right, I'm glad you told me." Lexi's informant didn't know about the connection between the operation and the murdered DA and she wanted to keep it that way.

"I'll keep you posted," he said, "on any further developments as they happen."

"Good. By the way, I'll make a new deposit to your offshore account today. Let's call it a bonus for all of your diligent work."

"I appreciate that, Lexi. I've been eying this new yacht, and with your generosity I may be able to get it now."

Lexi hung up the call. Then she stood and went to her liquor cabinet. She grabbed an oversized wine glass and poured herself a large amount of Merlot. She sipped the savory, oaky taste of the red wine and mulled over the next steps of Operation Tripwire.

Two glasses of wine later, she picked up the handset of her desk phone and punched in a number.

Within minutes, Lexi's head of security was in her office, standing ramrod straight in front of her desk. The brawny Canadian man with the buzz-cut blond hair was built like a football player, and in fact had a been a linebacker for a college team before going into security work.

"You wanted to see me?" he said.

"I did, Brad." She idly tapped her red Mont Blanc pen on her desk. "The man you hired to take care of the Atlanta problem. You told me before there was no way he could be connected to us. Isn't that right?"

"Yes. I hired this professional through a cut-out."

She tapped on her desk again. "That's good. Because it appears the FBI is intensifying their investigation into the murder of the DA."

"I see. What do you want me to do?"

"Nothing for now, Brad. But I needed to alert you. I may need you to take care of any additional Atlanta problems if they develop."

"Whatever you need."

"My dear husband Sergei always admired your efficiency," she said. "And so do I. You're a great part of my team and I'm lucky to have you."

He beamed and his large biceps bulged at the compliment. "Thank you, Lexi."

She nodded.

"Do you need anything else?" he asked.

"No, Brad. You're dismissed."

Chapter 39

Atlanta, Georgia

J.T. Ryan was sitting in his living room , jotting notes about the case, when the bedroom door opened and Rachel West stepped out, her long hair tousled. She was wearing one of his long-sleeve shirts and nothing else, the shirt-tails barely making her decent.

"Hey, beautiful," he said. "You hungry? Get dressed and I'll buy you breakfast."

She strolled over, leaned down and gave him a peck on the lips. "Come back to bed."

"Haven't you had enough?" he said, chuckling. "You wore me out last night."

Rachel laughed. "Poor baby."

He glanced at his watch. "We need to get going, okay?"

She folded her arms in front of her. "All right. I'll get dressed. But tonight I want a rematch. Deal?"

"Deal," he said with a smile.

After she showered and dressed they left his apartment, got breakfast at a Denny's, and stopped at a Bank of America branch where he made a cash withdrawal.

That done, Ryan drove to Sandy Springs, a suburb of Atlanta. He pulled his Ford Explorer into the parking lot of the strip club, parked, and eyed the seedy exterior of the place with its blinking neon sign reading *Gentlemen's Club*. The building looked even more decrepit than the last time he'd been there.

"Your CI works here?" Rachel asked, who was in the passenger seat.

"She does."

"Okay." Rachel reached for the door handle. "Let's go."

"No. I'll go in alone."

"Why?"

"It's not a very nice place, Rachel."

Her eyes blazed in anger. "Because it's a titty bar? Trust me, I've been in a lot worse."

"Calm down, okay? I'll go in and find her. She'll come out and we'll both talk to her in the car."

"Fine. But don't try to protect me, J.T. I'm a CIA operative, remember?"

"I know. I know. I'll be right back."

Ryan got out of his SUV, paid the cover charge at the door, and walked inside the strip joint. Since it was morning, the place was mostly empty, just a few customers at the bar, and a lone stripper on the stage, gyrating listlessly on a pole. The whole place reeked of stale beer, cigarettes and vomit.

He spotted Candy right away, serving drinks to a couple of rough-looking biker guys at one of the tables. He flagged her down and she sashayed over, a grin on her face. The waitress was a tall, statuesque brunette wearing only pasties, a G-string, and hooker heels. She had tired eyes, a pockmarked face, and a haggard look.

"Well, if it isn't John Ryan," she said, "My favorite customer."

"Hello, Candy. I bet you say that to all the guys."

She stuck out her chest, giving him a real good look at her double-Ds. "See something you like, honey?" she said in a throaty voice.

He tried not to stare at her huge breasts and almost nude body. Although she was not a pretty woman, she exuded a raw sexuality that was difficult to ignore.

"I'm here on business, Candy."

She shook her head slowly. "Figures."

"I'm looking for information."

"Bring cash? I don't take plastic."

He patted his blazer jacket. "I brought cash."

"Good. I'll take a break and meet you outside. Still driving the Chevy Tahoe?"

"No. I got an Explorer now."

"All right."

Ryan left the strip club and got back in his SUV to wait. Ten minutes later Candy came out of the building, now dressed in black leggings, a fake-fur leopard jacket and flats. She climbed into the back seat and immediately stared suspiciously at Rachel West, who was sitting up front with Ryan.

"Who's the blonde hottie?" Candy asked, acid in her voice.

"This is Rachel West," Ryan said. "She's a Federal agent and she's working with me on a case. Rachel, this is Candy, my CI."

Candy glared. "Well, I don't like her."

"Don't piss her off, Candy," Ryan said. "She's got a gun and isn't afraid to use it."

The CI folded her arms across her ample chest. "Whatever. Let's get down to business." Candy focused on Ryan, totally ignoring Rachel West.

Ryan nodded. "Sounds good. You remember the Atlanta District Attorney who was murdered a little while back? It was all over the news."

"Of course. Just because I waitress at a strip club doesn't mean I'm an airhead."

"The DA's name was Ed Roth."

"I remember," Candy said. "He was shot in a church. He was about to get married, right?"

"That's right."

"And I bet, J.T., you're looking for the killer."

"I am."

"I can ask around," Candy said. "I know a lot of people and they know a lot of other people. And most of them are drifters, criminals, and low-lifes."

"That's why I'm here."

"It'll cost you, J.T. Information isn't free."

"How much?"

"Two grand."

"Bullshit."

"All right, a grand."

"Still too much, Candy. I'll give you $500. Half now, the rest when you have something solid."

"I may have to shake my tits and ass all day, but I'm not stupid. My info is always solid, otherwise you wouldn't keep coming back, would you?"

"How much, Candy?"

"$800. Half up front."

Ryan mulled this over a moment. "Okay, 800 it is." He reached into his blazer, took out the cash he had there, counted out the money and handed it to her.

Candy took it and stuffed it in a pocket of her fake-fur jacket. She smiled sweetly and reached out with a hand and placed it on his shoulder. "If you get rid of blondie here, J.T., you and I can have some fun."

Rachel glared at the waitress.

"Cut it out, Candy," Ryan said, "you know we don't have that kind of relationship."

Candy laughed. "I know, sweetie. I was just having fun with you."

Ryan took out a business card and handed it to the waitress. "Call me the minute you find anything."

"You got it, sugar. By the way, I'm leaving the strip club soon. I've got a new job lined up. Next time we meet, it'll probably be there."

Ryan nodded. "Better pay?"

"Pay's about the same," Candy replied, "but I won't have to work almost nude at the new place."

"I'm glad for you. I always thought you were too smart to work at a titty bar."

"Thanks, J.T."

"How's your daughter doing?" Ryan said.

The waitress beamed. "She's doing great. She's in high school now. And getting straight A's."

"I'm glad to hear that. Give her my regards."

"Well, I've got to go now. My break's over."

"Talk to you soon."

The waitress climbed out of the SUV, shut the door, and hurried back into the strip club.

Chapter 40

Atlanta, Georgia

J.T. Ryan fired up the Explorer, drove out of the strip joint's parking lot, and got back on Route 9.

"Is Candy her real name?" Rachel asked, turning in her seat to look at Ryan.

"Nope," he said. "That's her stage name. She told me a while back she started using it and her tips got a lot bigger."

"She doesn't like me very much, that's for damn sure."

"She's a woman, Rachel. Women are like that."

Rachel frowned and crossed her arms in front of her. "I'm a woman too, remember."

He took his eyes off the road a moment and her gave her an up and down look. The blonde, as usual, was wearing casual clothes: jeans, a black polo shirt and a gray windbreaker, her Glock holstered at her hip under her jacket.

"So I've noticed." He grinned. "And a beautiful woman at that."

Her frown faded. "So what's next?"

"I need to go see another one of my CIs."

"Another stripper?"

"Candy's not a stripper. She's a waitress that happens to work at a strip club."

"Whatever."

"This other CI," Ryan said, "is an Army veteran, like me. But he's fallen on hard times. He went to prison for a few years and he's been in-and-out of drug rehab. But he's knows Atlanta's underbelly. A lot of shit goes down in this city, something the Visitor's Bureau never talks about. But it's there. My confidential informant, Stich, knows a lot of bad people."

"So that's you're next stop?" she said.

"It is."

"You don't need me for that, J.T. Why don't you drop me off at my hotel. I need to download another CIA program to my computer. I want to analyze all the data I've got about the DAs cases using this special software."

"You're good with computers too?" he said with a chuckle. "And here I thought you were just another pretty face."

She punched him in the arm. "Bastard."

"Just kidding."

She laughed. "I know."

Ryan drove to the Sheraton Hotel, dropped her off, and headed to his CI's house, a run-down bungalow with a sagging roof and peeling paint. There was a rusted-out Chevy pickup in the driveway so Ryan knew the man was home.

He parked his SUV at the curb, checked the load in his revolver and re-holstered the gun. Climbing out of the vehicle, he knocked on the front door several times. There was no answer so Ryan took out his lock-pick set and unlocked the door. He pulled out his handgun and carefully stepped inside the dimly-lit interior.

"Stich, you here? It's J.T."

He heard a groan from the living room sofa and flicked on the lights.

Stich was stretched out on the sagging couch, fully dressed, a hand covering his face. "Go away, J.T. Can't you see I'm sleeping?"

Ryan re-holstered his pistol, slid a chair over and sat by Stich. "Wake up. We need to talk."

"Give me a minute, okay?" the man said, rubbing his unshaven face with both hands.

Ryan glanced around the living room, which as usual was a shithole. Empty beer cans, pizza boxes, and wadded up Burger King wrappers covered the dilapidated furniture and heavily-stained carpet. The whole place stank of piss.

Stich sat up on the sofa and stared blankly at Ryan. The CI was a thin, wiry guy in his fifties with sunken eyes and long, greasy hair. He was wearing a wrinkled blue shirt and slacks.

"You been shooting up again, Stich?"

"Hell, no. The last rehab program you put me into? It took."

"Show me your arms."

The CI rolled up his long sleeves and held out his skinny arms. "See? I'm telling the truth."

Ryan inspected them and saw no track marks. The man had been a heroin addict for years. "I'm glad for you."

There was a half-full bottle of Jack Daniel's on a side table and Stich grabbed it and took a long pull. He burped and put the bottle back on the table. "I even got a real job now," Stich said. "I'm a janitor at a warehouse. Night shift."

Ryan nodded. "That's great to hear. I always hoped you could crawl out of the hellhole you were in."

"Thanks for believing in me, buddy. No one else did."

"We veterans have to look out for each other," Ryan said.

"So. What do you want to talk to me about?"

"I'm looking for information on a murder that took place in Atlanta. I'm sure you want to supplement the money you make as a janitor?"

Stich grinned, showing his crooked, stained teeth. "You bet."

Ryan described who he was after and the details of the case. When he was done, he reached into his jacket, took out cash and handed it to the other man. "This is a down payment. Find me something useful and I'll give you more."

Stich took the money. "I like the sound of that." He picked up the bottle of Black Jack and held it up. "You want a hit before you go?"

"No thanks. I'm good." Ryan stood, took out his business card and placed it on the side table. "Call me. Day or night. The sooner the better. There's a lot riding on me solving this case. A lot of people's lives are at stake."

Stich gave him crisp military salute. "You got it, Captain Ryan."

Ryan grinned. "You remembered."

The CI returned the smile. "My brain is half-fried from all of the drugs. But every once in a while, it all comes back to me. The Army days. Being in your unit."

"That's good, Sergeant. See you soon." Ryan turned, left the bungalow, and got back in his SUV, glad Stich was beginning to turn his life around.

Chapter 41

Vancouver Island, Canada

Lexi was on the third floor of her palatial home, in a windowless room she had converted into an office. She used the space when she worked from home, specially on days when the weather was bad and she couldn't have the helicopter take her to downtown Vancouver.

After making the room SCIF secure, she picked up the handset of her desk phone and punched in a preset number.

The colonel answered the call on the first ring. "Good afternoon, Lexi."

"It's morning here," she said, using her voice analyzer to verify his identity. Sometimes she preferred communicating with him without the video feed, to avoid having to see his horribly disfigured face. "I'm glad we connected so quickly, Colonel."

"You have something for me?"

"I do. I'm ready to give you the location for the next package."

"That's good, Lexi. Should I come to you? Or will you be coming to Russia?"

"Neither. We'll have to do this over the phone."

"I see. Any particular reason?"

"Under no circumstances can we be seen together, Colonel. I received information from my source that the CIA and FBI obtained a photo of the man they suspect being the ringleader of the bombing plot. I have a copy of this picture. It shows a scarred man. Lucky for us, they're looking for this man in Syria. Which means our ruse is working. But still, I'm not taking any chances."

"I understand," he said.

"When you come to the States, take no commercial flights. I don't want you spotted. I'll send my private jet to pick you up in Russia and fly you back. And my people in the States will rent any vehicle or equipment you require when you're in the USA. Now that this photo is out there, the fewer people that see you the better."

"Excellent idea."

"And one other thing, Colonel. Like when you delivered the package to the Philadelphia area, I only want you involved. No one else. Understood?"

"Yes, Lexi."

"Write this down. Then hang up, memorize the information, and burn the note." The auburn-haired woman then described the location in the United States in great detail. When she was done, she said, "Read it back to me."

He did.

"Good. Any questions, Colonel?"

"No."

"All right. I'll have my jet leave today for St. Petersburg. After you reach the U.S. and have the package in your possession, call me and I'll give you the details of the timing."

"Understood, Lexi."

She disconnected the call, exited her office, and took the elevator to the mansion's first floor, where she entered her spacious study. She turned on the gas-fired fireplace to warm the room. It was a rainy, gloomy morning on Canada's west coast and the flames from the burning wood brightened the study.

Lexi poured herself a large glass of cabernet and turned on her favorite music, *Stairway to Heaven*. She sat down on one of the leather armchairs facing the fireplace and hummed along to the song, occasionally glancing up at the large painting of her beloved husband Sergei, which hung over the fireplace mantel.

She sipped the savory crimson wine, relishing how well things were going. Operation Tripwire was working perfectly. And she reminiscence why she had chosen the name Tripwire. The nuclear explosions were the trigger, the tripwire, which caused the EMP blackouts, resulting in the stock market crashes and eventual recoveries, making her even more incredibly wealthy.

If Sergei were here, she mused, *he would be so proud of me.*

Chapter 42

Atlanta, Georgia

J.T. Ryan was looking over Rachel West's shoulder as she worked at her computer, inputting data into her CIA software program.

"You're really good at this stuff," Ryan said, admiration in his voice.

"Told you," she replied, continuing to tap at the keyboard of her laptop.

"I always thought of you as Action Rachel – a female version of 007."

They were in her hotel room at the Sheraton. She was sitting at the desk area and Ryan was standing next to her.

Rachel glanced away from the computer screen and looked up at him. "And if you're thinking of telling me a joke about dumb blondes, don't. That's a stereotype."

He shook his head and chuckled. "You must be able to read minds."

"No. I just know you, J.T." She faced the screen again and continued inputting the names of every criminal who could possibly have a grudge against the murdered District Attorney.

Ryan began rubbing her shoulders.

"Cut that out, J.T. I'm working here."

"Just trying to help."

"Bullshit. I know what you're trying to do."

"All right. I'll stop." He knelt next to her and brushed her long hair away from her face, then began nuzzling her neck gently.

Rachel kept her eyes locked on the computer screen and continued typing. But after a moment she stopped. "Damn you," she muttered, facing him. "If you keep doing that you know what's going to happen."

"I know," he said, caressing her face with a hand. "I can't help myself. You're a temptress, Rachel."

Just then his cell phone buzzed. He pulled it from a pocket and looked at the screen. "I got to take this," he said.

He stood. "Ryan here."

"It's Candy."

"My favorite CI. You got something on the case?"

"I do, J.T."

"Okay. But don't tell me on the phone. This call's encrypted, but still. I don't trust technology."

"You're such a caveman," Candy said, laughing.

"Probably. We'll meet in person."

"Sounds good. But this time, come alone, J.T. Don't bring blondie with you."

"All right."

"I've started my new job. Let me give you the address." She told him and they hung up.

"Looks like Candy's got a lead," Ryan said to Rachel.

"Great news. Give me a minute to close this software program and we can get going."

Ryan shook his head. "Candy wants me to come alone."

Rachel gave him a sly smile. "That girl's got the hots for you."

He shook his head again. "I told you before. She and I don't have that kind of relationship."

Her smile widened. "Tell me with a straight face you've never been tempted by Candy's double-Ds?"

"Cut that out. You know I only have eyes for you."

She stood and gave him a peck on the lips. "You're a sweet man. And I'm lucky to have you." She gave him a longer kiss and he returned it hungrily, wrapping his arms around her.

When they broke off the kiss a moment later, she said, "It's a good thing you're going on your own. That way I can get something done on my computer."

Ryan smiled, they said their goodbyes, and he left the room. He drove out of the hotel's parking lot, got on the 400 highway and a half hour later was in Sandy Springs. It turned out Candy's new job was only a block away from the strip club.

He parked the Explorer in the establishment's lot and eyed the one-story building. The neon sign read, *Superior Exotic Spa*. In smaller letters it said, *Atlanta's most exclusive massages. Open 24 hours a day*.

Ryan grinned, figuring out immediately what the place was all about. He climbed out of his SUV and went into the spa. He found Candy right away, sitting at the reception desk.

"Hey, J.T.," Candy said. She waved a hand around the reception room, which was almost full with men sitting on metal folding chairs. "What do you think of my new digs? And I'm not just the receptionist. I'm managing the place."

Ryan studied her appearance. Candy was wearing a black turtleneck and black slacks. "Good for you," he said.

"The best part is, I don't have to walk around nude. Or almost nude. And in case you're wondering, I don't give any of the massages myself. I hire other girls to do that."

Just then a new customer came in through the front door. The man stared at Ryan and quickly left.

"You've got that cop look, J.T.," Candy said. "We'll talk in my office before you ruin my business."

"Good idea."

Candy picked up the phone on her desk, spoke into it, and a tall, busty woman in her twenties came out of one of the back rooms. She was wearing a tight, low-cut halter top and short-shorts that left little to the imagination.

"Take over, Tammy," Candy said. "I'll be back in a few minutes."

Tammy nodded. "Yes, ma'am."

Candy led Ryan into a private office and they sat across from each other on the visitors chairs in front of the desk.

"You got a lead on my case?" he asked.

"You got cash?"

He patted his navy blazer. "Right here."

"Before I tell you, I want you to know I had to lay out some money on my own to get this info. More than I figured."

"How much?"

She told him and he thought about it a moment. "I don't have that kind of cash on me. I'll have to requisition it from Erin at the FBI."

Candy reached out with a hand and caressed his arm. "I trust you – you've never stiffed me before."

"Okay. I agree about the money. But your lead better be damn good." In a hard voice he added, "Otherwise I stop being a nice guy."

"Don't worry, honey. It's solid."

"Let's hear it."

"His name is Mitch Greer."

"He's the guy who murdered Erin's fiancée?"

"Yeah. He killed the DA."

"How'd you find out, Candy?"

"Do you *really* want to know?"

"No. Guess it doesn't really matter. What else can you tell me about this guy?"

"He's a gun for hire. A hit man. Apparently one of the best. Makes a good living, from what I could tell. He lives in Buckhead. Drives a Porsche."

"Okay. Who hired him to do the hit?"

Candy shook her head. "That I don't know."

"Can you tell me anything else about him?"

"No, honey. That's it."

"All right."

"Can I get my money now?"

He reached into his blazer, took out the cash he had there and handed it to her. "I'll get you the rest in a couple of days."

"Okay, sugar."

He got up from the chair and turned to go.

"J.T.," she said with a suggestive grin, "when you come back, I'll give you a massage. On the house."

"I thought you didn't do that."

"For you, honey, I'll make an exception."

Chapter 43

Vancouver Island, Canada

Lexi was in her mansion's study watching the roaring fireplace when she heard a knock on the door. She turned and saw her maid was in the open doorway.

"Yes, Sun-Yi?"

"Your visitor Shawn is here."

"Show him in."

Moments later Shawn walked in the room, carrying a briefcase.

"I brought the papers you needed," the young man said, setting the briefcase on the marble-top coffee table.

"Thank you, Shawn. The weather was so bad today I didn't feel like coming into the office."

"I understand," he replied in a low voice.

She studied the man's face, saw the troubled look there. "Are you okay, Shawn? You don't look yourself."

He shrugged his shoulders. "It's...."

"Tell me," she said, "I can see something's wrong."

"It's...it's my wife...she's sick...really sick...she's developed a serious heart condition...."

"Has she seen a doctor?"

He nodded. "Yes. A heart specialist here in Vancouver. She had tests." He shook his head. "They can't figure out how to treat it."

"There's a top-notch medical center in Toronto, Shawn. I've heard a lot about the place. They have the best heart doctors in Canada. I want you to take your wife there."

"But...the cost...."

"Don't worry about the cost. I'll pay for it. And you and your wife can fly to Toronto on my private jet. I'll make all the arrangements."

"I don't know...what to say, Lexi...."

She reached out with a hand and caressed his cheek. "You're not just an employee, Shawn. We're good friends too."

Chapter 44

FBI Field Office
Atlanta, Georgia

"All right," Erin Welch spit out in an irritated tone. "Enough with the damn suspense. Tell me why the hell we're meeting in the parking lot, instead of my office."

J.T. Ryan and Erin were in the front seats of his Explorer, which was parked in the FBI building's underground lot.

Ryan turned and faced her. "I have a theory."

Erin folded her arms in front of her. "I'm listening."

"We know," he said, "there's a leak high up in government. A deep-state mole. President Harris told us that himself when this whole thing started. And this mole keeps finding out information about our investigation."

"That's true. So you think my office at the FBI is bugged? I check it every morning when I get to work. I've found no listening devices or hidden cameras."

Ryan shook his head. "No, I don't think that's where the problem is."

"What then?"

"It's possible," he continued, "that the mole is someone really high up in the intelligence community. There's 17 law-enforcement agencies in the U.S. It could even be the director of any one of them."

She stared at him. "Like the FBI Director?"

"Maybe. Although he hasn't been involved in the investigation. You and I are reporting directly to the White House Task Force."

"That's true, J.T. Who then?"

"Like I said before. I have a theory."

"Tell me."

"What if," he said, "it's Alex Miller."

Erin grimaced. "Are you crazy? He's in charge of the task force. He's also the Deputy Director of the CIA. Why would he sell out his country? What's his motive?"

"Like I said, it's just a theory."

"Well, I think it's a stupid theory."

"I know it sounds far-fetched, Erin. But isn't it true that the conspirators always seems to find out what we're up to?"

"Yes, they do."

"We know for a fact that's it's someone high-up in law-enforcement. And Miller, since he runs the task force, knows every detail of what we're doing."

"That's true, J.T. Okay let me think about this a minute." She faced the windshield for a long moment, then turned back to him. "Well, if Miller is the mole, Rachel West, who works for Miller, could be a conspirator too."

Ryan shook his head forcefully. "Absolutely not. Rachel's on our side. I vouch for her 100%."

"Why? Because you're fucking her?"

He glared. "That's a cheap shot. And I resent it."

"Deny it then, J.T. I know you're doing her. Isn't that true?"

"My relationship with her has nothing to do with me vouching for her."

Erin stabbed a finger on his chest. "Men don't always think with their brains. Sometimes their other body parts think for them."

They scowled at each other for a long moment but said nothing.

Finally Erin said, "I really don't think Rachel is one of the conspirators. I'm sorry about what I said."

Ryan nodded. "Apology accepted."

Erin folded her arms in front of her. "Let's assume your theory is true, and Alex Miller is the mole. What do we do about it? He's still in charge of the task force."

"That's true," Ryan said. "We still have to report to him. So here's what we do. We continue giving him updates on our investigation, but don't tell him everything. Keep any new developments to ourselves."

"Okay, J.T. What you're saying makes sense. The FBI, CIA, and Homeland Security have flooded the Middle East with agents. It's just a matter of time before they locate the scarred man."

"In the meantime," Ryan said, "we'll keep investigating the killer of your fiancée. Now that we have a name, I plan on tracking him down."

"All right. Keep me informed on that. Do you need any help from me finding this guy?"

Ryan shook his head. "It's better if you don't get involved. I may have to break a law. Or two. This way your hands stay clean."

"When you find the assassin, I see no reason to use kid gloves. He needs to pay for what he did."

Ryan's hands formed into fists. "Don't worry, Erin. Once I'm sure he's the killer, I plan on hurting him."

Erin's eyes blazed with fury. "Hurt him bad, J.T. Hurt him bad."

Chapter 45

Atlanta, Georgia

J.T. Ryan had just returned to his apartment when he heard a knock at the front door. After checking the peephole, he opened it.

Rachel was there, a laptop under her arm. "I found the hit man," she said excitedly.

"Great," he replied. He let her inside and he closed the door behind her. Then he led her into the kitchen and she rested her computer on the dinette table.

They sat across from each other and Ryan said, "Before you tell me what you found out, we need to talk about something else."

"What?"

"I just got back from a meeting with Erin."

"By your tone, what you're going to tell me must be serious."

"It is."

"Spill it, J.T."

"As you know, there's a high-level leak in the U.S. government."

She nodded.

"I think I know who it is," he continued. "And you're not going to like it."

She frowned but said nothing.

Ryan tensed, knowing what her reaction would be. "I think it's Alex Miller."

"That's bullshit!" she spit out. She shook her head emphatically. "No way it's Alex."

He held his palms in front of him. "I know it sounds far-fetched. But we have to consider it. The criminals always seem to know what's going on. And even if it isn't Alex, it could be someone high up at the CIA, someone who communicates with Alex."

Rachel grimaced. "If you suspect Alex Miller, do you suspect me too? I'm Central Intelligence also."

"No. Absolutely not. I know you too well."

She sat there for a long time, deep in thought, not saying anything, obviously considering what he'd told her.

"All right," she finally said in a quiet voice. "Let's say it could be Alex. I still work for him. The task force – you, me, Erin, all of us report to him. How do you propose we deal with that?"

"On the surface nothing changes. We continue to be cooperative. At the same time we withhold any new leads on the case from him."

Rachel hand brushed her hair. "Okay. That would work."

He could tell she was still skeptical about Miller being the mole, but at least had accepted the possibility.

"Are we good, Rachel?"

She nodded, her expression softening. "We're good."

He pointed to her laptop which was resting on the dinette table. "What did you find?"

"It turns out," she said, "the person Candy told you about could definitely be the assassin who murdered the DA." She booted up her computer, opened a file, and turned the screen so both of them could view it. "This is the guy, Mitch Greer."

The photo showed a middle-aged man with black hair and a black mustache. He had a hard look, something Ryan recognized immediately – the man had ex-con written all over him.

"He lists his occupation as 'consultant', J.T., but from what I found out, he doesn't have any sources of income. It appears everything he makes is from illegal, under the table stuff. The thing is, he spends big. Lives in a condo in an exclusive high-rise in Buckhead. Drives a Porsche. Hires expensive call girls."

"Criminal record?" Ryan asked.

"Yeah. He's got a long rap sheet. I ran him through NCIC and AFIS. He's been in and out of prison several times for armed robbery, assault, attempted murder. But that was years ago. No arrests in the last five years. Looks like he figured out how to stay off the law-enforcement radar."

"What else, Rachel?"

"I did a deep-dive using my CIA software. It looks like he's got some mob connections. I think he's a hitman for those people."

"Italian mobsters?"

She shook her head. "No. That's what's curious. Greer has connections to the Russian mob."

"That's interesting. What else?"

"From what I can tell, the condo he lives in has top-notch security, so it's not going to be easy breaking into his place."

Ryan rubbed his jaw. "Can you print me out his picture and his other info?"

"Sure."

"Then I can take it from here."

"What do you mean, J.T.?"

"I'll track this guy on my own."

She shook her head. "No way that's going to happen. We're a team, remember?"

"True. But I made a promise to Erin. When I catch this guy and find out what I need, I'm going to hurt him bad. I don't want you involved with that. You're a Federal law-enforcement officer. What I'm going to do is illegal."

Rachel frowned. "Are you trying to protect me?"

"I don't want you getting arrested."

She bolted out of her chair. "You let me worry about that!"

He stood and in a calm voice said, "Please. Try to see it my way." He reached out his hand to caress her face and she swatted it away.

"Don't do that, J.T! Just because we have feelings for each other doesn't mean you have to protect me all the damn time!"

"I know, I know...."

Rachael's face was defiant. "I'm not giving up on this!"

He stared into her eyes and realized he wasn't about to change her mind. "All right."

Her face lit up with excitement. "We'll do this together?"

"Yes, Rachel. We'll do it together."

She flashed a beautiful smile, her vivid blue eyes sparkling. "You won't regret this."

He gave her a weak smile and felt glum inside. "I already do."

Rachel went up on her tiptoes, leaned in and gave him a quick kiss on the lips. "It'll be great, you'll see! The dynamic duo back in action."

Her enthusiasm was infectious and he grinned, this time for real. "Okay, Action Rachel. The dynamic duo it is."

They sat back down at the dinette table and started discussing the best way to catch Mitch Greer.

"We need to get him at home," Ryan said, "so I can interrogate him and go through his computer and records. That way we can trace it back and find who hired him to do the hit."

She nodded. "I told you his condo building has top-notch security. It won't be easy to break in."

Ryan thought about this a moment. "I know."

Her eyes lit up. "I've got an idea."

"I'm listening."

"If we go in the hard way and try to force our way in," she said, "there's going to be a fight, maybe shots fired and cops called."

"Yeah."

She smiled. "But what if we go in the soft way."

"Meaning?"

"Meaning I go in alone, J.T., and talk my way in."

"How is that going to work? This guy an assassin, a successful hitman. He's suspicious of everybody. That's what's kept him out of jail for the last five years."

She reached across the table and traced her fingers over the lapel of his jacket. "You'd be surprised how easily a man can be conned by an attractive woman. We already know this guy likes expensive call girls."

"So, you're suggesting you get dolled up and play the honeypot?"

She grinned. "It's just a tease, baby. Nothing's going to happen. I won't let it get that far."

"I don't like it."

"I figured as much, J.T. So I'll make you a deal. I talk my way into his place, get his guard down, then I'll let you in his apartment. Once you overpower him, I leave. That way you interrogate him and beat his ass into a pulp, all on your own. Then my hands stay clean, which if I remember, was what you wanted. Isn't that right?"

"Yes."

"So, do we have a deal, J.T.?"

"I really don't like you playing the role of a honeypot."

"It's the oldest trick in the spy trade."

"Yeah, Rachel. I know."

She grinned. "It's a great plan, isn't it?"

"It is."

"I know. So, are we good on this?"

"We're good, Rachel."

"I'd say let's shake on it, but I got a better idea." She leaned across the table and gave him a fierce kiss. He kissed her back hungrily and reached out for her with both arms.

Chapter 46

Buckhead
Atlanta, Georgia

"Let me out here," Rachel West said. "It's better if no one sees us together."

"Good idea," J.T. Ryan replied, slowing down the Ford Explorer and pulling to the curb. Greer's condo high-rise building was half a block away. The structure was one of many in Buckhead, an affluent suburb of Atlanta.

"You know the drill?" Ryan said.

"Yes. We've been over it a million times. I'll keep my cell phone on the whole time."

"Are you packing?"

In response, she opened her cocktail purse and showed him the small pistol inside. "See? And before you ask, yes, I've already racked the slide."

"Good." Ryan gave her a long up-and-down look. "But I'm not crazy about what you're wearing."

Rachel glanced down at her low-cut, curve-hugging, very short hot-pink dress. "I think I look good in this."

Ryan frowned. "Too good, if you asked me."

"You never mind it when I wear sexy clothes for you."

"That's different, Rachel."

She laughed. "You can't be a honeypot without the honey. But don't worry, nothing bad's going to happen."

"Okay. I'll go park the car and go in the building. They have a coffee shop on the first floor. I'll wait there. Call me immediately when he lets his guard down."

"Got it," she said.

**

Rachel climbed out of the SUV. Then she began walking on the sidewalk toward the building, pulling down the hem of her short dress. She rarely wore high-heels, much preferred flats, and she felt a bit unsteady at first.

Rachel reached the condo's entrance and strode into the impressive lobby. Cut-glass chandeliers hung from the atrium's high ceiling and large abstract paintings decorated the walls. The floors were polished, high-gloss marble. The place smelled of money.

Putting some hip action into her stride, she strutted to the armed uniformed security guard stationed at the reception desk.

"Will you buzz Mitch in 308, honey?" Rachel purred in a syrupy sweet Southern accent.

The security guard stared at her hungrily, taking in her provocative dress and manner. "You're here to see Mitch Greer, Miss?"

"That's right, sugar."

"Do you have an appointment?"

Rachel laughed. "Honey, Mitch and I are close friends. Really close friends. If you know what I mean...."

"Of course. What's your name, Miss?"

"Tell him it's Jen."

"Jen what?"

"Just Jen."

"Okay, Miss."

The guard picked up the phone and spoke into a moment. Then he put the phone down on the desk and said to Rachel, "Would you look up at that camera? Mr. Greer will be able to see you then."

Rachel glanced up at the CCTV security camera mounted on the wall, gave it a flirty wave and blew a kiss. Then for good measure, she smiled radiantly and leaned over so that Greer could get a real good look at her cleavage.

The guard picked up the phone and talked into it for another moment, then hung up. "You can go up and see Mr. Greer now, Miss. You can use the elevators behind me."

She smiled. "Thanks, sugar."

Rachel strutted past the stairwell and located the elevator. Getting in, she took it to the third floor. A moment later she pressed the buzzer of apartment 308. She heard a whirring sound and looked up at the security camera above the door.

Once again she smiled seductively and licked her lips. Leaning over, she let him get another good look down her low-cut dress.

She heard locks clicking and the door opened. Mitch Greer stood there, a slightly confused look on his hard face. The man was wearing expensive slacks and a white linen shirt.

"It's funny, but I don't remember you," he said.

Rachel gave him a 1000 watt smile, reached with a hand and rubbed his shirt front. She laughed a throaty laugh. "I'm not surprised, honey. You were drinking a lot that night. But you were hot to trot, baby. And I delivered."

Not waiting to be asked in, she strutted past him into the elegant foyer. "How about a drink, sugar?"

"Sure, Jen. Let's go in the living room. What would you like?"

"I'm partial to vodka. Straight up."

He led her into a sumptuously furnished room, full of leather sofas and teak wood tables.

Rachel sized up the man while he poured out the drinks. He was tall and heavily muscled. His body, like his face, looked hard and chiseled. Although she was well-trained in martial arts and able to defend herself, she realized she'd have trouble overpowering the guy.

He finished making the drinks and handed her a glass. "Should we have these in the bedroom?" he said with a leer. He gave her lecherous up-and-down look. "You look delicious, Jen."

She laughed. "Slow down, cowboy. I may be easy, but I like to be sweet talked first." She laughed again. "But don't worry, Mitch honey, Jen always delivers...."

"Yeah, sure, no problem. Let's sit over here for a bit. Okay?"

She sipped her vodka, weighing her options as they sat across from each other.

"Tell me again – when did we meet?" he said, downing his drink in one gulp.

"Don't you remember, honey? At the party three weeks ago...."

He grimaced and slammed down his glass on the coffee table. "I don't go to parties."

"You were drinking a lot, Mitch honey...."

In a suspicious tone, he said, "Who the hell are you?"

"Calm down, baby...."

He bolted off the sofa and planted his hands on his hips. "Answer me, bitch!"

Rachel opened her purse, slipped out the small pistol and pointed it at him. "Sit down."

With scowl he yelled, "Put that fucking thing down before you hurt yourself!"

She aimed the pistol at his crotch. "Take one more step, asshole, and I'll blow your balls off!"

He froze, staring at the gun and then at her face. "Look, there's no reason to argue. I know you're a call girl. I know you want to get the money part out of the way. Name your price, Jen. And put the gun away, okay?"

"Lay on the floor, Mitch. Face down."

"What the fuck? Are you crazy?"

"I've got a round in the chamber, Mitch. And I won't miss at this range. Now lay down on the floor or your balls go bye-bye."

He grimaced, staring at her intently, obviously trying to decide if she would pull the trigger. Eventually he nodded and slowly eased himself down to the floor.

She got off the sofa, and still pointing the gun in his direction, approached him cautiously. When she was next to him she took out plastic flex-cuffs from her purse. "Hands behind your back," she hissed. "And no sudden moves."

"No problem, Jen."

In a blur of motion, he grabbed her ankle and yanked.

Rachel toppled to the floor but held on to her pistol. She clubbed him with the gun, hard, on the side of his head.

Greer's eyes rolled white and his body sagged, unconscious.

Recovering the flex-cuffs from the floor, she rolled him face down and bound his hands behind his back.

"Asshole," she spit out.

After taking a moment to catch her breath, she took out her cell phone and made a call. "You can come up now, J.T. I'll let you in."

"Are you okay?" he replied in a worried tone.

"I'm fine."

"Any problems."

"Nothing I couldn't handle."

"I'm on my way."

"No rush," she said, glancing down at the unconscious man on the floor. "Greer's not going anywhere."

***

J.T. Ryan raced out of the coffee shop on the building's first floor and sprinted to the uniformed security guard at the reception desk.

Ryan pointed toward the lobby's front entrance and yelled, "The old guy fell on the sidewalk! He's bleeding. He owns one of the condos here. You better go out and help him!"

The guard's eyes got big and he stared through the glass door. Then he sprinted in that direction.

Ryan went around the reception desk, found the stairway and sprinted up, two steps at a time. A moment later he was on the third floor and Rachel let him into the apartment and closed the door behind him.

"You can put your gun away," she said, pointing toward the living room. "Greer's in there."

Ryan holstered his pistol and found the man face down on the living room floor, his hands bound behind his back. He wasn't moving, obviously unconscious. "Good work, Rachel."

"Told you I could handle it."

He nodded. "I never doubted your skills. I just didn't want you to get hurt."

She approached him. "You're a sweet man. Silly, but sweet."

"Your part's done," he said. "You can take off now."

"You sure? I can help."

"We had a deal, remember?"

"I remember," she replied, pouting. "How come you get to have all the fun?"

"What I'm going to do isn't fun."

"All right, all right, I'm leaving." She picked up her damaged high-heels, which were scattered on the floor. "But I'm putting in an expense report for a new pair of shoes. That asshole Greer broke one of them."

"Don't worry. Erin will cover it."

"Okay, J.T. See you soon." She turned to go.

"And Rachel," he said. "Do me a favor. When you get back to your hotel – can you please change into some decent clothes."

She laughed. "No more honeypot?"

"No more honeypot."

She laughed again, waved, and left the apartment, closing the door behind her.

Ryan checked to make sure Greer was still unconscious and bound tightly, then went through the three-bedroom condo. One of the rooms had been converted into an office and there he found a laptop and several notebooks. There was a messenger bag in the closet and he packed the computer and the other items into that. That done, he went back to the living room, where he found Greer beginning to regain consciousness.

Ryan propped the guy into a sitting position on the floor, with his back to a wall. Then Ryan squatted in front of him so they were at eye-level.

"Who the hell are you?" Greer spit out.

"That's not important."

Greer glanced around the room. "Where's that crazy bitch, Jen?"

"Call her a bitch again and you'll regret it, friend."

His eyes defiant, Greer said, "You a cop?"

Ryan shook his head.

"You look like a cop."

"I get that a lot," Ryan said.

"Is this a robbery? You picked the wrong guy," the man said, seething. "I'm connected."

Ryan nodded. "Yeah, I know all about you."

"You're fucking going to regret it!" the man shouted.

Ryan punched him hard on the mouth, splitting his lip. Blood began dribbling down, staining his white linen shirt.

"Shut up, Greer. I'm tired of you running your mouth. This is how this is going to work. I ask questions. You answer them. Got it?"

"Fuck you, whoever the hell you are!"

Ryan punched him again and more blood seeped from his mouth.

"Who hired you to murder the District Attorney, Ed Roth?"

"Fuck you! I'm not saying a word."

"I know you did it. What I need to know is who paid you."

The man shook his head. "I don't know what you're talking about."

"You're a hired killer, a hit man, mostly for the Russian mob here in Atlanta. You murdered Roth in a church a while back."

"You're full of shit."

Ryan punched him hard on the face a third time and the man's left eye began to swell up.

"Think you're tough?" Greer spit out. "I'm tied up. I can't fight back. You're not tough at all, you bastard."

Ryan sized the man up. He was over 6 feet, almost as tall as himself, who was 6'4". Both men were heavily muscled.

He stood up and took off his blazer. Then he unholstered his S&W Magnum revolver, unloaded it and put the bullets in his pocket. After re-holstering his pistol, he grabbed Greer and hauled him to his feet. He went behind him and unbound his hands. Then he faced Greer again and stood a few feet away.

"Take your best shot, asshole," Ryan said.

Greer seemed confused for a moment by Ryan's actions, then lunged at him.

Ryan sidestepped him and punched the guy hard in the kidneys. Greer grunted, then whirled around, swinging with his fist.

Ryan instantly stepped back and the punch only hit air. Then Ryan hit the man hard on the solar plexus with two punches, a left hook and right cross, and the criminal staggered back. He went down to one knee. He gulped in air, then stood and lunged at Ryan again, his eyes blazing with hate.

Ryan sidestepped him again, punching him savagely in the kidneys. Greer groaned and staggered back. Not giving him a chance to recover, Ryan punched him hard on the face twice, the hits cracking the man's nose, blood spurting freely. This time the guy collapsed to the floor, grunting, holding his face with both hands.

Ryan was exhausted from the fight and he gulped in lungfuls of air. Then he shook out his hands which were throbbing with pain. He examined his own knuckles, which were swollen and bleeding. Ryan had learned a long time ago that hitting something as hard as a person's head was painful.

He crouched by the other man, who was on the floor, groaning, his face covered in blood.

"Had enough, asshole?" Ryan said. "Ready to talk now?"

"Fuck you," the man responded with a grunt, as more blood and bits of broken teeth seeped out of his mouth.

"You leave me no choice, Greer." Ryan reached into his pocket and pulled out a set of brass knuckles, which he fit on his hands. Then he stood and said, "Get up, Greer. Let's finish this."

The man looked up and saw the brass knuckles. "Hell, no!"

Ryan kneeled next to him and growled, "This is for Erin." Then he began pounding on the man's face savagely with both his fists, blood spattering everywhere. When he stopped moments later Greer's face looked like raw hamburger meat.

The man howled in pain and began yelling, "Stop! Stop! I'll talk...."

"All right. I'll stop. But if I think you're lying, I'll start again. Understood?"

"Yes...yes...." he managed to say, as more gore and broken teeth came out of his mouth.

"Did you murder the District Attorney?"

"Yeah...."

"Who hired you to kill him, Greer?"

"I...don't...know...." the man said, gasping for air.

"Wrong answer!" Ryan reared back with a closed fist and the man put his hands in front of his face. "It's true! It was...it was...all done by phone...and wire transfer...I don't know who...hired me...."

"I've got your computer. I can check your bank records. If you're lying to me, I'll know. And next time we meet, I won't take it easy on you like I am now."

"No!...it's the fucking truth...I really don't know...."

Ryan sensed the man was telling the truth. He stood up, took off his brass knuckles and wiped the blood off his hands with a handkerchief. Then he took out his cell phone and punched in a number.

"It's Ryan," he said when Erin Welch answered the call.

"What's going on, J.T.?"

"I found Greer. He's our guy. He confessed to murdering your fiancée, Ed Roth."

"Who hired him?"

"He said he doesn't know. He was paid with a wire transfer and only talked to the people by phone."

"Is he telling the truth?"

Ryan glanced down at the man, who was gasping, groaning, and bleeding profusely on the floor. "Yeah. He's telling the truth. I've got his laptop and papers. Rachel can work some of her computer magic on it. I'm hoping we can figure out who it was from that."

"Okay."

"I need you to send some of your agents," he said, "to arrest Greer for murder." He gave her the address. "And one other thing, send an ambulance too. And put a rush on it. He's bleeding. A lot. And I don't want him to die."

"Why is he bleeding?"

"He fell off a ladder."

Erin was quiet a moment, then said, "Thank you, J.T."

"For what?"

"For hurting him."

"The bastard deserved it, Erin."

Chapter 47

San Diego, California

It had been an extremely long day for Colonel Mikhail Sharpov.

Lexi's private jet had picked him up in Russia early in the morning, they had flown to the United States and made a stop at the city where he stored the packages. After obtaining one of the backpacks, the plane had continued on its journey to its final destination, San Diego's International Airport.

The Gulfstream G700 jet touched down on one of the runways and taxied on the tarmac toward an unmarked hanger in the section of the airport allotted for private planes.

When the Gulfstream came to a stop next to the hangar, the colonel unbuckled his seat belt and stood. He put on the backpack, grabbed his duffel, and made his way out of the jet. There were no other passengers on the plane.

The pilot was waiting for him at the exit door. The man handed the colonel a set of keys and said, "There's a car for you by the hangar."

The colonel nodded, said nothing, and walked down the airstairs to the waiting Chevy Malibu. After storing the backpack and duffel in the trunk, he climbed inside the vehicle.

He drove out of the airport and stopped at the first motel he found, a Holiday Inn Express. He checked in under an assumed name and paid with a forged credit card. It was 3 a.m. and he was dead tired from his trip and knew he needed sleep before he continued on his journey. He had to be sharp for what was to come.

By 9 a.m. he was back on the road heading toward the marina area of San Diego. Lexi had done all of the research and he drove to the sprawling boat rental company she had selected. When he got there, he rented a 50 foot Cigarette Marauder speed boat, using a different identity and a different forged credit card. The very long and narrow boat had twin engines producing 1,075 horsepower. Capable of speeds of 90 MPH, the sleek and powerful boats were used for all types of watersports, and because of their amazing top speeds they were favored by smugglers.

The colonel stored the backpack and his other gear in the boat and started up the twin engines, the deep-throated growl of the powerful motors startling him at first. He casted off the moorings and piloted the boat out of the marina, then began heading north over the choppy water of the Pacific.

He inputted the coordinates Lexi had given him into the speed boat's NAV system and began following that course. He knew the distance between San Diego and Los Angeles was 120 miles. Using Interstate 5 he could have driven the distance by car in under three hours. But he also knew that traffic in the L.A. area could be hellishly bad, and because of his mission, getting caught in a traffic jam would be deadly for himself. After discussing it with Lexi, they had decided using a go-fast boat was the best option.

The colonel set the throttle to 50 MPH and continued north, the deep-V hull of the boat pounding over the waves. He hugged the coastline, staying about a mile west of the shoreline. It was a cold, windy day, the saltwater spray splashing the windshield and his scarred face. He zipped his parka up to his neck and tied his hood snuggly on his head so it wouldn't blow off.

Several hours later, he saw the coastline change from wooded rolling hills to the sprawling, overdeveloped congestion of metropolitan Los Angeles. Even from a mile offshore, the high-rise condos and other buildings were visible.

Watching the GPS map on the console, he realized he was close to his target. Pulling back on the throttle, he slowed his speed and continued motoring closer to the marina.

When he was in the center of the harbor, he shut off the engine, dropped his anchor, and gazed around. Situated six miles south of Santa Monica and four miles north of Los Angeles International Airport, Marina Del Ray is L.A.'s best known and largest marina. Home to approximately 5,000 pleasure boats, the harbor was the city's center for watersports and waterfront activities. It was also close to L.A.'s communications, banking, and transportation centers, the reason Lexi had chosen the location.

The colonel pulled out his handheld GPS device and verified the coordinates matched the ones from the boat's NAV system. Satisfied he was in the right place, he took out his SAT cell phone and punched in the woman's number.

Lexi picked up on the first ring. "Yes, Colonel?"

"I'm here."

"Read me your coordinates," she snapped.

He did so.

"Verify your location with your handheld GPS, Colonel."

"I've already done that."

"Do it again," she said testily.

"Yes, Lexi." He input the coordinates into his handheld device again and verified his location. "I'm in the exact spot."

"Good." She paused a moment, then said, "Describe the area around you. Are you close to anyone who might see you delivering the package?"

The colonel picked up a pair of binoculars he had brought with him and gazed around his location.

"There are boats in the marina," he said. "Sailboats and powerboats, but I'm not close to any one of them."

"Excellent."

"I'm going to set the timer now, Lexi. Then I'll deliver the package."

"How long?"

"Three hours. That will give me plenty of time to get back to San Diego."

"All right," she said. "Call me immediately and give me a status report when you're safely away from Marina Del Ray."

"Yes, Lexi."

"And one other thing. I'm counting on you. I'm depending on you. Nothing must go wrong."

"I won't disappoint you."

"I know you won't, Colonel. You're the most efficient and most important member of my team."

His chest swelled with pride and his devotion grew. "Thank you, Lexi. Thank you very much. That means the world to me."

The woman hung up and he put his phone away.

Going below decks, he picked up the backpack and placed it on the boat's small dinette table. Unzipping the pack open, he stared at the bomb's display panel. Like the first time he had armed a nuclear weapon, his stomach began churning and his heart raced. *One wrong move, and I'm dead.*

Carefully, he flicked a switch on the W-54 and a solid green light came on the device's control panel. *Don't let Lexi down. She needs me. I owe her too much.*

Methodically, he started adjusting the timer, adding minutes to the readout. He stopped when it read 180 minutes. Three hours.

The colonel flicked another switch and the control panel's solid green light began flashing. The readout now read 179 minutes.

Quickly zipping the backpack closed, he picked it up and slung it over his shoulder. Then he climbed the steps and went to the boat's cockpit on deck.

Picking up the binoculars, he gazed around the harbor and the sprawling marina to make sure there were no boats close by. There were none and he strode to the back of the Cigarette Marauder. Slowly easing the backpack off his shoulder, he carefully lowered it into the dark blue Pacific water. The heavy bag sank immediately.

He raced forward, quickly retracted his anchor, and turned on the boat's engines. The 1,075 horsepower motors roared to life. He put the Cigarette in gear and the boat went on plane, cutting through the choppy water with ease.

The colonel steered the craft out of the harbor area at a moderate pace of 15 MPH so as to not attract attention to himself. But once he was in the open waters of the Pacific, he pushed the throttle down quickly. The twin engines howled and the speedometer began climbing immediately. 40 MPH, then 50 MPH, then 60 MPH.

The Cigarette Marauder literally flew over the choppy ocean, it's deep-V hull pounding over the waves. He steered south as he studied the speedometer. 70 MPH, 85 MPH, the sound from the powerful engines deafening.

He grinned when he saw the speedometer hit top speed of 90 MPH.

"I did it," he yelled out loud. "I did it!"

The cold saltwater sprayed over the windshield, pelting his scarred face. But now the cold water felt good to him, his sense of accomplishment crowding his thoughts.

Lexi will be very proud of me, he mused.

His grin widened.

Chapter 48

Vancouver, Canada

Lexi glanced at the clock on the wall, counting down the minutes. It had been over an hour since the colonel had called her and she was beginning to worry.

Her thoughts raced. *Has something gone wrong? Did the package explode prematurely? Is the colonel dead?* Her stomach churned at the thought, knowing her plans were far from complete.

Lexi was at the workstation in her stock trading room, the program trades on her software ready to be put in motion. With a click of her mouse the final command would be activated.

She looked up from the computer screen to the six flatscreen TVs mounted on the wall. None of the channels were reporting a large explosion in Southern California.

Two of the televisions were tuned to local TV stations in the Los Angeles area. One was showing news, traffic, and weather, and the other was broadcasting a talk show.

Lexi's SAT cell phone was resting on her workstation and it buzzed to life. She grabbed it and took the call.

"It's me, Lexi," the colonel said.

"Is everything okay? I was worried."

"Yes, yes, everything is fine!" He was yelling into the phone and in the background she heard the deafening sound of the boat's engines.

"I'm halfway to San Diego," he shouted.

"The timer is set?"

"Yes." He paused a moment, then yelled, "The package will be activated in exactly 92 minutes."

"Excellent. Good work."

"Thank you, Lexi."

She stared at the clock on the wall, etching the time left in her mind.

"Get home safe, my friend," she said and hung up.

Putting the phone down, she studied her stock trading software, while simultaneously monitoring the L.A. area TV stations.

Periodically she glanced at the clock, her anticipation building as the minutes wound down.

Ten minutes left.

Then seven.

Then two.

Lexi typed in the final activation command, but didn't press the Enter key.

She stared at the clock, her heart thundering in her chest.

One minute.

45 seconds...30 seconds...15 seconds....

0 seconds.

She gazed at the television screens, her whole focus on the two local TV stations from the Los Angeles area. One was covering the weather, the other one broadcasting a commercial.

Nothing changed for the next minute, which to her felt like an hour, her anticipation at a fever pitch.

Suddenly one of the local channels flickered and the screen went dark.

Two seconds later the other Los Angeles TV station went dark.

Jubilant and ecstatic, Lexi pressed the Enter key.

Chapter 49

Atlanta, Georgia

Rachel West was working at her computer when she heard a knock on her hotel room door. Getting up, she checked the spyhole, then opened the door.

J.T. Ryan was at the doorway, a smile on his face. He was holding something behind his back and with a flourish, he brought it around and handed her a bouquet of pink roses.

Surprised and thrilled, she took them. "They're beautiful, J.T. What's the occasion?"

"I know you had a birthday a few months ago. But you were overseas on one of your super-secret agent missions to who-knows-where. So I figured now is a good time to celebrate it."

She grinned widely, went up on her tip-toes and kissed him. He returned the kiss hungrily, hugged her, and they stayed like that for a long, delicious moment.

When they broke it off, she let him inside and closed the door behind him. She placed the bouquet of flowers on the bed and faced him. "You're a sweet man, J.T."

He lifted his hands and showed them to her. His knuckles were badly bruised. "I beat a man half to death a few days ago," he said. "I'm not that sweet."

"That guy deserved it."

"Yeah, he did."

Rachel folded her arms in front of her. "When your time comes, hopefully a very, very long time from now, I know what you'll want inscribed on your gravestone, J.T."

"What?"

"John Taylor Ryan. He never killed a man that didn't deserve killing."

Ryan nodded. "You know me too well."

She reached out with her palm and caressed his handsome face, felt the light stubble on his cheek. "I do."

He glanced at her open laptop, which was resting on the small table in the hotel room. "How is that going?"

Rachel shook her head. "I still can't find the people who paid Greer to kill the DA."

"How about Erin's theory that the murder of her fiancée and the terrorists are connected?"

Feeling glum, she shook her head again. "I haven't found that connection. But I'm still looking."

"Okay."

Trying to lighten the mood a bit, she said, "How about a drink?"

He glanced at his watch. "It's only two in the afternoon."

She grinned. "C'mon. Just one. I need to thank you for the beautiful roses you just gave me."

"All right. But just one drink."

Rachel laughed. "You're such a Boy Scout." She went to the hotel room's closet, opened her suitcase, and took out the bottle of Absolut she had in there. She poured the vodka into the two glasses supplied in the room.

After handing one of the drinks to him, she said, *"Salud!"* and gulped hers down. It tasted bitter and refreshing.

He took a sip of his vodka. "Slow down. We still have work to do."

"Don't worry about me. Bet I can drink you under the table."

Ryan shook his head. "I'm not taking that bet."

"Smart man."

Ryan sat at one of the chairs by the small table and pointed to her laptop. "Okay. Let's get back to it."

She grimaced. "I've been staring at my spreadsheets all day. I got a much better idea." Rachel went to the bed and sat on it. With a grin, she patted the bedspread. "Come over here."

He smiled back. "You're such a temptress."

She laughed. "I'm your temptress. And no one else's." She patted the bedspread again. "Come on, baby, I want to fuck."

Ryan frowned.

"What's the matter, J.T. Don't you want to do it, too?"

"Of course I do. I just don't like it when you use that word."

"What word?"

"The 'F' word, Rachel. You're a classy woman. A classy and beautiful woman. And I want to make love to you in the worst way. But don't cheapen what we have by calling it fucking."

Rachel's jaw clenched and her eyes blazed. She stabbed her forefinger in his direction. "I hate it when you try to change me!"

He held his palms up in front of him, then stood, approached the bed and sat next to her. "I'm not trying to change you, Rachel. Really I'm not." He covered one of her hands with his.

Still angry, she snatched her hand away.

His deep brown eyes stared into hers. "I care about you, Rachel. Very much."

She looked down at the floor. "I know. And I care about you. More than any other man I've ever known. Still...."

He reached out, lifted her chin and smiled. "Let's not argue anymore, okay?"

She nodded. "Okay. Life's too short."

He wrapped one of his powerful arms around her and held her close. She leaned in and rested her head on his chest.

"This is nice, J.T.," she murmured.

"Yeah. It is."

They sat there for several minutes, not saying a word, both of them savoring the moment.

Then he said, "I know what would be even nicer."

She looked up to his eyes, saw the desire there.

"J.T.! You're such a devil!"

They both laughed, kissed, and hugged each other. Then their hands roamed all over each other's bodies, eager to take off their clothes.

Aroused and more than ready, Rachel was about to strip off her polo shirt when she felt her cell phone vibrate in her pants pocket. "Shit," she said, grudgingly. Standing up, she took out her phone and answered the call.

"Rachel West," she said.

"It's me," she heard Alex Miller say.

"Yes, Alex."

"It's happened again. The terrorists. This time in Los Angeles."

Her heart raced and she gripped the phone tightly. "When did it happen?"

"Just now, Rachel. The news broke a few minutes ago. Turn on your TV."

"Which channel?"

"All of them. Fox, ZNN, CBS, ABC, NBC, Newsmax. Take your pick."

"Okay, Alex."

"Do you have any new leads on the case? I just got a call to go to the White House about this latest attack. I need to fill in the President."

Rachel was tempted to tell Miller that the hitman, Greer, had been caught, but remembered what she, Ryan, and Erin had agreed to do.

"No, Alex. No new developments."

"All right. But keep working it hard. And keep me posted."

She hung up and stared at Ryan. "You heard?"

He grimaced. "The terrorists struck again."

Nodding, she sprinted to the TV in the room and turned it on. The television came on and using the remote she put on one of the cable news channels.

It showed an overhead view of a sprawling marina and harbor area, taken by a helicopter. The buildings nearest the water were flattened, rubble everywhere. Hundreds of damaged boats, or their remnants, bobbed on the choppy dark blue water. Fires were burning everywhere and plumes of black smoke towered over the marina.

Ryan came over and they both stared silently at the screen.

"As you can see," the off-screen reporter was saying, "Marina Del Ray has been destroyed. Authorities are telling us the casualties from the massive explosion are in the thousands, with many more thousands injured. To make matters worse," the anchorman continued, "all communication systems in the Los Angeles area are currently offline. No cell phones are working, and the Internet is down, along with local TV broadcasting. The authorities say this is the result of an Electronic Magnetic Pulse which was caused by the massive explosion. The bomb appears to have been detonated offshore, which caused a geyser effect, creating giant waves that flooded the Marina Del Ray area of Los Angeles...."

Chapter 50

The Oval Office
The White House
Washington, D.C.

Alex Miller was led into the Oval Office by a Secret Service agent, who left the room and closed the door behind him.

President Harris and General Foster were already in the office. The President was behind his historic wooden desk and he waved Miller to one of the wingback chairs in front of the desk. The CIA man sat and waited for Harris to begin.

"We already met with the Directors of Homeland Security and the FBI," the President said gravely. "They filled us in on the details of the attack. But I wanted to get your take on it, Alex."

"Yes, sir," Miller replied. "The attack in Los Angeles appears to be very similar to the one in Philadelphia. The terrorists could have detonated the bomb in the downtown area of L.A., where it would have killed hundreds of thousands of people. But instead they set it off about a mile offshore, which limited the casualties to approximately 15,000. It looks to me, Mr. President, that the terrorists' aim is not to inflict maximum damage."

"General Foster and I agree with you," Harris said. "Their motive is not to murder as many Americans as possible."

"Any ransom demands?" Miller asked.

The President shook his head. "None. Same as last time."

General Foster spoke up for the first time. "This bombing, like the last one, created a massive Electronic Magnetic Pulse, which we've known for some time is a side effect of a nuclear weapon detonation. So the whole Los Angeles area has gone totally dark. All electricity is down, with an area wide blackout. In addition, all electronic communication and data transmission has been knocked out. Cell phone, landline, TV transmission, and electronic banking are also down in that whole area."

"If there's any bright side to this whole mess," the President said, "is that the blackout may be temporary. We've seen the situation in Philadelphia improve recently. That city's electric power, cell phone, and TV transmission is being restored after several weeks."

"There's another aspect to this, Mr. President," Foster said. "And it has to do with the American stock market. After the L.A. bombing, the stock market went into panic mode. Stock prices cratered almost immediately. The Dow Jones Average has dropped 3,000 points today. This is very similar to what happened after the Philadelphia attack. We saw panic selling then. And after a week, prices began to go back up."

"What if," Miller interjected, "the motive of the terrorists is not to kill people and destroy cities as we saw on September 11, 2001. Maybe their motive now is to crash the stock market."

President Harris glared at him. "For what purpose? What would the terrorists gain?"

"Sir," Miller said, "there's a stock trading technique called short selling. Stock traders, in effect, are betting the price of a company's stock is going to go down. And when it does go down, they make a profit."

Harris leaned back in his executive chair and looked deep in thought. "I see. But how does that help us find the terrorists and stop them before they strike gain?"

Miller shook his head. "It doesn't, sir."

"The FBI Director told us," the President said, "that the Bureau is till blanketing Syria and the Middle East with hundreds of their agents, trying to locate the scarred man, the terrorist ringleader that John Ryan identified. Unfortunately, this terrorist has yet to be found."

"The CIA is doing the same thing, sir," Miller replied.

"Any leads?"

"No, Mr. President."

President Harris's face reddened and he slammed his fists on the desk. "God damn it, Alex! Find these terrorists! And do it now, before they strike again!"

Chapter 51

Vancouver, Canada

The Cadillac Escalade wound its way through Stanley Park, the driver going slowly, knowing his employer would want to make a stop at one of the many gardens that dotted the sprawling 405 acre park.

Lexi, who was in the backseat of the SUV, spotted one of her favorite gardens and said to the driver, "Stop here."

The man slowed the vehicle and pulled to the curb.

Lexi's assistant was sitting next to her and she turned toward him. "Walk with me, Shawn."

Lexi and Shawn climbed out and she led the way into the elaborately manicured garden. Her head of security, Brad Murdock, was in the front passenger seat and he also exited the vehicle and followed the two people at a discreet distance.

Lexi breathed in the foliage's fragrant scent and admired the beauty of the flowers and cultured hedges. Today the red-haired woman was wearing a scarlet silk jacket and matching skirt, with a white silk blouse. Instead of her usual stilettos, she had worn flats, knowing the shoes would be better for walking on the lush, carpet of grass.

She looked up to the cerulean blue, cloudless sky. It was a cool, crisp fall day and she found the park and the scenery invigorating.

Walking alongside Shawn, she said, "Beautiful day, isn't it?"

He nodded, but said nothing, deep in thought.

She stopped and turned toward him. "What's troubling you? You've been quiet for days."

"It's nothing."

She placed a hand on his shoulder. "I know you well. I can tell something's wrong. Is your wife okay?"

He nodded and his expression brightened. "She's doing very well. Ever since I took her to the doctors in Toronto, she's improved tremendously. Thank you, Lexi, for making that possible."

"I'm glad I could help." She began walking again and he strode alongside her. "So it's something else that's bothering you."

He gave her a sidelong glance and she could see the anguish in his face. "Lexi, what happened in Los Angeles recently. The bombing."

"What about it?"

"I've been watching the news," he said. "Over 15,000 people are dead."

"Yes, it's very sad."

"Were you involved in that, Lexi?"

"The bombing?" she replied and continued walking.

"Yes."

"Why would you ask me something like that?"

"Because I see your financial records," he said, "you've made a fortune in the last few days."

She nodded. "I have."

"The same thing happened after the Philadelphia bombing. I have a sense that somehow you're involved in all this. You and the colonel."

She mulled this over for a long moment. "Let's say, hypothetically, that I had some involvement in all this. Wouldn't you agree that the damage has been limited? Hundreds of thousands could have died."

Shawn grimaced. "Limited? Over 15,000 people were killed and many more were injured. I would call that wholesale murder!"

Lexi shook her head. "That's one way to look at it. Anyway, this plan of mine isn't just about making money, although that part has been incredibly satisfying. It's also about payback. Retribution. The American justice system killed my Sergei. I'm getting my payback, my revenge." Her voice dropped to a harsh whisper. "From my viewpoint, it's justified. Sergei is gone, taken away from me. Now American lives are my sweet revenge."

Shawn stopped in his tracks and gave her a hostile look. "I'm not sure I can continue working for you."

Her eyes flashed in anger. "You have no choice, Shawn. You're implicated in all this, by being my financial consultant."

He frowned. "I...."

"Face it, Shawn. You have no way out. My suggestion to you is, forget we ever had this conversation."

He stared at the ground and went quiet.

"In any case," she added, "the way I see it, you owe me big time."

"For what?"

"For what I did for your wife. Without the high-priced doctors I'm paying for, your wife would be dead right now. You could say I saved her life."

Shawn raised his eyes and looked at her, his expression tortured.

"What I just said is true, isn't it Shawn?"

He nodded, his shoulders sagging.

Lexi placed a hand on his cheek. "I care for you. Very much. Ever since my beloved husband Sergei died, I have only been intimate with you. You know that, right?"

"Yes. I know that."

Then she said, "I have an excellent idea for this afternoon. Let's go back to the office. We can relax, drink some wine, and make love."

He shook his head and in a hesitant voice murmured, "I don't know if I can...."

Lexi smiled brightly. "Don't be silly. Of course you can." She took his hand and led him back to the waiting Escalade.

Chapter 52

Vancouver, Canada

Lexi went into the penthouse office on the 80th floor of her building and quickly checked her email. Then she strode into the separate, windowless room at the back of the office. Once a storage area, she had converted the space into a bedroom. The room was outfitted with a king size bed, a dresser, a night table and a liquor cabinet.

Going to the liquor cabinet, she poured out two glasses of Merlot from one of the many bottles of red wine she stored there. She took a sip from one of the glasses and relished the strong, full-bodied oak flavor of the Merlot. Then she placed the wine glasses on the night table and glanced at the framed photo that was resting there. The picture was of Sergei. She caressed the photo and silently asked for his forgiveness. Taking off her wedding band and five-carat ruby engagement ring, she placed them in the drawer.

That done, she kicked off her flat shoes, removed her scarlet silk jacket, and lifted up the hem of her scarlet skirt. Then she reached underneath and removed her white silk thong. After smoothing down her skirt and unbuttoning the top button of her white silk blouse, she pulled the bedspread off the king size bed. Still clothed, she sat on the bed and continued sipping her wine, knowing he would be coming in soon.

Five minutes later there was a soft knock on the door.

"Come in, Shawn," she said.

The young man stepped inside and closed the door behind him.

Lexi immediately saw the worried, tense expression on his face. He was always a reluctant partner in these sessions, she knew. It appeared he would be even more reluctant today. *He'll need coaxing, Today more than ever.*

Lexi smiled seductively, picked up one of the glasses of wine held it up for him.

"I poured you a glass," she said.

"I'm not...I'm not thirsty, Mrs. Atwood...." he replied, with a tremor in his voice.

She motioned him over with a hand. "Sit by me."

"I don't think we should do this, Mrs. Atwood...."

"Don't be difficult. You know I hate it when you're difficult."

Shawn hesitantly stepped closer and sat next to her on the bed.

Lexi handed him the wine. "Drink this. It'll help. It always does."

He took the glass and sipped the wine, his hands shaking a bit.

"Drink it all down, Shawn."

He complied and she smiled. "That's better." She caressed his face with her hand and he flinched.

"Please, Mrs. Atwood...."

"Call me Lexi. This isn't our first time. Far from it."

"Yes, Lexi."

"That's better." She caressed his face again and this time he didn't flinch. She smiled and gazed into his beautiful gray eyes. "I love your eyes. That's your best feature."

He was a slender young man with a slight build, unlike her Sergei, who was big, muscular, and rugged, but Shawn had an innocence that she found highly attractive.

She took his empty glass and handed him her own, which was still mostly full. "Drink this. It'll help."

He downed the second glass quickly and closed his eyes.

"Feel better?" she asked.

He opened his eyes. "Yes."

"Good. Now get undressed, Shawn. You know what I like."

Without another word, the young man began taking off all of his clothes. When he was done, he lay on the bed, flat on his back and stared at the ceiling.

Still clothed, she lay next to him and snuggled close. His body was shivering slightly and she placed her palm on his chest, her anticipation building for what was to come.

His voice quivering, he whispered, "I don't...I don't think...it's going to work...today...."

Lexi glanced down at his groin and saw how limp he was. "Don't worry," she replied in a soothing voice. "I'll take care of everything, okay?"

Shawn glanced at her then continued staring at the ceiling. "Yes, Mrs. Atwood...I mean Lexi...."

She smiled and snuggled closer to him, pressing her curvaceous body tight into his. Her palm traced his chest then slid lower to his abdomen and finally rested on his groin. She began massaging him gently.

Shawn gasped a bit and closed his eyes tight.

She continued massaging him and started to feel him stiffen. She loved doing this and sensed herself getting wet. In a low voice, she said, "I care about you. Very, very much. And it's not just the sex. It's much more than that. I want to share everything with you."

H opened his eyes and faced her. "What do you mean?"

She stopped massaging him. "Exactly what I said. I want to share it with you. I have no one else. I want to share my wealth with you, Shawn."

"I don't understand. I work for you. I'm your employee."

Lexi caressed his chest. "You're much more than that to me. You're my companion. My lover. My confidant."

He frowned. "I'm your sex slave."

She continued caressing his chest. "That's a negative way of looking at it. I certainly don't see it that way." She smiled. "I see us as partners."

"Partners?" he replied in a nervous tone. "You tell me what to do and I do it. That's not a partnership...."

"I suppose you're right about that. I expect things from you. I require certain things from you. But that doesn't mean we can't become emotionally close."

"I'm a married man, Lexi."

"Yes, yes, I haven't forgotten. You can keep your wife and your children. I'll always provide for them. I won't interfere with your family life. But if we become closer, I'll share my wealth with you. Think about it, Shawn. I'm the richest person in Canada. You see the numbers. You prepare my financial statements. With my recent stock market gains, I'm sure I'm now one of the richest women in the world. And one day, God willing, I'll become the richest person on the planet."

She stopped talking and stared into his gray eyes. "Think about it, Shawn. I'm willing to share all of that with you. Think what that kind of money would mean to your family. You and they could live a life of wealth and leisure...."

He stared back and she could sense his uncertainty.

"I know it's a lot to take in," she said in a soothing voice. "Give it time. You'll see this is exactly what you and your family need."

He looked at her for long moment, saying nothing. His face showed a range of emotions – fear, but also eagerness and longing.

Eventually he nodded. "Maybe you're right, Lexi."

She grinned. "Of course I'm right. I always am. Now I want you to lay back on the bed and relax. I'll take care of everything."

The young man lay flat on his back and stared at the ceiling.

Lexi began massaging his groin again, gently at first, then more forcefully as he stiffened. She grinned fiercely, her own itch intensifying, her wetness growing. When he was fully erect she maneuvered her body, sat on his lap and straddled him. Then she pulled up the hem of her skirt so that it bunched up around her waist.

He was staring at her, his cheeks flushed, his face full of desire.

"Close your eyes, damn it!" she snapped. "You know you're not supposed to see this."

He shut his eyelids tight. "I'm...I'm sorry...."

"That's okay," she replied, now in a soothing tone. "I forgive you." She reached down with a hand and held him firmly. After stroking him a few more times she inserted his hardness inside her. She gasped from the pleasure, the sensation delicious.

Lexi leaned forward, placed both hands on his chest and began riding him, rocking back and forth, slowly at first.

She picked up the pace as her wetness intensified. She felt like she was on fire.

She gazed at him intently, noticing the satisfied expression on his face and knew he was enjoying it as much as she was. He was still flat on his back, his arms at his sides. His eyes were still closed and he was breathing heavy. A low moan was coming from his open mouth and his cheeks were flushed.

Lexi grinned fiercely and rode him harder, knowing her own itch would be satisfied very, very soon.

When they were both done a few minutes later, she rolled off of him and lay flat on her back to catch her breath. With a satisfied smile on her face, she looked over at him. Shawn was still on his back, his eyes still shut, his chest heaving.

She placed a palm on his chest and caressed it. "You were much better today, Shawn. You really pleasured me."

"Thank you," he said in a low voice. His eyes stayed closed.

"Was it good for you too?"

"Yes, Lexi."

"That's good. I want you to be happy. That's important to me." Her skirt was still bunched up around her waist and she tugged it down to make herself decent. Then she smoothed down her blouse and buttoned the very top button, the only one that had been open. When her clothes were in place, she said, "You can open your eyes now."

He opened them and looked at her. "What happens now?"

She smiled. "That's a silly question. Now we get back to work. Play time's over."

He nodded and said nothing.

"Get dressed, Shawn."

He climbed off the bed, picked his clothes off the floor and put them on quickly.

"I need you to call the colonel," she said, her tone all business now. "Find him, wherever he is. I have to talk to him. I want to make more money. And after you've found him, update my financial statements. I need to review them."

"Yes, Lexi."

Chapter 53

Vancouver, Canada

After Shawn left the bedroom, Lexi undressed, took a shower in the adjoining bathroom and dressed in fresh clothes. Then she went into her office and a few minutes later opened an icon on her computer screen

The colonel was already on the video call, as usual wearing an ill-fitting business suit. "Shawn said you needed to speak with me," the colonel said as he scratched one of the angry scars on his face.

"Yes, I did," she replied. "First, let me compliment you again on the Los Angeles operation. Everything went exactly to plan." She could see his chest swell with pride and he beamed, his crooked teeth showing.

"Thank you, Lexi. That means a lot to me."

"I'll wire you a bonus today, for a job extremely well done."

The colonel smiled again. "I appreciate that."

"I like to reward those who deliver results. And you have."

She placed her hands flat on the desk in front of her. "Now that the L.A. operation is behind us, I have a new opportunity to talk to you about."

"Another package needs to be delivered?"

"That's exactly right, Colonel."

"Will you be coming here to give me the details?"

Lexi mulled this over. She would love to visit Russia again, but realized she couldn't take the chance. Two trips to her home country in a short period of time was extremely dangerous. Russian security forces where everywhere.

"I'm afraid not," she replied. "We'll do this over the phone."

"As you wish."

Lexi spent the next twenty minutes giving him specific details of where she wanted the package delivered.

The colonel rubbed a scar on his face when she was done. "That's an ambitious target. Risky also. Are you sure this is what you want me to do?"

Lexi glared. "Are you questioning my judgment?"

"No...no...of course not...."

She stabbed her index finger toward him. "Don't ever fucking do that again! You hear?" She saw his face twitch and he looked down, his shoulders sagging.

Lexi gulped in several lungfuls of air and breathed them out slowly. In a calmer tone, she said, "I'm sorry I snapped at you. We're both under a lot of stress." She paused a moment. "You're right about this new target being very risky. But to get maximum profitability, we have to take higher risks."

He raised his eyes and looked at her. "Yes, Lexi. I'll start working immediately on the new package delivery. It'll take me several days to prepare."

"Very well. Call me when you have everything ready to go and I'll send my plane to Russia to pick you up. And remember, Colonel. I only want you to do the package delivery. None of your men are to be involved."

Chapter 54

Atlanta, Georgia

J.T. Ryan was driving home when his phone vibrated in his pocket. Slowing down the Ford Explorer, he slipped out the phone and took the call.

"J.T., it's Stich."

"How's my favorite CI?" Ryan said.

"That's a load of bull. Bet you say that to all your informants."

Ryan laughed. "Got something for me?"

"I do. The guy you're looking for? The one that murdered the DA?"

"Yeah?"

"I found out who did the hit, J.T."

"Who?"

"His name is Mitch Greer."

"Unfortunately for you," Ryan said, "I already know who did it. One of my other CI's gave me that info a few days ago. We've already arrested Greer and he's in FBI custody."

"Shit. Does that mean I have to give you the money back? What you paid me up front?"

"That's the way it works, Stich."

"Damn."

"Of course, if you tell me something useful about Greer, something I don't know, you can keep the cash."

Stich went quiet a moment, then said, "The people that hired him to do the hit. There's a Canadian connection."

"What kind of Canadian connection? You got names for me?"

"Sorry. It's all I know."

"All right."

"Can I keep the cash?"

Ryan considered this, recalling Stich's descent into heroin addiction and his recent recovery. "Yeah. You can keep it."

"Thank you!"

"Do me a favor, okay?"

"Anything, J.T."

"Keep on the straight and narrow, my friend. No more drugs. Okay?"

"I promise. I'm done with that."

"Good to hear it."

Ryan hung up the call then continued driving toward his apartment in midtown. Twenty minutes later he was at his front door, ready to unlock it, when he heard noises from inside.

Tensing, he pulled out his revolver and crouched by one side of the door. He unlocked it, turned the knob and pushed it open. Still in a crouch he peered inside, holding his pistol in front of him.

"Don't shoot," he heard Rachel West say, "it's just me." She was sitting on his living room sofa, her laptop open and resting on the coffee table in front of her.

Ryan holstered his pistol, went inside and closed the door behind him. "Jesus, Rachel. You almost gave me a heart attack. You should let me know when you're coming over."

She pouted. "That's a hell of a welcome. I thought you'd be happy to see me."

"I am. It's just – I thought you were a burglar."

She shook her head and waved a hand around the room. "Face it, J.T. There's nothing in here worth stealing."

He glanced around his living room. "What's wrong with my apartment?"

A smile appeared on her pretty face. "This sofa I'm on sags and is worn as hell. You probably bought it ten years ago." She pointed toward the chairs in the room. "Those are cheap, metal folding chairs. Who has that in their living room?" Then she pointed to the walls. "You have no pictures or anything on the walls."

He looked around again. "Yeah. I guess you're right."

"Of course I'm right."

"By the way, how'd you get in here? I didn't give you a key."

Rachel grinned. "I'm a CIA operative, remember?"

He smiled back. "And a very pretty one."

"Tell me something," she said, pointing to the chess set that was on top the wooden hutch in the room. "I didn't know you played chess. When did that start?"

"I was working on a case a while back, and the criminal I was after was an avid chess player. After I solved the case, I decided to check out the game. I found it fascinating."

Rachel nodded. "I never figured you'd be the type of guy who would enjoy a cerebral game like chess."

"Why? Because I'm a jock and I break down doors, kick ass, and shoot people for a living?"

"Something like that...."

"I'm highly insulted, Rachel."

"Bullshit."

They both laughed and he said, "Don't tell me you play chess too?"

"As a matter of fact, I do. Bet I can beat you."

He nodded. "Yeah, you probably can. You're not just a pretty face. You're smart too."

Rachel motioned to her laptop. "The chess game will have to wait. I came over for a reason. I found some information on the hitman, Mitch Greer. Using my CIA software, I've been combing his bank records. I've compiled a list of wire transfers that he received over the last six months."

"Show me," he said, sitting next to her on the sofa.

The computer screen was showing a spreadsheet with many dates, dollar amounts, and reference numbers.

Rachel pointed to a specific line on the spreadsheet. "This wire deposit was for the exact amount Greer told you he was paid for the job."

"Who sent the payment?"

"That's the thing. It was a local bank here in Atlanta. I checked on the sender of the money and found out it didn't originate here. It turned out to be a fictitious company, a cut-out. Criminals set up dummy corporations all the time to launder money."

Ryan nodded, knew this was true. "So. Are you telling me we're no closer to finding the criminals?"

"We're somewhat closer. At least now we have confirmation that Greer accepted blood money for committing a murder."

He mulled this over for a long moment. "I got a call from Stich today. He's one of my informants. I told you about him."

"I remember."

"Stich told me there's a Canadian connection to the people who hired Greer."

"Really?"

"Does that help, Rachel?"

She pursed her lips. "Maybe. I need to do some more work."

"Okay. What can I do to help?"

She glanced at him. "You're such a caveman when it comes to computers. It'll be faster if I work on my own."

"Ouch!"

"Is that not true, J.T.?"

"Maybe."

She grinned. "And I saw your gun when you came in here. I can't believe you went back to your revolver. You know, J.T., no one in law-enforcement uses wheelguns anymore."

"Yeah, I know. I'm kind of old school."

Her grin widened. "Kind of?"

"All right, smarty-pants. Get to work on that fancy laptop of yours. In the meantime, I'll make us a pot of coffee."

"There's none left in your apartment."

"What? I just bought a large can of coffee a few days ago."

"I threw that crap out, J.T. It was a generic brand from some grocery store I never heard of."

"I'm frugal, too."

"To a fault. If you really want to make yourself useful, go out and buy us some good Colombian coffee. And you're out of bread and eggs, too."

Ryan chuckled. "Anything else?"

"I'll take a kiss, if that's not too much trouble."

He leaned down and kissed her. She kissed him back and they stayed like that for a long moment. She tasted salty and delicious.

Rachel pulled away, her blue eyes sparkling. "You better get on your way or I'm never going to finish this spreadsheet."

He gave her a half-salute. "Yes, ma'am." He left the apartment, went shopping, and was back an hour later.

Rachel was still sitting on his sofa, poring over her laptop. She glanced up from the screen. "I found something."

"Great," he said. "I'll put these bags away and you can show me." He went to the kitchen, stored the food in the refrigerator and cabinets, came back and sat next to her.

Rachel pointed to her laptop. "I was able to trace the payment with my software. The wire transfer was routed through three different companies, all of them phony, then finally back to a real corporation. A company based in Vancouver."

"Vancouver, Canada?"

"That's right."

"What's the name of the corporation?"

She clicked her mouse and read from the screen. "Crimson Atwood Corporation."

"Never heard of it."

"Me neither, J.T."

"What kind of company is it? What do they do?"

"I don't know yet. But I'm sure as hell going to find out."

Chapter 55

FBI Field Office
Atlanta, Georgia

J.T. Ryan, Erin Welch, and Rachel West stepped into the conference room.

"You found something?" Erin said as she closed the door to the room and sat down at the conference table.

"We did," Ryan said, as he and Rachel sat down.

Erin nodded. "That's good to hear. We desperately need a break on this case. Have you seen the news this morning?"

Both Ryan and Rachel shook their heads.

"The EMP that caused the blackout in L.A.," Erin said, "is still impacting that area. All communication is still down. People there are panicking. Rioting and looting is rampant. The National Guard has been called in to restore order."

Ryan grimaced. "Damn."

"That's what I said too," Erin replied, "except I used stronger language. Now tell me what you've found out."

Ryan gestured to the CIA agent. "Actually it was Rachel who pieced it together. She should fill you in."

Erin tried suppressing a smile and failed. "That must be a blow to your ego, J.T. Having a woman figure it out before you did."

Ryan glanced at both women and saw the amused look on their faces. "I can see I'm outnumbered here."

"Yeah, you are," Rachel said. "But in your defense, J.T., you did provide me with an important clue. That the criminals have a Canadian connection." Then she faced Erin.

"Using my CIA software," Rachel continued, "I found that the hitman, Mitch Greer, was paid by a bank account of a company based in Vancouver, Canada. The name of the corporation is Crimson Atwood."

"Never heard of it," Erin said.

Rachel nodded. "Me neither. So I started checking into them. They're a holding company. They buy other companies. Crimson Atwood is a large firm, but not many people have heard of them."

"Who owns it?" Erin asked. "Is it publically held?"

"No. It's a privately held company. In my research I was able to learn there's a sole owner. A woman by the name of Lexi Atwood. Her full name is Alexandra Atwood, but she goes by Lexi. Apparently she's incredibly wealthy. A billionaire. Rumored to be Canada's richest person."

Erin frowned. "Why would a Canadian billionaire pay a hitman $100,000 to kill a DA in Atlanta?"

"I may have found an answer," Rachel said. "Atwood's husband died in prison. And the person who prosecuted him and sent him to jail was Ed Roth, your fiancée."

Erin closed her fists and she pounded the conference table. "That's the fucking motive! This Atwood woman wanted payback for the death of her husband. So she hired Mitch Greer to murder Ed." She shot Ryan a hard look. "Go to Canada, J.T. Find this Atwood bitch and take her out! I want payback too."

Ryan stared at Erin. "Are you telling me to murder someone? In cold blood? I want payback too, but we should arrest Atwood and put her in prison."

Erin glared at him and pounded the table again. "You beat the hell out of Greer because I asked you to. Why won't you do this?" In a pleading voice, she added, "I'm begging you. Please, J.T."

Ryan shook his head slowly. "I'm always pushing the limits, bending the rules, and skirting the law. But I've never murdered anyone in cold blood. And I won't start now."

Erin went quiet for a long moment and then her shoulders sagged. "You're right, J.T. I don't know what got into me. I'm a law-enforcement officer. You need to go to Canada and arrest her."

"That may not be that easy," Ryan said. "Lexi Atwood is a billionaire. I'm sure she's got the best attorneys on retainer. And since she's Canada's richest person, the authorities are probably not going to help us, at least not until we have solid proof she's guilty."

Erin nodded. "I see your point. So what's your plan?"

"Rachel and I," Ryan said, "will go to Canada and check her out first hand. We start turning rocks over and see what's underneath."

"Okay," Erin replied. "Are you going undercover or use your real names?"

"We have to go in as FBI agents. Otherwise she won't even talk to us," Ryan said. "It's better if we use our real names. But we have another problem, Erin. As far as we can tell, this Atwood woman has no connection to the terrorists. Which is the primary reason we started this investigation in the first place. It's why President Harris put us on the task force."

"That's true, J.T."

"Which leads us to another problem," Ryan continued. "If Rachel and I leave the Atlanta area and go to Canada, Alex Miller will know. Miller tracks us using the GPS on our cell phones. But Miller may be the mole. And the last thing we want is to have Atwood tipped off that we're on her trail. We need to question her first. Once we do, I think we'll have a good idea if it's her who hired Greer. Now you see our problem."

Erin placed her hands flat on the conference table and was quiet for a long moment. "Yes, that is a problem. Alex Miller may be the leak, the mole we suspect is feeding information to the terrorists. It's unlikely, but we have to continue with that premise. We know it's someone very high up in government. Someone in law-enforcement or the intelligence agencies. It could be Miller." She went quiet again for another minute. "What if," she said eventually, "you and Rachel give me your phones. You get new cell phones and forward your calls to ring to the new ones. So Miller will never know you're in Canada. As far as he can tell, you'd both still be in the Atlanta area."

Ryan grinned. "That's brilliant."

Erin returned the smile. "Yes, it is. I didn't get to be an Assistant Director in the FBI by chance."

Chapter 56

St. Petersburg, Russia

Colonel Mikhail Sharpov parked in the front lot of the old warehouse, shut off his car's engine and gazed around warily. He'd had an uncomfortable feeling recently that he'd been under surveillance.

Getting out of his sedan, he looked toward the street and saw no vehicles following him, or even in the area. He breathed a sigh of relief.

I'm being paranoid, he mused.

The colonel took several rolled up maps from the back seat and made his way to the warehouse. He input a security code on the door's control panel and had his eye's retina scanned by the device. After unlocking the padlock, he went inside and flicked on the lights. It was one in the morning and all of his men had left the building hours ago.

He took the stairs to the upper floor. Unlike the warehouse's decrepit exterior and first floor, the second floor had been converted into high-tech suites and work areas.

After unlocking his office, he turned on the lights and placed the rolled up maps he was carrying on the table in a corner of the room. Large maps already covered many of the walls near the table. Most were detailed diagrams of New York City, although several smaller ones were of neighboring areas in New Jersey and Connecticut.

He took off his jacket, rolled up his sleeves and began brewing a pot of coffee. It was going to be long night and he needed to focus on his task. He pinned the new maps he'd brought to the walls. One of them detailed the waterways around Manhattan, while another one outlined the city's subway system.

The colonel poured himself a large mug of coffee and stood looking at the maps, analyzing the sprawling metropolis of New York City.

He scratched one of the many scars on his face as he studied the area. When Lexi had told him where she wanted the next package delivered, he realized immediately it would an extremely difficult undertaking. He'd been wrestling with this dilemma for days, considering several options before discarding them. But he had to make a decision soon. Lexi had already called him twice, asking when he was going to implement her plan.

Soon, he'd told her, but he sensed she was becoming impatient and irritated. *I can't let her down,* he thought. *I must do this for her. No matter what the cost is to me.*

Still, he didn't want this to be a suicide mission and neither did she. There were more packages to deliver after this one. So the option he selected had to effective and fairly safe. *Nothing is risk free.* But he was sure he could limit his chance of capture if he selected the right approach.

The problem was the location. New York City.

Unlike the other package deliveries in Philadelphia and Los Angeles, Manhattan was unique. Unique because NYC had been the target of the terrorist attacks in 2001. The area had been fortified with maximum high-tech security, law-enforcement patrols, and security cameras everywhere. They even had bomb-sniffing dogs that could smell the nuclear devices in the backpack.

And Lexi had given him one other parameter, one that made the job even more difficult. She wanted it done in the middle of the night, when few people were out. He understood her motive, which was to limit the casualties, since many people who worked in Manhattan commuted in from other areas. He had hoped to use large daytime crowds in order to blend in and make it more difficult for police patrols to pick him out. Nevertheless, it was Lexi's operation and he had to abide by her rules.

The colonel spent half an hour considering a water approach to the target, as he had done in Marina Del Rey, but discarded that plan. The river and ocean that bordered NYC were heavily patrolled by police and FBI boats. Then he spent time analyzing the city's subway system to transport himself into and out of the area, but again felt that was unfeasible.

He traced his finger over one of the larger maps. He'd previously drawn a circle around the exact area Lexi had picked out.

It was the Freedom Tower, the new skyscraper that had been built on the rubble of the destroyed World Trade Center buildings. He had tried, without success, to talk Lexi out of bombing this location. She wanted to make a statement, he knew. And she wanted payback for her husband's death. *That's what she wants and that's what I'm going to give her. I will not let her down. Not now. Not ever.*

The colonel idly scratched another one of his angry scars as he sipped coffee and continued poring over the maps. Then after another two hours, it came to him like a bolt of lightening. *The perfect plan.*

He grinned, the gesture contorting his half-burned lips and mouth into an even more gruesome appearance than usual. Giddy with excitement, he forced himself to calm down and continue analyzing the approach to make sure there were no flaws. An hour later he was certain.

It's a perfect plan, he knew. He couldn't wait to call Lexi and give her the good news. *She'll be proud of me.*

The colonel glanced at his watch. It was already five in the morning. He was exhausted from the mental strain and decided to go home, sleep for several hours and then call her to give her the news. He needed his mind to be razor-sharp. Now that he'd selected the perfect approach, he wanted to make sure he had answers for her many probing questions.

He rolled down his sleeves, shrugged on his jacket and turned off the coffee pot. Then he made his way down to the first floor, set the security alarm and exited the warehouse. It was still dark outside and also frigid. Although it was only the beginning of November, St. Petersburg's long winter had already settled in. He buttoned his jacket, knowing it would snow soon.

When he reached his car, he heard the sound of footsteps from behind him.

He whirled around and saw them instantly. Five men, all wearing black, pointing large handguns at his direction.

"Halt and put your hands up!" one of the men shouted in fast Russian.

The colonel immediately raised his hands over his head. "Don't shoot!" he replied in Russian. "I'm unarmed!" His heart was thundering in his chest.

The men stepped closer and one of them came up alongside him and frisked him thoroughly.

"He's clean," the man said and stepped aside.

One of the other men dressed in black walked in front of the colonel and stopped. The colonel saw he was taller than the others and had a command presence. Obviously the man in charge.

"What's the meaning of this?" the colonel asked. "I've broken no laws."

"I am Captain Lorichenko of the FSB," the man replied in an authoritative voice.

When the colonel heard the word FSB, his heart raced even more and he had trouble breathing. No Russian citizen ever wanted to hear that. The FSB (officially known as the Federal Security Service) was the country's secret police, the dreaded government agency that had replaced the KGB years ago.

"What do you want?" the colonel said, trying to sound more confident than he felt.

"You are Mikhail Sharpov, is that right?"

"Yes, I am."

The FSB man nodded. "You were a colonel in the GRU for many years."

"Yes, I was."

"I am placing you under arrest."

"On what charge, Captain? I've broken no laws."

The FSB man glared. "We are in Russia, comrade. We don't need a reason to arrest you."

"But —"

The FSB officer turned to his men and said, "Take him."

Chapter 57

Vancouver, Canada

Lexi was on her way back to her office on the 80th floor when Shawn approached her in the corridor.

"Lexi," Shawn said, "two people are here to see you. They're from the American FBI."

The auburn-haired woman tensed. "FBI? What do they want?"

"It's about an ongoing investigation. They wouldn't tell me anything else."

Lexi mulled this over a moment. She knew she could refuse to meet them. The FBI had no jurisdiction in Canada. But still. It would be good to know what they were up to.

"Where are they now, Shawn?"

"In the lobby on the first floor."

"Let's go in my office. I want to see what they look like."

"Yes, ma'am."

They continued down the hallway and entered her office. Then she went to her desk and logged on to her computer. She tapped on the keyboard and a minute later the screen showed the CCTV camera feed from the lobby. Standing by the reception desk were two people, a man and a woman, both of them wearing business attire. The man was tall, handsome and ruggedly built. The woman was blonde, attractive and had piercing blue eyes.

Lexi pointed to the screen. "What are their names?"

"The FBI credentials he showed me confirmed his name is John Ryan."

"And the woman?"

"Her name is Rachel West."

Lexi pondered this, recalling the Ryan name. Her source had told her an FBI agent named Ryan was involved in the Atlanta DA's murder investigation. *Damn*, she thought. *Somehow the FBI has tracked me down. I have to talk to them. Otherwise I'll seem guilty.*

"What do you want me to do?" Shawn asked.

"Show them to my office. I'll see them."

Shawn nodded and left her office. Five minutes later he was back with the two visitors.

"Thank you, Shawn," Lexi said. "I'll take it from here."

Lexi ushered her guests to a sitting area which fronted the floor-to-ceiling windows of her massive office. As they sat, she smiled at the male FBI agent. "How may I help you? Shawn said this has to do with an ongoing investigation?"

"Yes," Ryan replied. "We're looking into the murder of a district attorney in Atlanta."

"I see. And what does that have to do with me?"

"Maybe nothing," the FBI man replied with a disarming smile. "But the name of your company, Crimson Atwood, came up in our investigation. According to some of the information we have, your company appears to have paid the contract killer hired to commit the murder."

Lexi frowned. "There must be some mistake. All of my business dealings are 100% legal and ethical."

Ryan nodded. "We've checked with the Canadian authorities and with our own State Department. Your company is above reproach."

"So, are we done here?" Lexi said.

"No, not by a long shot," the blonde woman said, speaking up for the first time. Lexi detected a high degree of skepticism from her, something she didn't sense from the FBI man.

Lexi glared at her. "I don't like your tone. Are you implying I'm lying?"

"Are you lying?" Rachel West stated in a harsh voice.

The red-haired woman stood abruptly. "You could learn a thing or two about common courtesy, Agent West."

Ryan shook his head slowly and stood. "I'm sorry, Ms Atwood. Agent West meant no disrespect." Then he faced the floor-to-ceiling windows, which showed a spectacular view of Vancouver's skyline and harbor. "What an amazing view."

"It is, isn't it," Lexi said. "I had this office building built on this exact spot to give me that view."

Ryan nodded and smiled. "You can see the whole city and the waterfront from here."

"Yes." Lexi approached him, stood next to him and began pointing out all of the scenic spots at ground level. When she was done, she said, "I have to be honest with you, Agent Ryan, you remind me of my beloved husband, Sergei." She pointed to a large framed photograph hanging on the wall. "That's him there, bless his heart. He died years ago and I still miss him every single day."

Ryan stared at the photo on the wall. "Yeah. I see the resemblance."

Lexi turned toward the blonde woman. "Tell me, Ms West, are all your male FBI agents so charming and handsome?"

Rachel rolled her eyes. "No. J.T. is unique. If you don't believe me, just ask him."

Lexi placed her hand on Ryan's arm and squeezed his bulging bicep. "Strong too. I bet you can last all night, like my dear Sergei could."

Ryan chuckled at this and Agent West just shook her head and glared. "Can we please get on with the investigation?" West said harshly.

"You're right, Rachel," Ryan said. He faced Lexi. "It would be helpful, Ms Atwood, if we could get a complete list of the employees at your company."

"Yes, of course," she replied. "I'll have Shawn prepare that for you." She went to her desk and pressed a button on the intercom device. "Shawn, will you please come in. Agent Ryan needs some information."

A moment later Lexi's assistant came in, talked with Ryan and they both left the office to compile the list. When they were gone, the red-haired woman said, "Can I get you anything? Coffee or some wine?"

"No, thanks," Rachel West replied. "I'm good."

Lexi went to the liquor cabinet in the office, opened it and poured herself a large glass of Cabernet. After taking a long sip, she turned to the other woman. "Tell me, Agent West, how long have you been fucking him?"

Rachel's eyebrows shot up. "What? Who the hell do you think you are?"

Lexi grinned. "You can deny it all you want. But I know you've been fucking John Ryan for a long while now."

Rachel West bolted out of her chair and gave her an icy look. "You're a bitch, you know that?"

Lexi's laughed. "I've known that for years. But I can see the sparks between the two of you from a mile away."

"Even if I was doing J.T.," Rachel spit out, her blue eyes like slits. "It's none of your damn business!"

Lexi laughed again. "Don't get your panties in a wad. I was just having fun with you. But I've got to be honest, this John Ryan guy gets me fucking wet."

Rachel's mouth hung open.

"And I bet," Lexi added, "he makes you wet too." She laughed again.

Just then Ryan walked into the office, holding a sheaf of papers in his hand. He said, "We'll, I've got everything I need."

"That's nice," Lexi said. "Does that mean you're done?"

"Yes, ma'am."

"Please, Agent Ryan. Call me Lexi. Everybody does."

He smiled. "Yes, Lexi."

"May I call you J.T.?" the red-haired woman said with a suggestive smile. "Your associate, Ms West, called you that earlier."

"Yes, of course."

Lexi walked up to him, rubbed his arm and squeezed his bulging bicep again. "Would you like a drink before you go?"

"We're done here," Rachel West said brusquely.

Lexi nodded and focused her whole attention on Ryan as she squeezed his bicep again. "You're welcome to visit me again, J.T. Anytime. Anyplace."

Chapter 58

Vancouver, Canada

After leaving the Crimson Atwood building, Ryan and Rachel went to their rented Chevy Malibu in the parking lot and climbed in.

"So what did you think?" Ryan said as he started up the car.

"I think Lexi Atwood is a real bitch. And a fucking liar."

Ryan chuckled. "Don't hold back. Tell me what you really think."

Rachel shook her head slowly. "Don't tell me you fell for her crap? The innocent damsel? The grieving widow? She makes me sick! She's a lying bitch and, I'm sure, a cold-blooded killer."

"Wow. Where's that coming from?"

Rachel's blue eyes blazed. "Men!"

"Men what?"

"Don't give me that look, John Taylor Ryan. I saw you checking her out."

"What are you talking about, Rachel? I just asked her questions. She seemed cooperative to me."

Rachel folded her arms in front of her. "Don't bullshit a bullshitter, J.T. Don't pull that choirboy act on me. I know you too damn well. Atwood is a gorgeous woman. I saw you checking out her tits and ass, not to mention her sexy red hair. And her bedroom eyes."

"C'mon. You know I only want you."

Rachel fumed for a long time, her expression hard, as she stared out the front windshield of the car. Eventually, she said in a low voice, "Tell me the truth. Weren't you attracted to her? Even a little bit?"

"Maybe a little," he replied. "But you're the only girl for me."

She turned toward him. "Don't call me a girl. I'm a thirty-five year old woman. Call me what I am. A woman."

"I'm sorry, hon." He reached out with a hand and stroked her long blonde hair. "I'm sorry I called you a girl. Let me rephrase. You're the woman of my dreams. You're the only woman for me."

She looked into his deep brown eyes. "And you're the only man for me, J.T." She paused a moment then said, "You need to know something about Lexi Atwood."

"What's that?"

"She's a man-eater. She'll fuck you and chew you up and spit you out. Then she'll stick a knife in your back and laugh about it afterward."

Ryan nodded. "You may be right. I know men are fooled by a woman's looks. It's happened to me before."

"Men are weak," she said. "They're enticed easily. Adam and Eve proved that a long, long time ago. "

"I'm not that bad, am I?"

"No, you're not." Rachel moved closer to him and rested her head on his chest. "Hold me, please."

Ryan wrapped his arms around her and squeezed. "You know I'm crazy about you, don't you?"

"I know," she said. "and I'm crazy about you."

They stayed that way for a long time, saying nothing, enjoying the warmth and comfort from holding each other.

Eventually Ryan said, "What do you think? Did Atwood hire the hitman?"

"Of course she did. No question about it. She's a cold-hearted bitch and a cold-blooded killer."

Chapter 59

Vancouver, Canada

Lexi paced her office, trying to control her rage. She turned to her head of security, the only other person in the room.

"You lied to me!" she shouted, acid in her voice. "You told me there was no way the American authorities could tie me to the murder."

Brad Murdock was standing in front of her, his broad shoulders sagging. "I'm sorry. I didn't think there was any way...I was very careful...."

"Not careful enough!" she yelled. Then she raised her hand and slapped him hard across his face.

The man flinched and his face reddened, but he accepted the punishment without protest. Brad was a big and brawny man, built like a football player. He was well over 250 pounds, all of it muscle. He towered over her and could have easily broken her in two if he'd wanted. He lowered his eyes to the floor. "I'm sorry, Lexi."

She glared at him, then continued pacing the office. "Lucky for me," she said, "I've got a lot of influence with the Canadian government. The FBI will have trouble arresting me. They have no jurisdiction here."

"You're right."

She stopped pacing and glared at him again. "Still. These agents who came to see me today can make trouble." She stabbed her index finger hard on his chest. "You need to fix this."

"Yes. Whatever you need. I'll do it."

"They need to disappear, Brad."

He nodded. "I'll take care of it."

She planted her hands on her hips. "Hire whoever you need. Whatever it costs. Just make sure it can't be traced back to me this time."

"Yes."

She started pacing the office again. "The woman FBI agent, West, I want her to feel pain before you terminate her. Lots of pain. Understood?"

"I understand, Lexi. What about the other agent, John Ryan?"

Lexi considered this for several minutes. "It's a shame about him. I rather liked him. He reminded me so much of my dear Sergei. Still, I can't be sentimental. Ryan has to be terminated also."

"Shall I torture him before I kill him?"

The red-haired woman shook her head. "No. No torture for him. Take him out quickly."

"Yes, ma'am."

"Any questions?"

"No," he said.

"Then get going. I've got other problems to handle."

Brad Murdock nodded and left the office.

Lexi pressed the intercom on her desk. "Come in here, Shawn."

Her assistant entered her office, closed the door behind him and approached her.

"I think we've got a problem," she said.

"The FBI people?"

"I'm already dealing with that, Shawn. Brad's taking care of it. It's something else. I've been trying to reach the colonel but I can't get a hold of him. He always checks in with me, every day, sometimes several times a day. But he hasn't called me in two days. I've called and left messages on his cell phone and his landline at his office and home. All I get is his voice mail. This has never happened before."

"I see. Should I try to call him, Lexi?"

"Yes. Make this your top priority. Postpone all of your other work."

Shawn nodded. "Of course." He paused a moment. "You look worried."

"I am. It's been a horrible day. This unpleasantness with the FBI people. And the colonel." She glanced toward the floor-to-ceiling windows with the spectacular view of the Vancouver harbor area. On most days she found the scene calming, but not today. "I wish Sergei was here. To help me with this. God, I miss him."

"I'll help you in any way I can, Lexi."

She turned toward him and stared into his beautiful gray eyes. Stepping closer, she placed her palm on his cheek. "I know you will," she said affectionately. "I don't know what I'd do without you. I know I usually come off as a real bitch. But I do care for you. Very much. I know I don't say that enough."

He smiled shyly. "Thank you, Lexi. I care for you too."

She gazed at him for another long moment, then in a business-like voice said, "Find the colonel, Shawn. Make it your top priority. Your only priority."

He seemed surprised by her abrupt change in tone. "Yes...of course."

"Get going. We don't have a minute to waste."

Chapter 60

Vancouver, Canada

J.T. Ryan peered through his binoculars at the skyscrapers that fronted the city's harbor area. It was easy to spot the Crimson Atwood building since it was Vancouver's tallest structure. He pointed the binos at the building's top floor, hoping to see into Lexi's office. But the office windows were constructed of mirrored glass and all he could see was the reflection of the sun.

Ryan lowered the binoculars and turned back toward his hotel room. He and Rachel had adjoining rooms at the waterfront hotel. Rachel was poring over her laptop, tapping her keyboard and occasionally writing things down. She'd been at it for hours and he was getting impatient.

"Find anything?" he said.

She glanced up from her computer. "Yes."

"Care to share?"

"Sure."

He put down the binos and sat next to her on the couch.

Rachel pointed to her laptop, which was resting on the coffee table in front of them. "Lexi," she said, "is a nickname she uses. Her full name is Alexandra Atwood. It appears she named her company Crimson Atwood because, from what I can tell, she loves the color red. When we visited her she was wearing a red dress and wine color heels, which complimented her long auburn hair. In the photos of her in local newspapers and magazines, she's always wearing crimson outfits."

Ryan nodded. "Okay. Anything else?"

"She told us that her husband was a man named Sergei Atwood, who died in prison in Georgia. Which I verified. And from everything I can piece together, she's the brains of the company. Her husband was somewhat involved, but she ran it and was the money-maker. And I found out she is definitely a billionaire. Self-made. Her husband had a much shadier past."

"Shadier how?" he asked.

She tapped her legal pad. "That's where it gets really interesting. Using my CIA software, I was able to track down her true identity."

"True identity? She's not Alexandra Atwood?"

Rachel shook her head. "Not always. She legally changed her name to that years ago. Her birth name was Alexandra Ivanova."

"Ivanova? That doesn't sound like a Canadian name at all. It sounds Russian."

"Bingo, J.T.! She was born in St. Petersburg, Russia. In her twenties she became rich as a day-trader, buying and selling stocks. Then she married Sergei, who it turned out, was a money-launderer for the Bratva."

"I've heard of the Bratva. It's the Russian mob."

"That's right," she said. "Eventually the authorities in Russia learned about his illegal activity and were about to arrest him, but he and Lexi fled to Canada. They changed their name to Atwood. She started Crimson Atwood Corporation and became a billionaire. Sergei, unfortunately, went back to his criminal ways. He was arrested and went to prison in the U.S."

"That's incredible. Good sleuthing, Rachel. You'd make a hell of a PI, if you ever decide to leave the CIA."

She gave him a peck on the lips. "Thanks for the compliment."

Ryan grinned. "You taste good. Damn good." He leaned in and gave her long kiss, which she returned hungrily. She tasted delicious.

Finally she pulled away, a little out of breath. "Let's slow down, cowboy. Or we'll never solve this case."

He smiled and gave her a half salute. "Yes, ma'am." Then he turned serious. "We still have a big problem. We don't have any direct evidence that Lexi is personally involved in hiring the hitman. She has hundreds of employees at her company. It could have been done by any of them."

"But Lexi's the only one with a motive, J.T. Her husband died in prison. She wanted revenge."

"I agree," he said. "But we have to prove it. In a court of law. A Canadian court, before she can be extradited to the U.S. And from everything we've uncovered, Atwood is one of the country's leading citizens. You said she was Canada's richest person. I'm sure the government here isn't going to turn her over without ironclad proof. Canada is no different than any other place. Money buys influence. And lots of money buys lots of influence."

"You're right, J.T."

"And we have another problem."

"What?"

"We have nothing," he said, "linking Alexandra Atwood to the terrorism case. Which is still our number one priority."

Rachel frowned. "Yeah, I know."

"Somehow we have to find the connection between Atwood and the scarred man."

Chapter 61

Vancouver, Canada

Lexi was worried. More than worried. She was panicked. It had been four days since she'd talked with the colonel. Every time she called him, she got his prerecorded answering message. She'd tried calling him on his cell, his office, and his home, all with the same result.

More ominous yet, she'd also called his trusted lieutenants, the men who worked for him in Russia. They were not answering their phones either – it always went to voice mail.

Lexi gulped down the rest of her red wine, then quickly refilled it from the bottle of Malbec on her desk. After taking another long pull from the glass, she stabbed her intercom device.

Shawn's voice came from the speaker. "Yes?"

"Have you found the colonel?" she growled.

"No, not yet."

"Keep at it, damn you! And don't stop trying until you find him!" She disconnected the intercom and went back to gulping down the red wine.

Chapter 62

Vancouver, Canada

J.T. Ryan had spent the day at the Vancouver police department, trying to get the chief to open an investigation into Atwood's possible involvement in the Atlanta DA's murder. Although the chief had been polite and respectful, he promised only to 'evaluate' the situation. It was clear to Ryan during their lengthy discussion that Atwood was a very prominent citizen and likely off limits. In other words, it would be a cold day in hell before any investigation was conducted.

Ryan had spent the previous day at the office of the city's Attorney General, pleading his case, with the same result. Tired and aggravated from the fruitless efforts, he went back to his hotel in the waterfront area. Before returning to his own room, he knocked on Rachel's and she let him inside.

"Any luck?" she asked as she went back to the couch and sat down in front of her computer.

Ryan shook his head. "None. Less than none. Everybody I talked with had only great things to say about Atwood. They refused to even consider she was involved in any criminal activity, let alone murder." He shook his head again. "It's a miracle they haven't canonized her to sainthood already."

Rachel folded her arms in front of her. "I was hoping they'd at least open an investigation. With local PD resources, we could get results much faster."

"You got anything to drink? I could use one."

She gestured toward the small refrigerator in the room. "I've got a bottle of Absolut in there. Help yourself. And get me one too, okay?"

Ryan found the vodka and poured out two drinks. He handed one to Rachel, then took a sip of his and set it down on the coffee table. He pointed to her laptop. "Any progress on your end?"

Rachel downed her vodka in one long pull. "No. It's slow going. Like we talked about, I've been reviewing the security footage from the lobby of Atwood's company, trying to determine if the scarred man visited her office in the last six months. I used a CIA facial recognition program to match the photo of him from the Albuquerque airport."

"And?"

"And nothing, J.T. From what I can tell, the scarred man never met Atwood there."

"Yeah," he said. "I figured that would be the case. Specially since Atwood was willing to give us a copy of the surveillance footage without giving us a hard time. I thought she'd ask to see a Canadian search warrant first, but she didn't. Atwood knew we wouldn't find anything incriminating."

Rachel stood up, went to the small refrigerator and poured herself another vodka. She took a sip, then said, "So we're back to square one."

"We've got to find a way to tie Lexi Atwood to this elusive scarred man – a man I think we should name Scarman, until we learn his identity. The only way we'll get the cops and DA here in Canada to cooperate is to two link those two people. They can stall us on the murder case, but there's no way they can ignore the terrorism angle."

Rachel sipped her vodka again and sat back down. "I agree. My guess is she met with Scarman not at a public place like her company, but at her home, where she'd have plenty of privacy. I found out Atwood lives in a walled estate on Vancouver Island, which is offshore from the city of Vancouver. We need to get the surveillance videos from that place."

"She'd never turn that over to us," Ryan said, "specially if it showed incriminating evidence."

"You're right." She considered this over for a long moment. "I know of a way to get the security videos of her home. But you won't like it."

Ryan sat down next to her. "Tell me what you're thinking."

"I propose we use CIA resources," she continued. "The Agency has multiple satellites that circle the earth constantly. They take photos of almost every part of the world. And the technology is so good, we can read a license plate number."

Ryan nodded. "I've heard about that. So why won't I like this?"

"I can't access satellite data on my own, J.T. Only one person can authorize me to obtain it."

"Who?"

"My boss, Alex Miller."

Ryan ground his teeth. "Shit."

"Yeah."

"But if he's the mole," he said, "asking him to give us this access will backfire on us."

"That's the problem. Plus, Miller doesn't even know we're in Canada. He still thinks we're in Atlanta. He'll be super-pissed I never told him about that."

They sat there silently for several minutes as they processed this latest twist in the investigation.

Ryan spoke first. "Let's get some dinner. I'm starved and all I've had today are three Snickers Bars and coffee. Maybe if we get some food, we'll come up with a plan on how to proceed."

"Okay. Want to eat at the hotel restaurant again?"

"No. I'm tired of that place. Anyway, you've been slaving over that laptop for days. I want to take you out to a great restaurant a few miles from here. We can hash out this Miller problem during dinner and drinks."

"Sounds good, J.T."

Ryan went to his room, showered and changed into fresh clothes. He met up with Rachel and they took the elevator down to the hotel's underground lot.

Locating his rented sedan, they climbed in and he fired up the car. Then he turned toward her. "Did I mention you look great?"

Rachel had changed into a form-fitting pencil skirt, a black turtleneck, and black flats. She was carrying a small purse, which he knew held her .380 pistol.

Her face brightened with a grin. "Well, thank you, kind sir." Then her grin turned mischievous and her azure eyes sparkled. "You play your cards right and you may get to see what's underneath these clothes later tonight."

He laughed. "I love the sound of that." He put the sedan into reverse and began backing up out of the parking space.

Suddenly a cargo van roared through the parking garage and came to a screeching halt behind their car, its tires squealing.

Ryan slammed on his brakes and stopped the car. Glancing back toward the van, he saw six armed men pile out of the vehicle, their pistols trained on their car. "Six bogey's with guns!" he yelled at Rachel, as he pulled out his revolver.

Rachel instantly retrieved her pistol from the purse, racked the slide and turned toward the car's back window, training her weapon toward it.

Just then the back window imploded from a hail of incoming bullets, all directed at Ryan's way. He felt one round whiz over his head and felt two others thud into the back of his seat.

His heart pounding, he fired off three rounds and one of the attackers went down, screaming in pain. Rachel fired also and hit one of the bogeys, who collapsed in a pool of blood.

Ryan heard one of the attackers shout, "Don't shoot the woman! We need her alive!" Realizing they were dead meat if they stayed in the car, Ryan yelled, "Get out, Rachel! Go to the front of the car! The engine block will shield you."

She fired off several more rounds and he did also, then she scrambled out of the sedan and took cover in front of it.

Ryan, his adrenaline pumping, saw another attacker race forward, the pistol in his hand bucking from the recoil as he shot through what was left of the back window. Ryan aimed and fired once and the man buckled, dropped his gun, and clutched his gut. Another attacker started firing and Ryan squeezed his trigger, only to hear it click empty. His heart racing, he knew he was out of bullets. He flattened himself on the front seat, pulled a speed-loader from a pocket, clicked open the cylinder and reloaded.

The front windshield of the car exploded along with several of the side windows as the sedan continued taking more incoming fire, shards of glass raining on top of Ryan. One round hit his headrest and shredded it. Another one blew off the rearview mirror. The booms from the loud shooting echoed in the cavernous underground parking lot.

"Cover me, Rachel!" he shouted, as he maneuvered his body, getting ready to exit the car.

She opened up, firing her pistol nonstop. There was a momentary lull in the incoming fire and he yanked open the door handle, dove to the pavement and rolled his body toward the front of the car. More incoming shots rang out, clanging into the sedan's bodywork. Leaning over the hood, Ryan took aim and squeezed off more rounds.

Just then he heard the van's engine roar to life and the vehicle lurched forward and then sped away.

Ryan crouched and cautiously made his way toward the back of the sedan, his gun in front of him. His heart thundering, he glanced at the area where the van had been. Four bodies lay on the pavement, bleeding and inert.

He approached them slowly and checked each man for a pulse and found none.

Standing, he went back to the front of the sedan to let Rachel know they were safe for now. His heart dropped and his stomach churned when he found her, sitting on the ground, groaning and gasping for breath, clutching her bleeding left leg.

A pool of blood was all around her.

Chapter 63

Vancouver, Canada

Lexi stabbed the intercom device on her desk. "Have you found the colonel?"

"I'm afraid not," Shawn replied.

"Keep trying, damn it!"

"Yes, Lexi."

She broke the connection and breathed in a lungful of air and let it out slowly. The feeling of dread crowded her mind and she had a difficult time thinking straight. It had been a full week and all her calls had the exact result. The colonel was nowhere to be found.

Lexi grit her teeth, knowing her well-crafted plans were on hold until she located the man.

The door to her office burst open and Shawn stood there.

"You found him?" she barked.

"No. It's something else. You have an incoming video call. It's...it's from the Kremlin, in Russia."

"What? Are you insane?"

"No, it's true. Prime Minister Pushkin wants to speak with you."

Lexi ground her teeth again. "Now I know you're crazy. I know no one in the Russian government, let alone the man who runs it."

"I verified the call, Lexi. It's originating from the Kremlin in Moscow. And I used a voice analyzer and compared it with a video I just downloaded from his public speeches. It's unquestionably him."

"And you say he wants to speak with me?"

"Yes. His aide and then he asked for you specifically. Lexi Atwood."

Lexi's mind raced, trying to process the enormity of this development. Not coming up with anything logical, she finally gave up. "All right, Shawn. Give me a moment to put my office into SCIF mode, then put the call through to my computer."

"Yes. I'll do that."

The young man left and closed the door behind him.

Three minutes later she clicked on the video conferencing icon on her computer's screen. There was a woman on there, who introduced the Prime Minister and then the camera panned left to a man sitting behind a desk.

Lexi recognized Vladimir Pushkin immediately. She'd seen news clips of him for years and he looked exactly the same. He was a short man with balding hair, coal black eyes and a cruel mouth. He was sitting behind an imposing desk, in an office that looked exactly like the publicity photos of the Kremlin.

"I assume you would prefer to speak in English?" he asked in flawless but accented English. He gave her a quick smile from his shark-like teeth.

She nodded. "Yes. My Russian is a bit rusty."

"Not a problem. I am Vladimir Pushkin, Prime Minister of Russia."

"Yes, Prime Minister. My assistant verified your identity."

"And you are Lexi Atwood." He gave her another shark-like grin. "Although I would rather call you by your real name, Alexandra. Alexandra Ivanova."

Her heart skipped a beat and her stomach began churning. "My legal name is Atwood. Alexandra Atwood."

He nodded. "Yes, yes, I am familiar with your name change. Clever, I must admit. But I headed up the KGB for many years and we have many ways to find out information."

She said nothing in reply.

"You may be wondering why I am calling, Alexandra."

"I am," she said. "I have no idea what this could be about."

"Everything will be clear to you at the end of this conversation." The man gave her an appraising look. "I must admit, Alexandra, you are even more beautiful than the surveillance videos we have of you."

"Surveillance videos?"

"Yes. We have had you under surveillance for quite some time now. Did you think, Alexandra, that you could slip in and out of Russia without us knowing?"

Her jaw dropped open and she tried to speak but nothing came out.

"For example," he said, "we have security camera footage of you visiting the Hermitage Museum in St. Petersburg recently. And that was not your only visit there."

"Why?...why, Prime Minister...are you keeping tabs on me?"

The shark-like grin flashed again. "Originally it was not you we were following. You see, we like to know what former members of our intelligence services are up to after they leave the employ of Mother Russia. One of those people is Colonel Mikhail Sharpov. A man you know well."

At the mention of the colonel's name, Lexi blanched. Bile rose up her throat and she fought the urge to retch.

"As you know, Alexandra, Colonel Sharpov served in the GRU for many years. I am sure you also know that the GRU is Russia's military intelligence unit."

She was speechless and simply nodded.

"Since we keep tabs on the colonel, we soon learned that he was working for you. At that point we placed you under surveillance as well. And since you met with Sharpov in Russia several times, your trips were monitored closely. If you doubt any of this, I can give you copies of the security footage."

She shook her head. "That won't be necessary."

"I know for a fact, Alexandra, that you have been trying to locate the colonel for a week. My people have been listening to the many messages you left on his answering machine and his cell phone."

Realizing Pushkin knew everything, she said, "Where is Sharpov?"

"The FSB arrested him. He's in our custody."

"Why was he arrested? He committed no crimes in Russia."

"Very true. He has not committed any crimes here. But we've suspected he was involved with something major in the USA. We were curious, since he has been traveling back and forth to the U.S. frequently. And his bank accounts have grown tremendously in the last year. At first we suspected he had become a spy for the Americans. So the FSB arrested him. They also did a through search of his office and home in St. Petersburg. He had encrypted his computers and files well, but our FSB people are better. We learned what he was up to. What he and you were up to."

"I don't know what you're talking about, Prime Minister."

"There is no use lying. We know everything. The bombing near Philadelphia and Los Angeles. Your planned bombing of New York City."

She shook her head forcefully. "I had no involvement in that."

The cold, shark-like grin appeared again. "No use denying it, my dear Alexandra. We know everything or almost everything. I must say it was an ingenious plan. The bombings, which caused the Electronic Magnetic Pulses. The EMPs shutting down all communications. We are familiar with how you made your wealth – by stock trading, in this case, short selling stock. Yes, as I said before, it was an ingenious plan. I am sure you have made billions of dollars in the last month."

"If you know all this, what do you want from me?" she asked. "I have not hurt Russia. I would never do that. I love the mother country."

"I am sure that you do. As I mentioned earlier, we know almost everything. But there's something we still need."

She leaned forward in her chair. "What do you want?"

"We want the bombs. The nuclear devices. The ones that are left. We in Russia do not have the technology to build them. They are extremely advanced."

"Why ask me, Prime Minister?"

"We still lack the last piece of the puzzle. The location where the bombs are stored. None of the colonel's records provide this information."

"You have Sharpov in custody. Ask him."

"We have. The colonel has been interrogated repeatedly. And I assure you, it was not pleasant for him. He is near death. Our FSB people are experts at torture. But he has refused to tell us what we need to know. If we torture him any more, he will die. We are sure of it."

"I see."

"It appears, Alexandra, that the colonel is very devoted to you. You have a strange hold over him. From everything he is saying, he feels he will be betraying you if he tells us where the nuclear bombs are located."

"Do you expect me to tell you where they are to save his life?"

Pushkin nodded. "If we get the bombs, we will release the colonel immediately."

"That's not going to happen, Prime Minister. Colonel Sharpov has been an excellent employee. But everyone is expendable. Including him."

"I suspected that would be your answer. So I propose a trade. I give you what you want and we get the backpack bombs."

"What could you possibly give me?" she asked, skepticism in her voice.

He nodded. "It is not money. We know you are already extremely wealthy. You have more money than God."

Lexi grinned, in spite of the tension she was feeling. "What then?"

"As I said, I propose a trade. I give you things you have always wanted and we get the nuclear devices. It is as simple as that."

"And I repeat my question – what could you possibly give me that I already don't have?"

"For starters, Alexandra, I would wipe your husband's record clean. Even though he is dead, he is still considered a fugitive from Russia. We would expunge his crimes and drop all criminal charges. And since you fled Russia with him and thereby were complicit in his crimes, all charges against you would also be dropped."

"Yes, that would be good. I still love Sergei very much and want his name cleared."

"There is more, Alexandra. My people have done a lot of research into your background. We know, for example, that you fancy the idea that you are a descendant of Empress Anna Ivanova, who as Tsarina ruled Russia from 1730 until 1740. Our research cannot prove your lineage to royalty. However, we cannot dispute it either. Because of that, the Russian government is ready to give you official recognition as a true descendent of Empress Anna Ivanova."

She flushed and her heart raced as she considered what the man had just said. *I love the idea.*

"Oh, my God!" she exclaimed. "You can do that?"

"Yes, of course. And since you then would be of royal blood, you would be welcome to live in Russia full time. You would be an honored citizen here. In fact, you would become one of the most respected and revered people in Mother Russia. It is something I am sure you have always wanted."

Lexi nodded furiously. "Yes! Yes, it is." Her thoughts swirled with anticipation. It had always been her dream. *Now it can be a reality.*

"There is one other thing we can offer you, Alexandra, in exchange for the bombs."

"There's more?"

"Yes. One thing you have always coveted. The painting at the Hermitage Museum. The one you always visit when you come here. The painting of Empress Ivanova."

"What about it?"

"It can be yours. We will give that painting to you," he said. "We will replace it with a forged copy at the Hermitage and give you the original."

Lexi's jaw dropped and she was speechless. Her heart pounded with excitement.

"I assume you would want this?" he asked.

"God, yes! Of course yes!"

He nodded. "I thought you would say that. So. Do we have a deal?"

"Yes, Prime Minister. We have a deal. But I have several conditions you need to agree to."

The Prime Minister frowned, then glared. After a moment his shark-like grin appeared. "Do not push me, Alexandra. I am not a nice man. If you do not agree to this trade, I will give all the information about the bombings to the Canadian government. I am sure you will be arrested immediately."

She swallowed hard, knowing what he said was true. *I would be arrested.* But she kept her fear in check and in a defiant tone said, "If that happens and I am arrested, you will not get the bombs you want."

Pushkin frowned, obviously considering her words carefully. After a moment he nodded. "You drive a hard bargain. What are your conditions?"

"The colonel is to be released immediately."

"I agree."

"Second, my plans for New York City have to go forward. I need that to happen."

"But why?" he said. "You have already made billions from your scheme."

"I want more money," she replied, her voice cold. "You can never be too rich. And then there's something else. Call it revenge, call it payback, call it retribution. My poor Sergei is dead because the Americans put him in prison. They need to pay a high price for that."

He shrugged. "Fine. Now do we have a deal?"

"Yes."

"Excellent, Alexandra. Now tell me the location of the nuclear devices that are left. You used one in the Philadelphia area and one in the Los Angeles area. Since ten were stolen, there are eight left. Tell me where they are and my people will get them and bring them to Russia."

"I will give you six of the bombs. I need one for New York City and I need one for another reason."

"What other reason, Alexandra?"

"Let's call it insurance."

He frowned and then finally shrugged. "I agree."

"Good. We have a deal."

"Now tell me where they are located."

"Tell me something, Prime Minister. Once I give you this information, what's to keep you from still giving me up to the Canadian authorities and having me arrested?"

"You are now a descendant of royalty. I have no intention of tarnishing your reputation. In fact, it is my fervent wish you return to Russia and live here." He gave her another one of his shark-like grins. "In fact, you are such a beautiful and desirable woman that it is my hope we will become very close friends one day."

Lexi nodded and spent the next ten minutes giving him detailed information on where the nuclear devices were located.

"Excellent," he said. He was quiet a moment and then said, "As a gesture of my good will, I will give you the painting now. The one at the Hermitage. The one of Empress Ivanova. Send your plane to Russia and we will load it on there for you."

"Thank you, Prime Minister. That means a great deal to me."

"I am sure that it does. Is there anything else we need to discuss?"

"I don't believe so, Prime Minister."

His cold, shark-like grin returned. "In that case, I will say goodbye. For now. By the way, I would like to invite you to dinner. After you conclude your...unpleasant business with New York City. I want you to come visit me in Moscow. I would be honored to dine with royalty. And maybe more than dine."

"Aren't you a married man, Prime Minister?"

He smiled and waved a hand in the air. "Of course. But I have a very understanding wife."

Chapter 64

Vancouver, Canada

J.T. Ryan entered the hospital room and approached the bed. Rachel West was on it, a sheet covering her. Medical equipment was behind and next to the bed, beeping in the way they always do in hospitals.

Rachel's face was pale and her long blonde hair was tousled, but she managed a wan smile. "Hey, stranger," she said, "long time no see...."

He pulled a chair close to the bed and sat. "I was here for the last couple of days but your were out cold. The docs have you on some really strong painkillers."

She nodded, her blue eyes a bit unfocused. "The pain killers are working. I feel like I'm floating on a cloud...."

He reached out and held one of her hands. "You look beautiful, Rachel."

She gave him another wan smile. "You're such a bullshitter." She looked down at herself. She was wearing one of those silly gowns hospitals give you, this one had tiny yellow flowers on it. "Admit it, J.T....I look like hell...my hair's a mess...and I'm probably white as a sheet."

"You look great to me." He squeezed her hand. "I thought I'd lost you."

She managed a grin. "I'm too tough to kill...you know that...."

"I know. Action Rachel."

Just then her eyes focused. "When can I get out of this dump?"

"I talked to the doc before I came in. You've lost a lot of blood. He mentioned they had to give you transfusions. He thought a week."

"A week? The hell with that."

He squeezed her hand again. "Please, Rachel. You need to recuperate. Okay?"

She grimaced but after a long moment her expression softened. "Fine. But I'm not happy about it. By the way, what happened at the shootout? I don't remember much...."

"We killed four of them. Two got away."

"Who were they?"

"Hired guns. Local talent from what I could tell."

"Who hired them?" she said.

"I'm pretty sure it was Atwood, but I can't prove it. At least now I've got the police chief's full attention. Vancouver is a tourist destination and a shootout leaving four corpses makes for ugly headlines."

Rachel nodded. "So. Where are we on the case?"

"We still need to tie Lexi Atwood to the terrorists. If we get proof that Scarman met with her, we've got something solid we can take to the Canadian authorities. They'll have to arrest her and we can extradite her to the U.S."

"That leaves us with only one option then, J.T."

"I know. I talked to Erin Welch. The FBI doesn't have satellites at their disposal. I have to call Alex Miller and get his help."

"I agree, J.T. We'll have to take a chance he's not the mole."

"After I leave here, I'm calling Miller."

She reached out with a hand and caressed his face. Her skin felt silky soft and warm and sensual, despite the hospital setting. "Don't go yet, okay?"

He grinned. "Okay. Let me tell you some new jokes. That'll cheer you up. Did you hear the one about the —"

She pressed a finger to his lips. "No. No corny jokes. You're sweet for trying to cheer me up. But I just want you to stay a little longer."

Suddenly a mischievous grin settled on her face. "I can't wait to get out of here so I can jump your bones!"

Ryan laughed. "Now I know you're feeling better."

Her mischievous smile grew and in a low voice she said, "Let me see your gun."

"My gun? What the hell for?"

"Just do it. Please?"

"All right. But I really shouldn't do it. Brandishing a pistol without cause could get me arrested."

"Please?" she whispered. "I promise you won't regret it."

He looked around the empty hospital room and toward the corridor to make sure no one could see him. He pulled his jacket aside and took the revolver out of the holster, then held the gun at his side, pointing toward the floor. "Happy now?"

"Unload it, J.T."

He gave her a puzzled look. "Why?"

"Please?"

"All right." He opened the cylinder, ejected the six bullets, then clicked the cylinder shut.

"It's safe now," she whispered.

"Of course it is."

She reached out with a hand. "Give me the pistol."

"Why?"

"Pretty please?"

"Okay, Rachel."

She took the gun and hefted it in her hand. "I love the chrome finish on this one."

"Okay. Now give it back."

Her grin changed from naughty to devilish. "Oh, I'll give it back when I'm done with it." She pulled the sheet down and in a rapid motion hid the weapon under it. Then she pulled the sheet up to her neck. He saw her hands fumble underneath the sheet and then her hands stopped moving when they reached her groin area.

Rachel grinned widely.

A dawning realization hit him. "You're really not going to do that, are you?"

Her devilish grin grew and he noticed her hands moving under the sheet again. "Oh! The metal is cold," she said with a laugh.

"Someone's going to see you, Rachel!"

She laughed again. "Don't be silly. Nobody's going to see anything. I'm all covered up." Then she lowered the sheet and handed him the pistol, which he re-holstered.

"All done," she said brightly, humor in her voice.

He felt his cheeks flush.

Rachel stared at him and laughed. "John Taylor Ryan, I believe you're blushing! Now that's a first!"

He shook his head slowly. "I can't believe you just did that."

Rachel's beautiful blue eyes sparkled with intensity. "Now, every time you hold your gun, you'll think of me."

"Tell me something – did the painkillers they're giving you make you do that?"

"Maybe – but then maybe not."

He shook his head again. Then he smiled. "You're bad. Very, very bad."

Rachel returned the smile. "Of course I am."

Chapter 65

Vancouver, Canada

J.T. Ryan picked up his cell phone, stared at it a long moment, then set it back down on the car's dash. He'd been dreading making the call for some time, still not certain it was a wise move.

Ryan mulled it over several more minutes as he stared around the empty parking lot of Stanley Park. The park bordered Vancouver Bay and the early morning sun was beginning to reflect off the water. Realizing he had no choice, he picked up the phone and tapped in a number.

"It's Ryan," he said when the CIA Deputy Director picked up.

"I'm glad you called," Alex Miller said. "Hope you're making progress, because we're at a dead end here."

"Yes, sir. We've got a solid lead."

"Good. Let's hear it. Is Rachel West on the call with you?"

"Actually, no," Ryan replied.

"Where is she?"

"Rachel and I were ambushed and she was shot."

"My God! Is she dead?"

"Thankfully, no. Right now she's recuperating at a hospital in Vancouver, Canada."

"What the hell? What are you talking about, Ryan? Her phone's GPS places her in Atlanta. The same place you're calling from."

"Sir, I hate to admit it, but we haven't been totally honest with you. Rachel and I have been in Vancouver for several weeks. We left our CIA cell phones in Atlanta and forwarded our calls to new phones."

"You lied to me?" he screeched. "Why the hell would you do that, Ryan?"

"Sir, I take full responsibility for this deception. Rachel is not complicit in this."

"That's crap!" the Deputy Director shot back, acid in his voice. "I talked to her last week and she said nothing about being in Canada."

"I know, sir. It was my idea to keep you in the dark. I talked her into it."

"But why? Why damn it?"

"Director, I thought you were the mole."

"You what?" he shouted. "You thought I was the leak?"

"Yes, sir. We knew it was someone high up in an intelligence service. Someone with access to top-secret information. The terrorists always seem to be one step ahead of us."

"I can't believe you thought I was the mole!" he barked. "I've been with the Agency for over twenty years. I've been a Deputy Director for ten of those years."

"I'm aware of that, sir. I'm sorry. And I take full responsibility for lying to you."

"You may take responsibility for it, Ryan. But Rachel is complicit. She is going to pay a price for this. A high price."

"But, sir, it wasn't her fault –"

"Enough! I'll deal with her another time." He paused and in a low growl added, "After this operation is over, I'll make her pay."

"Sir, please. Punish me."

"You're not part of the CIA. She is. Now, no more talk about that. Let's get on with why you called in the first place. You must really need my help or you wouldn't be calling me after the insane stunt you've pulled."

"Yes, sir. As I mentioned earlier, Rachel and I have a real solid lead. We've been trying to locate the person who killed Erin's fiancée. We believe we've tracked him down."

"Let me stop you there," Miller interrupted. "My first priority is to catch the terrorists and your first priority is to catch the terrorists. That's the mission the President assigned us to."

"Yes, sir. We, and by that I mean Erin Welch, Rachel and I are all convinced the terrorist bombings and the DA's murder are connected."

"I'm not convinced that's true, Ryan. On the other hand, our hunt for the scarred man in the Middle East has been a dry hole so far. So whatever lead you have is better than nothing. Who's the killer?"

"We believe the person who ordered the hit is a woman. A Canadian citizen named Lexi Atwood. She's a billionaire and she runs a company named Crimson Atwood Corporation, which is located in Vancouver."

"I see. Why do you suspect her?"

"Sir, the hit man was paid from a Crimson bank account. The money went thru several phony front companies, but we've been able to trace it back to Atwood's corporation. We also learned Lexi Atwood has a motive. Her late husband was a man named Sergei Atwood, who died in prison in Georgia years ago. He was a criminal and was prosecuted by District Attorney Ed Roth, who was Erin's fiancée. We also think that part of the reason for the bombings of U.S. cities may be Lexi Atwood's way of punishing the USA for the death of her husband."

"I see your point, Ryan. That's a hell of a good motive. Sounds like you have more than enough circumstantial evidence to arrest her for suspicion of murder."

"It's not as simple as that. Atwood is incredibly wealthy and probably Canada's richest person. I've tried to get the Vancouver police to at least bring her in for questioning, but they've refused. But if we can tie her to the terrorists, they'll have no choice but to arrest her."

"Good thinking."

"We learned something else about this woman," Ryan said. "Her real name is Alexandra Ivanova and she's Russian. She and her husband fled Russia many years ago when he was going to be arrested there for money laundering. They went to Canada, changed their name to Atwood and have lived there since. We believe Scarman, the guy directly involved in the bombings, is her employee. He also may be Russian."

"Russian? I see. So he may not be from the Middle East at all."

"That's right, Director. That's probably why we've had no luck finding Scarman in Syria."

"You may be on to something. So what's your plan now?"

"We need to find evidence," Ryan said, "that links Scarman to Lexi Atwood. We've reviewed CCTV camera footage from Atwood's company. From what we can tell, Scarman was never there."

"Where then?'

"Atwood has a gated mansion on Vancouver Island, which is near the coast of Vancouver. Her home is a very secluded, very private place. We believe Scarman met Atwood there. We need to get the surveillance feed from CIA satellites over that area for the last six months. From what Rachel told me, they capture precise images of earth in extreme detail. She said you can read license plate numbers from space."

"That's correct, Ryan. And only I can authorize the access to CIA satellite information."

"That's what Rachel told me."

"All right. Give me the details on Lexi Atwood and I'll get the process started immediately."

Ryan spent the next several minutes giving Miller all of the information he and Rachel had compiled on the Canadian billionaire.

When he was done, Miller, said, "Okay. I'll turn this over to my tech people right away. As soon as I have anything I'll call you."

"Thank you, sir."

"And another thing," Miller continued, the acid in his voice returning. "No more secrets, Ryan. Hold anything back from me in the future and I'll make sure you never do security work for any U.S. government agency for the rest of your life. Understood?"

Ryan swallowed hard. "Loud and clear, Director. I understand."

Chapter 66

Vancouver Island, Canada

Lexi stared at the painting, admiring the exquisite brushstrokes, every detail making the priceless artwork come to life. Her ancestor, Empress Anna Ivanova, looked even more lifelike here than she had at the Hermitage Museum. Lexi had hung the painting over the fireplace mantel in the study of her mansion. It was right next to the large photograph of her husband Sergei.

Prime Minister Pushkin kept his word, she mused. She'd sent her plane to Russia and, as promised, the painting of Tsarina Ivanova had been loaded in it. *Now it's here, where it should be. With me, Empress Anna Ivanova's only living descendant.*

A dark thought crossed Lexi's mind and she frowned. Pushkin has kept his word so far. *But can I really trust him?*

The man's cold, shark-like grin bothered her. It was obvious he wanted more than the bombs. That had been clear. *He wants me for a house pet. A sex slave.*

Lexi gulped down the glass of Cabernet and poured herself another from the bottle on the table. Taking another swallow of the wine, she decided then and there to be extremely careful in her dealings with the Prime Minister. She had never been any man's house pet and wasn't about to start now. Even her precious Sergei had learned early in their marriage that she was in charge and had submitted to her training.

Just then Lexi heard a soft knock and turned to the open doorway of the study. Sun-Yi stood there. The young Chinese woman with the doll-like face had been Lexi's maid for years.

"You have a call, Mrs. Atwood," Sun-Yi said.

"Who is it?"

"He would not say. But it sounded like the colonel."

Lexi's heart raced, hoping it was really him. "All right. I'll take it in my office."

Sun-Yi left and Lexi made her way to her office which was also on the first floor of her three-story estate. Sitting at her desk, she turned on the voice analyzer device and picked up the handset of her encrypted desk phone.

"This is Lexi Atwood."

"Lexi, it's me."

She recognized his voice immediately and relief flooded her mind. Just to make sure, she confirmed his identity with the voice analyzer.

"Colonel!" she said excitedly. "It's so good to hear from you. I thought I'd lost you!"

"I'm lucky to be alive. The FSB goons beat me half to death. I didn't think I'd ever get out of that dungeon."

"Thank God you're out of there. Where are you now, Colonel?"

"At home. I'm in bad shape. I should have gone to the hospital but I don't trust them either. After I was arrested, there's not much I do trust. Only you, Lexi. I trust only you. When the FSB let me go, the officer in charge told me it was because you interceded on my behalf."

"That's true, Colonel. But unfortunately circumstances are different now."

"How so?"

"I have a new partner."

"How is that possible, Lexi? This whole operation has been yours and yours alone from the beginning."

"The situation has changed. It's not something I wanted but I had no choice. As I said, I have a new partner. I can't tell you who it is, but trust me on this, we don't want to cross him. He's a very powerful and influential man."

"Yes, Lexi."

She paused a moment to formulate her thoughts. "The operation you were planning, before you were arrested. I need that to proceed."

"New York City?"

"Yes, Colonel. I'm counting on you."

"Of course. There's just one thing."

"What?"

"I'm in bad shape," he said. "I can hardly walk. The pain is excruciating. Every part of my body was beaten."

Lexi took another sip of her red wine. "I understand. How much time do you need?"

"At least several days."

"All right." Then her voice turned steely. "But no more than that. I need New York City to happen. The sooner the better."

"Yes," he replied.

"And one other thing. When you go to the place where the packages are stored, you'll find only one there."

"How's that possible?" he said. "There were seven left."

Lexi's stomach churned, still angry at having to give up her precious packages. "As I told you before, conditions have changed. My new partner has six of them now. Only one is left in the storage building."

"I see."

"All right, Colonel. Call me in a few days. I want the next phase to proceed as soon as possible. I'll send my plane to pick you up."

"Yes," he said. "You can count on me."

Chapter 67

Vancouver, Canada

J.T. Ryan entered the hospital room and approached the bed. Rachel West was on it, sleeping peacefully. He pulled a chair next to the bed, sat down and studied her features, noticing she wasn't nearly as pale as last time he'd visited her.

Ryan reached out and caressed her arm. "Wake up, sleepyhead."

Her eyes fluttered open. She looked startled a moment, then smiled. "J.T. I'm glad you're here."

He returned her smile and held up a box he was carrying. "Got something for you."

"What is it?"

"Doughnuts! The Breakfast of Champions."

Rachel laughed. "I'm a lucky woman. First you give me roses and now doughnuts. What more could I ask for?"

"You look great, Rachel."

"Bullshit. I look like hell."

"Not to me you don't." He squeezed her hand. "I have good news. I talked to the doctor on the way in. He said the blood transfusions have gone well. You should be out of the hospital by the end of the week."

She frowned. "I want out of this damn place now! I'm climbing the walls. And the food sucks!"

"Don't hold back," he said with a chuckle. "Tell me what you really think."

She stuck out her tongue at him and crossed her arms in front of her. "Easy for you to say. You're not the one in this hellhole."

"You'll be out soon, okay? In the meantime have a doughnut. You'll feel better."

"What kind did you bring me?"

He opened the box and showed her the contents. "Six jelly and six chocolate."

Rachel's frown melted. "They do look good." She reached out, took one of the jelly ones and munched on it.

"Feel better now?"

She nodded, finished the doughnut, and took out another and began eating it.

"I've got some other news," he said. "About the case."

She put down the doughnut and wiped her mouth with a paper napkin. "Tell me."

"I talked to Alex Miller. He's working on getting us the satellite images of Atwood's home on Vancouver Island."

Rachel made a face. "Yeah, I know. Miller called me here after you talked to him."

"How did that go?"

She shook her head. "Not well. His tone was icy, to say the least."

"I told him it had been all my idea, suspecting him as the government leak."

Rachel shook her head again. "It doesn't matter what you said. He's furious at us. Specially me."

"What's he going to do?"

"Nothing right now, J.T. He needs us to solve this case. But after that's done...."

She didn't finish the sentence, but she didn't need to. Both of them were expecting the worst.

Chapter 68

Special Operations Division
CIA Annex Building
Langley, Virginia

Alex Miller entered the conference room and glanced down at the large table, which was completely covered with black and white photographs taken by CIA satellites.

Miller's lead technician was already in the room. "Good morning, sir," the man said.

"What did you find?" Miller asked abruptly.

"Per your request, sir, we located Atwood's home on Vancouver Island and matched satellite overpasses over that area for the last six months —"

"Cut to the chase," Miller interrupted. "Just tell me what you found."

"Yes, Deputy Director." The tech picked up two of the photographs and handed them to Miller. "Sir, in the last six months we were able to locate two instances where Scarman visited Atwood's mansion. We were able to isolate these images by using facial recognition software and compared them to the photo John Ryan obtained of the man at Albuquerque airport."

Miller studied the two photos closely. The first one showed Scarman getting out of a car in the driveway of Atwood's mansion and going inside the home. The second photo showed Scarman climbing out of a helicopter in the back yard of the mansion. He was carrying a suitcase and he went inside the estate.

"Good work," Miller said.

The technician beamed. "Thank you, sir."

Alex Miller stood there and considered this new development. *This is it*, he realized. *This is the smoking gun that ties Atwood with the terrorists.* He grudgingly had to admit that Erin Welch, John Ryan and Rachel West had been right all along. The murder of Erin's fiancée and the bombings were linked. On one hand he was elated, but at the same time he was still furious Rachel had lied to him.

Pushing aside the negative thoughts, he said to the tech, "I need several copies of these two photos. One set for President Harris and another for General Foster. I'll meet with them right away. And one other thing – this new information you've learned is top-secret – only for the two of us to know."

"What about the CIA Director, sir? Shouldn't we let him know what's happening? This is a huge development."

Miller shook his head forcefully. "No! Do not tell the Director of the Agency! That's a direct order. If you disobey me, I will terminate your employment with the CIA."

"Yes, sir."

"Get going then. I need those photos immediately."

"Deputy Director, there's something else I have to tell you."

"What is it, damn it?" Miller snapped. "I'm not a mind reader."

"Sir, during our research we found out Atwood owns a jet. We were covertly able to obtain flight records for that plane. The jet traveled to St. Petersburg, Russia a total of seven times in the last few months."

"Russia?"

"Yes, sir."

"All right. Keep working on this. Find out who Scarman is. If we learn his identity, that will give us another solid lead."

"Yes, sir."

Miller pointed to the conference room door. "Go get me those photos. Now."

Chapter 69

The Oval Office
The White House
Washington, D.C.

"Thank you for seeing me on such short notice," Alex Miller said as he entered the Oval Office and approached President Harris's desk.

The President stood and extended his hand. "You said it was urgent?"

They shook hands and Miller said, "Yes, sir. It is."

Harris motioned to the wingback armchairs fronting the desk and both men sat.

"Where's General Foster?" the CIA man asked. "I was hoping to inform him also."

Harris shook his head. "He's not in D.C. today. Tell me what you have."

"Mr. President, we've found Scarman's employer. A Canadian woman named Lexi Atwood. We believe she's the ringleader behind the terrorist bombings. She's a billionaire, has plenty of money to fund the operation. And she has motive. Her husband died in an American prison. He was tried and convicted by Erin Welch's fiancée."

The President nodded. "I see."

Miller spent the next few minutes showing Harris the satellite images of Scarman at Atwood's mansion and filling him in on the other information he'd learned.

"Atwood, I believe," Miller continued, "had another motive for the bombings. She's a stock trader. We suspect she shorted stocks right before the explosions. The bombs triggered EMPs, which shut down all communication in those areas, causing panic in financial markets. I estimate Atwood made billions of dollars on those stock trades."

Harris rubbed his jaw. "That makes sense."

The CIA man then said, "J.T. Ryan found out that Lexi Atwood was born in Russia and lived there with her husband. Her real name is Alexandra Ivanova. She and her husband fled Russia when he was about to be arrested for money laundering. They moved to Canada, changed their identities and became Canadian citizens. We now believe Scarman is Russian also. We're trying to learn his true identity."

"All right. I want Atwood arrested immediately. If she's the ringleader of the terrorists I want her behind bars or killed, I don't care which."

"She's a Canadian citizen, Mr. President. And the richest person in that country. The woman is, from what we've learned, very well connected and very influential."

Harris closed his fists and pounded the armrests. "I don't give a damn who she is. She's killing innocent Americans. I want that woman arrested immediately!"

"Yes, Mr. President."

"I'll call the Canadian Prime Minister right now and get his ass in gear."

"Yes, sir."

"Where's Ryan now?"

"He's in Vancouver," Miller replied.

Harris jabbed his index finger on Miller's chest. "And if the Canadian's don't move fast enough, get Ryan involved."

"Ryan doesn't have arrest powers in Canada, sir."

"That's not what I meant."

"You're authorizing termination with extreme prejudice?"

"Hell, yes!" Harris growled. "I want that damn woman dead."

"Yes, Mr. President."

Chapter 70

Vancouver, Canada

Lexi paced her office on the top floor of the Crimson Atwood building, staring frequently at her desk phone, praying it would ring. It had been two days since the colonel had first called her and she was anxious to get the New York City operation underway.

"Heal quickly, Colonel," she muttered. "Don't disappoint me."

Just then there was a knock at her door and her security chief, Brad Murdock, opened it.

"What do you want?" she snapped at him.

"We've got problems."

Lexi's face burned. "Now what? I pay you big money to make my problems go away. But all you do is bring me more problems. What is it now?"

"People are watching this building," Murdock said.

"Who is it? That FBI guy, Ryan?"

"No. It's much worse. I think it's the Canadian police. Possibly even Canadian Feds."

"Shit." She began pacing her office again, her thoughts dark. She stopped in her tracks and her coal black eyes bore into his. "Why? Why would the Canadian's be monitoring me?"

"It could be connected to the DA's murder in Atlanta. The FBI agent, Ryan, has been meeting with the local PD trying to get them to open an investigation." The man paused a moment. "But I think there's a more ominous reason. The Canadian Feds may suspect your involvement with the terrorist bombings in the U.S. You're the richest person in this country. The Vancouver police know you're very well connected politically. They wouldn't jeopardize their own jobs unless they had a hell of a good reason."

Lexi's heart began to pound and her temples throbbed with an intense migraine. *Brad's right. Everything could be in jeopardy. Not just the operation, but even my own safety and freedom.*

Muttering to herself, she visualized an endlessly long jail sentence in a dark, foul-smelling, dungeon-like prison filled with hardened criminals. Dangerous, crude animals who would make the rest of her life a living hellhole. Lexi found it hard to breathe, felt like the walls were closing in around her.

"Are you okay?" Murdock asked, concern in his voice. "You're white as a sheet."

She didn't reply, just sank into her office chair, feeling as if a thousand pound weight had settled on her shoulders. She shut her eyes and breathed in and out slowly for several minutes, trying to get her heart to stop racing.

Lexi opened her eyes and glared at her security chief. "Find out more, damn it. Find out what's going on. And don't come back until you do." She pointed to the office door. "Now get the hell out of here! I need to think."

Murdock nodded and left the room, closing the door behind him.

She stood, went to her liquor cabinet, opened a bottle of Merlot and sat back down at her desk. Drinking straight from the bottle, she gulped down the red wine until the container was empty. Agonizing over what to do next, she massaged her temples trying to make the intense migraine in her head go away.

After an hour of tortured thoughts mulling over her options, she chose one. Lexi stabbed her finger on the intercom. "I need you now, Shawn. In here."

The young man came into her office and approached her desk. "Are you all right, Mrs. Atwood? You look pale."

She motioned to the chair fronting the desk. "Sit."

The man sat.

"I need your help, Shawn."

"Of course. Whatever you need."

She tapped her red Mont Blanc pen on the desk. "I need you to start liquidating my assets. I want you to sell half of my stocks and bonds. Put the cash into money-market accounts. Start immediately."

His eyebrows arched. "That's a lot of money. Billions of dollars."

Lexi scowled. "I know how much it is. Just do it."

"Of course. Whatever you say." He paused a moment. "You said only half your holdings. What about the balance?"

She shook her head. "Leave that alone. I'll need that for my last operation. I'm still hoping the colonel can pull that off."

"Yes, Lexi. By the way, where do you want me to put the money? In your Canadian bank accounts?"

"Absolutely not. Put the money in my Swiss numbered accounts."

"Will do," he said.

Then he frowned and seemed uncertain.

"Is there a problem, Shawn?"

"I was just curious...why are you liquidating your holdings?"

She almost barked out a response, telling him it was none of his business. But on second thought, decided on a softer response. She really liked Shawn and needed him to satisfy her emotionally and sexually. Deep down she knew she loved him, in her own twisted and perverted way.

"Things have changed," she replied in a soothing tone. "And not for the better. I may have to leave Canada at some point, and I want you to come with me. Nothing bad may happen, but I have to be prepared. Do you understand, honey?"

He nodded.

Lexi reached out with her palm. "Hold my hand, please."

Shawn took her hand and she held it tightly with both of hers. "I need you, Shawn. More than you realize. The money I have, the billions, I'd like to share that with you. You remember the conversation we had a few weeks ago? About me wanting us to become emotionally close?"

"Yes, I remember."

"I wasn't kidding then and I'm not now. I'm totally serious. We would make a hell of a team, Shawn. I've already trained you. You know what I like, what I need, what I must have." She smiled. "Think about it, honey. You'd be super-rich. Have wealth beyond your wildest dreams. You'd have access to billions of dollars."

"What about my family? My wife and children?"

She waved that away. "You could keep them. I told you before I wouldn't interfere with your family life. As long as you understand that I come first. That's the one cardinal rule you must never break."

He nodded and said, "I understand." But he looked sad.

Lexi smiled. "Don't worry too much. Things may turn out okay. My problems may resolve themselves. I may be able to make them go away. As we both know, money buys solutions. I may be able to stay in Canada."

"That would be best, Lexi."

"Yes, I agree. I love this city."

The red-haired woman contemplated happy thoughts for a long moment, then snatched her hand away. In a brisk, business-like tone said, "Now get going. Start liquidating my assets."

"Yes, Lexi."

Chapter 71

Teterboro, New Jersey

Colonel Mikhail Sharpov was exhausted and in pain. The last twenty-four hours had been a blur of activity. Ever since he'd called Lexi and told her he was ready to implement the next phase of the operation, he'd worked non-stop to get everything ready.

After packing what he needed, he'd spent the next twelve hours driving aimlessly through the outskirts of St. Petersburg, Russia insuring he wasn't being tailed by the FSB. Satisfied no one was following him, he had driven his car to the airport outside of the city. Lexi's private jet was already there waiting for him.

He boarded the Gulfstream G700 and it took off. He settled back on the seat but didn't feel totally safe until they had left Russian airspace. His time in the FSB prison was seared in his brain.

The colonel had tried to sleep during the long flight to the U.S., but it was difficult – the pain in his legs was intense from the multiple beatings. He hadn't been honest with Lexi. He really hadn't recovered from his injuries and was still walking with a severe limp. Still, he felt he couldn't disappoint her.

The colonel gazed out the plane's window as it circled over Teterboro Airport on its final approach. The jet landed moments later, he collected his bag and deplaned. There was a Buick sedan waiting for him and after storing his gear in the trunk, he headed out of the airport, which serviced mostly private planes.

Colonel Sharpov drove to the nearby storage facility and picked up the last remaining package. He insured it was fully functional and then stored the backpack in the trunk of his sedan. After spending several hours navigating surface streets to ascertain he wasn't being followed, he made his way to New Jersey's Route 3 and drove to the Lincoln Tunnel, which he used to enter New York City.

The colonel pulled into the first gas station he found and parked in the lot that fronted the convenience store. It was eleven in the evening and the place was nearly deserted. He stayed in the car and glanced around to insure there was no one nearby, then pulled out his encrypted SAT phone and pressed one of the pre-set numbers.

Lexi answered on the first ring. "Are you there, Colonel?"

"Almost there. I need to drive further south. I estimate I'll be in lower Manhattan in less than an hour."

"Excellent. Remember, I don't want the package to go off before midnight. I want to make a statement and make money. But I also want to limit the casualties."

"I understand, Lexi."

"We left a car for you at the parking garage," she said. "The one closest to the Freedom Tower. Call me as soon as you're safely away and give me the exact timetable."

"Yes, I will do that."

"And don't screw it up," she said, her voice low and sinister. "I have a lot of money riding on this."

"I won't let you down."

"See that you don't," she spit out. Then her tone changed and in a soothing voice added, "I'm sorry, Colonel, for being such a bitch. I'm just on edge. Good luck, my friend."

He was about to respond but realized she had already hung up.

Putting away his phone, he drove out of the gas station and headed south. Because of the late hour, traffic was light and twenty minutes later he located the designated multi-story parking garage near the Freedom Tower in lower Manhattan. On the way there he had spotted three separate canine police units, patrolling the almost deserted sidewalks.

With his adrenaline pumping, he realized there was no turning back now. He knew the NYPD used highly-sophisticated bomb-detection equipment. When Lexi had originally told him about this operation, he knew it would be extremely dangerous. Unfortunately she was a very headstrong woman and he hadn't been able to talk her out of it. Now, seeing the canine patrols and the security cameras positioned at every traffic light, he sensed his chance of getting away undetected was minimal. Still, he could not back out now. *I can't let her down.*

The colonel drove through the first level of the parking garage and headed to the second. He spotted the car Lexi's people had left for him and he parked in a slot nearby. Seeing no one around, he took in several deep breaths to calm his nerves.

Climbing out of his Buick, he limped painfully to the trunk, his legs aching with every step. He gazed around to make sure there was no one in the area and then opened the trunk. Unzipping the backpack, he flicked a switch on the W-54 and a solid green light came on the control panel. *One wrong move and I'm dead.* Methodically, he began adjusting the timer, adding minutes to the readout. He stopped when it reached 180 minutes. Three hours would give him plenty of time to exit Manhattan and be safely away in New Jersey.

The colonel's heart raced as he flicked another switch and the control panel's solid green light began flashing. Quickly zipping the backpack closed, he shut the trunk and limped toward the waiting car nearby. Using the key hidden in the sedan's wheel-well, he unlocked the car and fired it up. Then he slowly backed out of the parking slot and headed toward the exit on the first floor.

He drove out of the parking garage, turned right and headed north toward the Lincoln Tunnel.

Two minutes later all hell broke loose.

Two black-and-white police cars materialized out of nowhere, screeching to a halt in front of his sedan, blocking his way.

The colonel slammed on his brakes and threw his car in reverse. Glancing out his back window, he spotted a sea of blue lights and heard blaring police sirens piercing the quiet of night.

A small army of heavily-armed SWAT police surrounded his car, pointing their stubby automatic rifles at his face. With a sickening, stomach-churning feeling, he realized it was all over. *I'm sorry, Lexi. I'm sorry I let you down.*

Chapter 72

Vancouver, Canada

Lexi paced her stock trading room, staring tensely at the wall clock. *Something's wrong. Terribly wrong.* Her heart raced and her migraine pounded with a vengeance. *The colonel should have called me hours ago.*

Lexi gazed at the TV screens on the wall, all tuned to news channels. None had reported an explosion in New York City. She continued pacing, her thoughts dark and tortured.

Just then her intercom buzzed and she heard Shawn's voice. "There's a call for you, Lexi."

"Is it the colonel?" she asked, her hopes lifting.

"No. It's the other man. The man with no name."

"Put him through."

She sat down at her workstation, picked up the handset of her encrypted phone and took the call.

"I have something for you," the man said in his deep baritone. "And it's not good news."

Lexi verified his identity with her voice analyzer. "Go ahead, tell me," she said, steeling herself for the worst.

"Your man," he said, "was arrested in Manhattan."

She swallowed hard. "And the package?"

"It didn't detonate. A SWAT unit arrested your man before it exploded. The NYPD bomb squad defused it."

Lexi had trouble breathing. "How...how were they able...to catch him...."

"The NYPD anti-terrorism people are the best in the world. After Sept 11, 2001 they installed bomb-detection measures all over Manhattan."

The colonel warned me about this, she recalled. *But I didn't listen.*

"And there's something else, Lexi. Something worse."

"Worse? What the hell could be worse?"

"The Canadian government is now involved. I have it on good authority they're preparing an arrest warrant for you. They're coordinating with the FBI."

"Damn it all to hell!" she screeched into the phone.

"I'm sorry to be the bearer of bad news, but you need to know. That's what you pay me for. To keep you informed."

Lexi massaged her temple with a hand, trying to rub away the pounding headache. "Yes, yes, of course...thank you...I need to go...to get ready...."

"Of course, Lexi. Goodbye."

She hung up the call, her mind racing through several options. Coming to a decision a minute later, she stabbed her intercom. "Shawn, find Brad. I want him in my office immediately!"

"Yes, ma'am."

She sprinted out of her stock trading room and went into her office.

Her head of security came in a moment later and stood ramrod straight in front of her desk. "You needed to see me, Lexi?"

"I did. You were right. The Canadian Feds are on to me." She pointed at him. "Get everything ready. All the things we talked about. We need to go."

He nodded. "I understand."

"Don't just fucking stand there, Brad. Get going!"

He nodded, turned and left the office.

Lexi massaged her temple again for long moment, then stabbed the intercom device. "Shawn, please come into my office. I need to speak with you."

"Yes, of course."

The young man came in and closed the door behind him.

Lexi took an envelope out of her desk drawer, stood, and motioned to the couches in the office. "Let's sit over there, okay?"

They sat next to each other on one of the leather sofas and he said, "Would you like to review the financial statements? I've liquidated the stocks and bonds as you requested. The money is in your Swiss numbered accounts."

"I've already checked it. You did an excellent job," she said. "I have to speak with you about something else. I want to give you this." She handed him the envelope.

"What is it?"

"I've set up a trust fund for your family, Shawn. In the amount of twenty million dollars."

His eyebrows shot up. "You're kidding, right?"

"No. I'm absolutely serious. It's all spelled out in the documents. I've set up a bank account in the name of your wife and children. They can start using the funds immediately. Read it. It's all in there."

He opened the envelope and scanned the contents. "Oh, my God, Lexi! I don't know what to say. Except...thank you! Thank you from the bottom of my heart."

She caressed his face with her palm and stared into his sensitive and beautiful gray eyes. "I told you I would take care of your family."

"You did. I remember you saying that."

"I always keep my word, Shawn. Always."

Then his eyes grew wary. "There's more to this, though."

Lexi nodded. "I'm afraid so." She paused a moment to collect her thoughts. "I have some other less pleasant news. You remember the FBI people that came to see me a little while back?"

"Yes."

"Those people have spoken with the Canadian authorities and created a hornet's nest for me. The bottom line is, Shawn, I have to leave Vancouver. Immediately."

"Where will you go?"

"I don't know for sure yet. Maybe Russia. Prime Minister Pushkin has promised me a safe haven there."

"I see."

She reached out and covered one of his hands with both of hers. "I want you to come with me."

"But I live here, my family lives here. Are you asking for us to come with you?"

She shook her head. "That won't be possible. I can only take you." She saw the uncertainty and anguish in his eyes.

"Are you asking me to leave them, Lexi?"

"I am. I know this is hard for you, honey." She caressed his cheek. "But I need you. After my dear Sergei was taken away from me, you've been there for me. I care for you. Very much. In my own way, I do love you."

"I'm sorry," he replied. "I can't leave them."

"Please, honey. Think about it. I'll share everything with you. Billions of dollars. You'll never have to work another day in your life."

He stared down at the floor and sat there quietly for a long moment, deep in thought. Finally he raised his head and stared at her, his eyes sad.

"I'm sorry, Lexi. I can't leave them. And there's something else. I know how headstrong you are. I'd be a kept man. A junior partner at best."

"Is that your final answer?"

He nodded. "It is."

"All right. I understand. I'm not happy about it. I think we would have made a hell of a team. But I do understand."

"What about the money?" he said. "The twenty million dollars?"

"Don't worry, honey. That's yours. I'm not taking it back."

"Thank you."

"I have to go now, Shawn. Brad is getting everything ready. But before I go, will you at least share a glass of wine with me? Please? For old times sake?"

"Yes, of course."

"Excellent. I've been saving this one bottle of Merlot for a special occasion. It's a very rare vintage. And what could be more special than this? Two close friends saying goodbye for the last time."

She stood, went to the liquor cabinet and uncorked the incredibly expensive bottle of red wine. She poured out two goblets and walked back to the couch. Handing him one of the glasses, she sat next to him and raised her glass in the air. "A toast. To a bright future. For me, wherever I end up. And to you Shawn and your lovely family."

He smiled, clinked his glass to hers and took a sip of wine.

"Drink it all, honey," she said. "It's a very rare vintage. I paid ten thousand dollars for that bottle of Merlot."

Shawn drank down the whole glass, then leaned back and rested his head on the sofa. "I'm a little dizzy...." he managed to say, his empty glass falling from his hand and dropping to the floor.

After another moment his body twitched and his eyes rolled white.

"I'm sorry, Shawn. I really am."

Then Lexi stood and raced out of her office, in a hurry to leave Vancouver.

Chapter 73

Vancouver Island, Canada

J.T. Ryan was riding in the passenger seat of the police SUV when his cell phone buzzed. Ryan pulled out the phone and glanced at the info screen, which read *Langley*.

"Ryan here," he said, taking the call.

"It's Miller," he heard the CIA man say. "Where are you now?"

"Headed to Atwood's mansion. The Vancouver police just got an arrest warrant for her."

"Excellent. Good work on coordinating with them."

"Thank you, sir."

"I've got some great news, Ryan. We got him!"

"Got who?"

"Scarman. The NYPD arrested him. Scarman was about to blow up the Freedom Tower in New York City."

"Thank God." Ryan mulled this over a second. "What about the rest of the bombs? Where they found also?"

"No. Scarman's been interrogated but he won't tell us where they are."

"Damn it."

"The nuclear devices may be stored at Atwood's home," Miller said.

"I was thinking the same thing, sir. When we raid her house and arrest her, I'm hoping we'll find the bombs there. We know Scarman met with Atwood at her mansion."

"Call me as soon as you have her in custody," Miller said.

"Will do."

"By the way, Ryan, there's something else you need to know. Something critical."

"What's that, sir?"

"When I met with President Harris yesterday, he signed a Presidential Directive. If Lexi Atwood tries to flee before you arrest her, you're authorized to terminate her. With extreme prejudice."

"I can cancel her?"

"That's correct," the CIA man said and hung up.

Ryan put his phone away and turned to the uniformed officer driving the SUV. "How close are we to her house, Sergeant?"

"Almost there," Sergeant Baker replied.

Five minutes later the SUV slowed and then stopped in front of a gated estate. An eight-foot brick wall surrounded the large property. The squad cars and other police vehicles that were following Ryan's SUV continued on the residential street and took positions all along the walls to prevent escape. Ryan heard the rotors from police helicopters circling overhead.

Sergeant Baker lowered his window and pressed a button on the intercom by the ornate, wrought-iron entrance gate.

"This is the Vancouver police," he said. "We're here for Lexi Atwood. Open the gate."

A young woman's voice replied a moment later. "I'm opening it now."

The large wrought-iron gate creaked open slowly and the SUV, followed by two black-and-white squad cars, began driving through the immense wooded property. The SUV stopped in the circular driveway fronting the three-story mansion.

Baker turned off the vehicle and said to Ryan, "I'll take the lead and make the arrest. The FBI has no jurisdiction in Canada."

Ryan nodded. "I understand."

Baker, Ryan, and the two officers in the back of the SUV climbed out of the vehicle, drew their guns and cautiously strode up the flagstone steps to the massive front door. The uniformed cops in the squad cars got out of their vehicles also, and some of them joined Baker, while others went toward the side and back of the estate. A helicopter hovered overhead, the roar of the rotors clearly audible.

Before Baker had a chance to ring the ornate bell, the door was opened by a young Asian woman. Baker handed her a document. "This is an arrest warrant for Lexi Atwood," he said. "Take us to her now."

The Asian woman's face turned ashen. "Arrest? Mrs. Atwood? That's not possible."

Baker and Ryan pushed past her into a large marble-floor foyer, which was lit by an intricate cut-glass chandelier.

"Where is she?" Ryan demanded. "Which room?"

The Asian woman's eyes got big. "Mrs. Atwood...she's...she's not here...." She spoke in a shaky voice.

Sergeant Baker turned toward his cops. "Start searching the house. Find Atwood."

Baker and his men went deeper into the house, while Ryan stayed in the foyer with the frightened young woman.

"Where is Atwood?" he asked.

She shook her head. "I...I don't know...she left...."

Ryan's eyes bored into hers and he realized she was telling the truth. It was obvious from the tremor in her voice and her shaky hands.

Trying to calm her down and gather as much information as possible, he spoke in a soothing tone. "What's your name?"

"Sun-Yi," she said in her slightly accented English.

"What do you do here, Sun-Yi?"

"I'm...I'm the maid...I cook and clean."

"All right. You said Atwood left. Where did she go?"

The young woman shook her head. "I...don't know."

Ryan studied her pretty, doll-like face, trying to ascertain if she was lying. "When did she leave?"

"Two, maybe three hours ago."

"By car?"

She shook her head. "No. She left by helicopter."

"Who was with her?"

"Her head of security. Brad Murdock."

"Just the two of them?"

"Yes. Before she left, she had me help her pack some of her clothes and computers and files in large suitcases."

Ryan thought about the nuclear devices. "Did they take anything else? Think, Sun-Yi. It's important."

Her doll-like face scrunched in concentration. A minute later she spoke. "They took four large suitcases – but they were just packed with the clothing and files."

"Anything else?"

The young Asian woman mulled it over. "Yes. I remember now. Brad had a large bag on his back."

"A backpack? A black backpack?"

Sun-Yi nodded. "Yes. That's it."

One of the W-54s, Ryan realized.

"Is it true?" Sun-Yi asked, her eyes wide. "What the policeman said? That she's being arrested?"

"Yes, that's right."

"She's a criminal?"

"Yes."

"What did she do?"

"She's been charged with murder and terrorism."

Sun-Yi's face turned white again. "It can't be. Mrs. Atwood is a wonderful person. She treats me very well."

"Did you ever suspect she was a criminal?"

She shook her head forcefully. "No. Never." Then she said, "What happens to me? Will I be arrested also?"

"You'll be questioned, Sun-Yi. If the Canadian police determine you're not implicated in her crimes, you won't be arrested."

"Are you a policeman too?"

"I'm with the American FBI."

"Can you help me? Please help me. I don't want to go to jail."

"I will help you," he said, "if you tell me everything you can about Atwood. It will take the police time to search this large house, so we have plenty of time. If you cooperate with me I'll help you stay out of prison."

"Yes! Yes, of course."

"Start at the beginning. When did you first meet Lexi Atwood?"

Sun-Yi began talking and didn't stop for nearly an hour.

Then Sergeant Baker came back into the foyer, a dejected look on his face. "Atwood's gone," he said. "We've searched every inch of this place and the grounds. Twice. She's not here."

"What about the nuclear bombs?" Ryan said. "Did you find them?"

Baker shook his head. "No. They're not here."

Chapter 74

Vancouver Airport
Vancouver, Canada

Lexi settled back in the soft leather seat of her luxury Gulfstream G700 and closed her eyes, glad to be finally on her way. The jet could seat many people, but the only passengers were Lexi and Brad Murdock, who was seated a few rows toward the front.

The plane slowly rolled out of the private hangar and began moving on the tarmac toward the takeoff runway. The sound of the Gulfstream's jet engines increased from a muted whine to a roar and she realized they would be taking off soon.

Suddenly the engines powered down and the jet came to a halt a moment later.

Lexi's eyes snapped open. "Why did we stop, Brad?"

"I don't know."

"Find out!"

"Yes, ma'am." He bolted off his seat and sprinted to the cockpit and opened the door. He came back seconds later, shaking his head. "We've got problems, Lexi. Big problems. We're not cleared for takeoff. The police are here. And they have an arrest warrant for you."

As if on cue, she heard sirens in the distance. Glancing out of one of the windows, she spotted black-and-white squad cars and SUVs racing toward her plane. They came to a screeching halt all around the jet, blocking escape.

Heavily-armed police exited their vehicles, and using them for cover, pointed their weapons at the Gulfstream.

"What do we do now?" Brad said in a nervous voice.

She glared at him. "Shut the fuck up! Let me think!" She stared out the window as more police vehicles arrived. *Fuck!* her brain shouted. *It wasn't supposed to work out this way! Damn it all to hell!*

Then a thought occurred to her and she glowered at Brad. "Where's the package?"

"In the storage closet at the back of the plane."

"Go get it! Get it now!"

"Yes, Lexi."

The man raced back as she marshaled her thoughts. When Brad returned carrying the backpack, she said, "Turn it on. Set the timer to one hour."

His eyes looked uncertain. "Are you sure about this?"

"Just fucking do it!" she snapped, venom in her voice.

"Yes, Lexi."

Brad rested the black bag on one of the leather seats and unzipped it open. Then he flicked a switch and a green light came on the control pad. After that he adjusted the dial and began adding minutes to the readout until it reached 60.

"Turn it on, Brad."

This time he didn't question her and simply pressed another button on the controls. The solid green light started blinking.

"Now," she barked, "get me the phone number of whoever's running this shit show out there." She pointed to the cockpit. "Find out! Now!"

Brad ran forward and came back a moment later with a slip of paper. "This is the number of the police captain down there."

Lexi grabbed the paper, took out her cell phone and punched in the number.

"Captain," she said, "this is Lexi Atwood. I have a nuclear bomb on this plane. I've activated it, and I will blow myself up and everyone within a five-mile radius of here unless I get what I want. Do you understand?"

"Yes, ma'am," the captain replied. "Tell me what you want."

"Hell, no! I'll only talk to one person. His name is John Ryan. He's an FBI agent and he's here somewhere in Vancouver. Find him and get him here now!"

"I'm in charge here, ma'am. You can deal with me."

"Do you want fifty thousand people to die today?" she screeched. "Don't test me, Captain. I can make it happen!"

"Calm down, please."

"I will not calm down. Find Ryan! Bring him here! Or this bomb goes off."

Chapter 75

Vancouver, Canada

The police sergeant's cell phone rang and he took one hand off the steering wheel and picked up the call. "Sergeant Baker speaking."

He listened a moment, then glanced at J.T. Ryan who was sitting in the passenger seat of the police SUV. "Yes, Captain. Ryan is with me."

Baker listened some more and hung up the call. "Tighten your seatbelt, Ryan."

Ryan did so. "What's going on, Sergeant?"

"I've got two minutes to get you to the airport. If I don't, I'll lose my job." He pressed buttons on the dash of the SUV and a deafening siren blared. And blue lights flashed from the vehicle's roof-bar. The sergeant floored the accelerator and began weaving through the traffic around them.

Ryan hung on to the seat and put another hand on the dash to steady himself as the SUV roared past the other cars. Three minutes later Ryan spotted the Vancouver Airport sign, the vehicle swerved right, took the exit ramp at high speed, and with its sirens blaring and blue lights flashing, made its way toward the runway areas. Moments later it screeched to a halt on the tarmac, joining a sea of other police vehicles which had surrounded a red Gulfstream jet.

The sergeant pointed to one of the uniformed officers taking cover behind a squad car. "That's Captain Lewis over there. Get going!"

Ryan climbed out of the SUV and sprinted to the squad car. "I'm John Ryan," he said, crouching next to the police captain, as he flashed his FBI credentials.

"She'll only talk to you," the captain said.

"Who are you talking about?"

"Lexi Atwood. She's in that plane. And she says she's got a nuclear bomb and threatens to blow it up. I can't confirm she really has the bomb, but there's no way for me to dispute it either."

Ryan nodded. "It's true. She has one. What does she want?"

The captain shook his head. "Don't know. She wouldn't talk to me. Demanded she'll only deal with you."

"All right. Should I go to the plane now?"

"Are you armed, Ryan?"

"Yeah."

"Leave it with me. She said no guns and no cell phones."

Ryan unbuttoned his blazer, removed his .357 Magnum from the holster and handed the weapon and his phone to the other man. Then he reached down, pulled up his pant's leg and removed a snub-nose .38 revolver from his ankle holster. After giving the gun to the officer, he said, "Any advice you can give me?"

The captain shrugged. "I can tell you one thing for sure. This Atwood woman is insane. I got the impression she's not afraid to blow herself up."

"I agree with you. She is crazy. But she's also smart."

Ryan stood, strode around the squad car, and with his hands up in the air, began walking toward the red Gulfstream. When he got to the plane's airstairs, the side door of the jet opened.

He climbed up the stairs slowly, his hands up in the air. When he reached the open doorway, he called out in a loud voice, "I'm John Ryan. I'm unarmed."

"Get in here!" a woman shouted from inside the jet.

Ryan slowly went through the doorway and stepped inside. He saw Atwood right away, her arms folded across her chest. Standing next to her was a tall, blond man pointing a submachine gun at Ryan's head.

"It took you long enough," Atwood said. The woman was wearing a crimson pantsuit and her red tresses were pulled back into a ponytail. She looked just as beautiful as when he'd seen her last, but this time her coal-black eyes burned with a fierce determination that appeared insane and demonic.

"I'm unarmed," Ryan said, still holding his hands up in the air.

"Let's make sure," Atwood replied, picking up a wand device and walking toward him. "And no sudden moves, Ryan. Brad's a good shot and he's got an itchy trigger finger." Atwood stopped in front of him and slowly waved the wand device all over his body.

"Looks like you're telling the truth," she said and grinned wickedly. "But there's one last check I need to do. Hold still, Ryan."

Atwood reached out with a hand and cupped his pants at the groin. Her smile widened. "Just as I thought. You're hung like a horse." She began to slowly stroke him with her hand, the wicked grin not leaving her face.

She is insane, he realized. But in spite of the tenseness of the situation he became aroused from her erotic touching. He pushed aside the sexual thoughts and said, "What do you want, Atwood?"

Her grin faded and she walked back to where her accomplice was standing, still holding the submachine gun pointed at Ryan's head.

"You can put your hands down now," she said and he lowered his arms.

"It should be obvious what I want," she continued. "To get the hell out of here. Let my plane go."

Ryan shook his head. "That's never going to happen, lady. The Canadians will never agree to that."

"It will happen," she replied in a defiant tone. "Or I'll blow myself up and everyone within a five-mile radius of this airport. I figure there's fifty thousand people who will die. Maybe more."

"You won't do it, Atwood. I think you're crazy. But not that crazy. You won't kill yourself."

Her coal-black eyes blazed with fury. "Want to bet?"

He stared into her demonic eyes and realized she was willing to commit suicide. "How do I know you even have a nuclear bomb here?"

Atwood turned toward her bodyguard. "Give me the gun, Brad. Then bring the package. Show him."

The man nodded, handed her the submachine gun, then walked to a nearby seat, picked up a black backpack and rested it on a seat right by Ryan. He unzipped the bag so Ryan could see inside.

One look is all it took. The bomb was identical to the one Ryan had seen in Los Alamos. It was a W-54, he was sure of it. The green light was blinking and the timer was counting down the minutes and seconds. The screen read: 24 minutes.

"Satisfied now?" Atwood said, holding the submachine gun pointed at him.

"Yes," he replied.

"Call them now, Ryan. Call the police captain who's in charge of the cluster fuck down there. Clear the runway so I can get the hell out of here."

"They'll never let you go, Atwood. You're a wanted terrorist. Give yourself up. It's your only hope."

Her eyes flashed again. "You really think I could live in a hellhole of a prison? With those animals in there? Eating shit food? Wearing a foul-smelling orange jumpsuit?" She grinned wickedly again. "In case you hadn't noticed, I only wear red."

She really is crazy. That's obvious. But it's also clear she won't surrender.

He glanced at the bomb's digital screen. It now read: 19 minutes. He swallowed hard.

Lexi's bodyguard walked back to where she was standing and she handed over the submachine gun. Then she faced Ryan. "I propose a trade," she said. "I give you something extremely valuable and you let me go."

"What can you give me?" Ryan said.

"I tell you where the rest of the bombs are. The six that are left over."

"Where are they?"

Atwood shook her head. "You haven't agreed to let me go. Agree first and I tell you."

"It's not up to me to let you go." Ryan pointed to the windows of the plane. "It's up to them. The Canadian authorities."

"Then you have to convince them. Your life, my friend, depends on it."

Ryan thought furiously for a long moment.

Then she said, "I'll give you something else to sweeten the deal. I'll tell you who the mole is in the U.S. government. The spy I have in Washington, D.C."

"You'll give me that also?"

"I will." She motioned to the bomb's digital counter. "Call them now, Ryan. You only have fifteen minutes left."

"I don't have my phone on me. I left it with the police."

She took out her cell phone and handed it to him. "Use mine. Now hurry. Only fourteen minutes left."

Ryan took the phone and pressed on the last number called.

"Captain Lewis here."

"Captain, this is John Ryan. You have to let Atwood's plane go. She'll blow herself up otherwise. I saw the bomb myself. It's real. It's a nuclear device. There's only fourteen minutes left before it blows up. And if we let Atwood go, she'll tell us where the rest of the bombs are located."

"I can't agree to let her go, Ryan. I don't have the authority. I have to get my commander to agree, and he'll have to get the police chief to agree, and he in turn will have to get the Vancouver mayor to agree –"

"That's going to take too damn long!" Ryan shouted. "We only have twelve minutes left. Do you want fifty thousand people to die?"

"Of course not!"

"Then do it, Captain! Clear the runway!"

"I can't. I told you I don't have the authority."

"Are you married, Captain? Do you have children?"

"Yes, I do. But what does that have to do with anything?"

"If you want your widow to raise your kids without a father, then do nothing. Otherwise, clear the damn runway!"

There was silence from the other end. Then Ryan said, "Are you still there?"

"Yes, yes, I'll do it. I'll clear the runway."

Ryan clutched the phone tightly. "Thank you, Captain. Do it now!"

He hung up and returned Atwood's phone to her, then glanced out of the plane's windows. He noticed police cars moving away from the jet. He breathed a long sigh of relief.

Ryan faced Atwood. "Tell me where the bombs are."

"Good work," she said, grinning. "I knew you could do it." She cocked her head. "I could use a man like you in my organization. Pity we have so little time left for me to convince you to come join me. I could make you extremely rich. And now that I've lost my precious Shawn, I need a right hand man to take his place."

Ryan glanced at the timer readout, saw there were only ten minutes left. "Please Atwood, tell me where the bombs are."

She turned toward her bodyguard. "Keep the gun trained on Ryan the whole time, Brad. If he tries anything, shoot him." Then she faced Ryan. "All right," she said. "You've held up your end of the bargain. So I'll tell you. Prime Minister Pushkin has the nuclear weapons now."

"The Russians have them?"

"Yes."

"How do I know you're not lying?"

"Because I'm not. You'll have to trust me."

He stared at her coal-black eyes and sensed she was telling the truth. "All right, Atwood. I believe you. Now, who's the mole? The leaker in the U.S. government?"

Lexi Atwood told him and his mouth hung open in shock.

"He's the mole?"

She nodded. "Yes. He's the one."

Ryan shook his head slowly, saddened and horrified to find out who it was. Then he looked at the readout on the bomb. It read three minutes left.

"Turn if off!" Ryan yelled at her. "Or we're all going to die."

She grinned, her eyes blazing with a demonic intensity. "Yes, we are John Ryan."

"Turn it off, please," he said as he watched the seconds tick off.

"Can I call you J.T.?" she asked, the grin still on her face. "That's what that blonde woman called you."

"Yes, yes! Just turn it off or we're going to blow up."

"Come with me, J.T. We could make a hell of a team, you and I...."

The seconds ticked down. Now there was only one minute left. Perspiration ran down his face.

"I can't go with you, Atwood."

"Is that your final answer, J.T.?"

"Yes."

"Pity."

Ryan stared at the readout as seconds ticked off. 43...42...41...40...39....

The bodyguard kept the submachine gun pointed at Ryan the whole time.

"We could have made a hell of a team, J.T.," she said. Finally Atwood shrugged her shoulders and walked over to the nuclear device and pressed a button. The readout froze at 13 seconds.

Ryan breathed a long sigh of relief.

Atwood folded her arms in front of her. "Now get the hell off my plane, Ryan."

"Gladly."

She pointed a finger at his face. "And remember, if the police get any ideas about trying to double-cross me and stop my plane, I will blow up this bomb. You know I will do it."

He nodded. "I know."

She smiled and this time it wasn't a wicked or demonic grin. It was an endearing, beautiful smile. "I like you, J.T. I told you that a few weeks ago. You remind me of my dear husband, Sergei, God bless his soul. Pity you won't come with me."

Then her smile vanished. "Leave the plane now, J.T."

Ryan nodded and headed for the door, the submachine gun pointed at him the whole way. When he reached the airstairs, he climbed down and walked back to the squad car where Captain Lewis was.

Ryan and Lewis stood by the car as the Gulfstream's engines powered up and the plane rolled on the tarmac toward the runway. The jet reached it a minute later then the roar of the plane's engines became deafening. The red Gulfstream thundered down the runway and lifted off.

Ryan lost sight of the plane as it disappeared into the clouds.

Chapter 76

Vancouver, Canada

J.T. Ryan retrieved his weapons and phone from Captain Lewis and said, "I've got to make an urgent phone call, but it's too damn loud out here on the tarmac."

"Use my car," the captain replied. "I'm not going anywhere. I'll be answering questions from my superiors about this thing for hours."

Ryan got in the passenger seat of the sedan and slammed the door shut. He pulled out his cell phone and punched in a number.

The CIA Deputy Director answered on the first ring. "Miller here."

"It's Ryan, sir. I need to tell you what's happening."

"We already know. I'm at the White House with the President. The Canadian Prime Minister called us here at the Oval Office and briefed us about Vancouver. He even provided security camera footage of what occurred at the airport. We saw you walk into Atwood's plane and saw you walk out. Tell us what happened when you were in there, Ryan. I'll put this call on speaker so that President Harris and General Foster can hear you."

"Yes, sir," Ryan said. "By the way, where you able to track Atwood's plane after it took off?"

"The Vancouver airport tower and the Canadian Air Force tracked the jet's movement for about two minutes, then the plane dropped to a very low altitude and the radar lost it. All we know is she's headed west over the Pacific."

"Damn," Ryan said.

"We said the same thing," the CIA man replied, "but we used stronger language. Now tell us what happened."

"Sir, I had no choice but to let Atwood go. She had one of the W-54s on the plane – and it was clear to me she's insane enough to commit suicide. Up to 50,000 people could have died, including me, if she'd exploded the nuclear device."

"We figured as much," President Harris said, taking over the conversation from Miller.

"Mr. President," Ryan continued, "when I was negotiating with Atwood, I was able to obtain extremely valuable information from her."

"What is it?"

"Sir, she told me who has the rest of the nuclear devices. The six W-54s that remain."

"Who?" the President asked.

"The Russian government. Prime Minister Pushkin."

"Are you sure about this, Ryan? Maybe Atwood made this up."

"She's telling the truth, Mr. President. I'm sure of it. Remember, she's Russian herself. And Scarman was a colonel in the GRU at one time, that's the Russian military intelligence service. I suspect Atwood and Pushkin have some kind of deal going on. Possibly he offered her a safe haven, a place to hide in Russia in exchange for the bombs."

"That makes sense. After we get through with this call, I'll deal with the Russians."

"Yes, sir. There's something else I was able to obtain from Atwood."

"What is it?"

"Mr. President, she gave me the name of the leak. The traitor we've been looking for. The government employee on Atwood's payroll."

"Tell us."

Ryan told them who the person was.

"Damn!" the President shouted. "Him? I never suspected him. Are you certain this is true?"

"I'm positive. Atwood wasn't lying. Her own life was on the line. She's obviously insane and a killer, but she was desperate to escape prison and flee."

"All right, Ryan. I'll deal with the traitor as soon as I'm done with the Russians."

"Yes, sir."

"Excellent work on finding all this out," the President said. "Your country owes you a big debt of gratitude."

"Thank you, Mr. President." He paused a moment and then with a chuckle said, "Does that mean I get a bonus?"

"Don't push it," Harris said testily.

"Sorry, sir," Ryan replied, immediately regretting his glib remark.

"You're a hell of a good operator, Ryan. But your joking around is going to get you killed one day. I've read your military record when you were in the Army. You could have made colonel, maybe even brigadier, but instead you couldn't get promoted higher than captain. Your cavalier attitude held you back."

He's absolutely right, Ryan thought. "Yes, sir. That's true."

"All right," President Harris said. "I'm ending this call now. I've got the Russians to deal with."

Ryan heard a click on the line and knew the President had hung up.

Chapter 77

The Oval Office
The White House
Washington, D.C.

President Harris leaned forward in his executive chair and placed his hands flat on his desk.

He faced General Foster, who was sitting on one of the wingback chairs in front of the desk. "General, I want the U.S.'s military readiness raised to DEFCON 2 immediately. Go do that now."

The general stood. "Yes, sir."

When Foster left the room, Harris faced Alex Miller. "Do you think Atwood was telling the truth about Prime Minister Pushkin having the nuclear devices?"

"Ryan thinks so," Miller replied, "and I trust his judgment. Ryan may be a cowboy and a loose cannon, but he's the best covert operator in the business."

Harris nodded. "I agree." He pressed a button on the intercom device on his desk. "Margaret," he said, "call the Kremlin. Right now. Tell them I have to have a video call with Pushkin immediately. Don't take no for an answer. Tell them it's an urgent national security matter."

"Yes, Mr. President," the woman's voice came back. "I'll take care of it."

***

President Harris watched the large flatscreen TV, which was positioned in a corner of the Oval Office. A woman was on the screen, introducing the Prime Minister. The camera angle moved and Pushkin came into view, sitting behind an imposing desk.

"Mr. President," Pushkin said with that shark-like grin of his, "how good of you to call. It has been some time since we spoke last."

"This isn't a social call," Harris stated, a hard edge in his voice. "It's a matter of national security."

Pushkin's eyebrows arched. "I see. How can I be of help?"

"Prime Minister, we know for a fact that you are in possession of six of our backpack nuclear devices. Six W-54s to be precise. These weapons were stolen from our Los Alamos labs and we demand their immediate return."

A puzzled expression settled on the Russian Prime Minister's face. "With all due respect, Mr. President, I don't know what you are talking about. You must be misinformed."

"Cut the bullshit, Pushkin. You know exactly what I'm talking about. You got the bombs from a Canadian woman, Lexi Atwood. This woman was born in Russia and her real name is Alexandra Ivanova."

The Prime Minister's eyes bulged and he rubbed his face with a hand. He said nothing for a long moment. "If this was true," Pushkin said eventually, "which I am not admitting it is, why would we want to return them? Hypothetically, if we had obtained them, we paid a fair price for them. So they would now be our property."

Harris slammed both fists on his desk. "Do not test me, Prime Minister! You have them and I demand you return them immediately. Or else."

Pushkin said nothing, then his shark-like grin returned. "Or else what?"

"Or else I will fucking blow Moscow off the face of the map. Our military forces are now at DEFCON 2. If I give the order we will go to DEFCON 1 and 500 of our ICBM nuclear missiles will launch immediately and completely destroy you and a large chunk of your country."

The Prime Minister's face blanched. He motioned to someone off-screen and two uniformed military generals came into view. The three men huddled for several minutes and then Pushkin waved them away and faced Harris.

"I have been informed by my generals," Pushkin said, "that what you are threatening is true. In light of this, I agree to your request. We will return the six backpack bombs to you."

President Harris nodded. "Excellent. I will immediately dispatch one of our military transport jets to Moscow to pick them up today. Is that understood?"

"Yes, Mr. President. We will clear your plane into our airspace. Our people will coordinate with yours. I will personally make sure everything goes smoothly."

"I appreciate your cooperation," Harris said in a calm voice.

"Of course. By the way, there is a G-20 meeting in Paris a few months from now. I am sure we will see each other there."

"I look forward to it, Prime Minister. Until then."

The President pressed a button on his desk and the TV screen went dark. Then he faced General Foster. "General, arrange for the military transport plane. And follow this through to the very end. I don't want anything to go wrong."

The general stood. "Yes, sir. I'll take care of it."

When the military officer left, Harris faced Alex Miller. "Now that we've settled that matter, I need to take care of our other problem."

Miller nodded. "Yes, Mr. President."

Chapter 78

The Oval Office
The White House
Washington, D.C.

The door to the Oval Office opened and the FBI Director came into the room. His name was Scott Cooper and he was a tall, imposing-looking man with a florid complexion and distinguished silver hair. He was wearing an impeccably-tailored gray pinstripe business suit, a starched long-sleeve white shirt with gold cufflinks, and a royal blue silk tie.

Alex Miller watched as the FBI man approached the President's desk and stood in front of it. "You wanted to see me, Mr. President?" Cooper said in his trademark deep-baritone voice.

President Harris leaned forward in his executive chair. "I did." He waved the man to one of the wingback armchairs fronting his desk. "Have a seat."

Besides the President, Miller and Cooper, there were four other people in the Oval Office. They were Secret Service agents who stood silently at one side of the office.

The President faced the FBI Director. "How long have we known each other, Scott?"

The FBI man scrunched his face in concentration. "Many, many years, sir. Easily over ten."

Harris nodded. "And how long have you been my director of the Bureau?"

"Two years."

Harris nodded again. "Which makes your actions inexplicable, Scott. I've always considered you a man of integrity. An honorable man. And a man, who until very recently, I considered a close friend."

Cooper's face clouded with uncertainty. "What are you talking about?" he asked in his deep-baritone.

"I know for a fact, Scott, that you are a traitor to our country."

"Is this a joke, Mr. President? How can you even imply such a thing? I love the USA and everything it stands for."

Miller listened to the assured way the FBI Director spoke and realized Cooper was a consummate liar. *No wonder people always trusted him. No wonder the President never suspected he was the mole.*

President Harris shook his head slowly and had a pained expression on his face. "You can deny it all you want, Scott. But it won't help you. We know you've been secretly working for a Canadian billionaire named Lexi Atwood. You've been keeping her apprised of our investigation of the terrorist bombings."

Cooper opened his mouth and tried to speak but no words came out. His florid complexion drained from his face. He glanced at Alex Miller then faced Harris again. "Sir...sir...it's not true...." he managed to utter, but the self-assured tone was gone, replaced by a weak, pleading voice. "Sir, there must be...some mistake...."

"It's all over, Scott," Harris said. "Atwood gave you up to save her own skin. I assume you did it for the money, one of the oldest motives in the history of man." Harris shook his head again. "Greed. I never suspected you. Not once. But now that we know what's happened, I'm sure we'll be able to track the money she paid you. No doubt to some offshore bank account you set up."

The FBI Director closed his eyes and rubbed his face with both hands as if he was trying to make the meeting disappear. When he opened his eyes, he said, "What happens now?"

The President waved over the four Secret Service agents that were in the office. "These men will take you into custody. I suggest you don't resist, Scott. They're well armed. You'll be charged with treason and for colluding in the murder of thousands of Americans. You'll be tried, and I'm sure convicted. I expect you'll spend the rest of your miserable life in a Supermax prison." He paused a moment, then continued. "I wish this was the Wild West and we could dispense with a trial. We'd simply hang you from the nearest tree."

The President faced the Secret Service agents. "Take this traitorous bastard away. I can't stand to look at him anymore."

Chapter 79

FBI Field Office
Atlanta, Georgia

"I still can't believe Scott Cooper was the mole," Erin Welch said, shaking her head. "I worked for that man for two years and never suspected him."

"I agree, Erin," J.T. Ryan replied. "I never thought it was him either. But don't beat yourself up over it. Cooper fooled the President and everyone else in Washington D.C."

The two people were in Erin's office in the FBI building.

Ryan rubbed his jaw. "Any leads on Atwood's whereabouts?"

"None. The CIA, FBI, DHS, NSA, and every other law-enforcement and intelligence agency is on the lookout. She's the world's most-wanted terrorist. The manhunt for her is taking place in every country on earth. She'll be found eventually."

Ryan nodded. "When I left Vancouver, the Canadians were putting every available resource into catching her. The government there is extremely embarrassed that Atwood is a Canadian citizen, and a very prominent one at that."

"By the way," Erin said, "President Harris called me this morning and gave me good news. The Russians have complied fully and the nuclear bombs are now back in our possession. They're back where they started, in Los Alamos Laboratory."

"That is good news."

"Yes, it is, J.T. The President told me something else."

"What?"

Erin leaned forward in her chair. "He offered me the top job at the FBI."

Ryan grinned. "That's great! What did you say?"

"I told him I'd think about it."

"I'm surprised you didn't accept right away, Erin." He smiled again. "Erin Welch, FBI Director. It has a great ring to it."

Erin returned the smile. "It does sound good. But remember, I worked in Washington D.C. before, and I hated it. It's a swamp. A deep, snake-filled sewer that gets worse every day." She paused a moment. "And I'd hate to break up the team that's solved so many cases. You know, you and I. Welch and Ryan."

Ryan laughed. "I always thought of it as Ryan and Welch."

"Smartass."

He laughed again. "Guilty as charged."

Just then there was a knock on the door and it opened partway. Erin's assistant was there. "Erin," he said, "a video has just been released to the news media worldwide. The video is from Lexi Atwood."

"You have a copy of this video?" Erin said.

"I do." The young man held up a flash drive.

"Bring it in here," she said, "and put it on my TV."

The assistant came into the office, turned on the television and inserted the flash drive.

Ryan watched as Lexi Atwood came on the screen. She didn't look nearly as beautiful as when he'd seen her last. She had a tired, haggard appearance and had dark circles under her eyes. Her long, reddish hair was unkempt and the red pantsuit she wore was wrinkled.

"My name is Lexi Atwood," she began, her voice sounding nervous. The bravado of her usual tone was totally absent. "I am a Canadian citizen. And I want to direct my comments today to the people and the city that I love so much, Vancouver." She stopped talking and hand-brushed her long tresses.

"I love you, Vancouver," she continued, "the magnificent city where my beloved husband Sergei and I called home for so many years. Unfortunately, as you all know, I had to flee Vancouver because I've been charged with heinous crimes. Crimes for which I'm not guilty. Please know that. I admit I'm a greedy, selfish woman. But everything I did was completely legal."

Lexi Atwood paused again and stared right at the camera. "Two weeks ago, I fled Vancouver. At that time, I could have blown myself up. But I did not. I could not do that. I could never kill thousands and thousands of innocent Canadians. Instead I fled. I realize now, two weeks after I went on the run, that my situation is hopeless. I am, sadly, a wanted terrorist. A terrorist sought by every police organization in the world."

She paused again and when she continued, it was in the defiant tone Ryan remembered from their last meeting. "I am not guilty of these heinous crimes. I am an innocent woman. But it's clear to me now that I can never clear my name. The American FBI has tarnished my reputation forever. And once I'm caught, as I'm sure I will be, I'll be put in a foul, disgusting prison. For the rest of my life."

Atwood's coal-black eyes blazed with intensity. "I will never let that happen! I cannot let that happen. I am a proud woman. And I cannot accept the indignity of being caged like an animal for the rest of my life. That is why I have chosen the only path left to me."

She took in a long breath and let it out slowly. "As you all know by now, when I fled Vancouver I had in my possession a package. A very special package. I believe the technical term for the package is a W-54. Most people would refer to it as a backpack nuclear bomb. So, my beloved people of Vancouver, I saved all of you two weeks ago. But sadly it appears I cannot save myself."

Lexi Atwood stood up from the table she was sitting behind and moved a few feet to the left. Resting on the table was a black backpack, which she unzipped open so that the W-54 was clearly visible. Then she began adjusting the controls on the display panel.

Ryan could easily make out the details of the W-54. It was the one he had seen two weeks earlier on Atwood's plane.

When Atwood was done adjusting the bomb's controls, she stared at the camera again. "Sadly, I must leave you now. The time has come for my final farewell. Goodbye, my beloved people of Vancouver. Goodbye and Godspeed."

She glanced at the nuclear device's control panel and shut her eyes tightly.

Five seconds later the television screen glowed bright red and yellow and orange as a deafening roar emitted from the TV's speakers.

Then the screen went black.

Chapter 80

The Oval Office
The White House
Washington, D.C.

"Thank you all for coming," President Harris said, as he commenced the meeting.

Sitting in front of the President's historic desk, Resolute, were three people. They were J.T. Ryan, Erin Welch, and Alex Miller. Standing near the desk was General Foster.

The President leaned forward in his executive chair. "As you all know by now, one week ago, Lexi Atwood blew herself up with one of the nuclear devices. Our law-enforcement agencies and our military have confirmed she was on a small island she owned in the middle of the Pacific Ocean. From satellite images we have over that area prior to the explosion, this island had a runway that could accommodate her jet. Also on this island was a large home and a few other small buildings. As a result of the explosion, the island and everything on it was vaporized. It appears she had planned to live there when she escaped Vancouver, but obviously chose to commit suicide instead. The nuclear bomb's mushroom cloud towered over that area and was clearly visible on satellite images. And our naval ships that were dispatched to the area confirm the radioactivity of the region where the island once stood."

The President rubbed is jaw. "Atwood was correct during her final video statement. She would have been found. She would have been tried and convicted. And she would have spent the rest of her life in prison."

Harris leaned back in his executive chair. "I brought all of you here to commend you for the excellent job that you did in tracking down this terrorist."

The President paused and gazed at the meeting's attendees. "There's someone missing. Where's agent Rachel West? From everything I've been told, West was an integral part of this team."

"Sir," CIA Deputy Director Miller interjected, "Rachel West couldn't be here. Something urgent came up."

"That's too bad," Harris said. "All right, let's continue then. As I told you at the beginning of this operation, everything you've done must remain secret. You have all done an exemplary job in protecting our country and saving thousands of innocent lives. But unfortunately, as is the case with all covert operations, your participation will remain secret and you will not receive public recognition. A few years ago, when I created this team, you likewise did an exemplary job. At the completion of that operation, you received the Medal of Honor."

The President smiled. "This time I wanted to award all of you a different kind of medal. Something much more practical." He looked over at General Foster, who was standing a feet from the desk. "Let's have them, General."

The general was carrying an ornate wooden box which he placed on the desk.

The President opened the box and took out one of the medallions stored inside. He held it up in the air so everyone could see it. Ryan noticed it was a heavy gold coin about the same size and thickness of a silver dollar. The Presidential seal was embossed on both sides of the coin.

"This medallion," Harris said, "is a very special coin. Only a few have been minted. In fact, I'm the first President who authorized their manufacture. These coins don't have the status of the Medal of Honor you received last time. But as I said earlier, this is much more practical. Think of it as a 'Get out of jail' card. If any of you, in the future, get into a bad situation, you can bring me this coin and I will make your problem go away. It could be in the form of a Presidential Pardon or some other solution to your predicament. As President of this country, I can fix almost anything."

Harris's gaze focused on Ryan. "J.T, I'm thinking you'll be the first in this group to need a 'Get out of jail' card."

Ryan chuckled at this. "I believe you're right, Mr. President."

Harris handed the medallion to Ryan, who read the inscription closely, then pocketed it.

"Thank you, sir," Ryan said.

The President smiled. "You earned it, my friend."

Harris then took two coins out of the box, which he handed to Alex Miller. "Alex, one of these is for you and the other for Rachel West. Please see that she gets it."

"I will, sir. And thank you."

"You and Rachel did a great job," Harris said. "It's good to see that the CIA is still on my side." He laughed. "In this town, it's hard to tell the difference between patriots and back-stabbing snakes. Luckily for me, I have this team to watch my back."

The President removed the last medallion from the box and handed it to Erin Welch. "Erin, please accept this token of appreciation for your contribution to the team."

"Thank you, Mr. President," she said.

"You're very welcome. By the way, Erin, have you decided on my offer of the FBI Director position?"

"I'm still considering it, sir."

"You'd do a great job. I need someone fearless and intelligent and honest in that position. Now that Cooper's behind bars, I want someone with proven integrity. There's no better person than you."

Erin smiled. "I'm flattered, sir. And I will let you know my answer soon."

"Good," the President replied. Then he closed the lid on the wooden box and handed it to General Foster.

Harris faced the group. "Once again, thank you for your contribution to our country. You saved the lives of tens of thousands, possibly hundreds of thousands of innocent Americans. It's my fervent hope I won't need your services again." His eyes narrowed and a grim expression settled on his face. "At the same time, my tenure as President has taught me one important thing. There are always more evildoers out there who will stop at nothing to achieve their goals. Evildoers who wish to destroy this great nation of ours, the United States of America."

Chapter 81

Special Operations Division
CIA Annex Building
Langley, Virginia

Rachel West went into the conference room and closed the door behind her.

"You wanted to see me?" she said to Alex Miller, who was sitting at the table.

"I did," Miller replied in a curt voice. "No need to sit, Rachel. This meeting will be short."

Her eyebrows arched. "Okay."

"I was at the White House yesterday," the CIA Deputy Director said, "and while I was there, President Harris asked me to give you something." The man reached into a pocket of his suit, removed a large gold coin and handed it to her. "You," Miller said, his tone still brusque, "along with everyone else on the President's covert team, was awarded this medallion for solving the terrorism case."

Rachel held up the large medallion in the air, its brilliant gold reflecting from the overhead fluorescents. "It's beautiful, Alex."

"Yes, it is. The President described this coin as a 'Get out of jail' card, in case one of us ever needed his help with a problem."

Rachel grinned. "That's great. That might come in handy one day."

Miller nodded. "That day has come for you, young lady." His voice changed from terse to acid. "Give me back the coin."

Rachel's grin faded. "What? What do you mean?"

Miller extended his palm. "Give it back to me."

Frowning, she reluctantly handed it back.

"What the hell is going on, Alex?"

"From now on, I would prefer if you referred to me as Deputy Director Miller."

Her frown deepened. "We've always called each other by our first names."

"That stops now, young lady." He pointed his index finger in her direction. "You suspected me of being the traitor! And you lied to me. You lied to me for weeks!"

She was about to object and he glared at her.

"Be quiet and listen, Agent West."

A queasy feeling settled in the pit of her stomach. "May I at least sit down?"

"No, you may not!"

She nodded. "Yes, sir."

"Up until yesterday," he said, his voice a harsh whisper, "I had every intention to fire you. To terminate your position at the Agency. Lucky for you, you received this medallion from the President. Consider not being fired your 'Get out of jail' pass."

"So what happens now, sir?"

"As of this moment, you are suspended from covert operations at the CIA. You are off field duty. You will be assigned to work in the filing room."

Rachel gritted her teeth. "Shuffling papers? You've got to be kidding! I'm your best field operative. And you know it!"

He glared. "I'm hoping you'll hate your new duties and quit."

She was about to tell him to fuck off, but bit her tongue and kept quiet.

"And one more thing, Ms West. Hand over your duty weapon. You won't be needing it in the filing room."

Rachel's shoulders sagged. With deep regret, she un-holstered her Glock 43, ejected the clip and handed the gun and magazine to Miller.

Miller pointed to the conference room door. "That will be all, Ms West. You're dismissed."

Chapter 82

Atlanta, Georgia

J.T. Ryan was driving south on the 400 highway when his cell phone vibrated. He slowed the Ford Explorer, took out his phone and read the info screen. He smiled when he saw who it was.

"Hey, Rachel," he said. "How's the most beautiful CIA agent in the world doing today?"

"That damn bastard!" she screamed in reply, her voice as angry as he'd ever heard it. "That bastard screwed me!"

"Calm down, Rachel. What happened?"

"He suspended me!"

"Who suspended you?"

"Miller!"

Ryan tightened his grip on the steering wheel. "You've got to be kidding. You helped solve the biggest terrorism case in the last ten years."

"I know that, damn it! That's what makes this suspension even worse."

"Listen, hon, President Harris awarded us these gold medallions —"

"I know all about that," she said, her voice still furious. "That was the thing that saved my ass from being fired."

He tried to lighten her mood. "And it's a cute ass."

She didn't reply, his joke obviously falling flat.

"He suspended you for thinking he was the government leak?" he said.

"Yeah."

"So what happens now, Rachel?"

"I'm off field duty. Miller assigned me to a desk job shuffling papers. Can you imagine that? That's like a death sentence to me."

Ryan had known her for years and knew she was right. She was the most qualified covert agent in the intelligence business. She was also an action-driven adrenalin junkie, much like himself. A desk job was like a death sentence for her. He mulled this over a moment, then said, "Maybe I can help."

"How, J.T.?"

"I'm good at what I do. I can make Miller disappear. His body will never be found."

"Please," she said, her voice low and pleading. "Please don't even think about doing that. That's cold-blooded murder."

"I don't care!" he spit out. "I hate Miller for treating you this way."

"Thank you, baby. I appreciate the thought. I really do. But it won't work. You'll be suspected immediately. And so will I."

Ryan honked his horn at a semi that was edging too close to his SUV, then considered what she'd just said. "Yeah, you're probably right, Rachel. Everyone at the CIA would suspect us if Miller disappeared."

"I miss you, J.T."

"I miss you too. Look, I can drop everything and take the next flight out of Atlanta. I can be with you by tonight."

"I'd love that," she said, her voice breaking up a bit. "You know I would...you're the best man I've ever known...I'm crazy about you...."

"And I'm crazy about you."

"But please don't come," she replied, her voice close to tears. "I need to be alone for a while...I need to think things through...."

Ryan's grip on the wheel tightened again, feeling choked-up himself. "I love you, Rachel."

"I love you too...I'm saying goodbye for now, okay? I'll call you soon...."

He was about to reply then heard a click on the line and knew she'd disconnected the call. He felt depressed and sick in his stomach. He brushed away a tear and continued driving south.

Chapter 83

Atlanta, Georgia

J.T. Ryan pressed the buzzer at the front door of the townhouse and waited. The home was located in Buckhead, an exclusive area of Atlanta.

A few moments later he heard the door unlock and it opened partway. Erin Welch stood there, barefoot and wearing a bathrobe. She yawned and massaged her face a few times. "Do you know what time it is?" she grumbled.

Ryan glanced at his watch. "2:32 a.m. to be exact."

With a grimace, she opened the door fully. "You might as well come in, J.T. No way I can fall back asleep now. But this better be good or I'm putting you on my shit list."

"You got any coffee?" he asked. "I could use some."

She shook her head slowly. "You're insufferable sometimes, you know that? You barge in here at two in the morning and now you want coffee too?" The grimace on her face deepened. "Where do you think you are? The International House of Pancakes?"

In spite of the tension he felt, he chuckled. "That's a funny line. I think I'll borrow it."

"Let's go the kitchen, J.T. I'll make us some coffee. Then you tell me what the hell is going on."

"Okay."

He followed her into the high-end kitchen, which had granite countertops and stainless-steel appliances. He sat at the marble-top dinette and watched as the FBI woman prepared coffee on her chrome Keurig machine.

A few minutes later she brought him a steaming mug of coffee and sat across from him. She took a sip from her own cup. "Okay, J.T. What's up? And no bullshit, please. I'm in no mood for it."

"I'm sorry I woke you up. I really am. But I had to talk with you."

She frowned. "I have regular office hours."

"I know." He leaned back in his chair. "This couldn't wait. I've been in my car, driving around aimlessly for hours and hours, trying to sort things out."

"What's wrong? Did something bad happen?"

He nodded. "It's Rachel. She's been suspended from the CIA."

Her eyebrows arched. "What? How the hell could that happen? She helped solve the most critical terrorism case in years."

"I know. But it's true. Miller suspended her. For suspecting that he was the mole. Miller was going to fire her but the gold medallion the President gave us saved her from that."

Erin shook her head. "Alex Miller's good at his job. There's no denying that. But he does have a mean streak."

"That's for damn sure."

"I'm sorry this happened to her, J.T. I really am. I like Rachel. She's good people. And the two of you make a great couple."

Ryan nodded. "Now you know why I'm here."

"What's Rachel going to do?"

"Miller assigned her to a desk job, shuffling papers, hoping she'll quit."

"Is she, J.T.?"

"I don't know. She doesn't know. I was hoping...I was hoping since you're a senior level manager at the FBI, you'd hire her for a job in Atlanta. She'd be great. She's incredibly proficient. And you're a great boss. She'd love working for you."

Erin held up both hands. "I can't. There's no way."

He felt her words stab him like an ice-pick. "Why the hell not? You know she'd make a great FBI agent."

"That's not it," she replied in a soothing voice. "I have no doubt she'd be a terrific agent. But being suspended by the premier intelligence agency in the U.S. is a stain on her record. No law-enforcement agency can hire her."

Ryan thought about this for a long moment. "Then what do you think she should do?"

Erin took another sip of coffee. "She should wait Miller out. Maybe Miller will get transferred to another agency. Or maybe over time, he'll realize he needs her. Like you said, she's the top covert operator at Central Intelligence."

"Maybe you're right, Erin."

Erin yawned and rubbed her eyes for a minute. "Now that we've had a chat, could I get back to bed? I'm dead tired and I've got a long day tomorrow."

Ryan shook his head. "There's something else we need to discuss. Something equally important."

She glanced at the wall clock and sighed. "All right, J.T. But before that I need more coffee. I'll go make some more."

"Okay."

Erin took their cups, went to the Keurig machine and came back moments later with two steaming cups. After taking a long sip of coffee, she said, "Go ahead."

"I don't think it's over, Erin."

"What's not over?"

"The terrorism case."

"Are you nuts? Of course it's over." She folded her arms in front of her. "The President disbanded the team, remember? You were there."

"I know. But I've been thinking about this for a few days."

Erin frowned. "Lexi Atwood is dead. The stolen bombs are back safe and sound in Los Alamos. What the hell's left?"

Ryan rubbed his jaw. "I have a gut feeling it's not over."

"Based on what?"

"A hunch."

She rolled her eyes. "A hunch, huh?" She glanced at the ceiling. "God, please save me from the ravings of a madman...." Then she gave him a hard look. "Is this another one of your practical jokes? Another attempt at lame humor? It's three in the morning and I'm too damn tired for jokes."

"I can explain," he said earnestly, "if you give me a chance."

"All right. Go ahead."

Ryan spoke for the next thirty minutes without stopping.

When he was done, she said, "You *are* insane. That's the craziest idea you've ever had."

"You've always trusted my judgment before."

She glared. "I have. And I've regretted some of those times."

"Granted, Erin, I'm not always right. But we've solved a lot of cases together." He smiled. "You got promoted to Assistant Director in Charge of the FBI Atlanta office because of your case closing ratio. Isn't that true?"

"Yes."

He grinned again. "And you've been offered the top job at the FBI. Isn't that right?"

"Yes. A job I haven't accepted yet."

"You've got to admit, I've helped your career over the years."

She let out a long sigh. "That's true, you have." She pointed an index finger at his face. "But you're still a smartass and you get me into trouble sometimes."

"But I'm a lovable smartass," he said with a chuckle. "And you find my wit and charm and good looks totally irresistible."

Erin burst out laughing and he joined her. He felt a lot better now than before he'd come here.

"Okay, smartass," she said, "I'm sure you're going to need my help to pull off this next caper."

"How'd you know?"

"Because you always need my help." She took a sip of coffee. "What do you need?"

"First, I'll need some specialized equipment. Weaponry from your FBI armory downtown."

Erin rolled her eyes. "Boys and their toys. Okay, you got it. Come in the office tomorrow." She glanced at the clock. "That would be later today and I'll sign it out to you. What else?"

"I'll need some private wings."

"Why?"

"No way I'll be able to get sophisticated weapons on a Delta flight."

She nodded. "Okay. I'll have our FBI jet take you where you need to go."

"Thank you, Erin."

"By the way, where are you going first?"

"Back to Vancouver. I think I can get some answers there."

"All right."

Ryan stood. "I'll go now and let you get some sleep. Thanks for listening and thanks for the coffee."

"Before you go," she said, "I need to get something back from you."

"What?"

"The FBI badge you received from President Harris a while back."

"Really? You want that back?"

"I do. You're not really an FBI agent. You haven't gone through the proper training."

He nodded. "That's true. And since I don't know Bureau protocols, I can do pretty much anything I want."

"Hand it over, buster."

"You know, the President has another four years on his term. I figure I can keep the badge as long as he's in charge. And I'm sure you don't want to piss him off."

Erin shook her head slowly and then shrugged. "I can't win with you, John Taylor Ryan. Now go. Please get out of my house before I get my gun and shoot you."

Ryan laughed, gave her a half salute and left her townhouse.

Chapter 84

Vancouver, Canada

J.T. Ryan had just rented a Buick from the Hertz airport location and was walking toward the car in the parking lot. But before he got in the sedan, a police SUV screeched to a halt in front of him.

Three uniformed cops jumped out of the SUV and surrounded Ryan, their hands resting on their holstered guns. Ryan recognized one of the cops right away – it was Sergeant Baker, the policeman he'd assisted when they raided Atwood's mansion on Vancouver Island.

"What's going on, Sergeant?" Ryan asked him.

"I'm sorry to tell you this," Baker said, "but you're under arrest."

Ryan tensed. "What the hell? Is this a joke?"

"No joke, Ryan. This is as real as a heart attack. Put your hands up and don't try to resist."

Ryan stared at the three armed cops. It was clear they weren't kidding. He slowly raised his hands.

"Are you armed, Ryan?"

"I am. Revolver under my jacket."

The sergeant nodded to one of the other cops. "Frisk him and take his weapon."

Ryan was patted down and his gun was removed. "Can you at least tell me what this is about, Sergeant?"

"The arrest warrant states that you're obstructing a police matter."

"No way, Sergeant. All I've done is help the Vancouver police. It was me who found Lexi Atwood, a wanted terrorist."

Sergeant Baker nodded. "I know. I feel like crap for having to do this. But I'm just following orders. The police chief and the mayor of Vancouver are really pissed off. It's terrible PR that one of the world's worst terrorists was hiding in plain sight. It makes them look really incompetent."

"Maybe they are incompetent!" Ryan spit out.

Baker raised a palm. "Take it easy. This whole thing will blow over in a couple of weeks. The news media will focus on the next big story and everyone will forget about Atwood and the American FBI agent who found her."

"But in the meantime?"

Baker shook his head, a sad look on his face. "In the meantime, you'll be held in the city jail pending trial. Then the District Attorney will drop these lame charges and you can go home."

Ryan scowled. "This is bullshit!"

"I know. Like I said, I'm sorry about this." He turned toward one of his men. "Cuff him and put him in the vehicle."

Three hours later, after being processed into the Vancouver jail downtown, Ryan was able to make his one phone call. He dialed the number on the corridor wall phone, while a guard stood nearby, watching his every move.

Luckily, Erin Welch answered on the second ring.

"It's Ryan," he said, keeping his voice low so as not to be overheard.

"Hi, J.T.," she replied. "Are you in Canada now?"

"I am. And I'm in trouble and I need your help."

She let out a long sigh. "Already? You just got there."

"I've been arrested by the Vancouver PD."

"What? What for?"

"Some lame, made-up charge."

"The local PD should be giving you a medal for solving their biggest case in years."

"Actually, the Canadians are furious at me for making them look incompetent."

"Okay, J.T. Where are you now?"

"The city jail downtown."

"All right. I'll see what I can do to get you out of there. I'll get on this right away."

"Thanks, Erin."

"Don't thank me yet, I haven't got you out of there."

"But you will. You always get me out of jams."

In a stern voice, she replied, "I told you this whole trip of yours was a bad idea. I still think it's a crazy theory you came up with."

"I'm on the right track, I'm sure of it."

"That's because your ego, J.T., is bigger than your brain."

Ryan laughed. "That's probably true."

Erin hung up and Ryan was led back to his cell by the guard on duty.

Two hours later, as Ryan was sitting on his jail cell bunk, two men approached the cell's barred door. One of the them was the guard and the other was Sergeant Baker. The guard unlocked the door and Baker said, "Okay, Ryan, you're free to go."

Ryan's mood brightened immediately. "Best news I've heard in weeks." He walked out of the cell. "So what happened?"

"Looks like your friend, Assistant Director Welch, has some real clout. She got your charges dropped."

"That's great. Now I can get back to work."

"Tell me, Ryan. Why are you even here? The case is solved. It's over."

Ryan considered this and decided not to tell Baker the purpose of his trip. The man would think he was crazy, just like Erin did.

"I came to see the sights of your beautiful city, Sergeant."

Baker smirked. "A tourist trip, huh? I'm not buying it. I've been a cop too long. I know you're lying to me."

Ryan smiled but said nothing.

"One thing, though," Baker said. "You'll have to do all of your sightseeing in the next 48 hours. After that, you're a persona-non-grata in Canada. You will be arrested again. The police chief hates your guts."

Ryan grinned. "I'll make a note."

***

J.T. Ryan drove his rented Buick to Vancouver's General Hospital and parked in the lot fronting the ten-story building. He walked inside and talked to the administrative nurse on duty, who directed him to the man's room, located on the fourth floor.

A few minutes later he entered the hospital room and found Atwood's assistant, Shawn. The young man was sitting up on the bed, hooked up to an IV and looking much paler than the last time he'd seen him.

"I'm John Ryan," he said, "we met about a month ago."

A flash of recognition crossed his face. "I remember. You're the American FBI agent."

"I am. I read the police report and learned you'd been poisoned by Atwood before she fled. From what I've heard, you're lucky to be alive."

Shawn nodded. "I guess I am. I was in a coma for a week. But the doctors here have been great. If it hadn't been for them I wouldn't be here now."

Ryan pulled a chair close to the hospital bed and sat down.

"Why are you here?" Shawn asked.

"I had a couple of questions for you."

"Why? The police told me the case was closed. Lexi is dead. They've seized her assets. They told me if I cooperated, I could escape prosecution. So I was glad to help them. But to tell you the truth, the police seem pretty eager to put this case in their rearview mirror. They're embarrassed this whole thing happened on their watch."

"I got the same impression, Shawn. I, on the other hand, am not sure this case is over."

Shawn's looked perplexed. "Really?"

"Yes. But before we get into that, I need you to tell me something."

"Of course. Anything. Like I told the cops, I want to cooperate."

"Since Atwood tried to murder you," Ryan said, "you must really hate her guts."

The young man looked pensive and didn't reply for a long moment. Finally, he said, "That's a complicated question to answer."

"Why is that?"

"Before she fled, Lexi set up a trust fund for my family. A very generous trust fund. Once I get out of the hospital, I won't have to work another day in my life."

"Why did she set up the trust fund, Shawn?"

"Lexi wanted me to come with her."

"What for?"

"The simple answer is to help her run her business. But it was much more complicated than that." Shawn's eyes got a far-away look. "Lexi...Lexi loved me...in her own way. She and I...we had a relationship of sorts."

"A sexual one?"

Shawn nodded. "Yes. She's obviously a very evil woman. A murderer, as I learned. But still, she had, and maybe still has, a hypnotic hold on me. She has a way to touch your soul."

"But you still refused to go with her."

"I did. I couldn't leave my family."

"That's when she poisoned you."

"Yes."

"All right, Shawn. Now that I understand you better, I'll tell you the reason I'm back in Vancouver. It's because I'm not sure Lexi Atwood is dead."

The young man was shocked and his mouth hung open. "What? She's dead. She blew herself up. Everybody knows that. Every news station in the world showed her video."

"That's true," Ryan said. "I've seen the video. Many, many times. Still. I'm not certain it actually happened. I think she staged her own death and fled."

"Why do you think that, Agent Ryan?"

"I met her. Twice. It's clear she's a brilliant woman. Extremely evil and diabolical. But also incredibly smart and cunning. I believe she had an escape plan in place in case things went bad for her." Ryan paused a moment. "But you knew her better than anyone else, Shawn. You worked for her for years. What do you think?"

Shawn considered this for a few minutes. "It's possible. She planned everything to the smallest detail. She never left anything to chance. It's what made her so successful in business. And she is super wealthy. A billionaire several times over. Even after the Canadian government seized her assets here, I know she had hundreds of millions of dollars stashed in banks all over the world."

Ryan nodded. "Where do you think she would go?"

"Lexi is Russian. And she had some kind of deal with Prime Minister Pushkin. Maybe she's in Russia."

"Okay. Anywhere else?"

"She had numbered accounts in Swiss banks. Maybe she's in Switzerland. I know she owned property all over the place. I knew about her island in the Pacific."

"I see." Ryan mulled this over. He realized finding Atwood was going to be difficult, assuming she was even alive. "Is there anything else you could tell me that would help me in my search?"

Shawn stared at him. "I kept a copy of her financial assets."

"You did?"

"Yes. Not to steal from her. But just in case, if her criminal activities were ever exposed. I thought if I turned over this information to the police, it would help me avoid going to jail. Which is exactly what happened."

"The Vancouver cops have this list of her assets?"

"Yes. I gave it to them. But I kept a copy of it."

Ryan's hopes brightened. "Where is it?"

The young man pointed to the metal storage cabinet in the hospital room. "In there, there's a bag with my clothes and shoes. There's a flash drive in the bag also. You can have it."

Ryan walked over, opened the cabinet and rummaged through the bag of the man's clothes. Finding the flash drive, he pocketed it.

"Thank you, Shawn. You've been a huge help."

"Can I ask for something in return, Agent Ryan?"

"Of course."

"If you do find Lexi, please promise me you won't hurt her. Arrest her. But please don't hurt her. She loved me...and in a strange way that I can't explain...I loved Lexi also."

Ryan nodded. "If Atwood is alive and I do find her, my intent is to arrest her and bring her to justice."

Chapter 85

Vancouver, Canada

J.T. Ryan left the hospital and drove to the city's waterfront. Parking his Buick, he took the ferry to Vancouver Island. Once there, he taxied over to Atwood's walled estate, which was located on a remote part of the island.

After being dropped by the cab at the front gate, he noticed the large FOR SALE sign that was posted there. He pressed the buzzer at the gate and waited.

A woman's voice came from the speaker. "May I help you?"

"I'm John Ryan with the FBI. May I come in?"

"Yes," she said, and the massive, wrought-iron gate creaked open slowly.

Ryan strode in and followed the long, winding road to the impressive three-story mansion. The young Asian woman he had met previously was standing by the open front door.

"I remember you," the Asian woman said, leading him inside. "You're the American policeman."

"Yes. You're Sun-Yi, right? Atwood's housekeeper?"

"I am."

"I'd like to talk with you."

The young woman with the doll-like face appeared nervous. "Am I in trouble?"

"Of course not," he replied, trying to put her at ease. "I just had a couple of questions. But could I please have a cup of coffee first?"

"It will be my pleasure!" she said, seeming relieved by his request. She led him back into a vast kitchen, where she began brewing the coffee. He sat on one of the leather chairs at the granite-top table and a few moments later she brought him the coffee in a beautifully hand-painted china cup and saucer.

"I noticed the FOR SALE sign out front," he said after taking a sip of coffee.

Sun-Yi nodded. "The authorities seized the house and are selling it, along with all of her other properties. They told me I could stay here and take care of it until it is sold."

"I see." He motioned to a chair across from him. "Please sit."

Once she sat, he asked, "You worked for Mrs. Atwood for a long time?"

"Three years."

"Did you enjoy working for her?"

"Very much. She was very good to me. She paid me extremely well and treated me kindly."

"You told me last time you didn't suspect she was involved in criminal activities."

Her eyes went wide and the nervous tremor came back in her voice. "No! Never! Are you going to arrest me?"

"No. Of course not. You were extremely cooperative last time. I just had a couple of other questions about her."

"Anything! Just please don't arrest me."

He smiled to put her at ease. "It would help me, Sun-Yi, if you could tell me everything you know about Lexi Atwood. Her likes, dislikes, people she knew, people who visited this house. Even conversations you may have overheard. Anything that could help me understand her better."

"Why do you want to know? The policemen that came after her death told me the investigation was over."

"That's true, their investigation is over." Since he didn't know Sun-Yi that well, he had decided not to tell her the real reason for his visit to Vancouver. He smiled again to put her at ease. "Let's just say, I'm curious about Atwood's motives. So start at the beginning. Tell me about the day she hired you three years ago."

This seemed to satisfy and calm the young Asian woman and she began speaking in her flawless but slightly-accented English.

Ryan took out a notebook and jotted notes. She spoke for the next hour, with Ryan interrupting her at times, probing the woman as she recalled details about her employer.

"You said she spoke several languages?" Ryan asked.

"Yes. English and Russian of course. But other languages also. French and German. And Spanish. She spoke Spanish fluently. In fact, she had several long conversations in that language before she left."

"With who, Sun-Yi?"

"I don't know. I do know it was several conversations and they were long."

"Okay. That's helpful. What else?"

She continued talking and he continued asking questions and jotting notes. When she was done an hour later, he said, "You've done a great job, Sun-Yi." He pointed to his notebook which was now almost full of things he'd written down. "You've been very helpful."

"I'm glad I could help."

"You have. Could I bother you for another cup of coffee before I go?"

Her doll-like face brightened. "No problem. It would be my pleasure." She appeared relieved her part was done and that he was leaving.

She served him the coffee and he said goodbye and left the mansion. He was eager to go over the information on Shawn's flash drive and cross-reference it to the voluminous notes he'd just jotted down, hoping to ascertain Atwood's location.

Chapter 86

Asuncion, Paraguay

J.T. Ryan gazed out the jet's window at the scene below.

The FBI plane was now on final approach over the airport, its landing delayed due to bad weather. The strong winds and torrential rain buffeted the small jet and obscured the scene of the capitol city of Paraguay.

After meeting with Shawn at the hospital and with Sun-Yi at Atwood's mansion, he'd spent almost a full day correlating and researching the information they had provided. That had led him to this trip. Although he wasn't certain Atwood was hiding in Paraguay, he had a gut feeling it was possible. Atwood had done an excellent job of masking and hiding the properties and homes she owned, but Ryan had been able to decipher through the multiple layers of aliases and phony names and came up with clues that pointed to this backwater country in South America. He then spent several more hours doing Internet research on Paraguay.

Paraguay is a strange country, he soon realized. Nestled between Brazil and Bolivia, it had a turbulent and corrupt history. And because of its backwater, almost mysterious location, few people even know it exists. Paraguay is an extremely poor country. It has a population of seven million, of which 40% are considered poor and 19% live in extreme poverty.

The country was first explored and colonized by the Spanish in 1516. The indigenous Indian population that existed in the country at that time was ruled by Spain for the next 300 years. In 1811, the Spanish nobility was overthrown by the country's first dictator, Jose Gaspar Rodriguez, who ruled with an iron fist until 1840. For the next hundred years, Paraguay saw the rise and fall of many corrupt and infamous dictators, most of who were former military officers. One of the better known dictators who ruled was Alfredo Stroessner, who came to power in 1954. He remained in office as President until 1989, when he was overthrown. Eventually the country saw the rise of a duly elected democracy which began in the early 2000's and has lasted to the current day.

The climate of Paraguay is tropical and the eastern forest belt receives massive amounts of rainfall. During Ryan's research, he learned another interesting fact about the country. Over the years, it has received large influxes of immigrants. Italians, Germans, Russians, Koreans, Chinese, and Brazilians were all part of the influx of immigrants. In the aftermath of World War II, there was a flood of Germans, notably many ex-Nazi SS soldiers, seeking to escape capture and imprisonment by the Allied forces when Nazi Germany fell. Even in present day Paraguay, the German communities are extensive in the country and studies reveal that close to 10% of the total population is of German ancestry.

It was this aspect of the country's population that intrigued Ryan. He came to the conclusion that people seeking to escape from our modern-day, interconnected world could easily blend into a place such as Paraguay and live hiding in plain sight. Specially someone with the money and means like Lexi Atwood, AKA Alexandra Ivanova. She could easily buy her way into a corrupt country such as Paraguay, where poverty was widespread.

Ryan continued gazing through the plane's window at the scene below.

Although he'd been able to amass quite a bit of information on his own, he was still missing a piece of the puzzle. He still needed a local contact, someone who couldn't be bought off.

As he stared out the window, he noticed the torrential rain had intensified, the storm over the airport still raging. It would be a bit longer, he figured, before the FBI plane could land.

Ryan pulled out his SAT cell phone and punched a number on speed dial. Erin Welch picked up on the third ring.

"It's Ryan," he said.

"Are you still in Vancouver, J.T.?"

"No, not anymore."

"Where are you now?" Erin asked.

"In your fancy FBI jet," he replied with a chuckle. "I love the leather seats by the way."

"Don't be such a smartass. Where are you?"

"Asuncion."

"Where the hell is that?"

"Paraguay."

"The country of Paraguay? In South America?"

"Exactly that place, Erin."

"What the hell are you doing there?" she asked in an exasperated tone.

"Never been here before." He laughed. "I thought I'd play tourist for a while and take in the sights."

"Cut the bullshit, will you! Damn you, J.T.! You're so infuriating sometimes. I swear I could strangle you right now."

"All right, all right, I'll be good," he replied, his voice all business now. "I need some information."

"I figured that. I'm assuming it relates to your crazy quest to find Atwood? A woman who is dead?"

"Presumably dead. Anyway, I got quite a few leads during my trip to Vancouver. Those leads are the reason I'm currently on final approach over Asuncion Airport."

"Okay. Tell me what you need."

"I need the name of a local cop. Preferably a detective. One who works on the Asuncion police force. And someone not high up in the food chain. Probably a sergeant in the PD."

"There's probably a dozen of those, J.T."

"You're right. The guy I'm trying to find most likely lives in one of the poorer districts of the city. And he doesn't drive an expensive car. Use some of your FBI magic and find out the amounts in his bank accounts and see if they correlate with his paycheck."

"I'm guessing by your request that you're looking for an honest cop?" she asked.

"That's right, Erin. Paraguay is an incredible poor and corrupt country. My guess is some people on the PD are not above taking bribes from criminal elements to look the other way."

"All right. I understand. I'll work on this right away and call you back when I have something."

"You're the best, Erin. A class act. There's no one better at the FBI."

"Don't lay it on too thick, buster. I see through your bullshit. One day you won't be able to con me to do your work for you."

Ryan laughed at this. "I'm hoping today isn't that day."

He could visualize the grimace on her face right now. She said nothing for a long moment and then he heard a muted chuckle from the other end.

"No, J.T. Today is not that day. I'll get you the info you need."

"Thank you very much. I really mean that."

"I know you do," she replied. Then the levity left her voice and in a stern tone she said, "But I'm giving you fair warning, J.T. Don't get arrested in Paraguay. I know no one there. None of my contacts know anyone there. Most people have never even heard of that country. If you get arrested, I will *not* be able to get you out. You are on your own. Am I making myself clear?"

"Crystal clear," he said, swallowing hard. He was certain that what she had just told him was an absolute fact.

Chapter 87

Asuncion, Paraguay

The torrential rain finally eased somewhat and the small FBI jet was given clearance to land. J.T. Ryan spent the next few hours renting a Jeep Cherokee at the Asuncion Airport, loading his two large duffel bags of weapons and gear into it, and finding a nondescript hotel to check into.

Ryan grabbed a quick meal at the hotel restaurant, then went back to his room and spread out the paper maps he'd purchased at the airport. He familiarized himself with the layout and streets of Asuncion, the capitol city of the country. As he was doing this, he got a call back from Erin, who gave him the name and particulars of a local cop who fit the parameters Ryan was looking for. The man's name was Diego Cruz and he was a detective on the Asuncion PD. Before hanging up, Erin once again warned Ryan not to get arrested.

Now that he had a local contact, Ryan spent more time figuring out additional information about the man.

***

Ryan drove his Jeep through the narrow, grimy, and winding streets of one of the city's poorer districts. He spotted the cantina's faded sign, pulled to the curb and parked his vehicle. It was still raining, but the previous deluge had calmed. And even though it was nighttime now, the heat and humidity were oppressive. The description Ryan had read about the country's tropical climate appeared to be highly accurate.

Climbing out of the Jeep, he went into the mostly empty cantina and looked around the dilapidated place. To call it a restaurant would be an overstatement. It was more of a dive bar that served drinks and sandwiches. He spotted Cruz sitting at the long bar which ran along the whole length of the place.

Striding over, Ryan sat on a stool nearby and faced the other man.

"Puedo comprarte otra cerveza?" Ryan said in Spanish.

Cruz gave him a long up-and-down look. *"No, gracias,"* he replied. "I buy my own drinks," Cruz added, now in English. "Your Spanish is good – but your accent sounds American?"

Ryan nodded. "Guilty as charged, Detective Cruz."

A suspicious look settled on the man's face. "You know who I am?"

"Yes. Detective Sergeant Diego Cruz, Asuncion PD."

"And who the hell are you?"

Ryan took out his FBI credentials and held the wallet open so Cruz could read it.

After inspecting it closely, the cop said, "I'm not on duty now. If this is official business, come to my precinct tomorrow."

Ryan smiled, trying to disarm the man's suspicions. "No, it's not official business. I'm just looking for information."

"Since you're an American Federal agent, you need to see our police chief. He's the man in charge and can tell you anything you need to know."

Ryan shook his head. "I don't think so. I had him checked out. And I had your captain of Ds and the whole command staff at the PD checked out also. They all live in the ritzy part of town. What I'm looking for is an honest cop."

Cruz suppressed a smile.

"You, Detective Cruz, are the only police sergeant that lives on this side of town. And you drive a ten-year-old Chevy with over 100,000 miles on the odometer."

"You've done your homework, my American friend." Cruz nodded and got a far-away look in his eyes. "But sometimes I wonder if I'm doing the right thing. My wife is always telling me I need to make more money. I don't think she cares how I get it."

"You're doing the right thing. Trust me. I've seen cops who began taking little bribes. Here and there. Then the bribes got bigger. Once you cross that line, you can never go back."

Cruz smiled. "We think alike, you and I."

Ryan pointed toward a booth away from the bar. "Let's sit over there, okay? I'd rather no one overhear our conversation."

The police detective signaled the bartender and said, *"Dame dos cervesas mas."* Then he picked up the longneck he was drinking and headed toward the booth.

Ryan followed him and after the bartender served them the beers, he took a long pull from his drink. Just then the cantina's metal roof drummed loudly, the cascade of rain returning.

"Does it always rain so much here?" Ryan asked.

"Always." Then Cruz shrugged. "When you're born and raised here like I am, you get used to it."

Ryan glanced around the bar to make sure no one was paying attention to them and said in a low voice, "Like I told you earlier, I'm looking for some information."

"What kind?"

He studied Cruz's features, gauging if he could trust him. He had a good feeling about the man and after a long moment decided to tell him everything.

"I'm looking for a woman," Ryan said, "an incredibly wealthy woman. She's a fugitive from the law. A woman who everyone thinks is dead. But I think she's hiding here in your country."

Cruz nodded. "What's her name?"

"Lexi Atwood."

Shock registered on the man's face. But then a hint of a smile settled on his lips. "You had me going there a bit, John Ryan." He shook his head. "Now I see, you have a good sense of humor."

"I'm as serious as a heart attack."

"Even though Paraguay is a backward country," Cruz said, "we do have television news and the Internet here. I saw the video of her – she's the Canadian terrorist who blew herself up."

"Atwood is alive, I'm sure of it."

The cop stared at him for a full minute without speaking, then said, "Assuming this could be true, why here? Why Paraguay?"

"It's the perfect place to hide," Ryan said. "Someone as wealthy as Atwood could buy lots of silence. The Nazi SS did the same thing after World War II."

Cruz nodded. "I get your point."

"And there's something else. I found out she's fluent in Spanish and she appears to own some property here, although the information I have is sketchy."

"All right, Ryan. Let's assume she's here. She obviously wouldn't use her real identity."

"That's why I need your help. You've been a cop a long time here. You hear things all the time."

"That's true. But a lot of what I hear from informants is what you Americans call bullshit."

Ryan took another long pull from his beer, emptied the longneck, and signaled the bartender for more. When the guy served them their fresh drinks and left, the conversation continued.

"I did hear a rumor," Cruz said, "about a rich reclusive woman that bought a large property east of here. But she was from Bolivia." The cop scrunched his face in concentration. "Her name is...her name is Lopez. That's right, I remember now. Her name is Carmen Rosa Lopez."

Ryan nodded. "Lexi Atwood's real name is Alexandra Ivanova. Changing her identity to something else would be second nature to her."

Cruz shrugged. "This woman may not be who you're looking for. Like I said, it was a rumor."

"I'll take that chance. I've found criminals with less information. Anyway, I'm a long way from home. I'll check out this Carmen Lopez. By the way, if Lopez is the terrorist and I do arrest her, I'll give you the credit for it."

The cop's eyes got big. "Really? You would do that?"

"Sure. I'm not looking to make headlines or score points. I just want to catch a murderer. Plus, I'd like to help you out. Honesty should be rewarded."

The cop raised his bottle of beer and grinned. "I'll drink to that."

Chapter 88

Asuncion, Paraguay

J.T. Ryan drove to his hotel and went to his room. Pulling out his SAT phone, he punched a number on speed dial.

When Erin Welch answered, he said, "It's me."

"Where are you now, J.T.?"

"Still in Asuncion. Listen, I think I may have found her."

"Atwood?"

"Yeah. I met with the local cop," Ryan said. "He heard of a woman who owns a hacienda east of here. She's rich and reclusive. A Bolivian woman, goes by the name of Carmen Rosa Lopez. By the way, this woman's middle name is interesting. 'Rosa' means reddish in Spanish. Atwood loves the color red and she may have incorporated it into her new alias."

Ryan could hear Erin tapping away at her computer.

"I'll check her out," Erin said. "I'll cross-reference her name with the info on the flash drive Shawn gave you."

"Good. Use that FBI software you agents have to track people down."

"Glad you reminded me," she replied, her voice dripping with sarcasm. "I would have never thought to do that."

Ryan laughed.

"Okay, J.T., I'll call you back when I find something."

She hung up and two hours later his SAT phone buzzed.

"Found her," Erin said. "You're right about this woman, Carmen Rosa Lopez. She purchased a large track of land there six months ago. Looks like she planned ahead, in case things turned sour for her. According to the paperwork I found, Lopez is Bolivian, although she received her Bolivian citizenship without ever living there or having any relatives there. And she received her Paraguay citizenship the same way. And both of these things took place in a matter of a few days. It's pretty clear she bought and paid some highly influential people in both countries."

"I figured as much."

Erin then told him the exact location of Atwood's home. "I was able to pull up a map of that area and an overhead photo," she said. "The hacienda is comprised of a mansion and several other buildings. It's more like a fortified compound, ringed with walls and concertina fencing."

"Can you shoot that map and photo to my phone, Erin?"

"Will do."

"Once I have that, I'll get going."

"You have a plan, J.T.?"

"I always have a plan. In this case several. I have Plan A, B, and C."

"What are they?"

"Plan A," he said, "I go in quiet as a church mouse, sneak into her mansion, grab Atwood, and get out the same way I came in."

"And Plan B?"

"I blow shit up, grab her and run like hell."

"What's Plan C?" she asked.

"You don't want to know."

"All right. I guess the only thing I can do now is wish you luck. I know you're going to need it."

"Listen, Erin. Can I ask you one favor before I hang up?"

"Shoot."

"If I don't make it out of this hellhole alive, can you please call Rachel West for me? Tell her I love her."

"Why don't you call her yourself and tell her now?" Erin said.

Lee Gimenez

"I don't want to worry her. And if I told her now what I was up to, she'd drop everything and fly down here to help me."

"Okay, J.T. I'll do it. But try not to get killed."

"Yeah. That's definitely on my to-do-list."

"All right. Anything else before we hang up?"

"No, Erin. I'm good."

"Sure I can't get you a cup of coffee," she said, "and some doughnuts?"

Ryan laughed. "Now who's the smartass?"

"I learned from the king of smartasses. You."

He laughed again. "Goodbye, Erin." He hung up the phone and put it away.

Glancing at his watch, he noted the time. Then he opened up his paper maps and spread them out on the hotel bed. Now that he had an exact location, he wanted to figure out the best route.

Chapter 89

Cordillera, Paraguay

The Jeep Cherokee bounced over the mounds of mud and gravel, then sank into the deep ruts of the road, the heavy deluge of rain making the path a soupy mess of sludge.

Slowing the Jeep, J.T. Ryan put it into four-wheel drive and switched his headlights to high-beams, trying to make out the landmarks of the forested region. It was after ten p.m. and there were no lights anywhere in the desolate area, a place named Cordillera, a region east of Asuncion.

For the next hour he continued driving carefully on the muddy road, as it twisted and wound around the forest. His headlights suddenly lit up a large sign by the road which read, *'Propidad Privada. No entren sin permiso. Protegido con cercas electricas'*. Ryan knew this meant: 'Private Property. Don't enter without permission. Protected with electric fences'. Below the words on the sign was a skull and crossbones, the universal symbol of danger.

Ryan realized going any further in the Jeep was an extremely bad idea. He'd have to continue the rest of the way on foot. He steered the vehicle off the muddy road and deep into the woods, to a well-concealed place.

Turning off the engine, he pulled on the hood of his windbreaker and covered his head. But as soon as he climbed out of the Jeep, he knew the windbreaker and hood were no match for the torrential downpour. It was brutally hot also, even though it was nighttime. Making him hotter still was the vest underneath his jacket. It was a Level 3A Kevlar vest. The vest was five millimeters thick, its multiple layers of polymer matrix laminate able to stop a 9 mm submachine gun bullet, shotgun buckshot, and handgun ammo up to and including a .44 Magnum round. Police officers usually wear less protective Level 2A vests because they're lighter in weight and more comfortable during long shifts in squad cars.

He made a mental note to thank Erin again for lending him the Kevlar vest from the FBI armory in Atlanta.

With his boots sloshing over the muddy ground, he trudged to the back of the Cherokee and opened the cargo door. Unzipping the large rucksack that was in the cargo bed, he pulled out the modified Heckler & Koch MP-4. This particular short-barreled rifle was special in several ways. First, it had been converted to a fully-automatic weapon, capable of firing all the thirty rounds in the magazine in seconds. In addition, this MP-4 had an RPG launcher built in. The ability to shoot rocket propelled grenades was a handy feature, as he'd found out during his Army days in Afghanistan.

With a grin, he slung the sweet weapon over his shoulder and instantly felt more confident. *I may die today*, he thought morbidly. *But I won't be the only one to die.*

Besides the MP-4, he was also armed with his .357 Magnum revolver, already holstered at his hip. In addition, his snub-nose .38 caliber was in his ankle holster, along with a combat knife attached to his belt.

Then he pulled out RPG rounds from the rucksack, along with six loaded clips for the MP-4, which he stuffed in his pockets. After doing this, he removed a rolled up blanket and slung it over his other shoulder. Lastly, he took out night-vision goggles and strapped it over his head. Pulling down the eyepiece, he turned on the device and the darkness of night changed to a brightly-lit green hue. Once again he grinned, feeling like the soldier he used to be.

That done, he began hiking north deeper into the muddy woods, the torrential rain shadowing his every move. In five minutes, every part of his body was drenched, his clothes and socks clinging to his skin. Periodically as he continued north, he checked his handheld compass to make sure he was headed in the right direction.

Half an hour later he saw lights on the horizon and knew he was getting close to Atwood's compound.

Ryan trudged toward the lights, his boots sinking into the soft muck. He slowed his pace, his head on a swivel, looking for any movement or sound, anything that would tip him off that patrolling guards were nearby.

He saw nothing but trees and wild vegetation and tall grasses and mud. The scent of the vegetation was strong and the heat was intense. And the rain continued without letup, water cascading through the trees, creating pools of soupy mud on the ground.

He continued going north toward the lights on the horizon.

Ten minutes later his night-vision goggles clearly showed a tall chain-link fence topped with razor-wire. Posted by the fence were signs stating that the fence was electrified.

He stopped walking and dropped to one knee, swiveling his head to insure no guards were nearby.

Ryan grabbed the rolled up blanket off his shoulder and crept closer to the fence. Then he unrolled the blanket and, taking aim, pitched it up and over the top of the 8 foot fence. The blanket was insulated for electric current, making it possible for him to climb over the fence without being electrocuted.

After walking several paces away, he then turned toward the fence and ran full speed toward it. Leaping at the last moment, he outstretched his arms and grabbed the metal rod at the top. Using every bit of strength, he pulled himself to the top while trying to avoid cutting himself on the razor wire. He draped his right leg over the fence, then pulled his body over to the other side, crashing to the mud on the ground.

That done, he pulled the blanket off the fence, rolled it up and hid it under a tree. If everything went according to his Plan A, he'd follow the same procedure on the way out.

He advanced forward cautiously and a few minutes later the woods thinned out, giving way to low-lying vegetation. It was still raining, but the previous downpour had lost its intensity.

Atwood's compound was just ahead and he spotted lights coming from the mansion and the other structures. The road he had come in on was visible also, and it was to his right. Directly ahead of him was the wall that encircled the compound. Also ahead was a fortified front-entrance gate, which appeared to be constructed of heavy-gauge metal. It looked like Lexi Atwood had spared no expense with her security measures.

Ryan knelt behind a row of bushes and flicked a switch on his night-vision goggles. Through the green haze he now spotted beams of red light crisscrossing the areas in front of the wall. As he had suspected, those areas were secured with motion-detection beams. If he inadvertently crossed the red beams, alarms would sound.

Unslinging the MP-4, he made sure the sound-suppressor was tightly attached to the end of the barrel and then he racked the slide on the weapon.

Ryan slowly and cautiously advanced forward, avoiding the crisscrossing red beams of light. His heart raced and he gripped the rifle tightly as he made his way. Five minutes later the red beams were behind him and he breathed a sigh of relief.

He marched slowly toward the wall, picking up his boots and easing them down carefully, trying to be as quiet as possible. The steady rain that pelted him also muffled his movements.

Ten feet later, as he was walking between two large shrubs, he felt it. A tight pressure against his leg. Then he heard a snapping noise and knew instantly what had happened. But by then it was too late. He'd crossed a tripwire.

Damn, he mouthed silently. *An old fashioned tripwire!*

Instantly floodlights bathed the whole area, lighting it up like a nighttime football game. The lights blinded him and he ripped off his night-vision goggles and threw them to the ground.

A piercing alarm blared, a deafening sound that carried for miles. With his heart pounding, he dove to the muddy ground and rolled his body behind clumps of vegetation. He heard more sounds – men yelling, the shouts audible despite the piercing noise of the alarms.

Knowing his Plan A was now shot to hell, he immediately went to Plan B. He pulled down the bipod of his MP-4 and propped the rifle on a mound of wet dirt. He aimed toward the imposing metal gate, gauging the distance as best he could. After making several adjustments to the weapon, he slid his finger past the trigger guard and rested it on the trigger itself. Taking one last look through the MP-4's optical scope, he pulled the trigger.

The RPG round blasted away in a low arc, the fiery charge of the rocket propelled grenade lighting up the nighttime even more. The RPG round found its mark a second later, the explosion creating a fireball of shredded metal flying in all directions. The earsplitting detonation drowned out the strident sounds from the alarms.

Some of the shouting he'd heard previously changed in tone and he heard cries of pain. Wasting no time, Ryan inserted another RPG round into the rifle's launcher tube, took aim, and fired again.

This time part of the wall next to the gate exploded, shards of concrete spraying in every direction.

Then he heard it, return fire from semi-automatic rifles shooting out of the compound. But it sprayed over his head and to his left and right. It was clear the guards hadn't pinpointed his location. As best he could, he shoved mud aside and burrowed his body into the crude trench he had created. Stretching himself prone into the cavity, he pointed the MP-4 forward and kept feeding more RPG rounds into the weapon. Then he fired nonstop over the wall into the compound, aiming for the outer buildings around the mansion.

Fires erupted from the multiple explosions and the shouting diminished. Clearly, Atwood's guards had taken casualties. Ten minutes later all of his RPG rounds were gone, and fires and dark smoke towered over the buildings. He flicked a switch on the MP-4 and changed the bullet fire to fully automatic.

Ryan crawled toward the now crumbled wall on his hands and knees, his rifle pointed forward. Moments later he reached a hole in the wall and peered inside. Among the ruble he saw the bloody bodies of at least five men, apparently all dead. He spotted several more guards on the ground, severely wounded, clutching their stomachs or their heads, groaning and gasping for breath. Some of the floodlights were still operating and he could see the blood and shock that covered their faces.

Ryan felt sick to his stomach from the carnage he had created and the death he had caused. Bile rose in his throat and he almost threw up. Then he recalled something a Green Beret colonel had told him years ago, after one particularly gruesome firefight. *Kill or be killed*, the man had told him. *There is no other way.*

Ryan crawled through the ragged hole in the wall, and took cover behind the burnt-out hulk of a Ford pickup. He was about 100 feet from the mansion, which was situated in the center of the compound. The walls and roof of the three-story home had been damaged. The front door, which stood under an impressively-designed arched portico, had been partially destroyed. Through the haze and smoke he could see into the home's interior. There were no guards posted there, although he figured there were more of them inside the structure.

Atwood, Ryan was certain, was inside the mansion.

Gripping the MP-4 tightly, he raced toward the house in a zigzag pattern until he reached the front entrance. Hugging the wall, he peered inside. Through the smoky haze he spotted two bloody corpses on the foyer's marble floor.

Seeing no one else, Ryan cautiously stepped inside, his rifle trained forward. He picked his way through the ruble and broken furniture. Rain was dripping through the parts of the roof that had been damaged. He followed the wide corridor past a lavish living room and a few other vacant rooms. The RPG grenades had penetrated the walls, because damage was evident everywhere. A hazy smoke hung in the air and the odor of burning wood and cloth was strong. The electricity had been knocked out, but emergency lighting had come on, casting a dim glow along the corridor and rooms.

Suddenly he heard scuffling of boots on marble and out of the corner of his eye he spotted a man up ahead and to his right. Ryan instantly pulled the trigger of his weapon and the guy dropped to the floor, his rifle clattering on the marble. A second man emerged and Ryan threw himself to the ground as he fired again.

He heard a groan and kept shooting, some of the rounds ricocheting off the walls. Ryan, now flat on the floor, his adrenaline pumping, peered ahead through the haze of smoke. He'd shot the second man, who was slumped by a damaged bookcase, clutching his bleeding abdomen. The guy sank to his knees and pitched forward, crashing to the floor.

Ryan got on one knee, and seeing no one else approaching, stood and advanced slowly, his finger still on the trigger of his rifle. He passed a massive kitchen, which was unoccupied, and moved deeper into the mansion.

Then he sensed a blur of movement to his left and before he could shoot, he saw muzzle flashes and heard the roar of gunshots. The rounds slammed into this chest, knocking him backwards and off his feet. The blinding pain felt as if a sledgehammer had hit him in the chest and he gasped for air.

Then everything went black.

***

Ryan awoke sometime later, his brain foggy, the pain in his chest intense. He was bound to a chair and his windbreaker, shirt, and Kevlar vest had been stripped off. He still had his pants on, but his boots and socks were gone. Glancing down at his chest, he saw the large black and blue bruises where the bullets had hit him. Luckily, the vest had saved his life. He was sure, however, that several of his ribs had been cracked.

His thoughts were jumbled and hazy and he closed his eyes.

But a second later he felt the sting of a sharp slap to his face.

Ryan's eyes snapped open. Standing in front of him was a brawny blond man. He was holding a Glock pistol at his side. A second man stood off a few feet away – he was holding a submachine gun pointed at Ryan's head.

"Wake up!" the blond man shouted. "She wants to talk with you!"

Ryan, now fully alert, gazed at the two armed men and at the room they occupied. The room was a storage space and he noticed water dripping from the damaged ceiling to the concrete floor.

The blond man stepped aside and Ryan saw a woman walk into the room and stand in front of him. He didn't recognize her at first because she had dyed her hair black. And instead of her trademark red color clothing, she was wearing a gray blouse and black jeans. But she still looked beautiful.

"So we meet again, John Ryan," she said, folding her arms in front of her.

"I liked you better as a redhead," Ryan said.

The woman ran a hand through her long mane of hair. "Me too." She moved closer to him. "How did you find me?"

"It's a long story."

"You have time. I'm not going to kill you yet."

Still in intense pain from his cracked ribs and bruises, he stared up at her. "I found an honest cop in Asuncion. I know you spread a lot of cash in Paraguay to keep your secret. I got lucky and found someone you hadn't bribed."

Lexi nodded. "But how did you know I was even here? In Paraguay?"

"It turns out your assistant, Shawn, kept a flash drive with a lot of your financial information. From that I was able to track you down to here."

She grimaced. "That bastard. I trusted Shawn. And he betrayed me."

"Don't forget, Lexi. You tried to kill him."

"Obviously I didn't do a good enough job," she said, her voice dripping with acid.

"Don't be too bitter about Shawn," Ryan said. "When I talked with him at the hospital, he told me he loved you, even after you poisoned him. He told me that if I found you, I shouldn't hurt you."

Lexi nodded. "Yes. He did love me. But enough about him. Tell me, John, who else knows I'm here?"

"The FBI. There's an assault team on its way here. They probably have your compound surrounded by now."

"That's a lie," she spat out. "If a whole team of FBI agents are here, all of you would have attacked the house together. Instead it was only you."

It was obvious Lexi had seen through his bluff. "You're right. But others know where I am. Erin Welch knows."

"That part probably is true," she said. "And if you found me, others will follow. It's just a matter of time now." She waved a hand in the air. "Anyway, you've done a good job of fucking up my house. No way I could live here now." She paused a moment. "But to tell you the truth, I hate this fucking country. It rains all the time in Paraguay. And it is *so* damn hot."

"Where will you go?"

She laughed. "I'm sure you'd love to know. I can probably tell you, since you're a dead man walking." She glanced at her watch. "After we're done talking, if you don't agree to my demands, I will kill you. You can count it." She smiled a malicious grin. "Well, I won't kill you. I'll just tell Brad to do it." She looked at the brawny blond man. "How's that sound, Brad? I'm sure you'd enjoy doing that."

"It will be my pleasure," Brad said.

Lexi stared at Ryan again. "But before you die, we need to have a conversation."

She pointed to Brad. "Check his bindings. I want to make sure he's tied up tight."

The blond man walked behind Ryan and roughly checked his hands, which were securely tied behind his back. Ryan's arms were also strapped to the chair's armrests with flex-cuffs.

"He's not going anywhere," Brad said.

Lexi nodded. "Good. Now leave us, Brad. I need to have a private conversation with our FBI friend here."

"He's not our friend, Lexi. He killed fifteen of our men."

"Yeah, it is a pity about the men. Although what really pisses me off is that he ruined my fucking mansion." She pointed to the open doorway of the room. "Okay, Brad. Go now and take your goon with you."

"Are you sure, Lexi?"

She glared at the blond man. "Go, damn it! Stand in the hallway and leave the door open. If I need you, I'll call you."

Ryan looked at Brad, who still seemed reluctant to leave. But eventually he nodded to the guard with the submachine gun and the two men stepped into the hallway.

There was a chair in the corner of the room and Lexi walked over to it and slid it in front of Ryan. She sat across from him and stared into his eyes. "Now that we have some privacy, John, we can have a little chat."

"Is this the part where I talk you into giving up, Lexi?"

She laughed. "I see you haven't lost your sense of humor." She placed her palm on his broad chest, massaged it lightly, and stared at his extensive bruises. Then she made a fist and pounded his chest.

He winced from the excruciating pain.

"Does that hurt, John?"

"Yes!"

She grinned. "I'm sure it does. Tell me something. I'm curious about your name. In Vancouver you told me your name was J.T. Ryan. What does the 'T' stand for?"

In spite of the pain in his chest, he said, "Trustworthy."

The woman laughed. "You *do* have a great sense of humor. I like that." Then she ran her palm gently across his chest, gingerly tracing his bulging muscles. "There's a lot about you I like. When we met in Vancouver, I said you reminded me of my dear husband, Sergei. I wasn't kidding then, and I'm not kidding now." She slid her palm down his chest and gently cupped his pants in the groin. With a grin, she massaged him for a moment. "Yes, you're so much like Sergei...."

"What do you want?"

"I will spare your life, John. If you agree to join me."

"Join you?"

She moved her hand and placed it on his chest. "I need a man like you. A strong, intelligent man. To help me with my business."

Ryan shook his head. "You're a criminal. A murderer."

The woman laughed. "Well, there is that. But nobody's perfect. We all have our flaws."

"What do you really want, Lexi?"

"It's simple. Join me. Be part of my team. I need a strong, decisive guy." She traced his face gently with her palm. "Think about it. I can make you a wealthy man. Incredibly wealthy. Even though the Canadian government seized my assets there, I have money in banks all over the world."

"Why me, Lexi?"

"You intrigue me. You're highly intelligent and resourceful. You found me in this godforsaken country and you killed 15 of my men. I need a tough, clever man to help me run my business."

"You have Brad," Ryan said.

She shook her head. "Granted, Brad is big and strong and knows how to follow orders. But he's dumb as a rock and he's crappy in bed. No, Brad won't do. I was hoping Shawn would come with me, but the bastard refused."

"Shawn didn't want to leave his family."

Lexi nodded. "That's true. It's a real shame."

Then her coal-black eyes blazed with intensity. "So what's your answer, John? Will you join me? And share my billions? And share my bed, too? I could pleasure you and you could pleasure me. I'm convinced of that." She gently traced his broad chest again with her fingers. "Yes, I'm sure you could pleasure me in bed. I could train you to what I like in bed. I have very particular needs and wants. But I'm sure you'd be a fast learner. And as Shawn found out, I always gave him the sexual relief he needed. I always made sure of that."

She paused a moment and smiled. "Think about it. You'd be a billionaire. You'd live a lavish lifestyle. You could buy anything, have anything you ever wanted."

"It sounds like," he replied, "I'd become your house pet."

She shook her head. "It wouldn't be like that. Think of it as a partnership."

"I'd be lying to you, if I said I agreed to your terms. I can't agree, Lexi. No matter how rich I'd be."

She stared at him, her coal-black eyes blazing with a savage look. She was quiet for a long moment, obviously thinking about what he'd said. Then the fierce look softened and was replaced by a warm, calming gaze. "I'm not giving up on you, John. Not yet."

She placed both of her hands on his face and caressed it gently. "You must be in a lot of pain, John. Those bruises on your chest tell me that. You probably have cracked ribs. Is that right?"

"Yes."

"Are you in a lot of pain?"

He nodded. "Yes."

"I can make the pain go away. Would you like that?"

"Yes."

"Close your eyes," she said soothingly, "and I will make it happen. I'll make the pain go away."

Ryan shut his eyes.

"Now, John, I want you to think about a special, relaxing place you've been to in your life. Tell me where that is, John."

Ryan, his eyes still closed, thought about her question and knew the answer immediately. "St. Croix," he said. "The beaches there. It's always warm and beautiful there."

"The Caribbean. That's excellent. Keep those good, relaxing thoughts in your mind."

"Okay."

He felt her palms gently caress his face. Her hands were warm and soft and sensuous.

"Now, John, I want you to keep your eyes closed and keep thinking about the beautiful beaches in St. Croix. Will you do that for me?"

"Yes, Lexi."

He let his thoughts drift, her soothing, sensuous hands caressing his face. She began counting down from one hundred, slowly, rhythmically, in a low, soothing voice.

Ryan's mind kept drifting, the thoughts of St. Croix intensifying. He was laying on the warm, white sand of an isolated beach, the ocean water lapping quietly in front of him. There was a light breeze blowing, rustling the fronds on the palm trees. It was a beautiful, perfect day in the Caribbean.

Ryan awoke sometime later, his thoughts foggy. He opened his eyes and found Lexi still sitting across from him, her face close to his.

"Feel better now?" she asked softly.

Miraculously, the excruciating pain from his broken ribs was gone. "Yes. I do feel better now."

A warm smile was on her face and she reached out with both hands and cupped his face. "See? I told you I could make the pain go away. Now that you feel better, I want to continue the chat we were having. All right?"

Ryan nodded. "Yes."

He glanced down and noticed his arms were still secured to the chair with plasti-cuffs and he could feel his hands were still tied behind his back. But for some reason he didn't understand, he didn't feel he was in danger. All he felt right now was gratitude toward the beautiful, sensuous woman in front of him. The woman who had made his pain go away, and made him feel safe and comfortable. He loved the way she was caressing his face.

"Thank you, Lexi, for making my pain go away."

"You're very welcome." She smiled warmly again. "I want you to know, John, that I forgive you. Forgive you for wrecking my home and killing my men. And for hunting me down. That's all in the past. Think of this as a new beginning between us, John. You believe me, don't you?"

His thoughts were still foggy, but he sensed everything she was saying was true. "Yes, I do."

"Good." She gently ran a hand through his hair. "I want you to join me. Become my partner. My lover. I'll give you half of everything I have. That's billions of dollars. We'll have a beautiful life together. Yes, I'll be in charge, but that won't be so bad, will it? I'll be very good to you. You'll have everything you've ever wanted in your life. Everything. Doesn't that sound wonderful?"

It does sound wonderful, he thought. *Everything she's saying makes sense.*

"Yes," he replied. "It does sound good."

Her smile intensified and her sensuous black eyes were warm and inviting and hypnotic. "I will make you love me," she whispered. "Just like I made Shawn love me. As we spend more time with each other, you'll realize that our life together is going to be wonderful."

"You're right, Lexi."

She leaned in close and pressed her lips to his and kissed him slowly and sensuously. It felt delicious.

When she pulled away a moment later, she smiled radiantly. "Will you join me now, John?"

Even though his thoughts were still jumbled and foggy, he felt that life with Lexi would be perfect. "Yes. Yes, Lexi. I will join you."

She cupped his face with both of her palms. "Excellent. You'll see. We're going to have a beautiful life together."

Just then he heard an explosion from somewhere outside the mansion.

Lexi pulled her hands away from his face and stood up. "What's going on, Brad?" she said in a loud voice.

Brad appeared in the open doorway. "The storage building where we keep our fuel is on fire," he said. "One of the bombs Ryan set off must have ignited the gasoline."

The fog in Ryan's brain began to lift. The sound of the explosion and Brad's words brought Ryan back to reality and the extreme danger he was in. It was clear to him now that Atwood had hypnotized him. He suddenly realized he was bound to the chair and could be killed by Atwood anytime she wanted. The illusion of a perfect life with her faded from his thoughts. She was a murderer and a terrorist. A beautiful woman, but nevertheless a cold-blooded killer.

The severe pain in his chest from the cracked ribs returned with a vengeance. He winced and gritted his teeth, trying to will away the severe pain. Then his thoughts turned to escape.

Lexi, who was still standing, looked down at him. "What's wrong, John?"

"The pain...the pain came back," he managed to say, gasping for breath.

She shook her head slowly. "Damn. It was the noise from the explosion. Now we'll have to start all over, John. Don't worry, I'll make the pain go away again."

He nodded, but his thoughts were focused on coming up with a way to escape. He was still securely bound to the chair and he was in acute pain, but he knew he'd try anything and everything to get away.

Suddenly, he planted his feet solidly on the floor and jerked himself up into a standing position. He was still tied to the wooden chair and he whirled around, the chair knocking Lexi down to the floor.

Out of the corner of his eye he saw Brad reappear at the open doorway, raising his pistol at him. Ryan awkwardly staggered toward the man and crashed into him as a shot was fired, narrowly missing Ryan's head.

Both men toppled to the floor.

Ignoring the blinding ache in his chest, Ryan came up on one knee, twisted his body and threw himself against the room's concrete wall. The wooden chair he was tied to splintered and cracked.

Brad was now back on his feet, racing to get his Glock which was nearby on the floor. Ryan, his arms now free of the broken chair, kicked the gun away, then kicked Brad fiercely in the face. The man's nose cracked and blood splattered onto his clothes.

The guard in the hallway entered the room and leveled his submachine gun at Ryan, but stopped himself from shooting, obviously seeing that Lexi was nearby.

In that split-second when the guard hesitated, Ryan launched himself into the man full force, knocking him to the floor. Then Ryan ferociously kicked the man in the groin, and the guy howled in pain.

Ryan's hands were still tied behind his back and his heart raced as he frantically tried to think of a way to escape his bindings before Brad or the guard recovered.

The submachine gun the guard had dropped had a bayonet attached to the barrel of the weapon and Ryan dropped to his knees and maneuvered his body awkwardly until he was able to press his bindings against the sharp edge of the knife. After a moment he was able to cut off the plasti-cuffs and free his hands.

Ignoring the pain in his chest, he located the pistol on the floor and picked it up, just as Brad was recovering. Ryan fired two rounds and Brad's head exploded, brain matter and blood spattering everywhere.

Wasting no time, Ryan aimed the pistol and fired three more rounds into the other man. Then he looked around for Atwood but she was gone. She had obviously fled during the fight.

After making sure both Brad and the guard were dead, Ryan sprinted down the corridor and up a flight of stairs. He located Atwood in the lavish kitchen. The woman was frantically punching numbers into a cell phone. He knocked the phone away and leveled the gun at her face.

"It's too late for that, Lexi. No one can help you now. It would take hours for your bought-off Paraguayan friends to get here now."

Her eyes blazed with fury. "You bastard! I should have killed you when I had the chance!"

Ryan shook his head. "Half an hour ago, you had me believing you loved me. And that I loved you."

She glared defiantly. "What now? Are you going to kill me?"

He shook his head again. "No. Now I arrest you and take you back. You'll be tried under the Patriot Act for terrorism. You'll be imprisoned. You'll never be a free woman again for the rest of your life."

Her defiant expression vanished, replaced by fear. "Please, not that. I beg you, John. Please kill me. Do me that favor at least. I can't be caged up like an animal."

Ryan stared at her beautiful face and mulled it over for a long moment, his finger on the trigger. He almost pulled it, then grudgingly lowered the gun.

"I'm sorry, Lexi. But I can't kill you. You may be a cold-blooded murderer, but I'm not. I'm placing you under arrest, Lexi Atwood. Or Alexandra Ivanova, or Carmen Rosa Lopez, or whoever else you may be."

Chapter 90

FBI Field Office
Atlanta, Georgia

"Welcome back to the USA," Erin Welch said when J.T. Ryan came into her office.

Ryan sat on one of the visitor's chairs fronting her desk. "Thanks. Feels good to be back."

Erin closed the lid on her laptop and smiled. "Good job on finding Lexi Atwood and arresting her."

Ryan returned the smile. "All in a day's work. Where is she now?"

"After the FBI jet dropped you off in Atlanta, I told the pilot to take Atwood to ADX Florence, the Supermax prison in Colorado. She's facing multiple murder and terrorism charges. I'm sure she'll be tried under the Patriot Act. She'll get several life sentences."

"A Supermax is a good place for her," Ryan said. "That woman is cunning beyond belief. She's so intelligent, I'm certain she'd figure out a way to escape a regular prison."

Erin nodded. "And from the photos I've seen of her, she's quite beautiful too."

"I hardly noticed," Ryan said with a grin.

"You're such a bullshitter, J.T."

"Yes, I am."

Erin turned serious. "I watched the news reports on the Paraguayan TV stations. They said the man responsible for capturing Atwood was a police detective down there named Diego Cruz. Your name was barely mentioned."

Ryan shrugged. "I was glad to give him the credit. He's a good guy."

"Well, it's a nice thing you did, J.T. From what I heard, Diego Cruz is getting a promotion out of this whole thing."

"That's good. I'm glad for him. Anyway, I went to Paraguay to catch a criminal, not to make headlines or score points." Ryan paused a moment. "And if people found out I was the one who caught the world's most wanted terrorist, everyone would know who J.T. Ryan was. I wouldn't be a very effective covert operative, would I?"

Erin nodded. "You're right about that. But just so you know, I called President Harris this morning and told him what actually happened in Paraguay. He knows you arrested Atwood and brought her to justice."

"I appreciate that. By the way, Erin. Did you decide on the President's job offer to become the new FBI Director?"

She shook her head. "Not yet. To tell you the truth, it's been a difficult decision to make." She gazed out the window of her corner office, which offered a breathtaking view of the city's downtown skyline. It was a cloudless, azure blue day and the bright sunshine reflected from the glass and steel high-rises. "I like Atlanta," she said. "I really do. And I hate the swamp of Washington D.C."

"Plus," Ryan said with a chuckle, "you'd miss my charm and wit and dashing good looks."

Erin laughed. "And I'd miss your modesty too. Don't forget that."

Ryan laughed along with her, then winced from the pain in his ribs.

"Are you okay?" she said.

"Yeah. During the shootout in Paraguay, I got a few cracked ribs. It's going to take some time to heal."

"Too bad, J.T. I already had a new case for you to work on."

"Already?"

"Crime never sleeps," she said.

"That's the truth. But any new cases will have to wait. Once I feel better, I'm taking Rachel on a long vacation."

"I'm glad. How is Rachel doing?"

"I called her on the plane when I was heading home from Paraguay," Ryan said. "She's still under suspension at the CIA. I figure a vacation will do her a world of good."

Erin nodded. "Both of you deserve some time off. Call me when you get back and I'll fill you in on the new case."

Ryan's interest was peaked. "Tell me about it."

Erin opened a drawer, took out a folder and slid it across her desk.

He picked it up and began reading the contents.

Instantly, Ryan was intrigued. It was a mystery within a puzzle. It appeared that the perfect crime had been committed. And it would be a dangerous mission too.

Exactly the kind of case he loved to work on.

END

***

About the author

Lee Gimenez is the award-winning author of 16 novels, including his highly-acclaimed J.T. Ryan series. His novel FIREBALL was a Finalist for the Author Academy Award. Many of his books were Featured Novels of the International Thriller Writers Association, among them CROSSFIRE, The MEDIA MURDERS, FBI CODE RED, SKYFLASH, and The WASHINGTON ULTIMATUM. Lee is a multi-year nominee for the Georgia Author of the Year Award, and a Finalist in the prestigious Terry Kay Prize for Fiction. Lee's books are available at Amazon and many other bookstores worldwide.

For more information about him, visit his website at: www.LeeGimenez.com. There you can sign up for his free newsletter. You can contact Lee at his email address: LG727@MSN.com. You can also join him on Facebook, LinkedIn, and Goodreads.

***

Novels by Lee Gimenez

Tripwire
Blacksnow Zero
The Sigma Conspiracy
Crossfire
Fireball
FBI Code Red
The Media Murders
Skyflash
Killing West
The Washington Ultimatum
The Nanotech Murders
Death on Zanath
Virtual Thoughtstream
Azul 7
Terralus 4
The Tomorrow Solution

CROSSFIRE, a **J.T.** Ryan Thriller
is available at Amazon and many other bookstores in the
U.S. and Internationally.
In paperback, Kindle, and all other ebook versions.

The **SIGMA CONSPIRACY**, a **J.T.** Ryan Thriller
is available at Amazon and many other bookstores in the
U.S. and Internationally.
In paperback, Kindle, and all other ebook versions.

FIREBALL, a **J.T.** Ryan Thriller
is available at Amazon and many other bookstores in the
U.S. and Internationally.
In paperback, Kindle, and all other ebook versions.

FBI CODE RED, a J.T. Ryan Thriller
is available at Amazon and many other bookstores in the
U.S. and Internationally.
In paperback, Kindle, and all other ebook versions.

THE MEDIA MURDERS, a **J.T.** Ryan Thriller
is available at Amazon and many other bookstores in the
U.S. and Internationally.
In paperback, Kindle, and all other ebook versions.

SKYFLASH, a **J.T. Ryan Thriller**
is available at Amazon and many other bookstores in the
U.S. and Internationally.
In paperback, Kindle, and all other ebook versions.

KILLING WEST, a Rachel West Thriller
is available at Amazon and many other bookstores in the
U.S. and Internationally.
In paperback, Kindle, and all other ebook versions.

THE WASHINGTON ULTIMATUM,
a J.T. Ryan Thriller
is available at Amazon and many other bookstores in the
U.S. and Internationally. In paperback, Kindle, and all other
ebook versions.

Made in the USA
Columbia, SC
28 June 2021